Praise for *Midnight at the Blackbird Café*

"Perfect for fans of *Like Water for Chocolate* and *Fried Green Tomatoes at the Whistle Stop Cafe.*"

"Full of family secrets, undeniable charm, and that particular touch of magic so often found in the South . . . Webber creates a town as dynamic and real as her characters. I savored every word."
                                        —Kristy Woodson Harvey,
                national bestselling author of *Slightly South of Simple*

"Webber infuses her charming Southern small-town tale with lighthearted magic and gentle humor. . . . Readers of Sarah Addison Allen and Joshilyn Jackson will enjoy spending time at the Blackbird Café."   —*Booklist*

"Family, fate, and magic intertwine in this endearing Southern tale of long-held secrets, homemade pie, and building one's future from the remains of the past. A tantalizing, delicious delight."   —Kristin Harmel, international bestselling
                            author of *The Room on Rue Amélie*
                            and *The Sweetness of Forgetting*

"This novel is as warm as the cup of coffee you'll surely want to settle down with as you pick up this book and read straight through to the ending."   —*Bookstr*

SOUTH
of the
BUTTONWOOD
TREE

Heather Webber

A TOM DOHERTY ASSOCIATES BOOK
New York

SOUTH OF THE BUTTONWOOD TREE

A Forge Book
Published by Tom Doherty Associates
120 Broadway
New York, NY 10271

www.tor-forge.com

Forge® is a registered trademark of Macmillan Publishing Group, LLC.

The Library of Congress Cataloging-in-Publication Data
is available upon request.

ISBN 978-1-250-19858-7 (trade paperback)
ISBN 978-1-250-19857-0 (ebook)

Our books may be purchased in bulk for promotional, educational, or business use. Please contact your local bookseller or the Macmillan Corporate and Premium Sales Department at 1-800-221-7945, extension 5442, or by email at MacmillanSpecialMarkets@macmillan.com.

First Edition: July 2020
First Trade Paperback Edition: February 2021

Printed in the United States of America

0 9 8 7 6 5 4 3

For booksellers,
thank you for all you do.

SOUTH OF THE
BUTTONWOOD TREE

Chapter 1

"You'd be a dang fool to let her keep that baby. It should go to a loving home." Oleta Blackstock slapped her hand on the desk, nearly knocking over a pitcher of ice water with her bony elbow.

In his chambers, Judge Quimby pressed his fingers together under his double chin and tried to keep his expression neutral as he studied Oleta's orange pillbox hat. Mocking gravity, it perched on the side of her head, as defiant and stubborn as she was.

Oleta leaned forward. Coal-black eyes burned with conviction as she said, "Blue Bishop wouldn't know loving if it jumped up and hit her upside the head. I don't care one whit what that button said. You know the right decision to make, Judge, seeing as how you know the Bishop family better than anyone. Even better than me."

Good God almighty he knew the Bishops, all right.

He also knew anyone who truly cared about the infant or her welfare wouldn't call her "it."

Blue

It was the kind of day in Buttonwood, Alabama, where trouble slipped into town with the breeze, jarring awake sleepy springtime leaves on the massive oaks and sky-high hickories. It scraped parched dirt, sending dust skittering along the trail like it was running for cover. It whistled its warning, plain as day to anyone who cared to listen.

If anyone could recognize the cautionary tune, it was me.

I was a Bishop after all. My family name was practically synonymous with the word *trouble*. Daddy, Twyla, and my three brothers had embraced trouble like long-lost kin, consequences be damned. And look where that had landed them—each now dead and buried.

I'd done my best for most of my twenty-nine years to avoid trouble at all costs. It was the last thing on earth I wanted, and feeling it swirling around now set my nerves to jumping. I hated any kind of conflict, and my younger sister, Persy, all but personified the term *Goody Two-shoes*.

Bishop black sheep, both of us.

"What's wrong?" Marlo Allemand asked as she hiked up a billowy maxi skirt to high-step over a fallen log on the dirt path that led to the Buttonwood Tree, which marked the halfway point on the trail that curved around the town.

I hadn't realized I'd stopped walking. "Just sensing a bit of trouble in the air all of a sudden."

"Best just to ignore it," she said. "Like always."

The long, dark shadow of trouble had followed me my whole life. Teasing. Taunting. Humiliating. I snapped a sunny dandelion head from its stem and tossed it into a tin pail to join a small pile of other blooms that had suffered a similar fate.

I wiped my hands on old jean shorts, leaving behind a dandelion-yellow streak on the threadbare denim. It was that yellow color I had been searching for out in these woods this morning. Back at home in my art studio, I'd transform the decapitated dandelion into ink, along with any other flowers, roots, nuts, and bark I found.

Those weren't the only items I was looking for out in the woods this morning, however. I was always and forever on the hunt for . . . *something* else. Something I couldn't identify.

Something I'd been searching for my whole life long, pushed along by the hands of an insistent wind that was always seeking the lost.

Following its lead, I had a knack for finding things. Watches and wallets and Moe, Marlo's husband, who tended to wander. It was a skill I didn't fully understand since I had no control over it, but I couldn't argue it came in handy once in a while. But as of yet, that unique ability hadn't led me to the one thing I'd been looking for . . . forever. The thing that drove these adventures into the woods. The thing that gnawed my soul and made me restless.

The lost thing that had no name.

I had the feeling the wind would let me know what it was when I found it, but as of yet I'd had little luck.

So I kept looking. Turning botanicals into inks to supplement store-bought art supplies was a great excuse to wander the woods most mornings. I was a children's picture book author and illustrator, and I was grateful for any escape into my fictional world. I was almost done with another book in my popular series about a young, headstrong but shy rabbit who, like me, could find things, though her adventures were much more fun. In the book I was working on, Poppy Kay Hoppy would rather ballet dance than take a hip-hop class like the other rabbits, and it was near impossible to think about my worries while drawing a tutu-wearing bunny.

Marlo and I walked in comfortable silence for a while before I said, "I got a call last night about someone wanting to look at the farmhouse. Sarah Grace Fulton."

With every step she took, Marlo's hiking sandals and a glimpse of her vibrant-red toenails peeked out from the bottom of her skirt. "Well, isn't that interesting."

"Mighty. I gave her the code for the lockbox—she's looking at it today."

I'd been trying to sell the family farmhouse for more than

a year now, but showings were few and far between. Its value had plummeted in the decades my family had lived there, and even though I was selling it as a "for sale by owner" at a rock-bottom price, no one had made a single offer on the house, lowball or otherwise. I could hardly blame potential buyers. I didn't want to live there, either. I had moved out as soon as I could afford a place of my own six years ago.

A twig cracked loudly from within the woods, and Marlo and I both pivoted toward the noise. Something moved at a quick pace through the densely packed trees and brush.

"Deer?" she asked, squinting into the shadows.

"I'm not sure." The woods fell quiet as if they, too, were listening. After a moment, the birds began singing again, the bugs buzzing. Whatever had caused the snapping twig was gone now.

Marlo picked up the conversation. "I have a good feeling about the showing. That house only needs one person to see its full potential."

Cicadas droned as I plucked another dandelion and grinned. "Or it needs a wrecking ball."

Her dark skin glistened in the dappled morning light as she swatted at me, but there was a smile on her face. "Better to fix it up than knock it down. It's got good bones, that house. Seems to me Sarah Grace is the perfect buyer."

Good bones but a sordid history. My daddy, Cobb, had won it in a card game. *Cheating* at cards, though no one could ever prove it—and many had tried. "I hope so, because I could surely use the extra money." I held up a hand. "And before you ask, no, I haven't made the phone call to the adoption agency yet."

Marlo lifted the brim of her floppy straw sun hat, smoothed charcoal-gray hair streaked with strands of silver, and swatted a gnat away from her ear. A thin, judgmental eyebrow arched.

"I've been busy. My book is due in a few weeks. And with Persy being home from college for the summer . . ."

My sister had finished her freshman year of college at the University of North Alabama two weeks ago. After Twyla—my mother had always insisted her children call her by her given name—had died two years ago, I'd been granted legal guardianship of eighteen-year-old Persy, though that label had been a technicality at best. I'd always been Persy's caregiver.

Since the age of adulthood in Alabama was nineteen, she was my legal responsibility for another six months, but my house would always be her home for as long as she wanted to live with me. We were all the family we had left.

For now, at least.

More than anything, I wanted to grow my family, which was no easy task as a single woman with a fluctuating income. After more than three years of waiting to adopt an infant through the state, I had decided working with a private adoption agency was my best option at becoming a mama. I'd scrimped and saved to be able to afford the pricey fees, but now that I almost had enough saved up, I'd been dragging my feet on setting up the formal, in-person consultation.

Marlo's lips, tinted a deep red, pursed. *"Mm-hmm."*

She knew me too well, having pretty much raised me. She and Moe were both in their midseventies and were the grandparents Persy and I had never had, all but adopting us into their childless family nearly eighteen years ago, after Twyla had first sent us into the Allemands' children's bookshop, The Rabbit Hole. I'd been eleven years old and Persy just one.

We'd been in need of rescuing.

And the Allemands had saved us, plain and simple.

The Rabbit Hole was my happy place. There, among the colorful books and the kindness of Marlo and Moe, I'd found an escape from reality, a safe haven. A home. The shop was warmth and love and happiness.

I scrunched my nose. "All right, okay, fine. I'm scared to get the private adoption process started. What if no birth parents choose me? What if they want someone with a huge circle of friends . . . ?"

Previous feedback from state social workers strongly suggested I, especially as a single woman, get out more, become a "thread in the fabric of the community." The whole *it takes a village* mentality made me slightly queasy. My chest tightened as I thought of all the years in school when no one would sit with me at lunch or play with me at recess. I'd never hung out with friends, had a sleepover, or gone to any school dances. Even now, other than Marlo, Moe, and Persy, I had no close friends. If I'd had a choice, I'd have moved away a long time ago. A new town. A fresh start. A bright future. The past buried here in Buttonwood. Buried deep.

But I didn't have a choice. Not yet. As surely as the wind pushed me along, it also held me back, keeping me tethered to Buttonwood like a small bird in a big, pretty cage. Until I found the lost thing with no name, I was free to roam—but only within the confines of my ornate prison.

Marlo clucked softly. "If you let it, fear will always hold you back. Stand in your own light, Blue Bishop. Stand strong. Because I know that if you allow people to get to know you, they'll love you, same as I do. Opening yourself up, being *you*, is the only way to get what you want most in the world."

Stand in your own light. It was a favorite phrase of Marlo's, heard as often at the bookshop through the years as "thank you," "come again," and "the bathroom is down the hallway on the right."

I tried to stand in my own light, truly I did, but it was easier said than done. She didn't know what it was like to be a Bishop, every move under intense scrutiny, painted with the same crooked brushstroke as the rest of my family. My light had been dimmed by the bad choices others had made.

"And don't you dare tell me that opening up is easier said than done," she went on. "Because Persy has proven that point to be invalid. This town doesn't have an issue with you being a Bishop—most let that go a long time ago. *You* have an issue with you being a Bishop, and you're clinging to it as an excuse for your self-imposed exile, my shy, sweet girl."

I kicked another rock. This was a conversation we'd had a million times. Maybe more.

"You haven't had a good reason to change your hermit-like habits before. But now you do. You have the best reason of all: motherhood. Besides," Marlo added, "you don't really want to be cursed do you?"

I glanced ahead, toward the Buttonwood Tree, its upper canopy barely visible from this spot on the trail. According to local legend, the tree had come to be more than a hundred and fifty years ago after a woman named Delphine had warned her husband and son to delay their hunting expedition because of a storm rolling in. They hadn't heeded her advice and ventured into the woods, where they were struck down when lightning hit the tree they'd taken shelter under.

The grief-stricken woman sat so long in the woods where her loved ones had perished that she slowly transformed into a sycamore tree, known as a buttonwood tree in the olden days for the buttons produced from its wood. The Buttonwood Tree grew strong, fertilized by her broken heart, and her determination to prevent others from heartache had morphed into a small crow, almost ethereal in its luminous appearance, that led people in need of guidance to the tree. The tree's buttons had counseled many. But if people didn't listen to the advice . . . there was a steep price to pay.

While the Buttonwood Tree's buttons were made of wood, what was written on them was set in stone. If you asked advice from the tree, you'd best be ready to accept the counsel given. To defy the tree's guidance was to bring on everlasting unhappiness, a curse for ignoring the tree's wisdom.

I had gone to the Buttonwood Tree a few months ago,

brokenhearted after continually being passed over to adopt a newborn. I'd needed reassurance that I was making the right decision in continuing my adoption quest, even at the risk of being hurt again and again. The Buttonwood Tree's answer had given me strength to place the initial call to the private adoption agency.

LOVE IS WORTH THE RISK. LOVE IS LIFE.

I swallowed back a rush of emotion. It was true that I didn't want to be cursed by not heeding my button's advice and following through with my adoption plans, but more than that, I longed to be a mama, to have a family of my own to love, to raise up right and proper in a house full of happiness. "I'll call the agency as soon as we get back."

"And you'll start coming with me to Magnolia Breeze again? Mary Eliza Wheeler's been asking for you."

Magnolia Breeze was the nursing home and rehab center where Marlo volunteered every Monday night. I'd gone along with her a couple of times, but the facility had proven to be too close to home for comfort—several of the patients there had recognized me and wanted to gossip about my family's history, especially the bank robbery that led to the deaths of two of my brothers and sent nearly a hundred thousand dollars up in flames. A topic I most certainly had not wanted to talk about.

"Why? To finish the tongue-lashing she gave me last time?" Mary Eliza had all but cussed me straight out of the room. Marlo and the nurses had tried to tell me it was due to the brain injury Mary Eliza had suffered after a heart attack last year had deprived her of oxygen. But I knew better. She had never liked me or my family one little bit. Heathens, she'd called us among other things. For having been a preacher's wife, she was the most judgmental person I'd ever come across. How her son,

Shep, a local cop, had turned into an all-around good guy, I had no idea.

"Maybe she wants to apologize for her previous behavior."

I wrinkled my nose. "Thanks all the same, but I think I'll pass. I don't really want to get her riled up again. She has a bad heart, remember?"

Marlo crossed her arms. "Threads, Blue honey. Threads."

In my head, I could practically hear the adoption agency denying my application because I was a loner. I took a deep breath. Through clenched teeth I said, "All right, I'll go."

She looped her arm through mine and said, "And so cheerful about it! I can hardly wait for the residents to bask in your exuberance."

I pasted on a wide, fake smile. "I'd be *delighted* to go."

She laughed, a true laugh that nudged aside my dread and let in a sliver of happiness.

"Thursday at six it is, then. And, honey, if you have to fake it until you make it, I'm okay with that."

"Thursday? Not tonight?" I asked, not the least bit upset with the reprieve. Only curious, as Marlo had been trying to stick to a tightly controlled schedule since Moe's diagnosis. Magnolia visits took place on Mondays. Always.

"I have a late meeting tonight, so I had to reschedule to later this week."

I gave her a sideways glance. "Another mysterious meeting? It's the third in a month."

"It's not mysterious at all."

"Really? Who're you meeting with?"

"Someone."

I smiled. "About what?"

"Things."

"Oh, I see. That's as clear as a mud puddle." As we neared the glade surrounding the Buttonwood Tree, the wind picked up, and the trouble mixed in with it taunted me. I stiffened. Suddenly nervous, I said, "Wait. The trouble in the air doesn't have something to do with *you*, does it?"

"Me?" She pressed her hands to her chest and her eyes widened theatrically, as if she were reading aloud *Where the Wild Things Are* to a group of preschoolers. "Why would you think such a thing?"

I stopped midstep to look at her. "Your faux outrage, for one. And for another, your mornings with Moe are all but sacred. Yet, you're out here with me." He was at his best in the mornings. Nighttime was when he tended to lose his way, dementia leading him to places only he knew.

Before she could reply, a keening caw pierced the air. A glossy crow glided over the treetops.

Marlo's gaze followed the bird as she asked, "Are you in need of a button?"

"Not me. I've asked my one question this year. You?" Buttonwood Tree legend also stated that only one question could be asked of the tree per year, and I could understand why. Otherwise, people would constantly be trekking to the tree to seek help with every little decision.

"No," Marlo said. "All my big decisions have been made already. Odd that the crow is calling out, since it's rarely seen unless leading someone to the tree for counseling. Let's see what's going on, shall we?"

She strode over to the hollow in the Buttonwood Tree where flat, smooth buttons appeared after someone asked the tree's advice. "Empty," she said, peering into the crevice notched by nature into the mottled trunk, the bark a patchy mix of smooth and rough. She bent to look into the wide rabbit hole beneath the tree.

In all my years, I'd never seen a single rabbit emerge from it, though I looked every time I passed by the tree, endlessly hopeful. The tree's shallow root system had broken the ground's surface, creating a wide maze of twisted, outstretched arms, so vast and intertwined that it was hard to tell where each arm had originated. I watched my step so I wouldn't trip on a root as I walked over to her.

"C'mon, Marlo, tell me what's going on with you. You've been acting strangely for a few weeks now. Secret meetings and the like. Is it about Moe?" My heart nearly dropped straight out of my chest at the mere thought. "Is he worse than we think?"

She put her hand on my arm, settling me. Soothing me. "Don't go getting all worked into a tizzy. Moe's health is no better, no worse."

At her touch, I immediately calmed. "Then what?"

Inhaling deeply, she shot a look up the trunk of the Buttonwood Tree, then said, "It's the shop."

"The Rabbit Hole? What about it?" The bookstore had been named for the hole we stood next to, and Marlo often referred to her smallest customers as her "little rabbits."

"There are going to be some transitions. Starting tomorrow I'm going to need your help more than ever."

Even though I made a good living with my books, I still worked at the bookshop part-time, at least once a week. Partly to help out Marlo, especially now that Moe was unable to work; partly to be around all the kids who didn't care a bit that I was a Bishop; and partly because the store was my happy place, where my every worry seemed to fade away.

"Of course. You know you can count on me. What kind of transition are you talking about?"

"Since Moe has doctor appointments every morning for the rest of this week, I'm going to need you to train someone new," she said. "You're the only person who knows the shop inside out like I do."

"You hired a new employee? Oh, I'm so glad, Marlo. It'd be

nice if you could scale back your hours. You've been running yourself ragged, between caring for Moe and the store and with the Buttonwood Festival coming up . . ."

The festival was the town's biggest event of the year. There would be a parade, carnival rides, baking competitions, a petting zoo, food booths, vendors, and artisans. The Rabbit Hole's tent would have hourly story time, balloon animals, face painting, and refreshments.

Marlo took my hand, holding it tightly, and drew in a deep breath. "It's not a new employee." Pulling her shoulders back, she stared at me with a shiny, determined gaze and said, "Blue, honey, I've sold the shop. I'm handing over the keys tonight. The Rabbit Hole has a new owner."

The words swirled in my ears, slurring together. Certain I hadn't heard her right, I started shaking my head to sort the syllables properly.

She squeezed my fingers. "You must understand, Blue. I'm past due for retirement, and the time has come for me to be with Moe around the clock. I want the transfer to be as seamless as possible—I'll be staying on the staff for another month at least—but this week is just plain bad timing, especially with the festival. I'm throwing the new owner out of the frying pan and straight into the fire."

"I . . . I . . ." Tears welled and I blinked them away. I heard what she was saying, and I knew what she said to be true, but to be blindsided like this had stolen my breath. I pulled back, and the tin pail fell from my forearm, spilling cheerful dandelion heads across the tree roots.

She said, "I didn't tell you my plans ahead of time, because I knew you'd put up a fuss. You'd do something crazy like try to buy the shop yourself."

I nodded.

"But, Blue, the shop has been my dream, not yours. It would be a burden to you. Don't you shake your head at me. You know it's true. You want to leave Buttonwood one day, remember? Besides, the money you've saved up is earmarked for something more important—your dream to start a family, to be a mama."

"Who?" I managed to say. "Who'd you sell it to?"

A smile ghosted her lips. "He's a grade-school teacher. Someone—"

A cry cut her off. My chin came up at the sound. So familiar. So out of place here in the woods.

Marlo glanced around and said, "That didn't sound like a crow."

No, the cry hadn't sounded like a crow . . . It had sounded like a *baby*.

My head must've been playing tricks on me. Or it was my heart. Either way, I didn't appreciate it.

As trouble gloated, I looked around. It took only a moment to spot her. I blinked, convinced it was my eyes playing the tricks this time, until she opened her tiny mouth and let out another wail. I sprinted due south of the Buttonwood Tree, to the basket nestled in a patch of daisy fleabane. I dropped to my knees. Netting was draped over the wicker, and I peeled it away so I could pick up the baby, her pink blanket and all.

She couldn't have been more than a few days old, still wrinkled and looking like an old, wise, ticked-off woman. Warm and oh so soft, she was dressed in a simple white onesie. A headband made of pink ribbon that had a delicate scalloped edge was tied at the top of her head in a small bow that sat prettily in a fluff of pale-blond hair. As I tucked her close to my body, I was oddly reminded of a sack of flour, one big five-pound lump. My hands shook as I held her to my chest, and she quieted, her eyes squished closed.

Marlo came up behind me and gasped. "What in the everloving world?"

I stood up, keeping tight hold of the baby. There was no note. No explanation. Peering into the woods, I called out. "Hello?"

Surely someone didn't leave a baby out here in the woods all alone. Was this some kind of coldhearted prank, a cruel joke?

Twigs snapped in the distance, and I saw a quick-moving blur among the shadows. It seemed as though someone had waited to make sure the baby was found and then ran off.

"Blue, look," Marlo said as she crouched low to the ground.

My heart was pounding so loudly in my ears that I barely heard her.

"It must've fallen out of the blanket when you picked her up." She held out her open palm. On it rested a Buttonwood Tree button, made of wafer-thin sycamore about the size of a half-dollar. On the pale wood, a message was etched in chicken-scratch letters.

GIVE THE BABY TO BLUE BISHOP.

I glanced down at the baby, at her dark eyelashes, pink cheeks, and tiny pointy chin.

A tiny pink bundle of trouble.

And I'd be damned if I was letting her go.

Chapter
2

Sarah Grace

"I'd gut to the studs. New electrical, new plumbing." I glanced at the shafts of sunlight that shot through holes around the window frame, highlighting stains on an old orange couch. "New siding."

My father's gaze swept over the room. "New everything."

The 1920s farmhouse had good bones, but it had been sorely neglected. It reeked of stale cigarette smoke and mold but mostly of wet dirt, as though the earth were trying its best to reclaim the land and forget this house ever existed. "I've seen worse."

His grin came slow. "Sure enough."

Something skittered in a far corner behind a sideboard that was missing all its drawers, and I could only imagine what was living in the walls. "It's going to be a huge amount of work, but I can't seem to walk away. I just feel like this house . . . It needs me. That sounds crazy, doesn't it?"

My daddy, Judson Landreneau, had been mayor of Buttonwood for coming on ten years now, and there was no one around these parts more diplomatic. I trusted him to tell it to me straight.

"I don't think so, my little house whisperer." A spark of mischief flashed in his blue eyes. "But anyone else would think you're off your rocker."

I laughed. "My love of real estate came from you, so I get my crazy honestly."

Warmth filled his gaze. "Some things can't be avoided, I suppose."

Before becoming mayor, Daddy had run the biggest real estate company in the county and used to let me tag along with him to check out potential listings. It was a little surreal to have him here with me now, helping me with an inspection. I trusted his input and was grateful he'd taken the time out of his busy morning to be here.

He strolled across the room and ran a finger along a crack in the wall. "This house is going to be a challenge, Sarah Grace, for more reasons than the obvious. It might be too much to take on."

I glanced over at him, intrigued by his suddenly sober tone, to find that he was wearing what I called his *serious* face. Thick eyebrows had knitted together to become a unibrow, and his blue eyes were drawn into a deep squint. The corners of his mouth tilted downward, his chubby cheeks were sucked inward, and his jaw was pushed forward. He raked his fingers through short brown hair scattered with silver, lifting tufts into spikes—a dead giveaway that something weighed on his mind.

"You aren't trying to talk me out of offering on it, are you?" He had a way of talking me out of my decisions, and I really wanted this house.

"Truth be told, Sarah Grace, you need this house more than it needs you. There's a lot to be learned here once you start peeling back the layers. Valuable lessons. But it could also be a Pandora's box you ultimately wish you'd kept closed. Are you sure you're ready to take that risk?"

"I'm ready," I said. "I've yet to come across a house that couldn't be fixed one way or another. I'd love to take it back to its original footprint, the way it was before . . ."

Before Cobb Bishop had pretty much stolen it from my mother's family back in the 1970s. Granddaddy Cabot had cursed the Bishops until his dying breath. It was a grudge that had been passed down to my mother, as priceless to her as Grandma Cabot's lace tablecloths and Great-Aunt Mim's silver.

I didn't hold the same animosity toward the Bishops as my mother, but I wanted to finally right the wrong that had taken place long before I'd been born. I'd always been drawn to this house, and I couldn't help thinking that it was because I'd been cheated out of knowing it. It was high time this house once again belonged to a Cabot—even if it was only for a little while.

Through my company, Sweet Home, I located, bought, and rehabbed local fixer-uppers and then rented them at a deep discount to lower-income families. Prideful, hardworking people who didn't want something for nothing. To date, I owned fourteen houses. I couldn't be more proud of the work I'd done, and knowing how many families I had helped filled me with a contentment that was otherwise lacking in my life.

"It'll be beautiful once I'm done with it," I finally said, my gaze sliding over the threadbare furniture, the stained curtains, and the chipped cupboards.

He held my gaze for a long moment. "Okay. When will you present the offer?"

"As soon as possible." I, of course, didn't need his approval to bid on the house, but his support was everything. And I'd need that support when it came to my mother—she was not going to like that I was buying this place. I'd been warned against coming anywhere near here from the time I was old enough to understand the words.

Since Twyla Bishop's passing two years ago, the still-furnished farmhouse hadn't had any occupants, and it showed in the sadness that filled the house from cracked foundation to cobwebbed rafters. Determined, I aimed to change the vibes of this house as surely as its floor plan.

Out with the despair, in with happiness. Which might be easier said than done. It seemed to me that old houses tended to inherit the emotions of their former residents. I could see the pain and heartbreak here in cracked spindles and a bowed mantel that looked to be frowning.

It was why a full gut was in order. Exposing all the damage was the only way anything could be fixed properly. I gave the newel post a loving pat, silently promising to repair the destruction no matter how long it took or at what cost.

At the sound of something moving upstairs, Daddy and I both glanced upward. It was too loud for a mouse. A squirrel, maybe. I prayed it wasn't a raccoon. They became mean little devils when faced with eviction.

When quiet returned, he said, "The house hasn't changed much from the last time I was here. A little more age and a few more cracks, but the wallpaper's the same. The couch. The scent of cigarettes. Mac's father, Cobb, smoked like a chimney. Brings back memories."

Some, I imagined, weren't wrapped in fondness. I leaned against a door frame. "How long's it been?"

"Thirty years, give or take. It was after Mac's funeral service."

I knew Mac Bishop only through my father's colorful stories of their misadventures, most of which my mother refused to listen to. Mac and Daddy had been best friends in high school, but Mac had joined the military after graduating and had died in a bar fight not long after enlisting. But Mac wasn't the only loss this house had seen. Of the seven Bishops, only Blue and Persy were still alive.

It wasn't any wonder why this house wept with sorrow.

My phone chimed with a text message. It came from my part-time assistant—who was also my twenty-year-old cousin—Kebbie Hastings. She was on summer break from college and had already whipped my office into shape after only two short weeks.

HURRICANE GINNY COMING IN HOT. SHE'S IN QUITE THE TIZZY.

"Bad news?" Daddy asked, studying my face.

"Mama's on her way."

He snapped to attention. "Here?"

"Apparently." I held up the text message.

He stuck his hand in his hair, lifting strands into stressed-out spikes. My daddy was only afraid of one person on earth—my mama.

"Why?" he asked.

It had to be something serious for Mama to come out this way. This farmstead was on her personal list of places to avoid at all costs.

Panic needled my chest. Maybe she found out about . . .

No. She hadn't.

If she had, Ginny Cabot Landreneau would've self-combusted on the spot, leaving behind only her disappointment in me, due to it being an eternal affliction.

I walked to the window. My vintage white Ford pickup, with the Alabama state decal on the tailgate with the words SWEET HOME written in the middle of it along with the website for my real estate business, sat lonely in the driveway, but not a second later my mama's black BMW SUV came bumping down the pitted lane. "She's here now." I pushed my father toward the stairs. "You should hide. Mama doesn't need to know you're involved with my decision to buy this place. Not yet, at least. Let's keep the peace as long as possible."

This wasn't the first time we'd kept secrets from Mama. She'd never have approved of him playing touch football with me, or taking me mudding, or taking me to the casino to teach me how to shoot craps. Once, when he was showing me how to skin a fish and I'd cut my finger, we'd spun a whopper of a story to cover the truth. To this day Mama still had no idea I hadn't needed stitches because I'd been slicing strawberries to make shortcake.

For a moment Daddy looked like he wanted to argue but then nodded in agreement. "What she doesn't know won't hurt her."

I frowned as he hustled up the stairs. Those were words I'd lived by nearly my whole life—not just in regard to my mother, but with him, too. And it was true—what they didn't know hadn't hurt them.

It only hurt me.

A car door slammed, and I quickly stepped out of the house to head my mother off at the pass. A store-bought lockbox on the knob banged as I closed the door firmly behind me. The last thing I wanted was Mama's inspection of the house's interior—and her inevitable look of disapproval. She'd yet to come around on my chosen career choice, and five years in, I was starting to doubt she ever would.

My mother was all about perfection. In appearances, in behavior, in *everything*. My job refurbishing dilapidated houses was not what she would've chosen for me. She'd have me be an executive or lawyer or some other highly esteemed position. Certainly a career where I didn't get my hands dirty nearly every day.

As soon as I crossed the sagging porch, however, I saw that I needn't have worried about her coming inside. She was glued to the side of her SUV as though in fear of being contaminated by the sadness exhaled by the house. I suspected she had good cause to worry.

A large sticker on the BMW's passenger door touted BUTTONWOOD MAYOR JUDSON LANDRENEAU FOR GOVERNOR, and as I made my way down the broken front steps, avoiding the grabby reach of the ivy growing wild, a familiar panic poked me from the inside out. The primary was next month, and if he won that, he'd be on the ballot come November.

The thought of my life possibly being subjected to the media's microscope for the next four years almost made me break out in a cold sweat. But my secrets had been buried a long time now, and I had no reason to think they were in danger of being unearthed. I had to keep thinking that, or I'd lose my ever-loving mind.

Mama leaned against the car and stared at the house. She rarely looked anything other than completely put together. There wasn't a blond hair out of place, a single crack in her lipstick, or a wrinkle in her floral wrap dress. Her leather pumps were dust-free, and the two-and-a-half-inch heels lifted her five-foot-three-inch frame closer to eye level with me.

"Are you okay?" I asked, suddenly worried. She might look put together, but there was no denying she appeared to have had the wind knocked out of her. I'd yet to see her take a deep breath.

Her narrow jaw came up, as if only now noticing I stood there. Sunlight shimmered in her beautiful blue eyes as her gaze skimmed over me. She had turned forty-seven this year and still had a youthful glow about her. So much so that people often remarked that we looked more like sisters than mother and daughter. It was true. She'd married my father at nineteen and had given birth to me just shy of her twentieth birthday. I was an only child, but it felt like I had a sister in Kebbie, who had joined our family ten years ago after my aunt and uncle had died in a small plane crash.

"What? Oh, I'm fine, Sarah Grace. Just fine." Mama mustered a smile as if to convince me of that fact and quickly added, "But I'd like to know what're you doing at *this* house? I've told you a thousand times to stay away from here. I about died when Kebbie told me where you were. Don't you dare tell me you bought the Bishop house."

I braced myself for the storm ahead and said, "I haven't yet, but I'm going to."

Displeasure tugged at the corners of her lips. "Because of your granddaddy? If so, chase that thought right out of your head. This house has belonged to the Bishops for too long now.

It's *tainted*." Anger sparked a fiery light in her eyes, and her voice dropped deathly low. "You shouldn't be here. You know how I feel about the Bishops."

I knew. It was why I'd been hesitant to pursue the property for so long, but I'd finally had enough waiting. "Surely you can't hold those opinions against the *house*. It's been two years since a Bishop has lived here."

A pale eyebrow lifted. "Can't I? The Bishops have a terrible reputation. You shouldn't be associated with that family in any way."

"Good Lord, Mama. You act as though they were cannibalistic serial killers."

A police car drove slowly past the bottom of the driveway, and my breath caught and held until I saw it was the police chief behind the wheel, not Shep Wheeler. The car kept going, and I relaxed. I didn't know how much longer I could keep avoiding Shep, who'd come back to Buttonwood seven months ago after his mama, Mary Eliza, took ill. Forever would be nice. Lord have *mercy*.

Mama, oblivious to my inner turmoil, wagged a finger in my direction. "You're not too old for a switchin', young lady. Don't use the Lord's name in vain."

For such a petite woman, she was stuffed full of bluff and bluster. In all my years, she'd rarely disciplined me, and certainly never with a switch, despite threatening to do so at least ten times a year, every year, for as long as I could remember.

It was an understatement to say that I tried my mother's good nature.

I said, "It wasn't in vain. It was in astonishment."

"I swear your sassiness will be the death of me."

"So I've heard." A million times.

She rolled her eyes. "You know as well as I do that the Bishops trend toward criminality. You're a role model in this town, Sarah Grace. Do better. Be better."

I couldn't count the times she'd said that phrase to me while I was growing up. *You're a Landreneau, Sarah Grace. You must be above it all. You must set a good example. Do better. Be better.*

I'd heard it every time I climbed a tree. Or ran barefoot. Or tried to catch crawdads in the creek. I heard it when I wanted to dye my hair purple. When I wanted to wear trousers to church. When I wanted to join the cross-country team in middle school and not the cheer squad. When I got caught smoking in the attic. When I wanted to major in construction management. When I started training for a marathon, which was partly to keep in shape, but mostly because I constantly felt the need to run away.

Far away.

Guilt was my mama's weapon of choice, and she wielded it like a mighty sword.

"Not all the Bishops. Blue and Persy are hardly criminals." I couldn't rightly say that of the other family members.

"If I recall correctly, Blue had trouble with the law when she set that fire at the high school, and Persy will find her own trouble one day, too—mark my words. Bishops can't stay out of trouble. It's in their blood," she said, her tone laced with sadness, as though the house had, in fact, contaminated her by its proximity.

My chest ached with bottled-up secrets as I said, "Blue's charges were dropped, remember? And it's the only scrape with the law that she's had." Blue Bishop was now a successful children's author and illustrator. Persy was a straight-A student who'd earned an academic scholarship to college and was so straight and narrow that I was convinced she'd never even jaywalked in her life. Sometimes I forgot Persy was even a Bishop at all.

Mama was shaking her head. "Don't buy this house. *Please.*"

A gust of wind kicked up, whipping the house into a shuddering frenzy. Eaves groaned and the porch roof creaked loudly, telling me to go ahead and leave, that it was used to people walking away from it.

It had been a long time since I bucked one of Mama's pleas, and I told myself to stay strong and not give in.

Her voice softened to a near whisper as she said, "Think of your daddy, Sarah Grace. He's worked so hard on his campaign—we don't need any ties to the Bishop name coming up. Walk away from this house and buy another."

She wasn't playing fair, pulling my father into our disagreement. I was weak where he was concerned, and she knew it. But *I* knew he was hiding out on the second floor and that I had his full support to buy this house. The knowledge gave me strength to push back.

I dug in my heels, determined to stand firm. I held my mother's gaze, silently begging her to understand. I'd already given up so much for my parents—especially for my daddy's career. Things they'd never know about. I couldn't give up this house as well. It needed me. "You know I love you and would do almost anything for you, but I won't walk away, Mama. It's not fair of you to ask it of me. Personally, I don't care if the devil himself once lived in this house. It's empty now, and somewhere out there, there's a family who needs it. I aim to make that happen." I inwardly winced at how sharply the words had come out, old hurts bleeding into my tone. I kissed Mama's cheek. "Thanks for stopping by. Now, if you'll excuse me, I need to get back to my inspection." I started for the front door.

The house settled, letting out a weary, hopeful sigh.

Mama grabbed my arm. "Please wait a moment, Sarah Grace. My word. You know I only want what's best for you, even if we tend to disagree on what that is. I'm just trying to protect you."

I knew. Mama had a good heart, truly she did, and loved me to death, but she wanted what she always wanted: perfection. A perfect house, a perfect husband, and a perfect child. But

I was so far from perfect that it was laughable. And as much as I tried to fake it, it was nearly impossible to balance what I wanted and who I was with what she wanted and who she wanted me to be.

"Besides," she added, "I haven't even told you why I stopped by. It's interesting news. Good news, possibly. And oddly, it involves Blue Bishop."

"Oh?" At the mention of Blue, she had my full attention. "How so?"

Mama quickly spun an alarming tale of Blue finding a newborn baby near the Buttonwood Tree early this morning. It was almost too fantastical to be the truth. "Whose baby is it?"

With a bright smile, she said, "Nobody knows. The police are investigating."

I didn't understand my mother's delight at the news. An abandoned baby was a serious matter. I was grateful the little girl had been found to be healthy, thriving even, after having been checked out at the local hospital. That was the only good news I could see in all of this, but it was clear by my mother's glee that she saw something I didn't.

"Where's the baby now?"

"That's why I came. Apparently, Blue already had the proper paperwork on file to foster, so she was granted emergency guardianship of the baby by Judge Quimby. There's a rumor she wants to adopt the child, and once I heard that, I came straight to you."

"Why? How does this involve me?"

"Don't you see, Sarah Grace? It's a *temporary* order. You and Fletch need to get your own papers filed. *Adoption* papers. The sooner the better."

"*What?*"

"I know, I know; it's a lot to absorb. But listen to me. You and Fletch have been trying to have a baby for so long now. This perfect baby girl might just be the answer to your prayers."

My struggles were more complicated than she knew, starting with the fact that my marriage to Fletcher Fulton was in shambles, something Fletch and I went to great lengths to hide. Even from each other. The other being that I'd only told my mama we'd been trying to have a baby because she hounded me every time she saw me. The truth of it was that Fletch and I hadn't been trying at all. Our talks about babies always began with *someday,* as if we both knew bringing a child into our marriage was a bad idea.

Dumbfounded, I stared at her. "It's not as though we can just snap our fingers and adopt a baby. It's a process. One that a lot of people have already been through—ones who have been possibly waiting years. It's not right to cut in line, Mama. *Do better. Be better.*"

She frowned deeply at her favorite phrase being used against her.

"Plus," I went on, "there's the button to consider. You said it had instructions to give the baby to Blue. Do you really want to tempt a personal curse by challenging the Buttonwood Tree? I don't."

Even as I said it, I wondered if it was even possible for me to be cursed *twice.* I didn't want to find out. Once was enough.

Holding up a hand, she said, "Don't even talk to me about that tree. You know how I feel about it."

She hated it, and its legend, more than she did the Bishops, and that was saying something.

"It's utter foolishness to think a *button* can influence your life, and it's irresponsible to give it any power or control over decisions that should be your own." She crossed her arms over a heaving chest and looked to be building up a good head of steam.

To stave off a lecture on the dangers of folklore, I said, "Blue's already been granted guardianship. No one's going to take the baby away from her without just cause."

"Your daddy has connections, Sarah Grace. Just say the word and that baby will be taken from Blue Bishop and given to you." Mama lifted clasped hands under her chin. "I can just see the family Christmas cards, can't you? Our big, happy family?"

It didn't escape me that she seemed extra gleeful at the thought of taking the baby away from Blue. No doubt in her eyes, she felt it was the ultimate comeuppance. A house for a baby.

I wondered if she had any idea how alike she and Cobb Bishop were in this moment. Cheating to get what they wanted. But for as much as she was okay with it, there was simply no way on earth I'd ever use my father's power in the community to take a baby away from someone else. Judging by my mother's expression, however, she wasn't going to let this harebrained idea go anytime soon. That left me only one course of action to take: I needed to stall for time until she gave up on the idea. It was a defensive tactic I often used against her in our battles of will, and it had worked well in the past. "I need to think about it."

Mama let out a joyous squeak. "Don't think too long. Time is of the essence. Talk to Fletch and let me know as soon as you decide." She gave me a big hug, threw the house one last wary glance, and soon drove off.

Slightly stunned, I headed back up the steps, and the house whispered, "Welcome home."

I patted the doorjamb as I passed by. "You aren't mine yet, and when you are, remember it's only temporary."

"Sarah Grace," Daddy yelled from the second floor. "There's something up here you should see."

Daddy had been the one who taught me that houses had a lot to say if you listened carefully. I'd been so hopeful that he shared my ability to actually hear them and feel their emotions, but once, when I was eleven and with him at a potential listing, I mentioned that the house we were looking at was complaining about its rotting foundation, how it was causing a mighty ache.

Daddy had laughed and commented on my good imagination. From that day on, when I went to work with him he'd introduce me as his little house whisperer. The name had stuck, especially when I was able to point out problems with a house that no one else had been able to see.

At some point, he finally realized that I hadn't been kidding about hearing houses. He'd sat me down and told me how the South was full of magic and how it touched some more than others. He'd encouraged me to embrace my quirk and stood by my side in full support when I told Mama my career plans. Some around here, those who couldn't feel the magic, still believed my house whisperer nickname to be just that, but others found my abilities to be perfectly normal.

"Please tell me it's not a whole *family* of raccoons," I said as I climbed the maple steps, noting that the treads could probably be refinished instead of replaced.

"Worse," he said as I reached his side at one of the bedroom doorways.

"What's worse than a family of raccoons?"

"See for yourself."

I leaned in. Unlike the other dusty, grimy, smelly rooms in the house, there wasn't a speck of dirt to be seen in this bedroom. A rickety bunk bed made up with thin, faded pink cotton coverlets was pushed against the longest wall, and on the other side of the room, a deflated blow-up mattress sat like a scolded child in a far corner. A trash bag, soda cans, and snack wrappers littered the floor.

Daddy held up a crumpled take-out bag from Kitty's Diner, a local restaurant, and said, "The receipt is dated this past weekend. Seems to me this house has itself a squatter."

Chapter
3

All Judge Quimby had needed was a pack of light bulbs. He had to be in court in ten minutes.

"Blue's a Bishop, yes, but she's not like her daddy or her brothers or even her mama. Blue doesn't go looking for trouble. She's good-natured. Kind. Mild mannered. Not many see it, because they aren't looking. People see what they want to see."

Mrs. Tillman, a retired schoolteacher who owned the hardware store with her husband, Ike, held Judge Quimby's credit card in her hand.

Held it hostage was more like it.

He pointed at the card. "I really need to be on my way, Mrs. Tillman."

"Did you know I used to teach Blue? Had her in my fifth-grade class. One day she came to me, asked if I'd be willing to buy some rocks she found." Mrs. Tillman waved his card around as she talked. "Blue dumped a pile of stones on my desk. Smooth stones, clean as could be. She said the rocks could be painted for an art lesson and presented one she'd painted to look like a lamb. Cute as all get-out. What could I say? I was sold."

"I have court in seven minutes."

"I thought for sure Blue would keep the money for herself, seeing as how the Bishops rarely had two nickels to rub together, but later at lunchtime, I saw her slip every quarter I'd given her into Shep Wheeler's desk without him noticing. From what I could see of it, Mary Eliza had forgotten to send lunch to school with Shep, and when I asked around the lunch ladies, it seemed it wasn't an uncommon occurrence. Shep, despite coming from a good, middle-class family, went without more often than not."

Mrs. Tillman finally, blessedly, swiped his card. As she handed him a slip to sign, she said, "Goes without saying, I bought every rock Blue ever put on my desk—for years. And I still have the one painted as a lamb on my mantel at home. A priceless treasure, that's what it is. A priceless treasure."

Blue

A buttery scent floated through the air as I pulled a sheet of chocolate chip and coconut cookies from the oven and set it onto the granite countertop while glancing at the baby sleeping in the knee-high cradle in front of the sofa. "I thought I'd feel different."

I'd found the wooden cradle at a flea market in Birmingham a few years ago. It had been one of the first things I bought when I decided to pursue adoption, and it had taken weeks to strip the old paint off the cradle to reveal the beauty of its natural maple finish. The result had been worth the effort.

"How did you think you'd feel?" Marlo asked, sipping from a glass of sweet tea while keeping a watchful eye on Moe.

Elmore Allemand—fondly known as Moe by almost everyone—sat beside Persy on the purple velvet sofa and gently rocked the cradle, his long brown fingers wrapping around a delicate spindle.

"I don't know." I slid another cookie sheet into the oven and set the timer. I found solace in baking cookies, and at this moment, I was in need of a little cookie comfort, as Twyla used to call it. "Normal? Like a normal mom would."

As if finding a baby in the woods were normal, but still.

I'd always dreamed of a house bursting with children's laughter, family suppers, rooms filled with nothing but love and happiness. Over the past few years I'd gone to dozens of meetings, had assessments and a home study done, and had been officially licensed to foster *and* adopt.

But until now, I hadn't even come close to making that dream come true.

"How many times have I told you that there's no such thing as normal?" Marlo admonished as she fought a yawn.

She was doing her best to keep Moe at home and out of Magnolia Breeze, but even with the help of health aides who visited their house daily, the demands of the bookshop and being his nighttime caregiver were easy to see in the purplish circles beneath her eyes and the strain in her features. I wanted to ask about her earlier meeting with the new bookshop owner, but now wasn't the time. I didn't want any sadness to mar this night.

"Yeah, yeah." I carried a plate of warm cookies with me into the living room, set it on the coffee table, and sat next to Marlo.

"So how *do* you feel, if it's not normal?" Persy asked as she reached for a cookie, curiosity burning in reddish-brown eyes the same color as aged whiskey.

I'd called her from the hospital this morning, and she skipped her second class of the day to meet me there. I'd been glad to have her by my side. Since she'd been back in Buttonwood, she'd been busy with summer classes at the local community college, her job, and she often disappeared for hours late at night. I suspected she was dating someone on the sly.

Unlike me, Persy was outgoing and well liked in the community and didn't seem to be afflicted by the Bishop stigma. She had been too young to feel the town's condemnation in full effect, like I had. Plus, she had the remarkable—and enviable—ability to not care what people thought of her. I cared. I cared much too much.

I tried to put my feelings into words. "I thought mothering would bring a sense of warmth. The warmth that comes from true love, the kind that fills your chest until you feel like you might explode. But all I feel is a cold knot deep in my stomach."

Moe chuckled. "I think that's called parenthood, Blue."

"Oh, hush now," Marlo said to him. "Don't go scaring her off when she hasn't even been a mama a full day yet. That cold knot is fear, Blue. You're scared."

I wasn't just scared. I was petrified.

Not of being a mother, but of having to give the baby back to her family. Or the state. Or anyone.

Persy's phone buzzed with a text message, and she glanced at the screen before excusing herself. She took the stairs to her room two at a time, her long auburn hair flying out behind her like a cape.

I glanced at Marlo, and she had an eyebrow lifted.

Apparently I wasn't the only one who'd noticed that Persy might have a secret relationship going on. Ordinarily, she wouldn't have left the room to carry on a text conversation.

"What's her name?" Moe asked as he fussed with the purple cotton blanket tucked around the baby.

Marlo's brown eyes softened as I said, for the fourth time since they'd arrived, "Flora. I named her Flora."

Twyla had always said she'd named me Blue because that's the color I'd been when she first laid eyes on me. I'd been born on a bitterly cold December day, and my unexpected home delivery had apparently been traumatic because Twyla hadn't liked to speak of it, other than to mention the pallor of my skin. I'd thought about naming Flora "Violet" to carry on the color tradition, but it hadn't felt right. Flora fit her perfectly, especially since she was found near flowers.

"I bet this one will keep you up all night," Moe said, making goofy faces at the sleeping baby as though she could see him. He seemed completely enraptured by her and more mentally present than he'd been in months, especially considering it was past dark, when he was usually at his worst. *Sundowning*, the experts called the confusion and agitation that happened to dementia and Alzheimer patients after the sun went down.

I smiled. "I won't mind if she does."

Flora and I had a long road ahead of us, and I already owed a huge debt of gratitude to Marlo. She'd made several phone calls after we found Flora, and next thing I knew there'd been an emergency hearing before Judge Quimby. By its end, I had been granted temporary guardianship of Flora.

A probate court investigator would be here sometime this week to assess my living situation in preparation of me filing for full guardianship if Flora's parents weren't found quickly. And if they weren't, in four months' time all parental rights would be terminated by the court, and I could file a petition of adoption.

GIVE THE BABY TO BLUE BISHOP.

I couldn't help thinking the Buttonwood Tree had somehow played a role in how smoothly and quickly all the red tape had been cut through. It had wanted the baby given to me and was making sure it happened.

I hoped it kept on pulling those invisible strings, because Flora's abandonment was an active police case. I'd spent quite a bit of time this morning with an old schoolmate of mine, Shep Wheeler, who was now an investigator with the Buttonwood police department. He'd taken copious notes and promised updates as often as possible. If Flora's mother *was* found and wanted her back, then it was likely I would have to turn Flora over. Because, shockingly, in Alabama abandoning a child with no intent to harm was a *misdemeanor*.

Misdemeanors were *nothing*. My family didn't even bat an eyelash at misdemeanors.

Well, Persy did. She was an exceptionally law-abiding sort.

Misdemeanors were often slaps on the wrist. At most, a year in the county jail. With any kind of sob story, Flora's mother might get off with a fine or probation. The fact that I had only *temporary* guardianship of Flora made my stomach hurt.

Marlo stretched out her short legs, crossing them at the ankles. "The warmth will come when you make peace with your past, Blue, so you can have peace in the future."

She'd been telling me for years I needed to forgive my family in order to move on, but she never could quite explain how to do so. It wasn't as simple as saying so—that I knew for a fact. "Even if I could," I said, trying not to think of my mother passed out in a haze of stale whiskey, "Flora's fate is out of my hands. It's up to her birth parents, a judge."

Moe looked me straight in the eyes, his dark gaze burning with righteousness, and said, "Hogwash. This isn't the time for *peace*. You fight to keep this here little one. Fight *dirty* if you have to."

Twyla's voice echoed in my head, chasing Moe's like a tailwind.

Trouble will come for you, Blue—just you wait and see. And when it does, you'll embrace it same as me. Moral compasses are easily broken when dropped in between a rock and a hard place.

I'd refused to believe my mother. There were always other options. Always.

She didn't have to write bad checks or turn to a bottle to deal with her grief; Daddy didn't have to con people; Wade and Ty didn't have to rob a bank; Mac didn't have to fight.

They didn't have to die.

They didn't have to leave me.

I'd *never* be like them.

Anger simmered, and I took a deep breath. I avoided fights at all costs. I hated conflict and friction. I didn't even like to raise my voice. I wasn't going to compromise everything I'd ever stood for by fighting dirty. But . . . I would fight for Flora if I had to. *Legally.*

"Moe," Marlo said on a long sigh.

He ignored her. "Blue, you tell anyone who wants to take this here baby from you to go straight to hell and never come back. This is your baby. *Yours.* Y'hear?"

I nodded, simply to calm him down.

His eyes dimmed, the fire extinguishing before he glanced back at Flora. "She's a cute one. What's her name?"

Sarah Grace

The house, passed down from Fulton to Fulton for the past one hundred and twenty years, had been quiet when I arrived home, keeping oddly to itself. I'd been expecting its usual taunts.

It hated me, this house.

It was one of the first arts and crafts–style homes built in Alabama, and I adored the architecture with its arches and exquisite woodwork. But this old house had seen a lot of rage and suffering within its walls, and at some point it had adopted the callous personality it now possessed. Perhaps as a protective measure. Or perhaps 120 years of helplessness had hardened it to kindness and affection.

I wished the house had warned me what I was getting myself into when I first moved in, but houses were the best secret keepers. They tended to keep all proverbial skeletons in the closet until they were discovered by others. And as I'd learned, this house held a lot of skeletons.

Moving was out of the question. The house had been a gift from Fletch's widowed mother when we married. I could have sworn I'd seen relief—and pity—in Jasmine Fulton's eyes when she handed over the keys. Since then, she'd moved into a newly built house on a golf course in Naples, Florida, a house that was airy and peppy, full of happy energy. I tried not to let my jealousy show whenever I visited.

"Fletch?" I called out, the name echoing through a maze of hallways like the house was mocking my voice.

He had to know I was home. The motion detector on the video doorbell would've sent a chime to his phone. I despised that hideous doorbell, but he'd insisted we needed it for security, which was laughable. I suspected he wanted it because he liked to keep tabs on my comings and goings.

"In the kitchen," Fletch yelled back.

I dropped my workbag on the foyer table and took a fortifying breath. Life was so much easier these days when he wasn't home. Pasting a smile on my face, I went into the kitchen and immediately chilled when I saw the bottle of Jim Beam on the island next to a loaf of bread and sandwich fixings. "Have you been home long?"

"A half hour."

A half hour. He'd had at least one drink. Possibly two.

Fletch quickly put his phone into his pocket. "You're late. I was starving, so I ate without you."

I crossed to the sink to wash my hands. In the reflection in the window, I saw him pull his phone from his pocket, check it, then put it back in his lap. I dried my hands on a tea towel and turned toward him. I couldn't recall the last time we'd eaten together, just the two of us. Most of the meals we shared took place at my parents' table. Meals where we put on our best faces and told our biggest lies. The great pretenders.

"That's okay," I said. "I'm not very hungry."

He pushed his plate away. "Were you working?"

"Yes. Finishing up a proposal. I've decided to bid on the Bishop farmhouse."

Pale eyebrows lifted as he reached for his glass, a Baccarat crystal tumbler from a set that had once belonged to his great-granddaddy.

I despised those glasses. So much so that I'd *accidentally* broken four of the twelve already. One for each time I'd had to patch a hole Fletch kicked into a wall.

He downed the remainder of the dark-amber liquid in one gulp. "That isn't so much a house as it is firewood. You'd do best to set a match to it and start from scratch."

Fletch Fulton was a handsome man—and he knew it. Golden-brown hair, animated brown eyes. He'd been a football player in high school and college before being sidelined by a knee injury his junior year. He had a dazzling smile, a big personality, and the enviable ability to set most people at ease.

Having been born and raised here in Buttonwood, we'd known each other most of our lives. But we hadn't started dating until we'd finished college and come back home, connecting over cocktails at one of my father's fund-raisers. It hadn't been true love. Not even close. But it had been friendship, born from recognizing in each other, without speaking of it, a kindred spirit. A hidden spirit. A lost spirit. Both of us were living lives that we wouldn't have chosen for ourselves in order to please our parents.

In each other, we'd found things we both desperately needed at the time.

For me, it had been his shadow to hide in.

For him, it had been my family ties.

During his senior year of college, and at loose ends after having had his big NFL plans derailed, Fletch had gone to his dying father for advice and had come back with a life plan: Fletch would go into politics.

He'd finished college, barely, with a liberal arts degree. Buried his daddy. Married me. And he'd been working for my father for three years now. Everyone in Buttonwood knew Fletch had plans to run for mayor one day.

There were flaws in that grand plan he'd hatched with his daddy, however.

The biggest being that Fletch didn't want to be mayor. The only thing he liked about politics was the name recognition. He'd much rather be on a football field coaching or in a sport's booth announcing. Instead, he was stuck. Stuck in a job he didn't like, in a town too small for him, with a life he had to pretend to enjoy.

Even still, we'd been happy together for a while. Content.

But every pretender knew well that there came a time when the effort to keep up appearances took its toll. Especially when you couldn't even let your guard down at home. Tensions mounted. Unspoken regrets hovered over our conversations. We'd withdrawn from each other.

I'd thrown myself into work and marathon training.

Fletch found solace in liquor bottles and old demons.

He got up every morning to go to work, put on a good show among his coworkers, and no one was wiser to his bad habits.

No one but me. And this house.

Needing to defend the Bishop farmhouse from being called firewood, I said, "It has decent bones."

"Well, I wouldn't pay a dime for it. Blue's lost her fool mind if she thinks she's going to get full ask."

I crossed to the fridge, pulled out a pitcher of sweet tea, and asked myself for the millionth time how I'd ended up here, in this loveless marriage. Then I remembered.

The Buttonwood curse.

I'd brought this on myself.

Fighting an overwhelming urge to open the back door and go for a run until I could run no longer, I busied myself by taking a tall glass from the cabinet and filling it with ice cubes.

Standing, Fletch grabbed his plate. As he circled the island on his way to the sink, he said, "Jud spent some time in my office today."

Jud. My daddy. I had a feeling I knew what that conversation had been about. I finished pouring my tea and quickly capped the bourbon bottle while it was unattended. "Was he there to talk about the baby?"

"Yeah." He turned to face me full on and crossed his arms. "The baby Blue found in the woods."

"My mother paid me a visit, too, today. She says the baby is perfect."

He scoffed. "I'm not surprised. But if it's so *perfect*, why did someone dump it in the woods?"

I twisted the lid onto the Duke's mayo, and the grooves bit into my fingers. "Not everyone is cut out to be a parent."

I didn't know what it was like to give up a child, but I surely knew what it was like to lose one. It was a visceral ache I couldn't possibly describe—only feel. Whirling alongside it were painful memories I'd sell my soul to forget.

"*Whatever*," he said, taking a step toward me. "Jud wants us to adopt it, but Sarah Grace, I still want my *own* baby some-day."

One of Fletch's biggest goals in life was to be a father. Not so much because he wanted a child to love, but to prove, even if only to himself, that he'd be a better dad than his own had been. It was a short stick by which to measure.

He added, "I think it's time we start trying."

"I'm not so sure now's a good time." I shoved the mayo into the fridge and forced myself not to slam the door.

"You do want to have a baby, don't you?" he asked, moving closer.

"Of course I want to have a baby someday," I said, "but with the way things are between us, I'm not comfortable—"

"We're fine." He smiled wide, oozing charm. "Just hit a rough patch. Every marriage does."

Our relationship was exhausted and now lay dying at our feet, gasping for air. I didn't know how to save our marriage, but I didn't think having a baby right now was the answer.

"We should see a counselor," I suggested.

"Sarah Grace, we don't need someone butting into our business. Can you even imagine? You don't even like talking to me half the time."

"That's not true," I lied. Unsaid words clumped in my throat, choking me with regret and frustration. I wanted to point out all the conversations we'd had where he told me that renting my houses to lower income families was foolish. Or how often he commented that my time could be better spent in a gym lifting weights than on my marathon training. Work and running were two of the most important things in my life, two of the only things that brought me any measure of well-being and contentment, and he wanted me to change them. He wanted to change *me*. I was sick to death of having to explain myself, so if that meant I stopped telling him much about my job and training, then yeah, I guess he could say that I didn't like to talk to him all that much.

"This is why we should see a therapist," I added. I knew better than to try to explain my point of view, here and now, with just the two of us. He'd only get louder and louder trying to prove his points, and angrier and angrier when I refused to be steamrolled by what *he* thought was best for *me*. I wanted a mediator present when we talked. Someone to step in if our conversation turned heated.

He lifted an eyebrow, and his gaze hardened. "Therapy is not happening, no ma'am, so let it go, Sarah Grace. I've been thinking a baby might just be the thing we need to get us back on track."

It was a fine line I had to walk, considering the bourbon. I didn't want to stoke his anger, but I dearly wanted to give him a piece of my mind. I held my breath as I said, "You and I both know our issues won't be solved by having a baby."

I braced myself for a temper tantrum. I'd done more patchwork in this house than most of the houses I'd rehabbed. Fletch had yet to hit me, which spoke a lot of his determination not to be like his daddy, his granddaddy, and his great-granddaddy.

All men who'd lived in this house. All men who'd had trouble with liquor and tempers and demons. All men who'd used their fists on people they supposedly loved.

In addition to wanting to break the toxic cycle, Fletch knew if he so much as laid a harmful finger on me, it would be the end of us. And therefore the end of his political aspirations. I could pretend only so much.

Instead of lashing out, he put his hands gently on my arms, and I tried not to flinch. It had been months since he'd touched me in any kind of loving way. Two months? Three? I couldn't remember.

"We can make it work," he said. "I'm really thinking this baby thing is a good idea. We should've started trying sooner."

This baby thing. Good Lord.

His hands moved up to my shoulders and rested gently, but under the touch point of each of his fingers, my skin crawled. How had my life come to this? Unable to speak my mind? Unable to be *me* without feeling less than? Unable to stomach my husband's touch?

To stall, I said, "I have a checkup with my doctor soon. Let me make sure everything's in good working order, so to speak. Then we'll go from there."

"All right." Appeased, he backed away and added, "But we still need to decide about the baby Blue found. Jud gave me a name of a good lawyer. We need to get the ball rolling."

Stall, stall, stall. "We should think on the decision a little bit more. At least sleep on it. Adopting a baby isn't something that can be done on a whim. There's a lot involved."

"You know Jud can pull some strings."

It was the same message my mother had given me. Buttonwood was a small town, and my father held a lot of power. "I don't want preferential treatment."

"Hell, I don't particularly want the kid at all, but we'd be better parents than Blue."

"You barely know Blue. How can you say that?"

"Like you know her better than I do?"

"We're friends. We were in the same year in school, if you remember." She'd begun school a year late, setting her back a grade. And okay, we weren't quite friends, but we were *friendly*.

He snorted. "You don't have any friends."

I stiffened, and he smirked, having hit his target. I had very few friends. It was hard to maintain friendships when you had to keep so much of yourself *to* yourself.

"It's just that Blue is a *Bishop*." He sneered the surname.

"And you're a Fulton," I snapped, trying to make him see the inanity of his argument. "Spittin' image of your father."

He sucked in a breath and tucked his tongue into his cheek pocket—a sure sign he was reining in his temper. "Point taken. But we'd still be better parents, seeing that there are two of us."

"If anyone can raise a baby on her own, it's Blue. She practically raised Persy by herself, and look how well she turned out."

"Why're you defending Blue so much?"

Heat rose to my cheeks. "I'm just calling it how I see it."

He let out a long sigh. "Doesn't matter in the long run. Your parents are set on us getting that baby. The adoption will look mighty good for your daddy's campaign. And mine, too, if I run for mayor once his seat is vacant."

I tipped my head when I caught his *if*, surprised it hadn't been *when*. That was a new development. "*If* you run for mayor?" I questioned. "Are you having second thoughts?"

Broad shoulders stiffened. "I misspoke is all. My point is a ready-made family with a heartwarming backstory will sway voters. I'll call a lawyer tomorrow morning."

"Don't. I need time," I said again, feeling sadness wash over me. After all these years, it might be time to pay another visit to the Buttonwood Tree for advice. Surely there was some way to break my curse. Happiness. All I wanted was a little happiness in this complicated, muddled life I'd created.

A little voice inside my head whispered that I'd be happier if I left Fletch. Divorced him. It was a familiar voice, one that had started speaking up not long after Fletch and I married, telling me I'd made a huge mistake. As always, I silenced it. The last thing I wanted was a divorce. A messy, public airing of our grievances. It turned my stomach just thinking of it and the ripple effect it would have on my family—especially my father's career, a man whose whole platform revolved around the perfect family image.

Letting out a frustrated huff, Fletch said, "Fine, but you tell that to Jud."

"I will."

He checked his phone and said, "I need to get going."

"Going out again?" He'd either been working late or going out with his buddies nearly every night for weeks now. "Where?"

"Does it matter?"

"It just seems to me that it's not helping our marriage spending so much time apart. Is there a reason you're being secretive about where you're going?" If he could keep tabs on me through the doorbell, he could at least tell me where he'd be tonight.

"You're acting as if you don't trust me. And am I the one who worked late tonight and missed dinner? No. That was you, Sarah Grace. Maybe tomorrow you can get home on time. Don't wait up for me."

That little voice spoke up again, telling me to get far away from him, away from the threat that always seemed to be hanging in the air along with the scent of bourbon, away from the phony life we'd created.

And heaven help me, I wanted to run.

But then I thought of my parents and their expectations and stifled the urge. Fletch and I could make this work if we made the effort. *Do better. Be better.*

I opened my mouth to ask him to stay home, then snapped it closed again as he grabbed his keys. It had been a long day, and

I didn't have the energy to figure out how we could fix our marriage. My thoughts earlier about the Bishop farmhouse came floating back, teasing me.

Exposing all the damage was the only way anything could be fixed properly.

Except a full gut job was exactly what our marriage *didn't* need. The flimsy walls we'd put up were the only things holding Fletch and me together. If they were torn down, I had no doubt our marriage would completely collapse.

When I heard his car driving away, I grabbed my glass of tea, cut the kitchen lights, collected my bag from the entryway, and headed for my office.

The door tended to stick, so I gave it a good push, getting nothing but a splinter for my effort. I put my shoulder against the wood and shoved, and the door swung open easily, dumping me into the room.

"Not funny," I said, glad I'd managed not to spill my tea everywhere.

The house chuckled.

Over the past four years I'd tried to befriend this house again and again and was rebuffed at every turn. Like a fool, I kept trying. Not only for the house's sake but mine as well. It would be nice to have a friend around here.

"I still like you," I said as I picked the splinter out of my palm and pulled the Bishop offer out of my bag for another once-over.

Despite Fletch's suggestion of less than a dime, I planned to offer full ask, which would hopefully land me in escrow fairly quickly.

My cell phone rang, and I checked the screen before answering. If it had been either of my parents, I'd have muted the call. I couldn't deal with them right now. But it was Kebbie on the line, so I quickly answered. My cousin, Kimberlee "Kebbie" Hastings, had just finished her sophomore year of college at

Alabama, where she was well on her way to getting her bachelor's degree in interior design. She had great taste and often helped me stage my houses.

"I just wanted to remind you that I'm working at the bookshop tomorrow so I won't be at the office," she said. "Apparently something big is going on—Marlo called an emergency midday meeting for all the employees."

Kebbie was what I called a worker bee. Always busy. Always buzzing. She slept little, drank too much coffee, and was always on the go. I recognized the tactic. My way of coping with the pain of the past was running—hers was working. She currently held two part-time jobs: one with me, the other at the bookshop. But she also volunteered at the local vet's office, and she was Buttonwood's best pet sitter and babysitter.

My gaze went to a photo on my desk. In the picture, Kebbie had an arm around me during a pool party last summer at my parents' house. There was no doubt we were related, with our high foreheads and cheekbones, blond hair and wide smiles. But I was all arms and legs, long and lean, whereas Kebbie was short and curvy. We'd been sun bronzed and glowing, our smiles belying our inner sadness.

I wasn't the only pretender in my family.

"What kind of 'big'?" I asked.

Kebbie had held a steady job at The Rabbit Hole, a children's bookshop here in Buttonwood, since high school, and now that she was in college, she worked there whenever she was home on break. Her mother, my aunt Caroline, had taken her to story time there every week since she had been knee-high, and after her mama had passed, Kebbie often found herself back in that shop. It was a place of peace and comfort for her, which had a lot to do with Marlo and Moe Allemand and their giving natures as much as it did old, happy memories. There had been no way my mama could deny Kebbie's request to work there, despite the fact that Blue Bishop was also on the payroll.

Mama's fears of Kebbie being tainted by the Bishop reputation had thankfully proved unfounded, but Mama had banned all talk about Blue, as if even saying the Bishop name would rain damnation down upon our house.

Mama took her grudges seriously.

"I don't know," Kebbie said, "but I've seen a strange man hanging around the shop. I wonder if it has something to do with him."

"'Strange' as in an outsider, or 'strange' like he's touched in the head?"

She laughed. "Outsider. I'll fill you in when I have all the details."

We said our goodbyes and hung up. I worked for another few hours, enjoying the quiet, before deciding to turn in. As I locked up the house, sadness followed me up the stairs to my cold, empty bed, and I decided that a visit to the Buttonwood Tree needed to happen sooner rather than later.

Blue

I'd never been one for much sleep. A few hours of shut-eye saw me through most nights, but having Flora here, I didn't want to close my eyes at all. I just wanted to watch her.

I'd brought the cradle into my bedroom but had spent most of the night in bed simply holding her. Feeling her warmth against my skin. Trying to memorize the pattern of her breaths, the rise and fall of her tiny chest. I studied the fine lines on her palms, the shape of her surprisingly sharp fingernails. I longed to sketch her profile, but I didn't want to put her down long enough to pick up my drawing pad.

For the first time in my life I knew without a doubt that love at first sight was very real.

Flora hadn't been awake all night, like we had all suspected would happen. Instead she slept deeply, having awoken only at one a.m. in search of a bottle. As soon as she'd had her fill, I changed her diaper, and she drifted back to sleep.

It was now coming on four in the morning, and I knew I needed to sleep, but just when I decided to finally close my eyes, Flora woke up, crying pitifully.

"Hey now," I said softly as I cradled her head in my hand. "No need for such a fuss."

She quieted at my voice, then let out another irritated bleat as she wiggled in my arms.

"All right, okay. I'm going." I carried her through the house, the moonbeams providing enough light to guide me to the kitchen. I quickly fixed a bottle and soon we were back upstairs.

I paused at the top of the steps and tipped my ear toward Persy's room. All was silent. At Flora's earlier feeding, I'd heard the rumble of Persy's voice—she'd been on the phone, talking to someone in low tones. I hated that she was keeping something—someone—from me, and respecting her privacy was growing more difficult with each passing day.

Back in my room, Flora and I cuddled together in an old wicker rocker. A puddle of moonlight highlighted blue flecks in her gray eyes as she drank from the bottle, slurping loudly for such a little person. She blinked continuously as she drank, as if keeping her eyes wide open was too great a burden. Finally she gave up the effort, allowing them to close, her dark lashes falling heavily onto round pink cheeks. When I pulled the bottle away to burp her, she was already half-asleep, a warm, six-pound shapeless lump in my arms.

Six pounds even. Eighteen inches long. The doctors at the hospital had declared her to be no more than three days old. Though small, she'd been well cared for, and for that I was incredibly grateful.

"No, no, don't go to sleep yet, Flora. You don't want a stomachache, do you?"

Her lips smacked in answer, but I could tell by the rhythm of her breathing that she was already asleep. I stood and walked, trying to ease a burp out of her, refusing to give up. I was nothing if not stubborn.

As I passed the window, I caught sight of movement in the Allemands' backyard garden. For a moment, I thought it was Moe, wandering. But no. It was Marlo. It had been a while since I'd seen her out in the moonlight, and I took a moment to watch her as she went through a series of movements that reminded me of a mix of tai chi and ballet. I didn't think it had a name, this beautiful, rhythmic dance of hers she did every night the moon shined in the sky, but I called it her moondance. Her arms floated fluidly through the air, leaving sparkling golden swirls in the darkness as her skin absorbed the light.

I glided in tandem with Marlo's footsteps while still patting Flora's back. She let out a tiny burp, pulling me away from the mesmerizing scene outside, and reluctantly, I stepped away from the window. I changed Flora's diaper, kissed the top of her downy head, and tucked her into the cradle, only an arm's reach away.

I climbed into bed and pulled the covers up to my neck. My mind whirled, thinking about Marlo and Moe and the bookshop. About Persy and her secrets. About the old farmhouse, and the happiness I'd once known there, a long time ago.

As the minutes ticked by I finally drifted off, and I dreamed of a golden crow with pride shining in her black eyes, and a glittery piece of thread caught in her beak.

Chapter
4

Blue

By eight the next morning, I was showered and dressed. I sat on a stool in the all-season sunroom I used as a studio, staring at the drafting table in front of me. My gaze drifted from a drawing of ballet-dancing animals to a sleeping Flora in a Moses basket next to me, to the backyard.

When I had moved in, the yard had been a mess, sorely neglected by the previous owner, and I'd gone straight to work, trying to create the yard I'd always dreamed of as a child. Green grass instead of rutted dirt, wildflowers instead of weeds. Handblown fairy orbs in every color imaginable dangled from tree branches, giving the illusion that it was Christmastime year-round. Party lights skimmed the white picket fence, and a hammock hung between two oak trees.

Cool morning air and sunlight spilled through open windows. Birds sang, the bell in the church tower a few blocks over tolled the hour, and I was trying my mightiest to stay put. The wind beckoned, and the need to go searching nagged, nearly pushing me off my seat with its urgency.

"Later," I told it, hooking my toes on the stool's footrest. Much later.

While I was loath to go anywhere in public with Flora today, Marlo didn't often ask for help. In fact, I could count on one hand how many times she'd ever asked me for *anything*. I didn't want to let her down, so in another hour or so, Flora and I would go to the bookshop to meet the new owner to teach him the procedures for opening the store. Marlo planned to meet us there after Moe's doctor's appointment.

Finding Flora had taken some of the sting out of The Rabbit Hole news, but my stomach ached at the mere thought of someone else running the shop. As a deep sorrow settled into my bones, I forced myself to focus on all the good that would come of the sale—namely, Marlo having more free time and a bit of financial freedom. But there was no denying that it felt like I was losing something I loved deeply. The shop wouldn't be the same without Marlo. Like she'd said, The Rabbit Hole had been her dream, and her heart and soul had been poured into it.

"I can't believe Marlo sold the shop," Persy said from the kitchen as if reading my mind, her words punctuated by the clatter of silverware. "Well, what I mean is that I can't believe no one knew she sold the shop. Secrets are hard to keep in this town."

I didn't know about that. Persy was having no trouble keeping her late-night whereabouts to herself. "She had her reasons."

"Don't all secret keepers?"

If Persy was dating someone on the sly, why would she choose to keep him secret? While I wasn't thrilled she would have a hot-and-heavy romance at eighteen, I wasn't a prude. Life happened. I was less thrilled that she was keeping it from me. Why not bring her boyfriend home, let me meet him? Was there something about him that she was ashamed of? Was he older? Was he *married*?

"Apparently, she's been seen around town with a young-looking guy, but no one knows his name or where he's from. Definitely not a local."

"Really?" I asked, thankfully distracted from thoughts of Persy being a home wrecker.

"One of the vet techs saw them together at the bank the

other day. Tall guy, brown hair, dimples," she said as she came into the sunroom.

At the mention of the bank, my stomach turned. It had been almost twenty years since my brothers had robbed Button-wood's Blackstock Bank and Trust, and yet time hadn't less-ened the shame . . . or the grief.

Persy sat in an old armchair with a bowl of grits. Damp hair had been combed away from her face. As it dried, it would fall forward, framing her high cheekbones and strong jawline.

My oldest brother Mac and I favored Twyla's fairer side of the family, but Persy looked a lot like our daddy, Wade, and Ty, with her height, ruddy coloring, hair, and eye color. My mother had been over the moon when Persy had come along, since in her late forties, Twyla had believed she was long done having babies. Persimmon, named for the tree blooming in the yard the day she'd been born, had arrived nearly ten years after me, the pregnancy unknown until Twyla's seventh month when she suddenly realized why she hadn't been feeling well. Fortunately, it was a quicker time frame than when Twyla had learned she was pregnant with me—on the day of my birth. I'd been a com-plete surprise. An early one at that. The doctor my parents had taken me to after I'd been born had guessed that I'd arrived at least a month and a half early. I'd been tiny, at just a little over four pounds.

Persy dragged her fork around the bowl, carving deep im-pressions into the grits where melted butter pooled. "You need to text me as soon as you're done meeting with him. My curi-osity isn't going to wait until I see you. I need all the details."

She had calculus from nine to eleven Monday and Tuesday mornings. "You shouldn't be texting during class."

The community college where she was taking summer courses was only fifteen minutes away from home, unlike UNA, the University of Northern Alabama, which was an hour and a half northwest. She was enrolled in two summer classes, which would help fulfill some of the gen-ed requirements of her biology degree.

She pouted. "You're going to make me wait, aren't you? That's cruel. Just cruel. I'm going straight from school to work. I'll be middle-aged before I get all the details."

"Don't forget to sign up for AARP. I hear they have great discounts."

"Ha. Ha." She made a face at me.

I smiled and took a sip of coffee. "What time are you working till?"

"Five."

She'd been working with Doc Hennessey since middle school, starting out as a volunteer until eventually earning a spot on the payroll. Even though she didn't say so, I suspected she wanted to run the practice one day. First things first—her degree. She was one year into her biology degree, with her sights set on attending Auburn's College of Veterinary Medicine.

Persy set the bowl on a side table and pulled out her phone to snap a shot of Flora yawning, and Persy yawned, too. Dark shadows lurked beneath her eyes.

"I hope we didn't keep you up last night."

"Nope." She stuck the fork in her mouth and said nothing more.

I sipped my coffee, swallowing a thousand questions along with the dark brew.

After a long minute, she said, "Can I ask you something, Blue? Something that might be hard to answer?"

"Sure. You know you can ask me anything, anytime." I leaned forward. Was she finally going to tell me about the secret boyfriend? Lordy, I hoped so.

"Is it possible that someone else could adopt Flora right out from under you?"

I wasn't prepared for the emotional sucker punch, and it took me a moment to find any words. "I don't rightly know the answer to that question, but I don't think so. The court awarded me guardianship. As far as I understand it, for Flora to be taken away from me, something major would have to happen."

The words hurt just saying them. Flora had been in my life barely twenty-four hours now, and I already couldn't imagine a day without her. I was going to do everything possible to adopt her. I needed to find a good lawyer, and I was grateful I had a little nest egg saved up, because good lawyers were costly. I'd been intending to use the money to pay for a private adoption but life had a way of flipping upside down every once in a while.

"Major like what?"

I suddenly regretted telling Persy she could ask me anything. "Anything that would deem me unfit. Like if it was found that I abused her. Or I left her at home alone. Or I committed a felony."

Persy's eyebrow went up at the last one. "You are a Bishop."

I rolled my eyes. "Don't tease."

She laughed and went back to raking her grits.

Flora squeaked and fidgeted, and Persy immediately set her bowl aside and picked her up, rocking and cooing. The baby soon drifted off once again.

"You're a natural at calming her down," I said.

"Beginner's luck."

I narrowed my gaze. Ordinarily, I wouldn't have questioned the statement, but there was an unusual adamancy to her tone, and a faint blush stained her cheeks. Why was she trying to convince me of something that shouldn't need convincing at all?

Persy glanced at me and quickly tucked Flora back into the basket. "I best get going or I'm going to be late for class, where I won't be texting." She practically ran into the kitchen, rinsed her bowl, then grabbed my car keys and was out the front door with a hurried goodbye.

I tried to ignore a sudden ache in my stomach as I washed

paintbrushes and tried to organize the chaos that was my studio, so it would look put together when the court investigator stopped by later this week.

Next door, I spotted Moe sitting at the patio table on the deck. Shadows from the overhead pergola fell across his body, making him look like he was wearing prison stripes as he ate a banana and pretended to read the paper. Even from here I could see the *Buttonwood Daily* was upside down.

There were three calls on my voicemail from reporters wanting to interview me for a story on Flora, but I'd been advised by Shep Wheeler not to talk to anyone while the case was still active. Undoubtedly, Flora's abandonment would be old news soon enough, and the reporters would move on to the next big story.

As I continued to tidy up my studio, I promised Poppy Kay I'd find time at some point today to work on her. The sketches and text for *Poppy Kay Hoppy Finds Ballet* had already been approved, but I still had three pages of art to finish painting for the thirty-two-page picture book. The project was due to my editor in two weeks, which ordinarily would've been plenty of time, but now that Flora was here, I had to learn how to balance work with caring for her.

Next door, the screen door slapped against the house as an energetic Marlo flew onto the deck with a breakfast tray in hand. She left faint golden trails glittering behind her as she set the tray onto the table and then stood behind Moe's chair. She put her hands on his shoulders and whispered something in his ear.

As he sat up straighter, the glimmer around her vanished, and she slumped, as though suddenly exhausted, into the chair next to his. Laughing, he turned the paper right side up.

Flora whimpered, and I quickly scooped her up. When I turned back to check on Marlo, she'd gone back inside, and the sun had shifted position so that it shined solely on Moe's face.

He'd been temporarily freed from his prison and now possessed a glow all his own.

✦

The sweet scent of wisteria filled the air and fading purple blooms spilled over a rusted iron fence as Flora and I headed for the bookshop. I felt a little bit like a mama kangaroo as Flora's face peeked out of the fabric pouch of a baby sling. She made chirping noises as we walked along, not quite crying but rather making her presence known. As if it were possible to forget.

A small knapsack filled with a bottle of dry formula, a water bottle, and diapers bumped against my back as we walked— and as I ignored the wind's call to search the woods. It could wait until after we met with the new owner of the shop, which I hoped would be a quick meeting. Getting the shop ready for the day was a fairly simple routine, especially if the man had any retail experience.

I didn't know if he did—only that he'd most recently been a schoolteacher. I didn't even know his name. Marlo and Moe had already left for his doctor's appointment this morning by the time I thought to ask any detailed questions about the new owner. It was unlike Marlo not to thoroughly prep me for the meeting, which told me exactly how overwhelmed she'd become lately.

The heart of Buttonwood consisted of four blocks of shops, restaurants, offices, apartments, and a park. The rest of the town had risen up in concentric squares around it. On these outer streets were houses, churches, parks, baseball fields, and schools, with a few outlier businesses like Dodd's Electrical, which operated out of Mr. Dodd's old barn, and the woods.

Farther out from the center, the tidy grid of streets dissolved into county roads where one could find the car factory that employed many of Buttonwood's four thousand residents, the community college, the hospital, numerous farms, a few less popular churches, and the residents who valued privacy above all else, as evident by the NO TRESPASSING signs tacked to their fences and tree lines.

It was a small yet thriving community. Tight-knit with a long memory.

A very long, judgmental memory.

I received a few curious stares as I walked down Poplar Street, which divided Buttonwood neatly in half, east to west. I kept my gaze averted from the bank and noticed that workers were already in the park setting up for the festival taking place this coming weekend. Just as I'd passed Boon Hardy's barbershop, I heard my name being called, and I turned around.

"Oh my stars, Blue! You're the very last person I expected to see out and about today," Mrs. Tillman said as she rushed along the sidewalk. Fluffy white hair curled around her cheeks. "I just wanted to say hello and get a peek at your little one. I've never heard of such a thing. Finding a *baby* in the woods. It's unheard of. She's so precious! Do the police know who she belongs to yet?"

Mrs. Tillman had been my fifth-grade teacher but had been retired from teaching a good five years and now helped her husband at their hardware store a few days a week. Of all my teachers, she'd been my favorite, never treating me differently because of my family name. I couldn't say that of all my teachers, however. Or a certain high school principal.

And while I wanted to say that Flora belonged to *me*, I carefully chose my words. "The police are still looking for the woman who gave birth to her."

Wrinkles fanned out from Mrs. Tillman's bright-blue eyes as she excitedly said, "Might could be someone we know. Isn't that wild?"

Shep Wheeler was checking with all the local hospitals and midwives. If Flora's mother had given birth around here, we'd know soon enough. I ignored a jab of uneasiness and said, "We don't know that the woman is from around here."

"Don't we, though? What with the button and all? How'd she even know who you were otherwise? Or know about the Buttonwood Tree? Only locals know about the buttons. I hope the police are looking into the possibility that someone around here was hiding a pregnancy."

Cars and trucks passed slowly, people getting on with their day. People who could probably hear my anxiety as surely as the local country station they had playing on the radio as they rolled on by.

"Is that even possible in this day and age?" I mean, sure, my mother had been surprised by me—and hadn't known for seven months that she was pregnant with Persy—but Twyla had been a bit long in the tooth, as she would've said, and had always been a plump, round woman so she hadn't noticed a weight gain.

Mrs. Tillman laughed and tucked a curl behind her ear. "Haven't you seen all those TV shows about women who didn't even know they were pregnant?"

I shook my head. "I don't watch much TV."

"Well, it's possible. We'll leave it at that."

For reasons I didn't want to explore, I didn't like that possibility. Not one little bit. "I should be getting to work," I said, hooking a thumb over my shoulder. "I'm helping train someone new."

"Oh? Did Marlo finally hire on a store manager?" She stood on tiptoe and looked into the dark bookshop. "I bet it's that man who's been seen with Marlo all around town this past week. What's his name? Where's he from?"

My cheeks heated. Because I had no answers, I said, "You'll have to ask Marlo about that. It's been good to see you, Mrs. Tillman."

"You too, Blue. Don't be such a *stranger.* You've become

quite the hermit. Come by the store. We sell your books—I'd love for you to sign them."

I hadn't known the hardware store carried my books since I rarely went in there, preferring to shop online than run into neighbors. "That's mighty kind of you."

She waved a hand. "They're great books. I'm real proud of you, Blue."

My eyes misted, and before I could think of anything to say, she snapped her fingers.

"Oh! You should join the Buttonwood Moms Club!"

While I'd prefer a root canal, I thought about *threads* and said, "I didn't know there was such a thing."

"Sure, sure. *Everyone's* welcome. The group is a great source of support, especially in these early days when it feels like you're living with an adorable little alien." She smiled wide. "I'll get the information to you. The group would love to have you. Both of you."

Everyone's welcome.

I searched her face. She was either a great actress or she truly believed what she was saying. I was at a loss, on unfamiliar ground. "Thank you."

"You'll be at the festival, right?"

"Yes, at The Rabbit Hole's booth." Though, even as I said it, I wondered if I would be now that Flora was here. Yet, the thought of leaving Marlo shorthanded sent guilt flooding through me. I'd have to figure out a way to make it work.

"The Moms will have a booth, too. I'll bring you by. Make introductions."

I smiled so tightly my jaw hurt. "All right."

She peeked into the wrap once again, then rested a gentle hand on my shoulder, like she used to do when I was little and had earned her praise. "I can't rightly say I know who this little one's mother is, but I do know she's in good hands with you. You'll be a fine mama, Blue Bishop. A fine mama."

With a wave she headed back toward the hardware store a block down the street, and I watched her go with a lump in my throat until finally turning toward The Rabbit Hole.

Diffused sunlight glinted off the bookshop's picture window that held a multilevel display of books, and I smiled when I saw *Poppy Kay Hoppy Finds a Tadpole* surrounded by a variety of stuffed frogs and a small notecard with LOCAL AUTHOR written on it sitting in front of the book.

Marlo was a proud mama hen.

Sometimes when I saw my name on a book cover, it still didn't seem real. Until Marlo and Moe had taken me under their wings, I hadn't had much of a career goal. I'd wanted only to be normal. A normal girl in a normal town with a normal family. I'd never dreamed my love of painting could ever be anything other than a hobby.

But I fell in love with this shop and had been inspired by Marlo's love of rabbits and by all the books in the shop, especially the ones that focused on how being different wasn't a bad thing. *Chrysanthemum. Little Quack's New Friend. The Story of Ferdinand. Whoever You Are. Princess Smartypants.*

I'd started sketching a rabbit. A rabbit much like me, who found things. I sketched drawings of her for years before Marlo and Moe started encouraging me to write a story around that rabbit. Once I'd done that, they then pushed for me to submit the book to a literary agent. As if the stars had been aligned just right, I signed with that agent, and it wasn't long before a large publishing company in New York wanted to publish it. My career took off.

Just as I pulled the store key from the pocket of my shorts, to my right, the door to Kitty's Diner opened and a woman came out, to-go cup in one hand, a phone in the other. When she glanced up from the screen and saw me, the soft lines of her face hardened. Her gaze dropped to Flora for a split second before she pivoted and marched away.

"That's Ginny Landreneau," I said to Flora. "She doesn't like us on account of my father stealing her family's house. There are certain people around town you'll learn to avoid. She's one of them. Oleta Blackstock is another. She'll give you nightmares."

For a split second I let my gaze wander to the bank. Oleta's bank. She never let it be forgotten that the Bishop boys had shot the place up, stolen her money, then let it burn. Never mind that the bank had insurance. Or that it wasn't really her money. Or that two of my brothers had paid the ultimate price for their bad decision.

She was . . . loathsome.

Before I got too caught up in the past, I quickly unlocked the bookshop's door and stepped inside. I was early for the meeting and glad to have some time alone in the shop as I turned off the alarm and quickly shut the door behind me, making sure the CLOSED sign still faced outward.

I rested my cheek on top of Flora's head as I breathed in the scent of the shop, which smelled a whole lot like *love*. I blinked away sudden tears in my eyes and cut on the lights. I had to be *strong*. Marlo had made her decision, and I needed to support her, as she'd done for me all these years.

Flora blinked at the sudden light and spit out a pacifier clipped to the baby sling to squeak a protest.

"Give it a second," I told her as I rubbed her back and walked around the shop. "You'll adjust."

I took a moment to admire the mural above a dozen waist-high bookshelves that extended the length of the shop. The painting was of a tree with a wide green canopy and long, gnarled roots. In the middle of the tree's trunk was an empty hollow, on a low branch sat a shiny, wise-looking crow, and at the base of the trunk was a family of rabbits standing round a warmly illuminated hole in the ground: two taller caramel-colored rabbits and a dozen little ones, all with different colored fur, ears, and noses.

Moe and Marlo had commissioned the mural long before I'd ever stepped foot into the shop, but I couldn't help thinking that two of those little rabbits in the mural were Persy and me. But I also had the feeling that every child who came into this shop also saw themselves in one of those rabbits. The rest of the walls were wallpapered to look like a dark forest, where occasional sparkles hinted at fairies and colorful toadstools suggested gnomes hid nearby.

The main part of the store was divided into sections by bookcases, separating the books into age groups. Board books, picture books, early readers, middle grade, tweens, and young adult. The story time and craft room was at the back of the shop. Cozy, upholstered chairs and beanbags invited long sit-downs. Stuffed animals and other sideline items like journals, tin banks, coloring sets, puppets, giclée prints and notecards of Poppy Kay, small backpacks, and mugs with wry parenting and grandparenting quotes filled nooks and crannies. These gift items helped keep the store afloat, often selling better than the books themselves.

Flora fussed and I offered her the pacifier back, and she happily took it. She was, without a doubt, the most good-natured newborn ever.

I strolled in front of a bookshelf that stood alone near the front door. It was The Rabbit Hole bookcase, filled with books featuring rabbits. Poppy Kay Hoppy had a shelf to herself, while the other shelves held the likes of *Bunnicula, Peter Rabbit, Marshmallow, Knuffle Bunny, The Velveteen Rabbit, Little Rabbit Foo Foo,* and, of course, the White Rabbit from *Alice's Adventures in Wonderland*—among many others.

I glanced upward as I heard footsteps in the room above the shop. I hadn't realized the new owner was staying up there and would likely be downstairs any second. A ball of nerves rolled around my stomach as my gaze fell on the signboard that would sit out on the sidewalk once the store opened.

I couldn't help myself. I set my knapsack on the counter and found the bucket of chalk behind the counter. I went to work.

HOME! THAT WAS WHAT THEY MEANT, THOSE
CARESSING APPEALS, THOSE SOFT TOUCHES WAFTED
THROUGH THE AIR, THOSE INVISIBLE LITTLE HANDS
PULLING AND TUGGING, ALL ONE WAY.

After attributing the quote to *The Wind in the Willows*, I drew a rat, mole, badger, and toad under the words. I carefully stood up and turned to find a man leaning against the counter, watching me.

Startled, I nearly dropped the chalk, and Flora spit out the pacifier again to lodge a protest.

"Good gracious. Didn't anyone tell you not to sneak up on people?" I asked him, my voice sharper than intended. I jiggled Flora and added, "You're lucky you're still standing."

A smile teased his lips as he held up his hands in surrender. "My apologies to you both. I didn't want to interrupt your drawing." He reached out and picked up the dangling pacifier to offer it back to Flora. She blinked slowly at him, blew a drooly bubble, then sucked the binky back into her mouth. "I take it this is Flora. Marlo talked my ear off about her last night. How in the world is she staying in that wrap? Is it safe?"

He had such a serious look in his deep-blue eyes as he studied the way the fabric crisscrossed that I almost smiled. I put the chalk back behind the counter and tugged on the baby sling's knot at my hip. "You'd be surprised how much so. I'm Blue Bishop."

"I know. We've met before. I see you're still finding things." He nodded to Flora with an amused look in his eyes.

Surprised, I studied his face. "Did I help you find something?"

Because, heaven knew, I'd helped a lot of people find things. Not exactly willingly, I might add. The wind always led me to the lost, but explaining that was near impossible.

Once when I was little, I tried to explain my relationship with the wind to Twyla, how it pushed and pulled, and how sometimes, most times, I was the only one that could feel it blowing. How, without fail, it called to me every morning to walk the Buttonwood trail, and how every once in a while, it would summon me at other times of the day to lead me to something that was lost, like the set of keys one of my teachers had dropped in the school parking lot.

Twyla had told me that my gift of finding things was right special, so special that I shouldn't tell anyone else my secret. As an adult, I wasn't sure whether her warning was to protect me from people thinking I was plumb crazy or if she was just humoring me, thinking my imagination was at play. Over the years, I told only those closest to me—Persy, Marlo, and Moe—mostly to explain my strange hiking habits.

"Actually, yes. You helped me find myself, and I've never forgotten the kindness. I'm Henry Dalton."

He held out his hand, and I reluctantly shook it, trying to place his face. Blue eyes, brown—almost black—wavy hair that was tamed around his ears. Shallow dimples sat in lightly stubbled cheeks. He looked to be a little older than I was, in his early thirties. I truly didn't meet many new people, so I wasn't sure why I couldn't place him.

"It was a long time ago," he added, clearly taking pity on my memory. "Right here in this shop, in a blanket fort in the back room."

Suddenly, I was twelve again, hiding inside a makeshift blanket fort in the craft room, sitting alongside a sleeping Persy, a stack of books, and my embarrassment. He'd found me there, naked shame shining in his expressive eyes, and apologized for the kids who'd called me names earlier in the day. He'd asked if he could stay awhile, and I'd moved aside to let him in. We'd sat side by side in silence that afternoon, but I hadn't read a single word of the books we'd shared. I hadn't known the teenager's name. I'd never seen him before that day, and I'd never seen him again. Until today.

I'd actually used that afternoon as inspiration for *Poppy Kay Hoppy Finds a Friend* and wondered if he'd read it.

"Henry," I said, liking the way the name rolled off my tongue. "I don't quite understand how I helped you find yourself. You're the one who found me that day."

"It's a long story. One best saved for another day, since the store is due to open soon."

"Right. We should get to work," I said, feeling somewhat bereft to not hear the details. "Before I forget"—I reached into the knapsack—"I have these for you." I handed him a treat bag filled with cookies. It had a notecard tied to the top that said WELCOME TO THE RABBIT HOLE.

Faint lines fanned from the corners of his lips as he smiled, and his dimples deepened. "These aren't poisoned, are they? Marlo also mentioned you were upset with her selling the shop to me."

I eyed the cookie bag and blinked innocently. "Chocolate chip, coconut, and arsenic. One of my special recipes."

When he laughed instead of taking offense, I relaxed a little. "I've come to peace with Marlo selling. I just want her to be happy. These are some of Marlo's favorite cookies. They're also highly addictive. Fair warning."

"I appreciate the kindness. Thank you."

I nodded and quickly walked him through the store's opening, from the alarm to the air-conditioning, the cash register, the software that tracked time sheets, to finally the signboard, which needed to be placed on the sidewalk.

He said, "*The Wind in the Willows* has been a favorite of

mine ever since hearing Moe read a passage once. He has quite the memorable delivery."

I smiled. "That he does. How long has it been since you heard it? Seventeen years now?"

"Actually, that was probably twenty years ago—my family used to visit Buttonwood quite a bit when I was younger. But Moe's reading is still as fresh in my mind now as it was then. It stays with you."

My gaze went to the mural on the wall. *All the little rabbits.* I shifted foot to foot, rocking Flora. "He definitely leaves a lasting impression."

"I kept in touch with Marlo through the years. Pen pals. When she mentioned selling the shop, I jumped at the chance to buy it. I love teaching, but owning a bookstore has been a dream of mine. And I've always wanted to come back to Buttonwood. There's something magical about this place. You're lucky to have grown up here."

I raised an eyebrow at that but said nothing. He'd wanted to come back, but I couldn't wait to leave. "Where are you from?"

"Ohio, born and raised." He picked up the sign and held open the door for Flora and me as he nodded to the quote. "Is home on your mind?"

Sunbeams shot through trees branches, creating lacey shadows on the sidewalk. I backed into the shade so Flora was protected from the sun. "This shop is a lot like home, so yes." My heart was in my throat when I asked, "Are you planning to make any changes?"

"Only one right away."

"Please don't tell me you're painting over the mural." I'd go to war for that mural if I had to, my feelings about conflict be damned.

"The mural is staying." He stepped back from the signboard, glanced at me, and said, "I'm going to add a blanket fort to the back room."

Chapter
5

"Did I ever tell you about the time Cobb Bishop swindled my daddy out of a hundred dollars, twenty acres of land, two sides of beef, and his favorite pipe?" Calvin Underhill asked, holding his hat as he blocked the judge's entrance to Cal's Feed and Seed.

The judge had been on a mission to pick up some birdseed to refill Mrs. Quimby's feeders when Calvin had stepped in front of him, asking for a moment. He noticed the man's hands. Thick, calloused. Dirty fingernails cut short. Scars that spoke of hard work. Calvin's farm was one of the most profitable in the county, and he was known to be a God-fearin', good, honest man. "How'd Cobb do that?"

Twin spots of color appeared on Calvin's cheeks. "Cheatin' at pool, sir."

If anyone had been foolish enough to play pool with Cobb Bishop, the judge reckoned they got what they deserved. Cobb, the Bishop family patriarch, had been a charismatic and accomplished con man.

Calvin went on, saying, "Mac Bishop busted my lip once when we were in grade school for doing nothing but pointin' out the holes in his shoes. He was always the first to throw a punch. I wasn't surprised when I heard he was killed in a bar fight. No one was."

There were five Bishop children. Three boys and two girls: Mac, Wade, Ty, Blue, and Persimmon. Mac, the oldest, had been just twenty years old when he'd been killed in a bar near

Fort Jackson. If he had lived, he would've been the same age Calvin was now: forty-eight. And it seemed to Judge Quimby that if Calvin had been pointing out the poor boy's shoes, he'd been the one picking the fight, not the other way 'round.

"And as you know," Calvin said, "my mama was working at Blackstock Bank the day the Bishop boys, Wade and Ty, busted in and robbed it. I swear it took ten years off her life, God rest her soul."

Maybe so, but Wade and Ty had been the only ones to lose their lives that day, when their getaway car flipped off an overpass and went up in flames. Blue had been eleven years old at the time. All three brothers—and her father—had died before she had even seen her teen years. That was a whole lot of death and grief for anyone to deal with, let alone a child.

"Why're you telling me all this now?" the judge asked, though he had the feeling he knew. People had been stopping him all over town to give him a piece of their minds regarding Blue Bishop and her foundling.

"I've never had any dealings with Blue to speak of," Calvin said, "but she's a Bishop, and that's condemnation enough for me. You need to protect that baby she found at all costs."

Blue

"Doesn't this just bring you right back?" Persy asked a few days later as she knelt beside me on the hardwood floor in the living room, a wet rag in hand. Her ruddy cheeks were brighter than usual from exertion.

The court investigator would be here this afternoon, and we had been giving the house a deep cleaning. Thankfully, this was the last room on the to-do list because I was worn out, and it wasn't even eight in the morning.

I glanced over at Flora. Swaddled, she was nestled in the Moses basket set below an arched toy strung with colorful, patterned cutouts of animals. "The scent of vinegar alone takes me back."

A mixture of water and white vinegar had been Twyla's solution to most of life's dirty problems. From cleaning windows, floors, and stubborn laundry stains to getting rid of bad smells and even warts.

"I swear I smell vinegar sometimes even when I'm not using it," Persy said. "It's like using it so often has caused it to become part of my genetic makeup."

"I wouldn't doubt it."

I scrubbed a stubborn scuff on the white baseboard. The court investigator would be a big factor in whether I'd be able to keep Flora for the foreseeable future. I was trying my hardest not to let my nerves get the best of me, but my stomach ached, twisting and turning. Right about now, I'd much rather be at The Rabbit Hole than on my knees cleaning and worrying.

I'd spent the last few mornings at the bookshop with Henry. Every day it seemed Marlo needed me to teach him something new. The accounting program. The inventory process. Ordering. Returns. I hadn't minded. Henry was a nice guy and a quick learner. Business had been booming, too, which I thought had more to do with the town's nosiness than the community's sudden desire to buy books.

Because of the busier schedule at the bookshop, I hadn't spent as much time in the woods as I normally did, and oddly the wind hadn't been as insistent, as if it knew I had my hands full. I glanced out the window and saw branches swaying on the crepe myrtle in the front yard. I promised myself that after the court investigator left, Flora and I would take a long walk in the woods. Hawthorn would be blooming soon, and from its flowers I could make a nice yellow ink. And maybe, just maybe, today would be the day I'd find the lost thing with no name.

As I washed baseboards in the living room, I tried to keep my mind from drifting down memory lane. But the truth of it was that the scent of vinegar had called forth old ghosts. Now they haunted my thoughts and took me back to one of the worst days of my life: the day after Wade and Ty had been buried in the Buttonwood cemetery, in the same small plot where Mac had been laid to rest years before. The sun had shined in betrayal, but the wind had been howling. It shook the house, rattling everything and everyone in it, mourning the same as we were.

"I have to leave," Daddy had said to Twyla while she'd sobbed silently on a kitchen chair, her shoulders shaking so hard it was like cruel invisible hands had hold of her. "I've made up my mind. Don't try to stop me. It's best for all of us."

"It's *not* best. Don't go," Twyla begged him. "Please don't go."

"I have to," he said, and only those who knew him best would have heard the cracks in his firm tone.

He'd quickly packed what little he owned, and when he'd walked out the front door, he'd never looked back at who he left behind.

As soon as he was gone, a broken Twyla had taken to her bed, where she had stayed for nearly a full month. Despite her convictions for check kiting, shoplifting, and assault from the time she slapped a cop trying to arrest Wade, she somehow landed a job at Dulcette's Orchard during the day, and at night she did her best to drown her sorrows in a bottle of whiskey. She'd retreated into herself, trying to close herself off to the possibility of more pain—and any chance at happiness.

We'd received word of Daddy's death two months later by way of a knock on the door from a neighboring county's sheriff, a visit we'd been expecting so it hadn't come as much of a shock. Daddy had been buried next to his beloved boys in a quiet ceremony with few attendees.

At only eleven, I'd taken on the household cleaning—and almost every other chore as well, including tending to the chickens Twyla had stolen from a neighboring farm so we'd have fresh eggs. And since Persy had been my shadow from the time she'd learned how to walk, she could always be found at my side eager to help. Cleaning together felt just like old times.

"Blue? Did you hear me?"

"Hmm?"

"I asked what time the investigator would be here."

"About one."

She sighed. "It's going to be a long morning."

"The longest."

Persy dipped her hand into a gallon bucket, squeezed excess liquid out of a rag, and rubbed it along the wood grain of the oak floor. To bring up the shine, she followed the motion with a swipe of her other hand, which held a dry microfiber cloth.

It was a tedious process but worth it. Experts would say not to use the vinegar spray on wood. That it'd damage it. But revealing what's been hiding underneath the surface, allowing it to fully shine, was worth the risk.

I knee-walked over to the Moses basket and peeked in. Flora had fallen asleep, her angelic face slack, her cheeks a healthy pink. Her mouth was slightly puckered, and there was a formula bubble on her lips. I used the tail of the blanket to dab it away. After a moment, I reluctantly left her side and went back to the baseboards.

Persy scooted along the floor and used her fingernail to pick a piece of lint from a knot in the wood. "Do you really think the investigator is going to check the baseboards for dust and scuff marks?"

"I'm not sure, but I don't want to leave anything to chance. When I had my home study, a social worker even checked the closets for cobwebs."

"Dang."

"They take their jobs very seriously."

I ran down my mental checklist of chores to finish before the investigator showed up this afternoon, wishing I had more time to accomplish all the jobs I'd been putting off. Like replacing the window with the broken seal in the sunroom. Swapping out the broken tile in the downstairs bathroom. Having the area rugs dry-cleaned. Painting the house. *Becoming a thread in the community.*

I hadn't done much communitywise since finding Flora, but tonight I was going with Marlo to Magnolia Breeze to read to patients there. It was pretty much the last thing I wanted to do, but I knew how important community was to social workers and the court, so I was forcing myself out of my comfort zone.

Since I couldn't take Flora with me, Persy was going to babysit, and I was already dreading leaving her.

I walked over to the basket again and smoothed the blond fluff at Flora's forehead. She wiggled at my touch but quickly resettled.

No, I wasn't looking forward to tonight, but I'd put on a fake smile and go, because I'd do anything for her.

She was worth every hard step out of my comfort zone.

Every. Single. One.

And I had the feeling there were going to be a lot of them.

Sarah Grace

"Just call her, Sarah Grace," Kebbie said from the desk across from mine. "Blue's been wanting to sell the house forever. It's not like she's in seclusion. I saw her and the baby at the bookshop yesterday."

"You did?"

My Sweet Home office was located on Oak Street, three blocks west of the main square—and The Rabbit Hole. The small cottage had once been home to a hair salon. Six years ago when the owner retired and put the place up for sale, I bought it with some of the money Grammy Cabot had left me. I'd been just five months out of college at the time, running from my past and trying to salvage some hopes and dreams by starting my own business.

This cottage had undergone a complete transformation after I bought it, turning from a seventies-era salon complete with brown vinyl flooring and orange- and yellow-striped wallpaper to a cozy space with seafoam-green walls, heart pine floors, and ivory wainscoting. The front door of the cottage opened into what Kebbie and I called the meeting room, which looked a lot like a typical living room with comfy sofas, armchairs, and a coffee table. It was where I interviewed potential Sweet Home renters.

The back half of the cottage was one large room that had a small kitchen on one side, a pub table with four barstools in the middle, and a dedicated office space on the other side, where our desks were.

As the company had grown, the office area had become more cramped as I'd added additional shelving and more filing cabinets. I'd thought many times about expanding the building off the back but just as many times considered moving to another location. The cottage approved of the latter idea—it mourned the busyness of the salon with its endless chatter and wanted it back. It even complained about missing the vintage wallpaper, calling my décor choices boring.

I'd always countered with "classic," but the cottage was a whiner and hardly ever let me forget that it considered pale green to be bland.

There were days I was beyond grateful that over the years I'd learned how to tune out houses. Some droned on endlessly, and without a way to block the noise, I'd never get anything done.

"Blue's been at the bookshop nearly every morning." Kebbie fought back a yawn. "She's helping the new owner, Henry, get acclimated."

"With a newborn in tow?"

"Marlo's been busy this week with Moe. Doctors' appointments and assessments."

My heart fluttered. "Oh." Poor Moe. Poor Marlo.

There was a slight catch in her voice when she said, "Yeah. So Blue has been coming in before the store opens, so Flora—that's the baby's name—isn't around all the customers. Apparently newborns have weaker immune systems, so it's best to keep them out of crowds."

"That makes sense." And it made sense why Blue was helping out, even after becoming a new mom. Everyone in Buttonwood knew the Allemands were more like family to Blue than her own had been.

Kebbie smiled. "Blue carries Flora around in a baby sling, and it's all kinds of adorable. I'll probably see her again tomorrow. If you want, I can talk to her about your offer, kind of break the ice, and tell her to expect a call."

It had been three days since I'd seen the Bishop farmhouse, and as much as I wanted to present an offer to Blue, it felt like an intrusion so soon after her finding the baby. "No, no. I'll call her. Maybe I'll stop by the bookshop tomorrow. I'd love to meet the baby, too."

Kebbie yawned again. "She's sweet as can be."

It was obvious my cousin had spent some time getting ready for work today. She'd curled her blond hair and applied full makeup. But even from here I could see darkness beneath her eyes that no concealer could hide. Slackness in her face and a dullness in her blue eyes hinted of exhaustion. Too much work, and not enough rest and relaxation. "You seem extra tired today. Do you want the afternoon off? I don't mind."

She laughed and went for the coffee pot. "No. I'm fine. I just need more caffeine."

"Or a vacation." I shuffled papers on my desk, trying to find the file I needed. Sweet Home had two houses in differing stages of renovation, and hopefully I'd be under contract with Blue's house soon. The business was a labor of love, but it was also demanding and time-consuming. I often arrived here at the office early and left late. In between, I was usually at a job site.

"If anyone needs a vacation, it's you," she countered as she filled a mug with coffee. "When did you last take time off?"

It had been my honeymoon, four years ago. Truthfully, I wasn't sure I remembered *how* to relax. Especially not lately. I couldn't even imagine vacationing with Fletch these days.

Just thinking about him caused an ache near my sternum, like a thorn was stuck there. He had barely been home this week, continuing his cycle of working late, then going out with the guys. While I didn't mind the peace and quiet at home, ignoring the rut we were in wasn't helping the tension between us.

Abruptly, I said, "We should go on a girls' trip. Just the two of us. It'll be good to get away for a while."

"That sounds nice. Let me just check your calendar to see when you're free to get away." Kebbie set her mug onto a coaster, sat down, and quickly tapped away on the computer keyboard. Her gaze cut to mine. "Just what I thought. Never. You have no free time."

I rolled my eyes. "No need for sarcasm, Keb. I'll make time. Pick a long weekend, four days at least, and move some of my appointments around." I'd figure out a way to make it work with my job commitments. "Mama and Daddy's vacation house is sitting empty down on West Beach. We might as well make use of it. It's probably lonely."

I could practically hear it pouting from here. It had been a long time since I'd been down there. Ten years, in fact. I tried not to think about that time with Shep Wheeler too often.

Kebbie squinted as though not believing me. "Seriously? You really want me to plan a getaway?"

"Yeah. Do it."

"But really. You're serious?"

I laughed. "*Kebbie*. I'm serious."

She tugged on a curl. "Have you been sniffing too much construction glue? A vacation. *Dang.* What's next? Don't even tell me you're actually considering adopting Flora like your parents want." Kebbie leaned forward in full gossip mode, and generous cleavage spilled from the empire bodice of a flowy maxi dress. "They've been talking about it all week. I can't believe they're willing to risk going against the tree's advice. The button said to give the baby to Blue. I don't want you to have any part of a curse. A lifetime of unhappiness sounds like hell to me."

Little did she know I was already cursed. "*Mmm,*" I mumbled in response, thinking that hell was proving to be an apt description.

"You're not, right? Considering it?"

Suddenly she looked very serious, as if it were my life at stake and not just my happiness.

"You know how my mama gets when she has her mind set on something. It doesn't matter, though. As far as I'm concerned, Blue is the right choice for that baby. She'll be a good mom."

"Oh, thank goodness." Kebbie let out a dramatic sigh that was cut off by a chime that sounded when the back door opened.

"Please don't mention my decision about the baby," I said under my breath to Kebbie as my father stepped into the office.

"Don't you worry none. I know how to keep secrets."

The words were meant to reassure, but instead they sent a spiral of worry through me. Was something going on with her other than exhaustion?

"Hi, Daddy," I said. "What brings you by?"

It wasn't often he dropped in during the day, and I hoped to the heavens above that he wasn't here to talk to me about Flora.

He kissed my cheek, then Kebbie's. "I thought you might want to take a look at this, Sarah Grace." Daddy handed me a manila file. "Hot off the press, so to speak."

Kebbie's cell phone rang, and she glanced at the readout and quickly said, "Be right back." She hurried out the back door onto the deck that overlooked the parking pad at the back of the cottage.

I skimmed the pages inside the folder and was relieved to find no mention of a baby at all. "The Dobbinses' house? I didn't know it was for sale."

"It isn't yet," he said. "I bumped into Clark Dobbins earlier at the bank and he mentioned he and Edna were planning a move to Florida, to be closer to their grandkids. We got to talking about his property, threw around some numbers, and he agreed to give you first look, since you pay cash. I took the liberty of drawing up a mock listing, and I pulled the lot survey. I think it's a good deal, but you need to act fast. The market's hot right now, and he's close to signing with a realtor."

I often suspected that Daddy missed his old real estate business, and the listing he'd put together proved it. He'd gone above and beyond when he simply could've told me what Clark Dobbins was asking.

"The Dobbinses have a nice house with lots of potential, but I can't make an offer on it." Paying cash for the properties I bought meant that I had to budget carefully. "My funds are going to be tied up with the Bishop farmhouse once Blue accepts my offer."

He gestured to the folder and raised bristly eyebrows. "This here is a great deal. Bigger return on investment."

He was in full salesman mode, and suddenly his visit made a lot more sense. "Daddy."

"Sarah Grace," he said, mimicking my exasperated tone.

"Did Mama put you up to this?" I held up the folder.

Blinking innocently, he pulled a long face. "I surely don't know what you mean."

For a politician, Daddy was a terrible liar. I should've known my mother would fight dirty when it came to the farmhouse. But dangling something shiny in front of me wasn't going to detract me from my goal.

I set my hands on my hips. "I thought you were on my side about the Bishop house."

"I am," he said with a smile. "It's just that your mother is a force of nature when she has her mind set on something. I was hoping you had enough money in reserve to buy both. A compromise she can't argue."

I thought about my personal bank account. I had just enough saved to float myself a loan, but then I came to my senses. "Tell her I'm making an offer on the Bishop house and that's that."

His eyes flared, and I swore I saw a bit of pride shining in them.

"Now, I've really got to get going." I peeked out the window. Kebbie was still on the phone, talking animatedly.

"You and Fletch should come to dinner tonight," he said. "I'll throw some steaks on the grill. Real casual. It's been a while since we've all gotten together."

I eyed him. "Is this another one of Mama's ideas?"

He gave an exaggerated shrug. "I surely don't know what you mean."

I couldn't help but smile, even though the dinner had to be about forcing Fletch and me to listen to Mama's adoption plans. It was probably best to set her straight on the idea before it got too far out of hand. "I'll have to check with Fletch. He's been working late these past couple of nights. I'm not sure if he is tonight, too."

Daddy pushed a hand into his gelled hair, raising up sharp spikes. "Working late?"

I stared at those spikes of hair and felt a stab of dread. "Yes. Why're you sounding shocked by that?"

Daddy wouldn't look me in the eye as he said, "I'm confused is all. Fletch hasn't been working late. In fact, he's been leaving early. Wherever he's been, Sarah Grace, it's not at the office."

Chapter
6

Blue

An hour before the court investigator was due, I walked the house, my nerves preventing me from keeping still. I was hyperfocused on making sure the man found no reasons to terminate my guardianship order.

It was, I'd decided, the only thing *I* could control. I'd covered every outlet. I made sure every cabinet door had a childproof lock. I had a cupboard full of formula. I had diapers enough for an entire army of babies. The house was spotless and smelled faintly of vanilla, thanks to a batch of sugar cookies I'd made earlier. As I looked around for the millionth time, I couldn't see anything the man could fault.

Marlo watched me from a spot on the sofa, a laptop propped on her legs. A pair of reading glasses sat low on her nose, and she looked at me over the top of the frames. "You should sit down, take a breather."

"I can't sit. I'm too nervous."

Marlo shook her head and turned her attention back to the screen. She was updating The Rabbit Hole's website.

As I stepped into the sunroom, I surveyed my studio. I'd cleared my desk, set my paints on high shelves, and had organized my canvases as best I could—storing canvases was an art form in and of itself, one I had never mastered.

Persy, who didn't have classes on Thursdays, couldn't bear to watch me pace, so she'd volunteered to pull weeds in the backyard, a task she despised only slightly less than my nervous anxiety. She was crouched low in front of a hedgerow of camellias and was yanking crabgrass with steely determination. Moe worked alongside her, pulling more flowers than weeds, and looking right proud of it. If it made him happy, he could pull every last flower out of the garden for all I cared. He'd been more like his old self since Flora had arrived, and we were all grateful for the reprieve. And we knew it was one. Soon enough, the dementia would take him away forever.

I could hardly bear thinking about it. My gaze went to Flora in my arms, and she looked up at me, blinking slowly. Her tongue pushed at her lips, and I hugged her more closely.

"Child. You're going to wear a hole in the floor if you don't settle down," Marlo said, her voice taking on a motherly timbre I knew well.

Flora squawked from the crook of my arm, apparently agreeing with the advice. Her arms flailed as though she finally realized she could move them, and her skinny legs kicked, stretching the daisy-printed fabric of her one-piece sleeper.

"Do you think it's physically possible for a stomach to actually knot?" I asked.

Marlo smiled. "No."

I wasn't so sure.

As I kept pacing, my gaze went to the bookcases, to the pictures atop them that kept watch over the room. Most of the frames held faded Polaroids, their surfaces crackled and crazed. Images that were slowly disappearing over time, fading as surely as the memories would someday. They were snapshots of my family. Twyla and Daddy in happier times, playing cards. Wade, whose grin was almost as big as the bass he held up proudly. Ty and me, covered in mud from playing in the creek. Baby Persy sleeping under a small Christmas tree. Mac in his camouflage uniform shortly after he graduated from boot camp, the brim of his patrol hat shadowing serious eyes. I never even got the chance to meet him. He'd gone and gotten himself killed when I was only a few months old.

Until Wade and Ty died, I'd had a happy enough childhood. We were poor, yes. The police were around a lot, yes. No one had a steady job. And I went without more often than not. But there was love. Ty was my best friend, never making me feel like a pesky little sister when I trailed after him and begged him to play hide and seek in the woods. Daddy favored those search-and-find puzzles in the weekly paper, and one of my earliest memories was sitting on his wide knee, helping him look for letters while he sang my praises for knowing the alphabet so well. Mama enjoyed baking and patiently taught me how. Wade mostly came 'round on Sundays—he was a good bit older than me, eighteen years, and had long since moved out—but every so often he'd come by early to take me to the river to catch fish for dinner. Sundays were my favorite day, when we were all together, sharing a meal, even if there wasn't always enough to go around. It was overwhelmingly loud and rowdy, but for a few hours every week it felt like we were a somewhat normal family.

As my gaze shifted from one photo to another, grief and anger pulsed in my throat. They should be here. With me. With Persy. With Flora. Why hadn't they fought harder to stay out of trouble? Why hadn't they made different choices? Why had they left me alone to deal with the fallout of their behavior? Left me alone to raise Persy.

Left me.

Swallowing hard, I closed my eyes, trying to banish questions I'd never have answers to, questions that had haunted me for years. Questions that tended to resurface when I was most anxious, as if they knew precisely when my emotional guard was down.

Flora wiggled, and I repositioned her so that her head rested on my chest. She continued to fuss, no matter what I tried to do to calm her.

"Is she hungry?" Marlo asked.

"She shouldn't be." Flora was freshly bathed, fed, and changed. Wisps of her blond hair curled around a lace headband that had a small bow, making her look somewhat gift wrapped. "She finished a bottle half an hour ago. *Shh, shh*—it's okay, Flora."

"She probably senses your nerves."

"If that were true, she'd be all-out squalling." Just as I said the words, Flora let out a high-pitched wail. I pulled her forward to look at her. "What's the matter, eh? Oh no—she scratched her cheek." I bent and kissed it, trying to take the pain away with love alone.

Marlo was instantly at my side, her dark-brown eyes shining. "She'll be just fine. Give it a second to let the sting fade."

A thin red line marred Flora's fair skin. "I knew I should've cut her fingernails." My voice rose, almost to the same pitch as Flora's. "Oh God, do you think the investigator will hold this against me?"

Marlo held out her hands. "Give me the baby. Hand her over."

"But—"

She beckoned with long fingers. "Come on, now. Sometimes being a good mama is knowing when to ask for help—and accepting it when it's being offered."

Drowning in emotions, I reluctantly passed Flora to her.

Marlo curved Flora to her body, swaying gently. "You go get yourself a glass of water, Blue, and calm down. Go on," she said, her voice steely.

I knew her firm tone almost as much as her encouraging one. I'd heard both often over the years as she helped shape me into the person I'd become. I strode into the kitchen and yanked a cup from the cabinet.

Marlo hummed soothingly as she swayed, her thumb sweeping over Flora's cheek. The crying stopped just as I heard a car door outside.

"Looks like your guest is here," Marlo said. "I best be taking Moe home. It'll all be fine, Blue. Believe it, and it'll be true. Y'hear?"

I couldn't help but notice that her eyes had lost some of their bright shine. "Yes, ma'am."

She passed Flora back to me, gave me a squeeze, and it wasn't until the back door closed behind her that I noticed the angry scratch on Flora's cheek was gone.

⤹ ⤸

"And how old is Persimmon?" Sam Mantilla asked as we toured the house.

"Eighteen." So far the home visit had been fairly painless. A lot of questions, a lot of poking around, opening cupboards, checking windows and doors.

Mr. Mantilla jotted something in the portfolio he held. "When will she be nineteen?"

I tried to ignore the fact that the paperwork in the portfolio had the name Flora *Doe* on it. "In November. Why?"

"As you probably know, the age of adulthood in Alabama is nineteen. Any adult living in the home needs a full background check done," he said. "Since her birthday is still six months away, it's not necessary."

Not necessary, because one way or another Flora's fate where I was concerned would be decided by then.

We stepped into the nursery, and I cut on the lights. "Well, if it helps set your mind at ease, Persy's a straight arrow. She's never been in a lick of trouble her whole life long."

Not that I could say the same.

It was only once that I'd found myself in deep trouble. When

I'd made that fateful choice in high school on the day of the fire, I'd never dreamed of the long-reaching impact it could've had on my life. I was beyond thankful that I'd escaped that incident without it causing lasting damage to my reputation—in the eyes of the law, at least. Yes, I'd been arrested for misdemeanor criminal mischief, but thanks to a civil agreement, the charges were dropped in lieu of a fine. My record had been expunged a few years ago.

Mr. Mantilla opened the window, checked the screen and the lock. He ran a hand over the dressing table, dresser, and crib, feeling for sharp edges, and finally made his way back to me, checking the lock on the door as well. "Do you have plenty of clothing for Flora?"

"More than enough." I opened dresser drawers to show him all the items.

"A local doctor?"

"Flora has her first appointment next week."

He nodded and said, "What about your support system?"

My heart rate kicked up a notch. "Well, there's Persy. And Marlo and Moe Allemand, my neighbors, though they're more like grandparents."

After making a note in the file, he glanced up. "Any other family? Close friends?"

I shook my head.

"I see. How involved are you with the community? Do you volunteer?"

A bead of sweat slid down my spine. "I read to the patients at Magnolia Breeze every once in a while. In fact, I'm going there tonight."

"How often have you been there? Say, in the last six months?"

"Twice," I said, trying not to wince.

"*Hmm.*"

"Oh! I'm looking into joining the Buttonwood Moms Club."

He made another note. "I strongly suggest you do so. Community is an extremely valuable resource when raising a child. Even more so when you don't have much familial support."

He walked out of the nursery, and I fought the urge to stick my tongue out at his back. As if I didn't know that already. Truly, I was sick to death of hearing it.

Downstairs, I saw that Persy and Flora were in the backyard, where they swung on the hammock in the shade of the oak trees.

Mr. Mantilla stepped into the sunroom and smiled at one of the paintings on the wall—the first I'd ever done of Poppy Kay, back when I'd been just fourteen years old.

He said, "My nieces and nephews have a few of your Poppy books. They enjoy them."

I felt heat rise in my cheeks—I'd yet to learn how to take a compliment without blushing. "Thank you. I love creating them."

Deep lines formed between his eyebrows as he glanced around, his gaze narrowing on the shelves that held jars of colorful pigments, inks, and paints. "Is this your art studio?"

I didn't like the troubled look on his face. Not one bit. The knot tightened in my stomach. "It is."

"I was afraid you were going to say that. It can't stay here."

"What do you mean?"

"Your studio. It can't stay here. There's no door. Plus, all these paints need to be in a locked cabinet, and I don't see where you can add any more furniture to this room. It's already cramped. Too cramped—even if you removed this chair, it would still be tight. There should be enough room to have a clear passage through here and there's not. I'm surprised this wasn't raised as a concern in your previous home study."

"My studio was in a different location then." It had been in what was now the nursery.

"If you keep your studio in this house, it needs to be in a

room with a door, and *all* your paints, inks, thinners, and any other supplies you use need to be locked up."

"There aren't any spare rooms. Can I put it in my bedroom?"

"Not if you intend to sleep in there. A bedroom cannot be used for two purposes." Mr. Mantilla closed his portfolio. "I can give you until Monday to relocate your studio."

"I just . . ." I was at a loss for words.

My mind spun with options. Since there was no room in this house to move my studio, I had to look elsewhere. I could rent space in town, but not only would that take time I didn't have, it would use money I needed for an adoption attorney.

His dark eyes were full of empathy as he added, "If you can't find another solution, then Flora cannot stay here. I'm sorry."

Chapter 7

"I once caught Blue Bishop sneaking onto my property like a thief in the night. Two, three in the morning. Fool girl. I coulda shot her dead if she hadn't spoken up when she heard me cocking my rifle." Moses Kehoe shook his head at the memory and tugged hard on his scraggly white beard as he stood in line in front of Judge Quimby at the pharmacy.

The judge asked, "How long ago was this? When Blue was in high school?"

Ten years ago, before he'd become a probate judge, he'd been a magistrate working in the municipal court, overseeing parking tickets and other misdemeanors. It had been the end of Blue's senior year at Buttonwood High when she had been called before him, the first and last time she'd been in his courtroom. It was a doggone miracle he hadn't seen more of her, considering her circumstances.

Moses said, "It was last year. Right after the missus had her girly surgery and was laid up for four weeks."

Last year? Judge Quimby let the words sink in. This changed everything. Blue's sneaky behavior couldn't be attributed to childish mischief. She'd been twenty-eight years old. "Did you catch Blue breaking in?"

"Nah," Moses said, a smile spreading. "She was returning our cat Vera, who'd done run off the week before. Found her out in the woods. And with Mrs. Kehoe laid up, Blue thought we might like a sweet ham, some mac and cheese, a dozen cookies, and a few other sundries she was able to pull together right quick. She'd been planning to leave them on the doorstep when I caught her. You know, she still drops items off every now and again. The missus is teaching her how to play pinochle. She's a good girl, that Blue. And she'll be a good mama. Mark my words."

Inching forward in line, the judge said, "I don't understand. Why hadn't Blue waited until morning to come by?"

Moses shrugged. "When I asked, all she said was that she hadn't wanted to bother us none."

Sarah Grace

My mind had been on Fletch as I ran along sidewalks, pathways, and wooded trails. Late afternoon sunlight peppered the dirt, and my father's words echoed with each step I took.

Fletch hadn't been working late at the office.

And ever since hearing those words, I couldn't stop thinking about Fletch's overly clean soapy scent as he'd slid into bed late last night, as though he showered before coming home. He usually returned from a poker game smelling like an ashtray, not lavender. All the men smoked while playing, a variety of cigars and pipes and cigarettes, as if it were a prerequisite to sit at the card table.

I hadn't given the scent too much thought with everything else weighing on my mind, but now I could practically smell the soap as if it were haunting me. Lavender and roses. It drove out all other outdoor scents, the earthy loam and familiar pine, shoving them aside as though saying, "Pay attention to me!"

It was the decidedly *feminine* scent that bothered me. Coupled with what my father had said, it made me question something I'd never doubted before, no matter how secretive Fletch could be: his faithfulness. Despite our rocky marriage, I'd never dreamed that he'd step out on me. Was his sudden uptick in *hanging out with the guys* and working late a cover for something more sordid?

No, I told myself. *No.* He had too much to lose if he was caught: His stellar reputation, which he'd painstakingly crafted from the loathsome legacy his father had left him. His political aspirations. Me.

Yet I couldn't shake the suspicion. I couldn't outrun it, no matter how hard I was trying. I'd ended up turning down my father's dinner offer—it was the last thing I wanted to do tonight. Well, no. That wasn't quite true. The last thing I wanted to do was confront Fletch about his fidelity. But a family supper was a close second. Everyone watching us. Wondering.

I hurdled a log on the trail on my way to the Buttonwood Tree, found my feet, and kept running. My breath echoed in my ears, and perspiration ran in rivulets down the sides of my face and along my spine.

I picked up my pace, praying with each footfall that there was a way to break my curse. I had to ask. I had to know. It had been more than a year since I last asked for advice, so there was nothing stopping the tree from answering. There had to be a way to be happy again.

Please let there be a way.

My stomach churned as I reached the Buttonwood glade, relieved to find the small clearing empty of reporters and busybodies who wanted to see where Blue had found the baby earlier this week.

I took a moment to catch my breath before I looked up the ridged bark of the tree, deep into the green canopy. "How do I break the curse? Will I ever be happy again?"

A moment later, I heard a soft thump from inside the tree and reached into the hollow for my button. I read the message once. Twice. Three times.

"Is this some kind of joke?" I yelled.

The button I held in my hand was identical to one I'd received almost exactly ten years ago.

FOLLOW YOUR HEART TO FIND YOUR HAPPINESS.

"It's not funny if it is! This is impossible advice. Impossible!" I slumped against the tree, my body going limp from the weight of my desperation and the burden of my secrets. Tears welled.

"Sarah Grace? You okay?"

I straightened, realizing I was no longer alone. Swiping away tears with the back of my hand, I said, "I'm fi—"

The words died in my throat as I turned and saw who'd asked the question.

Shep Wheeler stuck his hands in his pockets. "I gave it a month, tops, but we lasted seven months, twelve days."

Behind him, a black feather drifted slowly to the ground, and a mix of musk and cinnamon swirled around me, a smell so familiar it made my chest ache. "I don't know what you're talking about," I said, lying through my teeth.

The corners of his eyes turned up in amusement, as if knowing the truth of the matter, but he didn't call me out on my fib. "That's how long it's been since I've moved back to Buttonwood. Somehow we managed, with great calculation, I suspect, not to run into each other. It's got to be some kind of record for a town this size."

My cheeks heated as I thought of all the times I'd seen him in the distance at the park, the gas station, the grocery store, and forced myself to turn around, to turn away. To not run up to him, hug him, and not let go this time around.

I'd dreaded a face-to-face meeting, afraid I couldn't hide my feelings. No one in town knew my connection to Shep. Well, that wasn't quite true. Blue Bishop knew some of it. But not all.

No one knew *all*, except for Shep and me.

My gaze swept over him, trying to take in every detail. It had been ten years since he'd last stood an arm's length away. His eyes, an unforgettable milky green, were still filled with pain and hunger. His light-brown hair was shorter than the last time I'd seen him on a sandy beach, the sun glinting off the clear waters of the Gulf—the day I'd watched him walk away from me for good, taking my heart and happiness with him.

His face had thinned and hardened with age, all strong lines and chiseled planes. His body had filled out—once tall and lean but now tall and muscular. The short-sleeve polo shirt he wore pulled taut against his chest and revealed tattoos he'd added over the years. The slim cut of his khaki chinos showed off long, strong legs. But I barely saw the differences. To me, I suspected he'd always look like the broken and scarred eighteen-year-old boy I'd fallen in love with.

"It's good to see you," I finally said because it was the truth. "I'm sorry about your mama. How's she doing?" I couldn't count how many times I'd picked up the phone to call him. To console him. I couldn't imagine what it had taken for him to forgive Mary Eliza.

He'd been a preacher's son, but his mama had been a devil in disguise. Only a few around town knew the damage that had been inflicted on Shep by his mother, despite the warning signs. After all, it was incomprehensible that a pastor's wife, a godly, upstanding woman, could be emotionally and physically abusive and had become even more so after his daddy had died when Shep was seventeen.

"Not well. The doctors don't think she has too much time left. They're keeping her as comfortable as they can. I visit often, but she keeps ringing for the staff whenever I drop in to see her at the care facility. Tries to hide her valuables, too. She has no idea who I am, which I admit makes it easier for me to be in the same room." He offered a hint of a smile. "She thinks I'm a thug with all my tattoos."

My heart hurt for him. After all these years, she still couldn't see what a good man he was. "Do you try to set her straight?"

"Sometimes. Some days it's just best to let it go."

"I'm sorry."

He nodded an acknowledgment.

"What are you doing out here in the woods?" I finally asked, wanting to change the painful subject.

"Working. I'm sure you've heard about the baby Blue found. I'm investigating the case. Thought I'd come take another look around, see if there's anything I missed the first go-round."

"Everyone's heard about the baby. I'm glad she's okay."

The sun shifted overhead and flashed off a badge at his belt. I stared, still not quite believing that he was law now. An investigator. I wanted to beam with pride with how far he'd come. He'd been a bit of a troublemaker in high school. Petty stuff, like pulling the fire alarm, cutting class, failing classes, and getting tattoos. Acting up had been his way of rebelling against his home situation. Showing he had some control over his own life. But underneath it all, he'd been a young man with a big, tender, broken heart. It would've been so easy for him to continue down the wrong path, especially after we'd broken up, but he'd held strong in the faith he had in himself to rise above his raising.

"Me, too." His eyes darkened as he said, "You know why I'm here, but why're *you* here, Sarah Grace, crying to the Buttonwood Tree?"

My grip tightened on the button I'd received, and I stepped around him to pick up the fallen feather. "I was in need of a little guidance."

"Did you get it?"

My gaze wandered to his left hand. He wore no wedding ring.

But then again, neither did I. Mine was at home, tucked away in my jewelry box. Out of sight, but not out of mind.

The button dug into my palm. "Not really."

"Sorry to hear that. Anything I can do to help?"

If only there was a way for him to go back in time to talk me out of making the worst mistake of my life: letting him go. By doing so, I'd cursed myself to a lifetime of unhappiness. "What I want is impossible." Our gazes locked until I couldn't take it anymore and looked away. "I'll let you get back to work."

"And I'll let you finish your run, though I have to confess I'm a little surprised you're still running after all these years."

"You don't run anymore?" I couldn't imagine it. We'd been on the cross-country team together in high school, and he'd been fairly obsessed with the sport, running nearly sixty miles every week.

"Not since I've moved back."

I tried for a smile, but sadness wouldn't allow it. "I have the feeling I'll be running forever."

He set his hands on his hips. "Or, like me, only until forced to face what you're running from."

"Maybe so," I said to appease him.

We said our goodbyes, but as I returned to the trail to jog back to town, I hoped to God that never happened.

Because if I stopped running from my secrets, all hell was sure to break loose.

⤳⤶

I'd picked up a running buddy not long after leaving the Buttonwood clearing.

"Shoo," I said, looking over my shoulder at the dog who, well, dogged my every step.

I hadn't seen which direction he'd come from and had only known he was behind me because of the heavy breathing. He panted loudly.

As a runner, I often came across loose dogs. Some friendly. Some not. This one, fortunately, seemed to be an agreeable sort. When confronted by a dog, I'd always found it best to simply stop running. That usually gave the dog's owner time to track him down or it gave the dog plenty of time to investigate me and decide me unworthy of attention.

This dog, however, wasn't budging from my side. I walked. He walked. I stopped. He stopped.

"Who do you belong to?" I asked, giving him a good once-over.

He sat and his tail swished the ground, creating a cloud of dust.

I let him sniff my hand, then tucked the Buttonwood Tree button and feather between my arm and rib cage as I carefully checked for a collar in the thick fur at the dog's neck, but he wasn't wearing one. He appeared to be some sort of Irish setter mix, one that looked painfully thin. His rich mahogany coat was covered in dirt and clumps of matted fur, and I could only imagine the ticks and fleas I couldn't see.

I freed the feather and looked at the button.

Follow your heart to find your happiness. I shook my head as I thought about the words, wondering what they even meant, since my heart went with Shep the day we broke up. Why hadn't the button just said what I needed to *do*?

I jumped as the dog suddenly licked my hand.

"No kissing," I said, smiling at him. "For goodness' sake, we just met."

He wagged his tail harder.

I patted his head and walked onward, toward town, not surprised in the least when the dog followed me. "You can't come home with me. Fletch doesn't like dogs. I'll take you into town. Doc Hennessey at the vet clinic is real nice. He'll see to it you're healthy, check for a microchip, and if there isn't one, he'll find you a good home."

Fletch.

I needed to call him out on his lies. Last I'd heard, he'd said he'd be working late, then playing pool with the guys at the Dishwater, the local bar. I'd wait up for him to see what he had to say for himself, and I couldn't help wondering if he'd come home smelling of that lavender soap again.

Pant, pant, pant. The dog stared up at me with baleful brown eyes.

Letting out a sigh, I scratched his ears. He pushed his snout against my palm, and I gave in to him and offered up a good petting. "I wish I had some water for you."

I didn't carry much with me when I ran. Only a small key ring secured to my shoelaces and a five-dollar bill in the small zipper on my shorts. No phone. No music. No water.

The closest stream was a half mile away through dense woods. It would be faster to go back to town, almost a mile away, and buy a bottle of water at the general store. "Come on, then."

As much as I wanted to run, I kept a steady walking pace for the dog's sake. His panting eased but didn't stop.

About ten minutes later, we were almost to the trail's starting point when the dog started barking. I looked ahead and saw Blue Bishop walking toward us, wearing some sort of baby contraption that looked like a scarf gone very wrong.

A year older than me, she was about my height, five foot seven, maybe an inch shorter, but her long, dirty-blond hair was pulled up in a wobbly topknot that made her seem taller. She wore a pair of denim shorts, a white tee, and old sneakers. There wasn't a speck of makeup on her suntanned face, but I'd never seen her look prettier.

The dog kept barking and raced circles around me until I said, "Hush now. You'll scare the baby. Sit."

He sat at my feet, panting heavily once again.

"I didn't know you had a dog, Sarah Grace," Blue said as she approached, curiosity sparking in her amber eyes.

"I didn't know you had a baby." Then I laughed. "Kidding. Everyone in town knows you found a baby. Can I see her?"

There was something about being around Blue that allowed me to relax. I never felt as though I had to *pretend*. I could be myself. Of course, it helped that she knew one of my deepest, darkest secrets.

Because it was her secret, too.

Blue peeled back the fabric near her shoulder, revealing a tiny oval face. The baby's eyes were closed tightly, her cheeks rosy. Her lips were puckered as though she was sucking in her sleep. "I named her Flora."

"She's beautiful, Blue."

Perfect. For once, my mother had been right to use the word.

"I think so, too," Blue said with a smile. "Your dog is . . ." She tipped her head and seemed to be searching for an appropriate word. "He's . . ."

I rubbed the dog's floppy ears and decided to spare her from potentially hurting my feelings. "Not mine. He's been following me for about half a mile."

"I think he's yours now. Check out the way he's staring at you. MoonPie eyes if I ever saw them."

I glanced down. Big, brown, woeful eyes stared up at me. Begging me. "I'm going to take him straight over to Doc Hennessey's. If the dog isn't chipped and no one shows up to claim him, then I'm sure Doc will find him a good home."

Fletch would have a cow if I showed up at home with a dog. Yet . . . I'd always wanted a dog. I hadn't been able to have one growing up, because my mama was allergic. Taking this dog home with me might be worth any trouble with Fletch. He wasn't home much, anyway. How much of a fight could he put up? I decided I didn't want to think about that particular question too hard.

"You best hurry. The clinic closes at six tonight."

Of course she'd know the vet's schedule, between Persy working there and all the animals Blue had found in her lifetime . . . Honestly, I was surprised she hadn't found this dog first—and I said so.

"Only one reason for it," Blue said.

"What's that?"

"He's not lost. I'm going to guarantee you this dog doesn't have a microchip. No one's looking for him. He's meant to be yours, Sarah Grace."

Impossible.

But suddenly I wanted it to be possible. I wanted it more than anything. "Let's see what Doc Hennessey says; then I'll make a decision."

She smirked, as though she already knew what the outcome would be. "I have some water in my knapsack if you want to give him a drink. Side pocket. Just pour some into your hand."

Turning, she presented me with her back. I tugged the reusable water bottle from its nylon netted holder, crouched down, and tucked the feather and button under my arm again.

"Do you want me to hold those for you?" Blue asked.

I hesitated only a moment before nodding, and she immediately put out her hand, accepting my treasures without comment. I carefully poured water into my palm, and the dog slurped it up happily. While crouched, I noticed something rather important. "Seems I made a bit of a mistake."

"About?" Blue asked as she studied the feather closely.

"The dog."

"Are you finally willing to admit he's yours now?"

"Don't get carried away. It's just from this angle, down here close to the ground, I can see that he's very clearly a she. I'm sorry, dog." The dog stopped drinking and licked my face. I laughed. "Okay, okay. All right. That's enough of that."

Blue was smiling as I stood up. "Have you picked out a name for her yet?"

"No. Don't be ridiculous." Hazel. I'd name her Hazel. Hazey for short. I replaced the bottle in Blue's knapsack and said, "Thanks for sharing."

Flora made a squeaking noise, and Blue shifted foot to foot while rubbing her hand along the baby's back. "Happy to."

It was then that I noticed the sadness in Blue's eyes. "Hey, you okay?"

"Hmm? Oh. I'm fine. Thanks. Just a bit of bad news. I'll sort it out."

"About the baby?"

"No," she said, shaking her head. "No. Everything with Flora is fine."

"Moe?"

"He's holding steady."

"The bookshop?"

She laughed at my persistence. "No. The bookshop is doing well. The new owner has been great. It's about my art studio. No big deal."

Yet her eyes told me it was a very big deal indeed. "Anything I can do to help?"

"No, but thanks for offering. I'll figure it out."

I hadn't intended to ask about the farmhouse, since I planned to present a formal, professional offer, but after seeing that glimpse of sadness, I wanted to cheer her up. "I do have some good news for you. At least, I think it's good news."

Curiosity lit her eyes. "What's that?"

"I want to buy your farmhouse, Blue. Full asking price. No inspection, either."

"You're kidding."

"Not in the least."

"I don't suppose I need to ask why you want it so badly, considering how my father acquired it."

"There is that," I said. "And it will be nice to have it back in the family for a while, but why I want to buy it goes beyond its history. Have you ever felt a connection to a place that you don't quite understand? It's just this feeling, deep inside, that you're meant to be there?"

"These woods," she said with a faint smile.

"I have that with the farmhouse. I've always been drawn to it, even when I was little and simply driving past."

"Makes sense, considering your grandfather built it."

"It's more than that." I shook my head. "It's hard to explain."

If I was being truthful, I'd always been drawn to Blue, too. And not just because my mother had teased temptation by warning me to stay away from the Bishops. There was something so genuine about Blue that I'd always wanted to be her friend. She didn't expect anything from anyone or need me to be perfect, which was why I could be myself around her. But wanting to be her friend and being one were two completely different things. She had a wall around herself that was near impossible to break through—and I was too withdrawn to keep trying to knock it down.

I added, "I want to take the farmhouse back to its original footprint and update it inside and out." I didn't mention my desire to chase away its melancholy, because Blue had lived with that sorrow, and there was no need to remind her of her painful past.

"I can't tell you how long I've wanted someone to buy that farmhouse. To take it off my hands and out of my life."

"I can bring the contract over straightaway; just let me know—"

She held up a hand to cut me off. "But I can't sell the farmhouse right now, Sarah Grace. I'm sorry. I'm going to be taking it off the market."

"What? Why?"

"My art studio." She shook her head. "It's a long story about clear passageways and a room not having two purposes."

I felt like crying right there on the trail. Hazey must have sensed my distress because she whimpered. I patted her head and tried to get hold of my composure. I'd had offers turned down before, but this one hit a little too close to my heart.

"I'm truly sorry, Sarah Grace."

Not as much as I was. "Is there anything I can do to change your mind?"

She glanced down at the baby and after a long moment shook her head.

We stood in pained silence for a moment before I finally said, "I should get going, since the vet clinic is closing soon." Then I remembered something I probably should've mentioned before. "You aren't currently renting the farmhouse out by any chance, are you?"

"No, why?"

"I didn't think so, but I wanted to make sure. When I was there on Monday, I noticed a blow-up mattress in one of the upstairs bedrooms, some trash, and a recent take-out bag from Kitty's."

Her inner eyebrows dipped low as she frowned. "A blow-up mattress? That wasn't there the last time I was in the house a couple of weeks ago."

"It's possible it's a squatter. I probably should've told you before now, but it slipped my mind with the news about Flora."

"It's all right. I'll check it out. Thanks for letting me know." Blue held out the feather and the button; then her gaze shifted to mine. "I'm curious, Sarah Grace. Where's your heart leading you these days?"

Some ten years ago she'd seen the original button and knew where my heart had led me back then.

I glanced over my shoulder again, in the direction of the Buttonwood Tree . . . and Shep. "I honestly don't know, Blue. For some reason it feels a whole lot like I'm just going 'round in circles."

Blue

"Now, aren't you glad you came?" Marlo said as we walked down a long corridor on the third floor of the Magnolia Breeze Nursing and Rehab Center—the inpatient hospice care floor.

Well, Marlo walked. I trudged.

She pushed a library cart ahead of us, and I had to admit, if only to myself, that I had enjoyed myself so far tonight. The cart held a variety of books, mostly enjoyable short story or poetry compilations, and the patients for the most part were grateful for the companionship. No one had asked about my past or about Flora, allowing me to simply enjoy the camaraderie that came from sharing a good story.

It was the perfect therapy after my world had been knocked off-kilter by Mr. Mantilla's visit and having to turn down Sarah Grace's offer.

Remembering the look in her eyes made my heart hurt all over again. At this point I just wanted to go home, bake some cookies, cuddle Flora, and try my best not to think of what tomorrow would bring.

Marlo bumped my arm. "Are you still stewing about the farmhouse? My offer stands. We'll make do. Call Sarah Grace right now and tell her you've changed your mind."

That Marlo could read me like a book always took me slightly by surprise. When she heard what had happened with the court investigator, she had offered up space in her house, but I couldn't do that to Moe. It wasn't worth upsetting his day-to-day routine and changing his environment, both precious commodities to someone with dementia.

I had only one option left for my studio.

Tomorrow, I would start packing up my art studio to move it over to the old farmhouse, which felt a little like cruel and unusual punishment.

"I don't want to upset Moe since he's been doing so well

lately. I'm hopeful that using the farmhouse as studio space is only a temporary situation. A few months at most. When I find another solution, I'll check with Sarah Grace to see if she's still interested in buying the place. I'm just trying to make peace with the decision to go back there, but peace isn't coming easily."

She smiled. "You know, maybe going home again is where you'll find the peace you're looking for so badly."

Not this again.

At the look on my face, she smiled wider and said, "Yes. I do believe it's just what you're needing. God provides, honey. He provides." She walked off, wheeling the cart down the hallway toward a room at the far end.

Marlo and I had been here at Magnolia for nearly two hours and would wrap up our visit after one final stop.

Mary Eliza Wheeler's room.

I eyed the EXIT sign above the stairway door and thought about making a run for it, but as I watched Marlo call out a cheerful hello to the nursing station, I forced myself to follow her lead.

The hallway's décor tried for light and cheerful but came off as trying too hard to feel natural with flashy colors, murals painted on the walls, faux flowers, and six-panel doors that seemed like they belonged in a home rather than a care facility. But if you looked closely, the colors were trying to mask the fact that there wasn't a lot of natural light, the flowers were coated in a fine layer of dust, and the doors weren't wooden—the panels had been painted on steel security doors.

I had to give the place credit for trying to look homey. The facility had great reviews and provided necessary palliative and hospice care. According to the staff, Mary Eliza had been relentless in asking for me, and I couldn't imagine why. She had never liked me. She called me white-trash trouble, which was the least of her insults.

Marlo waited for me outside the door, and when I caught up, she leaned in and whispered, "Still making her hats. I'm glad to see it. Bless her heart."

Wearing a pink housecoat that was buttoned to her jaw, Mary Eliza sat up in her hospital bed, her gaze intent on the knitted hat she was working on. Her mind might not be the same as it once was, but her hands moved slowly yet surely to complete the project, knitting needles clicking in a mesmerizing rhythm. Three small hats sat stacked on a bedside table. Baby hats. Each identical to the other.

Mary Eliza had been making baby hats for the community for as long as I could remember. Each the same pattern, though different colors. Pink for girls. Blue for boys. As traditional as it got.

Mary Eliza's face, normally thin and narrow, appeared puffy and swollen. I hadn't seen her in a little more than a month and was taken aback at the changes in such a short time. Her thin, shoulder-length hair was a stark, brilliant white, and even with the obvious swelling, she seemed to be shrinking within herself.

"Hello, Miss Mary Eliza!" Marlo said as she knocked on the door.

Mary Eliza glanced up. She breathed loudly, wheezing as though she couldn't take a full breath, despite being hooked up to an oxygen cannula. "Do you hear it?" she said, her voice low, weak.

Marlo stood at the foot of the bed. She tipped her head. "Hear what? The TV? It's not on. Would you like me to turn it on? It's about time for *Wheel of Fortune*. Do you like game shows, Miss Mary Eliza?"

"The wind," Mary Eliza said louder, stronger. "The wind, the wind."

My skin prickled and my heart beat faster.

"The wind? Why, no, I don't," Marlo said, peeking out the window. "It's a calm night."

Mary Eliza turned her head toward me and stared, her eyes cold and empty. She dropped her knitting to point a finger at me. "Blue! Bad, bad, atone, atone," she hissed. "The wind, the wind! The wind knows! Blue is trouble. Trouble, trouble."

Marlo glanced back at me, horror in her eyes.

Mary Eliza's gaze bore into me. "The wind, the wind! Took the baby. Trouble! Took the baby! The wind knows! The wind saw! Atone, atone!"

Marlo walked slowly backward toward the door, easing her way out of the room. "Take a breath, Miss Mary Eliza. We're going to go now. Try to get some rest, sweetie."

Mary Eliza dropped her head back against the pillow. Her chest heaved from the exertion of speaking, but her hard gaze didn't waver from mine. "Took the baby. Trouble, trouble. No more trouble. Atone . . . atone."

With that, she picked up her knitting and went back to work, as if we'd never been there.

Out in the hallway, Marlo and I stood rigid side by side, leaning against one of the peppy murals. She drew in a shuddering breath. "Good heavens above. What just happened?"

Rocked to my core by the visit, I started to tremble. I gave Marlo a sideways glance and jokingly said, "At least I didn't get her riled up."

She looked at me, and we began to laugh, but before I knew it, I was crying.

"I'm so sorry, honey," she said as she hugged me. "I don't know why I insisted you come with me."

"Threads." I wiped tears from my eyes.

We collected ourselves and made our way downstairs. Marlo said, "You don't ever have to see her again. Poor woman obviously doesn't know what she's saying. I can't even imagine what's going on in her head that she thinks you took Flora."

I wasn't sure either, but the way she'd said the wind *knew and saw* made me wonder if it was possible Mary Eliza had a similar connection to the wind as me. I'd never heard the wind talk, but I didn't think it impossible. Perhaps with her brain injury she'd misinterpreted what the wind had been saying?

As Marlo and I walked through the front doors, I paid careful attention as a breeze rustled the leaves of the magnolia trees flanking the building's entrance. More attention than I had paid in years.

As Marlo had said—it was a calm night.

And I couldn't help feeling that it was the calm before the storm.

Chapter
8

Blue

"Can I borrow the car this afternoon?" Persy asked early Friday morning as she grabbed the flour from the pantry and set it on the countertop.

I held a ceramic bowl in one hand and a wooden spoon in the other as I creamed butter and sugar together, the base of my chocolate chip cookie recipe. "You can take it. I only need to go to the bookshop, then stop by the old farmhouse, and I can walk to both. Where are you off to?"

Concern flared in her whiskey gaze as she dipped a measuring cup into the flour. "You're going to the farmhouse? Why?"

Persy had very little attachment to the house. Growing up, when she hadn't been in school, she'd spent most of her days in the bookshop. For the last six years, many of her nights she slept here with me. Twyla had done her best to push us out of the nest early on, in an effort to distance herself from everyone she loved.

I tucked aside old pains, cracked an egg against the bowl, and said, "Sarah Grace mentioned that she thinks someone has been living there recently. A squatter. I need to check it out."

She blinked in confusion. "Why would Sarah Grace think that?"

"She was at the house on Monday to take a look at it and saw some stuff that made her suspicious. She was thinking about buying the house, but now that I pulled it off the market, that's not going to happen. If there's a squatter, they need to be evicted before I move my studio there."

The scent of vanilla wafted up and wrapped around me like a comforting hug as I poured a teaspoonful into my batter. Cookie comfort had started when I was old enough to drag a stool over to the counter to help Twyla bake away her troubles. It was a phrase she used often when explaining why she baked so much. Back then she mostly made Bisquick sugar cookies—cheap yet tasty. Sometimes when money was a little less of an issue, she'd splurge on chocolate chips.

Making cookies with her was one of my happiest childhood memories. After I moved out, I'd drop off cookies for her every week. Sometimes, she'd return my tin with a heart drawn on it. Some weeks, though, I wouldn't hear from her at all and would have to track her down to make sure she was still alive. This went on for years until the week I'd shown up to check on her and found my worst fear had come true.

Across the room, Flora was throwing her fists around inside her Moses basket on the sofa, and I made a promise to myself to tell her of the Twyla who loved to bake. And I'd teach her how to make Bisquick sugar cookies just the way Twyla had taught me. Some things were too important to leave buried in the past.

Persy added baking soda and salt to her bowl of flour and whisked it with vigor as she said, "A squatter? That's crazy. I mean, who'd want to stay there?"

Snowy clouds erupted from the bowl and landed with wild abandon on the countertop, coating measuring spoons and cups, the box of baking soda, the canister of salt, and the vanilla extract bottle in a blanket of white velvet. "Anyone looking to get out of the elements, I suppose. I didn't mean to upset you by bringing it up."

"I'm not upset."

I lifted an eyebrow at the white landscape that used to be the countertop. Her actions belied her words; Persy wasn't ordinarily a messy baker. But whatever I'd triggered within her was bound to stay stubbornly locked away with the other secrets she'd been guarding lately. "Where are you going this afternoon?" I asked again, suddenly realizing she'd never said.

She slid the floury bowl my way. "Just a thing I need to do."

"A thing," I echoed as I began incorporating the dry mix into the wet.

"Yeah. For school." She washed her hands. "But Blue, don't you have a book due soon? Your time would be better spent by staying here and working. I can check the farmhouse on my way home to make sure the squatter is long gone."

I studied her as I scooped cookies onto a cookie sheet lined with parchment paper. "You don't have to do that."

Wiping her hands on a dish towel, she said, "I want to! I don't mind at all. So it's settled?"

As I slid the cookie sheet onto a rack, I leaned away from the blast of heat that shot out of the oven. It felt a lot like a taunting gust of hot wind, and I couldn't help but consider it a warning of impending trouble.

Trouble that involved Persy.

I made a noncommittal noise as I grabbed a sponge to clean up. The only thing settled in my mind was my determination to find out why Persy did not want me at the farmhouse.

᭥

Today the signboard outside the bookshop read:

> IT IS ONLY WITH THE HEART THAT ONE CAN SEE
> RIGHTLY, WHAT IS ESSENTIAL IS INVISIBLE TO THE
> EYE
> —*The Little Prince*

There was a decently drawn crown as well, and I smiled at the effort. Henry had certainly taken to writing the daily quotes.

The CLOSED sign hung on the door, but I could see Henry inside. He glanced over as if sensing someone watching him and waved me in. This morning we were going over the last-minute details for tomorrow's festival.

"Coffee's hot," he said as I pushed open the door. "Want a cup?"

"Would love one. Thanks."

Flora started to fuss as I walked over to one of the reading couches, where Henry had already set up a laptop and a notepad. I shrugged out of the knapsack and tried to settle her at the same time.

He set two mugs on the table and said, "Do you need any help?"

"Actually, could you hold Flora for a second while I get a bottle ready? She might be hungry."

"Yeah. Yeah, I can do that."

I unwrapped Flora and she shot her arms out, stretching them as she yawned. "Careful with her head," I said as I passed her over to him. My heart tripped a little as he drew her to his chest, her small head nestled in the palm of his big hand. Because he looked slightly shell-shocked, I said, "Not much experience with babies?"

He laughed. "Does it show?"

"Only a lot," I said, hurrying toward the restroom to wash my hands.

"I have two nieces and a nephew, my sister's kids, but I never held them much until they were old enough to beg me for piggyback rides."

"How old are they now?"

"In their teens and barely have time for the likes of me."

I came back to find them sitting on the sofa. Flora held on to his finger and studied his face as he studied hers. "Are they in Ohio?"

He nodded. "I'll see them at Christmas. I have to admit I

kind of miss them ignoring me. They probably haven't even realized I moved yet."

"I doubt that. When Persy first went off to college, I about drove her crazy texting her all the time. I had to learn to let her go, which wasn't easy—trust me. But what I found was that soon she was the one texting me all the time." I poured water into a bottle that already had formula powder in it. "The point of that was your nieces and nephew will miss you soon enough."

"I hope you're right." He glanced up at me, then back down at Flora. "You know, I swear she looks like you. She has your eyes. Those pretty, downturned eyes."

At his soft gaze, I grew warm and flustered. I focused on studying her features. "Really?"

Now that he pointed it out, I saw it. It was a prevalent shape among many people, not just me, but I liked having something in common with her.

"It's not just her eyes. It's her chin, too."

"Come on, now—my chin is a good four times that size. Maybe five." I shook the bottle, keeping a finger over the hole in the nipple so formula wouldn't fly out.

He laughed as he wiggled his trapped finger. "She'll grow into it."

I held up the bottle as Flora smacked her lips and let out irritated chirps. "Do you want to feed her while I get our checklist started for tomorrow?"

His gaze caught mine, and he slowly smiled. "Yeah, I do."

Flora thrashed her head side to side as he held the bottle near her mouth, then clamped down on the nipple as a drop of formula touched her lips. She made eager, noisy sucking sounds, and Henry laughed.

"She's a good eater," I said as I picked up the laptop and sat next to him.

"I'll say."

He fed Flora as we discussed the booth's setup, takedown, and everything in between. We went over the schedules for the day, who was slated to do what, and I had to admit to him that I needed to play the day by ear. I had no choice but to bring Flora along, and I'd need to leave if it got to be too much for her . . . or me. "I haven't been to the festival in years."

He set Flora against his shoulder like he'd burped her a hundred times before. It made me realize just how close he'd been paying attention to me this past week, and the knowledge made my cheeks heat.

"You don't like festivals?" he asked as he rubbed Flora's back, his hand looking enormous against her small body.

"I like festivals just fine. I'm just not— My family—" I took a deep breath.

"Say no more. I get it. In the book of life, everyone has chapters they don't like reading out loud."

I'd never thought of it that way. "Do you?" Suddenly I was very curious about this man.

"Yours isn't the only family with issues, Blue. Some are just better than others at hiding it."

He sounded so serious that I suddenly felt the need to lighten the tension. "Fess up. Are you the grandson of D. B. Cooper? Or Jack the Ripper? Or . . ." I grinned, suddenly unable to think of another unsolved mystery.

He laughed. "No. Well, not that I know of. I've actually been meaning to talk to you—"

The door pushed open and Kebbie came inside. "I just heard a storm's coming in this afternoon. I hope the festival doesn't get rained out tomorrow."

I looked at Henry. "We didn't even talk about a backup plan if it rains."

"We'll just wing it," he said.

Winging it didn't sound like a good plan to me. "We can always open the store. Funnel festivalgoers over here. Maybe we should take only a few book displays, ones we can cover quickly . . ."

"Blue," he said, finally easing a burp from Flora, and she began to cry from the effort. "We have a tent. It'll be fine. Don't worry about it."

Don't worry. I didn't know how to *not* worry.

Kebbie dropped her purse on the counter and rushed to the couch to look over Henry's shoulder. "Flora's already gotten so much bigger in just a few days."

Henry passed Flora over to me. "No wonder. You should see the way she eats."

I curled Flora against my chest, and she immediately quieted. As her heart beat against mine, I felt a wave of emotion, of pure, simple love for her. I rested my cheek on her head and tried to remember this moment forever.

"I've seen," Kebbie said with a smile, watching us closely.

She wore a blue sundress that showed off her curvy figure and brought out her eyes, and she'd pulled her blond hair back in a slick ponytail. But when I looked a little closer, I noticed that she appeared . . . unwell. Tired, with bags under glassy eyes, and her coloring was off. She had a flush to her cheeks that didn't look natural and hadn't come from makeup.

"Are you feeling okay, Kebbie?" I asked. "Your color is high."

She pressed her hands to her cheeks. "I think it's just allergies. Pollen is the devil, I swear."

"Are you sure you're okay to work?" Henry asked as he folded the diaper cloth and set it on the table.

"I'm fine," she said. "I look worse than I feel. I took an allergy pill a little bit ago. It should kick in any second."

I tucked Flora into her sling. "We should get going, before the store opens. We're off to the woods for a quick forage." I didn't mention stopping by the farmhouse—Persy's reaction to the news of the squatter had made me uneasy about sharing the information. Thinking of the squatter also brought forth the image of Sarah's Grace disappointed face yesterday when I'd turned down her offer, and I tried to tamp down the guilt. I'd had no other choice. "Kebbie, did Sarah Grace end up keeping the dog she found yesterday?"

"Dog?" she asked. "What dog? Sarah Grace found a dog?"

I nodded. "Last I heard, she was taking the dog to Doc Hennessey's to see if she had a microchip."

Kebbie said, "I haven't heard anything, but I also haven't talked to Sarah Grace since yesterday morning. A vacation, now a dog. Wow. Good for her. She's always wanted a dog, but Aunt Ginny's allergic. I'm going to text her right now to get the scoop." She whipped a phone out of the pocket of her dress and her fingers flew over buttons.

I tensed at Ginny's name, as always. My father's sins weren't my own, but I still felt the shame of them, even now, more than forty years later. I had the uneasy feeling that would never change.

Henry stood up. "Blue, are you headed past the Buttonwood Tree by any chance?"

I nodded. "Why?"

"Would you mind if I tagged along? Kebbie can watch the store for a bit." He looked over his shoulder. "Can't you, Kebbie?"

She looked up from her phone. "Sure can."

When he turned back to me, she wiggled her eyebrows.

I rolled my eyes as I finished packing Flora's things, but I could feel a blush starting.

Henry said, "I've always been fascinated by the folklore of the tree, but I haven't seen it since I was a little kid. I'd go on my own, but with my sense of direction, I'd be lost in no time at all."

"You shouldn't worry about that," Kebbie said. "Blue would come find you."

My cheeks were now as red as hers as I intently focused on packing the knapsack so I wouldn't have to look at Henry.

"True enough," he said. "Let me just run upstairs and change. I'll be right back."

Kebbie's phone pinged as he headed for the back staircase. "Sarah Grace says that Doc H didn't find a microchip, but he did find an infection. Hazey had to stay overnight for treatment, and she's been looking at lost-dog listings." Kebbie smiled. "*Hazey?* If she named her already, I bet she's fixin' to keep her."

I remembered the MoonPie eyes—on both of them. "I hope so."

The phone pinged again. "And she says not to say anything to anyone, because she hasn't told Fletch yet."

"Fletch doesn't like dogs?" I asked.

She looked annoyed as she said, "Fletch doesn't like sharing attention."

"Ah."

"Yeah." She shook her head. "I'm not quite sure what Sarah Grace sees in him."

Me, either. Not when she'd been head over heels for Shep Wheeler back in high school, planning on marrying him as soon as they graduated. I didn't know what had happened between them. I only knew that when she came back from spending the summer at her family's house on the Gulf, she'd been alone.

Thinking of Shep reminded me of his mother, Mary Eliza, and what she'd said last night. *The wind, the wind.*

I shook her voice out of my head, determined to forget the incident ever happened.

Henry was back downstairs in a flash, and soon we were on our way to the trailhead, shaded by the spindly outstretched branches of cherry trees that lined the sidewalk. A Ferris wheel had been erected in the middle of the park and loomed over

Poplar Street, its colorful cars glinting like jewels in the sunshine.

Henry glanced up at the sky and said, "It certainly doesn't look like it's going to rain."

"It's going to."

He glanced my way. "How can you tell?"

"The leaves on the silver maple trees are turned, which means extra-high humidity, which means rain."

"Isn't it always humid down here?"

At his suspicious look, I shrugged. "I spend a lot of time outside and notice these things."

"All right, Blue Bishop—I'll trust you."

I nearly tripped on a crack in the sidewalk. I don't think I'd ever heard the name Bishop and the word *trust* together in a sentence. He grabbed my arm to steady me, and I mumbled a thanks as I checked on Flora. She'd fallen asleep in the baby sling, her heart against mine, her head nestled on the soft spot under my collarbone, one leg hugging each side of my rib cage.

I came to a full stop as the wind suddenly picked up, stirring to life the serrated leaves on the cherry trees.

"Something wrong?" Henry asked.

"I—" The wind gusted again, pulling me in the opposite direction. It would have to wait. I'd take Henry to the tree, then see where the wind would lead me. "No. The tree is about a half mile from the trailhead."

We walked in silence for a bit before he said, "It must've been something for you to find Flora in the woods."

"'Something' is one way of putting it. She's only been with me for a few days, but I really can't imagine life without her now."

"Have there been any updates with her case?"

"Not really."

"I'm wondering why her birth mother didn't just contact you about a private adoption. Why did she choose to follow you into the woods, leave Flora, and run? She had to know there are legal repercussions if she's found. Abandoning a baby in the woods, even if she knew Flora would be found imminently, isn't covered by the safe-haven law, right?"

"Right." In Alabama, the law allowed a newborn up to three days old to be dropped off with an emergency room employee of any licensed hospital, no questions asked. But *only* emergency room employees.

"She must be confident she won't be found, and for some reason she doesn't want her identity to be known." Mrs. Tillman's speech about hidden pregnancies floated through my thoughts, and I pushed them straight back out.

"Then there's the button. The tree must think highly of you."

"Maybe, but it also knows how much I wanted a baby. I've been trying to adopt a newborn for years now."

"I didn't know that. For what it's worth, I've seen what a good mom you are to Flora and think the tree made the right choice."

My heart swelled. "Thanks for saying that. I didn't have the best role model." I winced. "That sounds harsh."

"From what I've heard, you had a bit of a harsh life."

"There were some happy times. They were few and far between, but still. I just wish—"

"What?"

"I wish my family had made better choices." The wind gusted again, pulsing and insistent. I slowed to a stop and turned around, toward the direction of the ball fields.

Henry stopped walking, and I could feel him looking at me, waiting.

"Do you mind if we take the scenic route?" I finally asked, turning to look at him.

His gaze searched my face, the blue in his eyes lit with curiosity. "Not at all."

"C'mon," I said, speed walking away from the trailhead.

He easily kept pace with me. "Where are we going?"

"I'm not sure yet."

"All right, then. Lead on."

It was a quick walk to the fields, five minutes at the most, and I kept a hand on Flora's back to keep from jostling her too much. As we approached the chain-link fencing, the wind died down. As soon as I saw why, I sighed.

"Is that Moe?" Henry asked, squinting.

Moe sat on a small set of bleachers set up behind home plate. "He must've slipped out of the house. Marlo's probably going crazy right about now." I took a step forward, but Henry grabbed my hand.

"How'd you know he was here?"

I smiled. "I find lost things, remember?"

"But seriously, Blue. How?"

Moe must have heard us, because he glanced over his shoulder and grinned. "Fine morning for a ball game, but best they get it in soon. Rain's coming." He patted the spot next to him. "Come sit down. I've saved some seats."

I gave Henry's hand a squeeze, then let it go without answering him. "Moe, that's real kind of you to save us some seats. Thank you."

He wore an Atlanta Braves ball cap, and he lifted it up and wiped his brow. "Ain't no problem at all."

I sat down next to him, and he leaned over and kissed Flora's head. "How's the little flower today?"

"She's good. Real good." Henry slid onto the bleacher next to me. "This is my friend Henry. I think you might've met him before, some time ago."

"Sure, sure," Moe said, eyeing Henry like the stranger he was. Apparently, he measured up because Moe stuck out a hand. "Good to see you again."

"Yes, sir," Henry said as he shook hands. "Always good to see you, too. Blue speaks so fondly of you."

Moe smiled. "She's a good girl, that Blue. You two a couple?"

I coughed. "No, no. Just friends." I pulled out my phone from my back pocket, texted Marlo, and then said, "*Dang*. I just got a message that the umpire called the game off early, on account of the rain coming."

Moe looked at the blue skies. "People be going soft. There's hours still until the rain comes. Calling the game. *Sheesh*. Back in my day, we played in the rain. A little mud never hurt anyone."

I nodded. "Sure enough, it doesn't. I can't count the times I played in the rain. Ty and I would make our own versions of a Slip 'n Slide using trash bags."

"How's Ty doing these days?" Moe asked. "I ain't seen that boy in forever."

My heart ached. "I haven't seen him in forever, either, but I have a feeling he's just fine. Hopefully he's at peace."

Moe patted my hand. "I bet he misses you just as much as you miss him."

Tears welled and I blinked them away. "I bet so, too. You know, Moe, I've got some of your favorite chocolate chip cookies at home. Just made them this morning. How about we go get a snack?"

His gaze narrowed. "You didn't put any nuts in them, did you?"

"No—no, sir. I wouldn't do that to you."

Moe glanced at Henry. "I told you she was a good girl, didn't I?"

"You surely did."

"You two a couple?" Moe asked.

I stood up and took hold of Moe's hand to help him off the bleachers. "Nope. We're just friends."

Henry hopped off the bleachers and stepped up on the other

side of Moe as we headed back toward town. "Actually, Moe, I've been thinking about asking Blue out to dinner or to see a movie. What do you think she'd say?"

I threw Henry a questioning look, but he didn't pay me any mind as he focused solely on Moe.

"Well now," Moe said as he scratched his chin, "she'll probably say no. At least at first. She's been hurt a fair time or two, and she's closed herself off from most people. To protect herself, you see."

"*Mmm*, yes, I can understand that," Henry said.

Moe leaned into him. "She's like her mama that way, not that Blue sees it for what it is. She's different from her mama in the way that she *wants* to be around people. She just doesn't want to be hurt again. What she hasn't learned yet is that she's hurting herself by keeping herself closed off. Opening up is the only way she'll find her happiness." His voice turned sharp. "You aren't planning on hurting her, are you?"

"Never," Henry said. "I like her."

Moe nodded. "Good, good. She's a good girl, that Blue."

"The best," Henry said as I swiped at the tears streaming from my eyes.

Moe glanced upward. "We best get a move on. Looks like rain is coming."

Chapter
9

Hayward Granbee placed Judge Quimby's groceries into a paper sack, his hands trembling slightly. Hay was up there in age, eighty if a day, but often said the day he stopped working would be the day he was set into the ground. The judge hoped the tremor was from age rather than a medical ailment. Hay was a stalwart of the community, everyone's granddaddy, and losing him would be like losing a piece of the town's heart and soul.

Hay's eyes, pale with wisdom, narrowed as he glanced across the scarred wooden countertop. "Heard you been gettin' some grief over Blue Bishop's foundling, Judge."

The judge lifted a bristly eyebrow. "Don't tell me you've got an opinion on the matter as well."

"Opinions change. What I know about Blue Bishop is fact."

Hay was an old friend so the judge humored him. "What fact is that?"

"This goes a way back. To the spring her two brothers died. Did you know Ty Bishop worked for me a couple days a week?"

The judge feigned surprise. "No, I didn't."

"Sure enough. Spent an afternoon or two a week out at the farm, mucking stalls and helping with other chores. It was an agreement we came to after I caught him nicking a few items here at the store. Milk. Bread. That boy was hungry more often than not. At eighteen he was a big boy and still growing. He worked off his debt, showing up early, staying late. Even after his debt was paid, he kept coming back. I didn't have the heart to let him go. Mrs. Granbee neither. She stuffed him full as she could every time he was out at the farm. Since his debt was paid, Ty worked for store credit. He used the credit to buy food for his family. Always food, except for the marble. A single twenty-five-cent marble."

"An odd purchase for a grown boy."

"It wasn't for him. It was for Blue, only eleven at the time. Apparently they had a game they played, racing marbles for keeps. He always let her win." Hay's eyes drifted closed for a moment. "He had a good heart, that boy."

The judge didn't often hear kind words about the Bishop boys, and he was glad he'd let Hay say his piece.

Hay said, "A few days following the purchase of the first marble, I was surprised to see Blue come into the store alone, acting suspicious like. I watched from afar as she put the marble Ty had bought back into the bin. She ran out before I could question her. Later, I asked Ty about it. Turned out he hadn't told his family that he worked for me—and wanted to keep it that way. He guessed that Blue thought he'd stolen the marble, and that's why she gave it back. It became a game between him and me, wondering what marble she'd covet so much that she wouldn't return it."

"Was there one?"

His eyes suddenly misted. "No. That girl is as honest as the day is long. I ain't saying the Bishops are saintly, but there's goodness there, if you look for it. I wanted you to know that fact."

"I appreciate it, Hay. But I'm curious. Don't you wonder why Ty never told his family he worked for you?"

"Pride, I figured. Mostly I've wondered two other things all these years."

"What's that?"

Hay's hands shook as he pushed the sack across the counter.

"I'm wondering how hungry you'd have to be to rob a bank. And who played with little Blue once Ty was gone?"

Sarah Grace

The sun glinted off the bell of Buttonwood Baptist Church as I drove past, winking like it was a coconspirator privy to my secrets. I supposed in a way it was.

The belfry was where I'd first kissed Shep Wheeler on a long-ago Sunday after one of his daddy's long-winded services. While everyone else had trickled into the gathering hall for coffee and refreshments, I'd sought out a hiding spot from my life and climbed as high as I could. I'd found Shep in the tower. It turned out he had also been seeking a quiet place. From that day on we were nearly inseparable, sneaking off to be with each other as much as possible.

Thoughts of Shep were welcome after spending the last couple of hours simmering over Fletch. Last night I hadn't had a chance to talk to him about my suspicions, because he hadn't come home until after I fell asleep. When he woke up late this morning, grumbling about being late for work, I decided I'd wait until he was less stressed before starting such a hard conversation. I'd made it until lunchtime before I couldn't stand the suspicions a moment more, and had gone to his office, hoping he'd take a walk with me and tell me that there was a perfectly good reason why he'd been lying to me.

Only, he hadn't been at work.

Turned out, he'd taken the day off.

And he wasn't answering his phone, either. I'd left several messages and texts, asking him to call me as soon as possible. The notes had started off laced with curiosity, then shifted to angry, and then had dissolved into apprehension. My gut insisted he was fine, but my overactive imagination began picturing his car crashed at the bottom of a cliff.

Not that there were any cliffs nearby, but my imagination stubbornly refused to alter the image.

My cell phone rang as the haunting rosy lavender scent suddenly swirled around me, and I rolled down the window, hoping the wind would carry the aroma away. I saw the call was from my mother and put her on speakerphone, grateful for any reprieve from thoughts that Fletch was with another woman.

"Darling, I know it's short notice," Mama said, her voice echoing through the truck cab, "but I'm throwing together a simple dinner party tonight to celebrate Kebbie making the dean's list."

"Tonight?"

I glanced at the empty passenger seat and wished Hazey were with me, but Doc Hennessey had called to let me know he was keeping her another night. Kebbie, after learning the news about Hazey from Blue, had taken over the online search for lost-dog postings and was texting me the results. So far she hadn't found any that matched Hazey's description, and I secretly hoped she wouldn't. Blue's words about how Hazey was meant to be mine floated through my thoughts and made me smile. Maybe Blue had been right all along.

"Yes, tonight, Sarah Grace," Mama said. "I just found out about the list this morning. Supper won't be anything fancy—a roast chicken, whipped potatoes, a cake. But I'm just so pleased for her that I couldn't let the occasion go without marking it. Don't you think making the dean's list is an accomplishment worthy of celebration?"

I was surprised that syrup wasn't dripping out of my phone from her overly sweet tone. It wasn't the celebration of it all that concerned me. It was the sense that I was being baited. My mother didn't do spur-of-the-moment gatherings. She planned elaborate parties with embossed name cards and expensive catering. A birthday party took weeks of planning. A sudden, weekday party? Never. No doubt this get-together had little to do with Kebbie and everything to do with Flora.

"Of course it's worthy." I slowed to a stop at a red light. "But I don't know if Fletch and I can make it. I'd need to check with him."

If I could find him.

My imagination added shooting flames to the car crash, and I took a deep breath.

"Your father spoke with him already. His schedule is free and clear. He said to check with you."

I gripped the steering wheel. "Daddy spoke with him? When?"

"I heard them on the phone about half an hour ago. Why?"

"Did he say where Fletch was?" My knuckles whitened, and I forced my fingers to loosen on the wheel.

Her voice dropped. "Is Fletch not at work? Is he missing? What's this about, Sarah Grace?"

I quickly explained the situation.

"Oh," was all she said.

It was all that needed to be said.

Now my imagination had *me* pushing Fletch's car off the cliff.

I didn't find that image to be as disturbing as it should've been.

I lowered the window all the way down as the lavender and rose scent threatened to suffocate me.

"I'm sure he has a perfectly reasonable explanation," Mama said, sounding like she didn't believe a word she said. "Perhaps he's planning a surprise for you." Her voice rose as she latched onto this idea. "Yes! A surprise."

A car honked behind me, and I glanced up in time to see the green light flash to yellow. I waved to the driver behind me as an apology and waited for another green.

"Where are you?" she asked.

"In the truck. I'm on my way to one of my properties," I said, lying through my teeth. She didn't need to know I was on the way to the OB-GYN's office for my yearly checkup—and to get a refill on my birth control pills. My suspicions about Fletch only solidified my opinion that this definitely wasn't the time to be having a baby.

"Did you have a chance to look at the Dobbinses' house?"

"No," I said. "I don't want to buy the Dobbinses' house." Sometime last night while trying to stay awake until Fletch got home, I'd decided to talk to Blue one last time about the farmhouse. I couldn't bear the thought of walking away from the place. I'd offer her more than asking price, an amount that would be enough to cover rented studio space for a year at least. "I'm going to offer on the Bishop house."

"I see." She sighed heavily as if she were a woman long burdened by a rebellious daughter, then tartly said, "Drinks tonight are at five; supper is at six p.m."

Her tone was unmistakable: if I was going to defy her about the Bishop house, I sure as heck better be at her table tonight.

The light turned green, and I eased off the brake. "I'll be there," I said reluctantly, wondering how on earth I was going to pretend everything was fine between Fletch and me. "I need to go, Mama. I'll see you tonight."

The wind through the open window blew my hair about my face as I drove through town, past the high school, and turned onto Highway 119, which would lead me into Alabaster, the closest big city to the north.

I took a deep breath and let it out slowly as I glanced at the clock, trying to figure out my schedule for the rest of the afternoon.

Doctor appointment at two.

Dinner party at five.

Have it out with Fletch when we finally got home tonight.

In between all that, I'd pay a visit to Blue and present my new offer.

I took a deep breath, and the landscape blurred as I sped past, woods fading into soybean fields, weathered fences, and lazy cows. It only came into focus as I slowed down with the approach to Alabaster's city limits.

The doctor's office was housed in a one-story, square brick building a few blocks off the main road into town. I found an empty spot as far away from the door as possible and parked. Since I was a few minutes early, I took a moment to check my cell phone for any new messages or emails before I went inside.

None from Fletch.

Maybe my mother was right and he was planning a surprise. Earlier this week, he'd been so gung ho on baby-making plans that it was possible he was putting some extra effort into our marriage.

But even as I thought it, the lavender and rose enveloped me, forcing me out of the truck. Why was it haunting me with truths I didn't want to acknowledge? Why couldn't it just leave me alone?

My stomach ached as I headed across the parking lot toward the building's front door. Even though ours was a troubled marriage, the thought that he could be cheating hurt, a deep, unfamiliar pain.

Swallowing back a rush of emotion, I blindly stumbled toward the door, stopping short to avoid a couple I hadn't seen come out. They stood on the sidewalk playing kissy-face.

I did a double take as I passed by. Certain I was seeing things, I took off my sunglasses, and my stomach launched into my throat. "*Fletch?*"

He turned my way. His jaw dropped and his face flushed crimson. "Sarah Grace?"

The woman he was with stepped in close to his side. "Babe, you know her?"

I took a good look at her but no recognition sparked. She was young, about Kebbie's age, and pretty with black hair and blue eyes. She was also quite obviously pregnant. Maybe four or five months by the look of the rounded belly housed in a skintight hoochie dress.

I couldn't stop staring at her stomach.

"Sarah Grace, I can explain," Fletch said.

Feeling as though I might be sick, I slapped a hand over my mouth and turned on my heel. I needed to get out of there. My feet felt heavy, like they were melting into the asphalt as I walked away. With effort, I broke into a jog, and before I knew it, I was running as fast as I could across the parking lot.

Brakes screeched and the odor of burning rubber bloomed in the air. A car halted, mere inches from my body. Shaken, I stumbled away from the hood and sent a quick, apologetic glance to the driver, and was stunned to see Persy Bishop gaping at me from behind the wheel.

"Sarah Grace!" Fletch yelled.

I glanced back at him and saw the young woman still clinging to his arm like a desperate barnacle. I had to get away. I couldn't think. I could barely breathe. I sprinted for my truck.

My hands shook as I found my keys and started the engine. I didn't look back at Fletch as I pressed my foot on the gas, jumped the curb, and drove over the sidewalk. Out on the main street, I floored it.

Gulping air, trying to catch my breath, I realized I didn't know where I was going, or where to run.

All I knew was that I could never go back to what once was.

Chapter
10

Blue

The skies had darkened and the scent of rain clung to the humid air as I headed back into the woods, this time without Henry. After taking Moe home, Henry had decided to take a rain check on seeing the Buttonwood Tree and had gone back to the bookshop. I was more than okay with parting ways.

I wasn't sure at all what to think about his dating questions.

On one hand, my life was fairly busy these days between Flora and work. On the other, the way he looked at me made me feel things I never had before. I'd never had a serious boyfriend, which felt all kinds of ridiculous to say at twenty-nine years old.

She's been hurt a fair time or two, and she's closed herself off from most people. To protect herself, you see.

Moe's words made me ache just as much now as when he'd first said them. I hadn't been able to argue with him, because what he said was true. I had closed myself off, and opening myself up again terrified me.

I like her.

Henry's honest, simple words made me smile, because I had to admit that I liked him, too.

I just didn't know what to do about it.

For now, I pushed it all out of my mind and focused on the task at hand. Checking the farmhouse for a squatter—and trying to figure out why Persy hadn't wanted me to.

The shortcut to the farmhouse through the woods was well marked from my many trips back and forth through the years. My forays into the woods never failed to take me past my old home, pulling me along like the wind had me by the hand.

Flora slept on my chest, the wrap keeping her secure against me as I strode down the wooded path, past towering trees I'd seen grow from saplings, over the fallen butternut tree where I'd harvested bark to make a pale orange-yellow ink, and across rocks that lined a shallow creek bed, the water barely deep enough to cover a tadpole. My arms pushed against swaying branches that reached out to hug me like I was an old friend.

As the path widened, opening into the farmhouse's back-yard, I paused at the edge of the tree line. My gaze swept from the old chicken coop across patchy, overgrown grass to the sagging back porch and the back door, which hung from one hinge. Paint peeled from the clapboard like it was trying to escape, the gabled roof was in desperate need of repair, and bricks were missing from both chimneys. My stomach churned at the thought of being regularly back inside this house, enveloped in old memories, but I had little choice.

I cupped the back of Flora's head and carefully picked my way across the knee-high grass, heading toward the front porch. As I rounded the corner of the house, I was surprised to see Sarah Grace's truck parked on the gravel drive.

Confused, I wondered what Sarah Grace was doing here. I stepped over ivy that shot upward through porch slats and pushed open the front door, which stood ajar.

Sarah Grace sat on the floor of the living room, her back against the staircase wall. She had her arms wrapped around her knees, which were drawn up to her chest. She glanced up at me, and I saw dried tear tracks on her face. She looked away, and I noticed that both her jaw and hands were clenched tightly.

I walked over to her, carefully eased the knapsack off my shoulders and put it on the floor. Keeping a firm hand on Flora,

I slid down the wall and sat next to Sarah Grace. I took quick stock of the house, noting how much it hadn't changed since Twyla had passed away. It was dustier and dirtier, but everything was the same. The couch sat slightly off center from the front windows, a chipped ceramic pot on the sideboard held a dust-covered plastic fern, and an old throw blanket was draped over the back of the threadbare armchair.

"Sorry for trespassin', but I didn't know where else to go," Sarah Grace said, her voice strained. "I just needed somewhere to think. Somewhere I can simply be. I like it here."

"Stay as long as you'd like." I glanced her way, but I didn't see any visible injuries. No bumps. No bruises. But I also knew that some deep wounds didn't show.

At the sudden sound of rain pounding the roof, I looked upward. It didn't take but a minute for water to start dripping onto the living room floor and flow toward the front door.

Sarah Grace watched the stream. "Foundation problems."

"The floor has sloped as long as I can remember. For years, every Saturday Ty and I used to have marble races, and the slope added to the fun. Winner got to keep the other's marble. Ty used to give me a head start. He pretended he didn't, and I pretended I didn't know. Every week he showed up with a new, shiny marble, ready to roll, ready to make me laugh with his over-the-top color commentary."

I could practically see him now, crouched here in this living room the last time we'd played, marble in hand, a mischievous spark in his russet eyes, his shoulder-length hair pulled back in a low ponytail. He'd been eighteen at the time, big and burly, but his cheeks had still been round with baby fat and peach fuzz. My chest ached with the longing to hug him.

"That's sweet," Sarah Grace said, relaxing her fingers.

"It was. Though I also pretended not to know that every week he'd steal his marble from a bin at the general store. Each time I won, I snuck the marble back into the store the following

Monday. I only have one marble left, from the last game we'd played together. It was a few days before he died."

She released her hold on her legs and let them slide out in front of her. "I don't blame you for not giving that one back."

As rain beat against the house, I said, "Oh, I tried to. I held on to that marble a good two weeks after my brothers' funerals, wanting to keep it. It was a tiger's-eye marble and looked so much like Ty's eyes—Wade's, too, for that matter—that it made me both happy and sad to see it. But it was burning a hole in my pocket, knowing it was stolen. I couldn't keep it. It wasn't mine to keep. So I took my broken heart on down to the general store, and just as I was about to drop that marble back into the bin, a big hand clamped around my wrist. Old Mr. Granbee. I about died myself. I thought for sure he was about to accuse me of stealing and call the police and that I'd be sent to juvie and there'd be no one to take care of Persy since Twyla had taken to her bed. It was all I could do not to burst into tears."

"Good gracious, Blue. I'd have been a puddle. What happened?"

Flora snuffled, wiggled, and settled, her lips puckering as she slept. I wrapped my arms around her and said, "Mr. Granbee asked me what it was I thought I was doing. But before I could come up with any sort of sensible answer, he said that tiger's-eye marble was a right special marble, and that he'd been hesitant to let it go, but Ty had been determined to buy the best of the bunch for his little sister and would likely be real sorry if he knew I was planning to swap it out for another."

"No," Sarah Grace said, dragging out the word, her bloodshot hazel eyes wide. "Do you think he really believed you were planning to swap it out?"

I recalled the way his big, calloused hands had folded my small, dirty fingers around that marble and the soft look in his eyes. "I don't know. All I do know is that day, as I ran all the way home, I felt as though I'd been given the greatest gift in the whole world."

"Wow," she said. "I'm not sure I've ever heard you talk of your brothers."

"I don't talk about them often. It still . . . hurts." Yet twice today I talked of Ty, and though it hurt, I realized I'd missed talking about him. I missed *him*. In a small way, telling these little stories had brought him back to me, if only for a little while.

"That's understandable, but I like seeing them through your eyes." She relaxed against the wall, her shoulders loosening. "I have a feeling you knew different people than we all did," Sarah Grace said. "Mac is the only one of your brothers I feel like I know anything about. My dad talks about him from time to time."

Mayor Jud talking about Mac? "Really? Why? Had Mac done something to him? Beat him up?"

She laughed. "No, nothing like that. Mac saved my dad from a hallway bully once in middle school. Broke the kid's nose. Mac and my dad became friends."

"I didn't know that." But I wasn't the least bit surprised to hear that Mac had busted someone's nose. According to Twyla, he'd always been a scrapper.

The only reason Mac was in the army was because a local judge had taken pity on him, offering him enlistment instead of jail time after a fight had landed him behind bars. It had been a fateful choice. But I also couldn't help wondering what would have happened if Mac had chosen jail. Would he have ultimately ended up a bank robber like Wade and Ty? Or a con man like our Daddy? Or would he have been able to overcome it all to break the cycle, like Persy and me? I'd never know, which both broke my heart and soothed it.

"I'm sure you know a different Jud and Ginny than most

people." She for certain knew a different Ginny than I did, but I had to admit that my interactions with her weren't the norm around here.

Sarah Grace dragged a finger across the floorboard, rubbing a spot clear of dust. "Not really. For the most part, my parents are open books. My mama does tend to be intensely private about matters that would put her in a bad light. Like the fact that she was pregnant with me when she married Daddy. It's the worst kept secret in Buttonwood, but she's never spoken openly of it, and I doubt she ever will."

I noticed Sarah Grace mentioned only her parents and not herself, which made sense, because if she were a book, her binding would be pristine, and her pages would be glued together to hide what was inside.

"Even still, as far as families go, yours is pretty picture-perfect, even with you being the chubbiest preemie ever known to be born at Buttonwood Hospital."

"My mama would be giddy to hear you say you think our family is perfect," she said with a weak smile.

We sat in silence for a moment, with only the dripping rain and Flora's soft breathing filling the emptiness.

"It seems like you've had some good memories here," Sarah Grace said, looking around. "The house misses you."

I glanced at her. It was such an odd thing to say.

Redness flared on her cheeks. "I mean, I bet the house misses having you here."

"Being here is painful," I said simply. "For every good memory, there's a bad one. Maybe two. This house is full of hopes and dreams and hunger and heartache. Mostly heartache."

"I'm sorry. I never stopped to think about how hard life must have been for you back then. I'm embarrassed to admit that, and more than ever I regret what happened in high school."

"You have regrets? Why? It was my idea to take the blame."

Her hands fisted again. "I shouldn't have let you talk me into it. I should've spoken up and set the record straight."

Suddenly I was back in high school on the day of the senior prom. Crews had been hard at work on prettying up the gymnasium, and everyone had been buzzing around, anxious for the day to be over with and night to come. I'd had to stay after school that day to make up a quiz I'd missed when out sick the week before, and had stopped in the restroom before walking over to the bookshop. The smell of cigarette smoke and sobbing had drifted out from one of the stalls.

I'd tried to mind my own business, but the sobs broke my heart. "Are you okay in there?"

Sniffle. "Fine."

"You don't sound fine."

"Leave me alone."

Maybe I should've listened, but I hadn't. I pretended to leave, then stood still in the corner until Sarah Grace walked out of the stall, a cigarette between her lips and a pregnancy test in hand.

She'd dropped both when she saw me standing there.

"I just wanted to make sure you were really okay," I'd said.

She started sobbing again, and before I knew it, she was pouring out her heart and all its troubles. She showed me her Buttonwood Tree button and told me she loved Shep, someone her parents wouldn't approve of because of his rebellious nature and multiple tattoos, and that they were going to get married down in Mobile . . . and that they were going to have a baby. She didn't know how to tell her parents. Her heart was breaking at the mere thought of it.

At some point, she'd tossed her stubbed-out cigarette into the trash can. Neither of us realized until later that it sat smoldering among paper towels, which finally burst into flames not long after we had left the building. Thankfully the damage had been limited to the bathroom, but the prom had been canceled, a fact that was still brought up from around town to mark time. *The year Blue Bishop ruined prom for everybody . . .*

"Even if you had confessed, who'd have believed you?" I asked. "No one. They'd have thought you were covering for me, taking pity."

If she believed otherwise, she was delusional. A teacher had seen *me* coming out of the restroom shortly before the fire broke out, not Sarah Grace. And the principal had been a blowhard, intent on seeing someone pay for ruining the prom. He'd sent the police to question me. When they asked me what I knew of the fire, I kept thinking about a sobbing, pregnant Sarah Grace who had everything in life to look forward to.

And me, who was trapped in this town by the wind.

So I confessed to smoking in the restroom but insisted I'd stubbed out the cigarette—as I'd seen Sarah Grace do it.

I smoothed Flora's hair, letting my fingers linger in the softness, and bit back questions about what had happened between her and Shep. Now wasn't the time. Not when she was sitting here with tear tracks on her face. "The fire was an accident, Sarah Grace. No one was hurt. The school eventually dropped all charges after restitution was paid. Thank you for that, by the way. If you hadn't stepped up and paid the fine anonymously, it's likely charges would've been filed. My whole life could have turned out differently."

Her eyes widened. "Blue, I didn't pay the restitution, though I wanted to. Someone else beat me to it."

I'd always thought Sarah Grace had paid the fine. "If it wasn't you, who was it?"

"Maybe it was the Allemands?"

"Maybe." But I felt like they would have told me—why wouldn't they have?

She looked my way. "I envy you, Blue."

"Me?" I said, unable to keep the shock out of my voice. "Why?"

"Do you know what kind of freedom you have because you're a Bishop?"

"I'm not sure I'd call it freedom. More often than not, it feels like punishment."

"Everyone in this town thinks you lit a fire in the high school restroom, yet no one dwells on it. It's as though it was expected, and even though it's brought up every once in a while, there isn't really any censure in the reflections. Just matter-of-factness."

Her viewpoint was interesting, because it felt a whole lot like censure to me.

"If I skipped church on Sunday, I'd be hearing whispers for a month and would probably get a visit from the pastor. My mama doesn't want me to buy this house, because I might get *tainted* by the Bishop name. How ridiculous is that? But God's honest truth, I'm starting to hope it's true."

There were sparks in her eyes as she talked, and I was starting to notice it happened when she spoke her mind instead of tempering her words and feelings. I was about to jokingly welcome her to the family when what she said hit home, and my heart sank. "I'm sorry about the house. I really am."

She turned her body toward me and crossed her legs. "You just told me that this house makes you hurt. How are you going to create peppy books here?"

Feeling suddenly overwhelmed, I said, "I don't know. I just know that for Flora, I'll find a way."

"I need to buy this house, Blue. I can't explain why I need it so badly, but I do."

The desperate look in her eyes almost did me in. "I want to sell it, Sarah Grace, but I have nowhere else to set up my studio." I explained about the court investigator. "I have to move the studio by Monday, and I have a book due soon. There's no time for any other options."

"We can work out a way for you to work here," she said, the sparks in her eyes flying. "For as long as you need. Escrow will take a week or two since it's a cash offer, and then I can renovate around your schedule, focusing on smaller projects until you can find another place for your work space. Have you thought about adding a studio to your backyard? It's plenty big enough for one."

It was true—it was. And if I sold the farmhouse, I'd have the money to do it. But it would take time . . .

She pressed her hands together. "Please say yes."

"I don't know how long I'll need to be here. Could be four months or longer."

She smiled and the whole mood in the room shifted, filling suddenly with light. I hadn't even noticed it had stopped raining. "It doesn't matter how long. We'll make it work."

I studied her face, taking note of the tear tracks, inky stains that mocked the sudden joy in her eyes. "Before I say yes, I have one other condition."

"Anything," she said, still smiling.

"I want you to tell me why you're hiding out here." It was a lot to ask, but she tended to keep her feelings locked up, and I wasn't above a little strong-arming if it was a way to pry open her emotional vault.

Her smile fell, and she looked at me in silence for a good minute. Just when I thought she was going to deny my request, she cleared her throat and said, "I found out this afternoon that Fletch has been cheating on me. Not only that, his young girlfriend is pregnant. I came straight here to try to figure out what to do. To say my life is a hot mess at the moment is an understatement."

"Oh no, Sarah Grace. I'm so sorry." I wanted to give her a hug, but I didn't know her well enough to know if she'd accept it.

She looked upward as if seeking advice from the leaking ceiling. "I can't go back to him; I *can't*. But a divorce would be so messy. The gossip alone would be mortifying. And my father's primary is coming up, so it's bad timing to be making waves."

"Your father's campaign is *his* campaign. It has nothing to do with you."

"I wish you were right about that, Blue, but you're not. Being in a political family is like living under a microscope. His opponents are looking for anything to bury him. His platform is centered around family values. The messy divorce of his only child? It's a political nightmare. The last thing I want is to hurt him in any way. He deserves to be governor. He's a good man. I don't want to be the person to ruin his chances."

I let out a sigh, wanting to help but not knowing how. "I can't imagine your parents would want you to stay with Fletch if they knew the truth."

"They shouldn't have to suffer because of my bad choices. I never should've married him."

"It's not like you set out to hurt them."

I stiffened as I said the words, suddenly realizing they pertained to my family as well. They hadn't set out to hurt me with their choices. But they had.

Letting out a sigh, I said, "It won't change how much they love you. They want what's best for *you*."

"That won't take away their pain, though, will it?"

"Sometimes," I said softly, "I use a mixture of water and vinegar to clean my wooden floors. It's potent, yes. And there's a chance of damaging the floor, yes. But, Sarah Grace, revealing what's been hiding underneath the surface, allowing it to fully shine, is worth the risk."

Her voice cracked as she said, "I don't know what it's like to be happy anymore."

The plaintive honestly in her voice broke my heart. "Follow your heart to find your happiness," I said, repeating the advice from the button Sarah Grace had received yesterday. "Where's your heart right now?"

"Right now?"

"Yes. Right this minute."

She swiped at her face, erasing some of the tear tracks, and then took a deep breath. "You know what? It's here. This house makes me happy, and I'm thankful you're going to sell it to me. I actually have the contract in the truck in my messenger bag. Are you willing to sign it now? I can go get it."

Her smile was so contagious that I was suddenly glad I'd accepted her offer. "I'll sign it. While you do that, I'm going to check out the squatter situation."

"I was up there earlier. Nothing's changed from Monday that I could see, so hopefully whoever it was is long gone. I'll be right back."

As she walked outside, I stood at the bottom of the staircase looking upward. I'd been determined to find out why Persy hadn't wanted me here, and I wasn't leaving until I knew.

At the top of the steps, I turned to the right and peeked into the room I'd shared with Persy. The first thing that struck me was its spotlessness. As I went inside for a closer look, I wasn't sure I'd ever seen this room so clean. What Sarah Grace had thought was a blow-up mattress was, on further inspection, an inflatable sofa. It most definitely had not been here a couple of days ago, when I'd last stopped by.

The almost-imperceptible scent of vinegar swirled around me as I noticed a faded stain on the sofa and shuddered, absolutely certain I didn't want to know what it was. There wasn't much else to see—only junk food wrappers.

Had Persy been hanging out here with her secret boyfriend? She had to know I'd put two and two together and realize that *she* was the squatter, especially after how intensely she had reacted earlier. Now that I was selling the farmhouse, she wouldn't be able to use this place as a love nest any longer, but it still bothered me that she'd go to such great lengths to keep the relationship to herself.

I was turning to leave when the sunlight shifted and a flash of color poking out from beneath the sofa caught my eye. I bent to pick up the scrap of fabric. As I held the pink ribbon to the light, I felt the blood drain from my face as I recognized it, the telltale scalloped edge a dead giveaway.

It was the same kind of ribbon that had been in Flora's hair when I found her. I glanced between the ribbon and the sofa . . . my mind filling in the rest of the story. Suddenly it seemed very possible that this room was where she had been born. Not only possible. Probable.

I looked down at Flora and tried not to think of Persy and how she hadn't wanted me to come here today . . . Maybe it hadn't been about a secret boyfriend at all.

Was *Persy* Flora's mama?

Mrs. Tillman's words about secret pregnancies came to mind, followed by images of Persy tugging on her oversized shirts. Then Henry's comment this morning about Flora having the same eyes as me wound through my head, snaking through a lush field of sudden fear.

Leave, a small voice at the back of my head said. *Don't look back. Pretend you didn't see anything at all.*

Flora started to wiggle and protest. Her whole face puckered as she let out a cry. I rocked back and forth, trying to soothe her, soothe myself. I prayed for guidance, because leaving meant breaking the moral code I'd lived by my whole life in an effort to prove my worthiness, not to the people of this town, but to myself. Because when people constantly judged you as unworthy, you started to believe it was true. But all that seemed so distant, when all that mattered at this very moment was protecting Persy.

I loved her so much that I'd sacrifice myself, my principles, and everything I'd strived to be to save *her*.

Moral compasses are easily broken when dropped in between a rock and a hard place.

Oh, how Twyla had been right.

I closed my eyes against the memory of a long-ago Sunday

evening, the remnants of the cookies Twyla and I had made sitting next to the medical bills stacked on the kitchen table in front of my daddy, his eyes red, his cheeks gaunt, his skin ghostly pale.

A tear tracked down my cheek at the memory of my brothers saying they'd find the money for treatment, someway, somehow, and that they were Bishops and wouldn't let the leukemia win. The acute leukemia that was stealing Daddy away, one cell at a time.

My heart broke flat open as I recalled the stoic look on Daddy's face the day after my brothers were buried as he walked out the front door, leaving so Twyla and I didn't have to watch him die, too.

All three of them had died trying to spare someone else pain, but it had been the wrong choice. They'd only made the pain worse. So much worse.

Yet here I was in the same position, ready to do the same. All I had to do was go downstairs and not look back.

But if I left, I'd *always* be looking back, over my shoulder, wondering, worrying. If I *stayed* and faced the trouble head-on, then maybe, just maybe, this situation wouldn't end in the kind of heartbreak I knew well.

"Blue? Shep's outside." Sarah Grace lowered her voice as she added, "He says he got an anonymous tip in Flora's case to check out the farmhouse. And Persy."

My head snapped up—I hadn't heard Sarah Grace come into the room. Her blurry face swam in and out of focus.

Sarah Grace took one look at me and said, "Oh, Blue. Oh no."

She rushed over, throwing her arm around my shoulders, anchoring me to her as the decision to stay or leave had been made for me. And at that moment, all I could hear was my mother's voice.

Trouble will come for you, Blue—just you wait and see. And when it does, you'll embrace it same as me.

It hadn't just come for me, but Persy, too.

We were Bishops. And while our family name was practically synonymous with the word *trouble*, I had thought Persy and I were different. Black sheep. But I'd been wrong, so very wrong.

Chapter
11

Sarah Grace

"You're late." My mother pulled me through the kitchen doorway. "Why haven't you been answering your phone? Fletcher has been here an hour now, and we've all been worried sick. I've been pacing the kitchen."

"I'm here now, Mama," I said.

The house, one of my earliest friends, blew a sigh of relief, and the scent of warm bread and roasted chicken wrapped around me like a blanket, chasing away the chill that had started when Blue had looked at me with tears in her eyes and fear etched onto her face.

My mama's words from earlier in the week echoed in my mind, about Persy eventually finding trouble, because it was in her blood. I hadn't believed it to be true, but now . . . Now I had to admit my mother might've been right.

A thread of guilt wove through me at the sight of the foil-wrapped platters on the counter and the bowls sitting on a warming tray—dinner waiting to be served. Waiting on me. I should've called. Or texted. *Do better. Be better.*

It wasn't the only guilt eating at me. Earlier, when I answered Shep's questions about the squatter, I'd kept quiet about seeing Persy Bishop in the doctor's office parking lot this afternoon, an OB-GYN's office. I'd asked myself a hundred times since why I hadn't volunteered the information, and I still wasn't sure. I suspected it had a lot to do with my past, when I'd been young, pregnant, and scared.

Shep had seemed to sense that I was holding something back because he had me put his phone number into my phone's contact list and told me to call him if anything came up. I wasn't going to call. Persy's secret was safe with me as long as it wasn't hurting anyone else. If she was truly Flora's mother, we'd know soon enough without me saying anything.

Mama took a step back and looked me up and down. "Are you still in your work clothes? You're filthy. Where have you been?" She sneezed and picked a glossy mahogany hair off my shirt. "Have you been near *dogs*?"

From the farmhouse, I'd walked to Doc Hennessey's clinic to visit Hazey since my truck had been blocked in by police cars. Hazey had cried when she saw me, and it was all I could do to leave her when the office closed for the night. She was responding well to treatment, and Doc Hennessey assured me I'd be able to take her home tomorrow. The news was a bright spot in this gloomy day.

Mama sneezed again. "I swear, Sarah Grace. You could have changed and washed up."

I glanced at her, silently pleading with her to please see *me*.

"This is a special occa—" She finally looked me in the eye, and instantly all the air went out of her. Her shoulders slumped, her irritation vanished, and her blue eyes misted, making them look gray. She lifted her hand and cupped my cheek. "Oh, my baby girl. What's happened?"

As tears filled my eyes, I shook my head. I couldn't talk about the chaos in my life right now if I was going to make it through this night. For Kebbie's sake. Because this *was* a special occasion. Something to celebrate. Her success made me happy.

FOLLOW YOUR HEART TO FIND YOUR HAPPINESS.

I was determined to allow my heart to lead me, even if it felt more like I was tripping my way along. "I'm sorry if I ruined dinner."

She tossed a look over her shoulder. "It's kept beautifully. Don't you worry. More important to me is why you're late. Is it about Fletch's disappearing act? Did you two have a fight?"

"Mama, please," I whispered, pressing my cheek into her palm. "Not now."

Resignation flashed in her eyes; she sneezed again and then took a deep breath. "All right. But whatever's happened is fixable. *Everything* is fixable. C'mon now. You look like you could use a drink."

Fixable. Fletch having a child with another woman certainly was not fixable.

I could blame the Buttonwood Tree curse all I wanted, but deep down it hadn't been the tree who had married Fletch. It had been me. I hadn't followed my heart when I married him. I'd done it because it was easier to hide in his shadow than stand in my own light. Now, I didn't know who I was anymore, and I was paying the price for my foolish, cowardly decisions.

Mama took hold of my hand and towed me through the kitchen like I was a small child in need of maternal direction. I didn't mind. If I'd ever needed her guidance, it was now. I had no idea how to navigate my way through what lay ahead. How did I admit to her that my marriage had failed? And not only failed, but crashed and burned spectacularly? How did I let Fletch go without hurting my family?

"Is that Sarah Grace?" Fletch asked as he strode into the kitchen. He stopped short when he saw me, his cheeks slowly turning red.

By the glassy look in his eyes, he'd had at least three drinks. Maybe more. As much as his drinking worried me, God help me, I was grateful his bourbon-scented haze obliterated the rosy lavender scent that had been haunting me. He still wore the same clothes he'd been in at the doctor's office earlier, a pair of blue trousers and a white dress shirt with a pale-gray paisley design. I wondered if I'd ever be able to look at paisleys again without feeling betrayal.

Fletch put his hands on his hips. "We need to talk. You shouldn't have run off earlier," he said to me in a tight, chastising tone, his words slurring slightly.

The massive kitchen was primarily white except for the gold fixtures, knobs, and handles, and the heart pine floors and exposed ceiling beams. Several mirrored cabinet doors caught the evening sunlight and reflected it throughout the room. It was big and airy with sky-high ceilings, but as soon as Fletch had walked into the space, it seemed to shrink, making it feel claustrophobic. He'd sucked the energy out, and it wheezed, trying to catch its breath.

Did he really think that *talking* would solve all our issues? I searched for a way to respond to him that wouldn't stoke his anger, but I couldn't find one. And I suddenly realized I was doing it again: holding back my feelings and emotions to keep the peace.

But, Sarah Grace, revealing what's been hiding underneath the surface, allowing it to fully shine, is worth the risk.

I wanted to shine. Lord, how I wanted it. If revealing what's been hiding under my surface all these years was the only way to do it, then so be it. After all this time, I was finally going to allow myself to *be* myself.

"It was either run or run you over in the parking lot," I said, my words sharp. As soon as they were out of my mouth, I felt a lightness bloom within me. It floated in my chest, an unfamiliar, but not uncomfortable, feeling.

He chuckled, trying to brush off my statement as a joke, but the corners of his mouth were pinched. His tongue pushed at the inside of his cheek.

Mama turned a shocked, assessing gaze on me, and I wasn't

sure what she saw, but when she looked back at Fletch, she held up a single finger in warning in front of his face. "Whatever you have to say to Sarah Grace can wait."

I swore Mama could control an army with that one finger. It had kept me in line most of my life.

"Now, Miss Ginny." He gave her a big smile, trying to charm. "No offense, but this is between Sarah Grace and me."

"It can wait," Mama said again. Icicles clung to each word. She drew her shoulders back and lifted her chin, ready to go to war for me. She had drawn a line in the sand, and her deadly glare was daring him to step over it.

"Mama's right," I said. "It can wait. Tonight is about Kebbie. If you have a problem with that, you can leave. Perhaps you should go play poker with the guys?" I squeezed her hand and pulled her along as I carefully skirted past him, not even wanting my sleeve to brush against his arm and those dang paisleys.

As we stepped into the dining room, Daddy and Kebbie suddenly found fascination with their drinks. By their guilty demeanors, I figured they'd been eavesdropping. I couldn't blame them—I'd have done the same.

The dining table looked beautiful, covered in one of Grammy Cabot's old lace tablecloths, a treasured heirloom. Mama had claimed this was a casual dinner party, yet she had used Grammy's gold leaf china for the dinner plates, usually reserved for our fanciest get-togethers. She'd used her own tobacco leaf–patterned china for the salad plates, and a Bibb salad with candied pecans had already been served. Gold flatware and crystal glasses gleamed. Candles flickered. Dinner rolls were mounded in a basket. Small vases of pink peonies dotted the table, and I was glad they weren't roses.

Mama said, "Kebbie, as the guest of honor, you should sit at my right tonight. Sarah Grace, you can sit in Kebbie's usual seat."

Daddy's head snapped up, and Kebbie looked like she was

about to argue until she glanced at me. "All right. I'm game for switching things up."

Kebbie would now be sitting next to Fletch with me across from him. I had a feeling the decision was a spur-of-the-moment one by Mama. Keeping me out of Fletch's easy reach. Unfortunately, though, now I had to look at him all night. His wineglass was full, and his angry gaze was on me.

Daddy came over to kiss my cheek, and there was a mix of concern and anger in his eyes. "Are you okay?"

I nodded and tried for a reassuring smile.

Mama let go of my hand and filled my wineglass. "Sit, sit."

I set my napkin in my lap and dared a glance at my father. He was glaring at Fletch, who was still glaring at me.

"I'm sorry I'm late," I said again.

"I was late, too," Kebbie said as she slid into a lightweight sweater that had been hanging on the back of a chair. "The bookshop was extra busy. It's arts-and-crafts Friday, and I had to help ten preschoolers make a fish out of construction paper to go along with the book *Rainbow Fish*. It was hectic but fun. I'm worn-out."

She looked it, too, with the dark circles under her eyes and the general air of exhaustion, but I didn't buy that her tiredness came solely from working at the bookshop. She'd been just as tired yesterday. I didn't want to ask at the dinner table if she was feeling poorly, but I'd ask her later, when I could pull her away in private. The flush in her cheeks looked an awful lot like she was running a fever.

I sipped my wine. "The *Rainbow Fish* brings back memories. I remember Marlo reading it at story hour when I was little."

In the book, the rainbow fish had learned that sharing pieces of himself brought him happiness, and I wondered at the coincidence of Kebbie mentioning that book today of all days.

"Marlo is a gifted storyteller," Mama said. "She simply

glows when speaking, doesn't she? The way she draws you into a book like you're living in the story is a talent I admire."

I admired the way the three of us were carrying on conversation while ignoring the fact that the men in the room were silently simmering, saying nothing at all.

Ignoring and pretending felt an awful lot alike, but I decided now wasn't the time to pick apart those particular semantics.

"Marlo was the one who read the story today," Kebbie said. "I soaked it up like I was one of the littles. Now that she's retiring, I'm not sure how many more readings I'll get to hear."

Mama passed the bread basket to her. "How is Moe faring these days?"

Kebbie shook her head. "Usually he does pretty well in the mornings and fades at night, but today he snuck out this morning after getting home from a doctor's appointment. Blue and Henry found him while they were out walking, thank goodness, and brought him back home. Caring for him looks like it's been hard on Marlo. I just wanted to hug her the whole day long."

Mama *tsk*ed sympathetically, then sneezed.

Kebbie and I blessed her.

"Blue and Henry were out walking?" I asked.

She nodded, her eyes glimmering. "He asked her to take him to the Buttonwood Tree. I think he's sweet on her."

Mama abruptly stood up. "Go ahead and get started without me. I'll be back in a moment. I need to take an antihistamine."

"Sorry," I said again. I was apologizing an awful lot, I realized, and I had the feeling that I still had loads of apologies ahead of me. "I didn't realize how much dog hair I had on me."

Kebbie buttered a roll. "If you're keeping Hazey, Sarah Grace, Aunt Ginny might want to look into allergy shots."

"Hazey?" Mama and Fletch said at the same time.

Kebbie said, "Oops. Sorry, Sarah Grace, I didn't realize . . ."

"It's fine," I said, meaning it. I reached into my pocket for my phone to show a picture of her, but the pocket was empty. I'd last had my phone at the clinic—I had set it down to snuggle with Hazey and must've forgotten to pick it up again. "Hazey is a dog I found in the woods yesterday. She's at Doc Hennessey's for an infection, but she'll be coming home with me tomorrow. I'm adopting her."

Fletch's grip tightened on the bread basket. "What? No you're not."

My gaze narrowed on the paisley on his cuff, and I noticed for the first time how much the design looked like a baby in an early ultrasound picture, all curled up, not quite fully formed. I raised my gaze to meet his. "I most certainly am."

He set the basket down and in the process upended his wineglass. Red wine seeped into the white tablecloth, making it look like a bandage helplessly trying to stanch a fatal wound.

"Oh no!" I dabbed at the stain with my napkin. "Will it come out?"

"I'm not sure," Mama said as she blotted the stain as well.

Fletch didn't seem to care that he might have ruined an heirloom. Anger peppered his tone as he said, "We're supposed to be adopting a baby, not a *dog*. Isn't that why we're here tonight? To talk about the baby Blue found?"

Mama had the grace to blush as she said, "We're here to celebrate Kebbie."

Kebbie pasted on a big smile and drolly said, "Yay, me." She nodded to the stain. "Is there anything I can do to help?"

Mama shook her head.

As I gripped the damp napkin, I tried to keep my temper. "*I'm* here for Kebbie. I thought I made that clear earlier today in Alabaster," I cryptically warned so he'd take the hint not to pick a fight with me right now.

"You're lucky no one called the police on you," Fletch said, the words running together. "You could have killed someone."

So much for taking the hint.

"Police?" Daddy sat straighter.

There was no more wine to sop up, so I carefully laid the napkin on my dinner plate and jabbed a finger in Fletch's direction. "You're lucky I didn't kill *you* on the spot, because trust me, I thought about it. I'm still thinking about it."

He rolled his eyes. "So dramatic. You need to calm down and think rationally. This is a party, remember?"

Mama's worried gaze flitted between Fletch and me. She let the stain be and walked over to stand behind my father's chair. "What happened exactly?"

"Sarah Grace jumped to conclusions and made a fool out of herself." Fletch's eyes zeroed in on me. "Didn't you?"

With his statement, I saw the truth as plain as day on his face. He was going to try and brush the whole pregnant mistress situation under the rug, where it would share space with the scattered pieces of our crumbled marriage. He fully believed I'd go along with his plan once I *calmed down*. That I'd keep pretending. That I'd happily keep living in the prison I'd built for myself, high above all the secrets I'd buried. Because that's what I'd always done. I'd never wanted to rock the boat or draw attention to myself. I never wanted anyone else to be hurt because of my actions. I'd been there, done that, and I never wanted to repeat it. But I'd done it at a cost to myself, and I was done paying the price.

Done.

"I admit to being a fool," I said evenly. "I was a fool for pretending we've had a happy marriage all these years. For pretending what *I* wanted didn't matter. I'm not perfect. I've never been perfect, and I doubt I ever will be. But I deserve a better life than I have now. I'm done pretending. We're through. I suggest you don't fight the divorce, because I'm ready to tell all, Fletch."

He folded his arms across his chest. "And what is it *you've* wanted, Sarah Grace? Shep Wheeler? Is it a coincidence your newfound backbone coincides with his return to town? I thought you were over him, considering you divorced him ten years ago."

I sucked in a breath, rocked to my core.

There it was. My biggest secret finally revealed. It hung in the air over the beautifully set table, glinting under the light of the chandelier like an unearthed gem now polished for all to admire.

Fletch smiled smugly at me. "Since we're telling all, perhaps you should start with your own secrets, Miss High and Mighty."

Under her breath Kebbie said, "Sweet baby Jesus."

Mama sank onto a chair, her hand covering her mouth.

"That's *enough,* Fletch," Daddy warned as he stood up.

Fletch ignored him, either his anger or the liquor making him brave as he said, "You best rethink your divorce plans, Sarah Grace, because I'm not throwing away everything I've spent years building. If you tell my secrets, I'll tell yours, and I'm sure the media will be happy to share all the sordid details. I'm surprised they haven't already uncovered your first marriage. Your divorce record was easy enough to find with a background search of court documents, something my family attorney did before I married you."

"You've known all this time?" I said, my voice raspy, my chest tight.

"A good poker player always knows when to hold his best cards. Your past didn't matter to me then, but it matters now, when *my* future is at stake. And not only my future, but your father's. It's best we forget this night ever happened. All of us. Now, let's go home."

As he voiced my every fear, I didn't even flinch. Instead, I stood my ground, more determined than ever that the time had come to peel back my layers, one painful secret at a time. His threat had done nothing but motivate me.

"Your future?" I snapped, losing any semblance of staying

calm. "What future is that? Becoming mayor, a job you don't even want because you hate politics? Drinking yourself to death and hitting things because you're unhappy living a life you didn't choose for yourself? You can talk to the media all you want. Will my secret elopement hurt Daddy's campaign? Maybe. Maybe not. It was a long time ago, and I was just a young woman in love with a young man, and oh, I was pregnant, too. Did your lawyer know that, Fletch?"

He blanched, and his tongue went into his cheek pocket and stayed there.

I took a breath, expecting someone to stop me, but it seemed as though shock had rendered my family speechless, which was fine with me, because I had more to say. The more I spoke, the lighter I felt as the weight of my burdens melted from my shoulders. That bubble in my chest grew.

"But when I miscarried early on, Shep and I started to wonder if we'd rushed into marriage for the wrong reasons. Before we gave ourselves time to sort out our feelings, Daddy announced he was running for mayor, and Shep and I decided a secret divorce was best to keep things hush-hush for the sake of Daddy's campaign. Because he *deserved* to be mayor. You don't."

"*Whoa*," Kebbie murmured, her blue eyes wide as could be.

"Once you sober up, Fletch, you should probably take a deep look inside yourself for what you truly want in this life, because as much as it pained me to see it, I've never seen you happier than you were today when you had your hand on your pregnant girlfriend's stomach. Now, I'm leaving—alone. Do not come home tonight, understand? I need some time to be by myself, and I know you have a place to stay."

He offered no rebuttal, and I hoped that meant that he finally understood our life together was over and no amount of manipulation was going to change that fact.

I tested the limits of holding myself together as I glanced

around the room, first at Kebbie, whose expression was one of pure astonishment, eyes wide, mouth open. I braved a look at my mama, who had tears in her eyes and devastation written across her face in broad strokes. Then I stole a fleeting glance at my daddy, and I nearly bawled at the heartbreak on his face.

It took everything in me to walk away, to hold my ground, to stand in my own light and not collapse under the weight of my many emotions. As I stepped outside and began walking home, I started shaking—the adrenaline wearing off. The pace of my footfalls picked up, turning into a jog, then I kicked it up another notch, and the sidewalk flew past under my shoes. For the first time in so very long, I wasn't running from my past. My past had caught up, keeping pace with me, easily matching my every stride. Side by side, we'd go forward together to build a new life. A *true* life. I was running now because I finally felt alive again, a dark cloud lifted. The bubble in my chest kept growing, and I finally recognized that it was *happiness*.

My deepest secrets were out in the open, and I was never again going to let a secret stop me from living my own life. Somewhere nearby, a crow cawed as the pink glow of late evening sunshine fell across my path, making it shine. I realized suddenly that I was crying, the tears sliding down my face, falling across my lips.

Freedom had never tasted so bittersweet.

≥⅄

I ran all the way home, and I'd barely been inside a few minutes when I felt a ripple of dread roll through the house. It shook the picture frames on the wall and rattled vases.

Unnerved, I glanced out one of the living room windows. A red-faced Fletch raced up the porch steps. When he let me walk out of that dining room without stopping me, I should have known that he'd follow. He always had to have the last word, even when he was perfectly sober.

I crouched low and my gaze shot to the front door—the door I hadn't locked behind me when I'd come in. The knob jiggled but didn't turn.

He pounded on the wood. "Sarah Grace! Open up! We're not done talking."

Maybe I'd locked the door after all, out of habit. Thank goodness. My hands shook as I reached for my phone in my pocket—then remembered I'd left it at the clinic.

I heard metal against metal—the key in the lock and the tumbler clicking. The door didn't budge. He kicked it and yelled, "What the hell! You already had the locks changed? You can't do that! This is my house, Sarah Grace. My house!"

I didn't know what he was talking about—I hadn't changed the locks. In his stupor, he'd probably confused his keys. I watched from my low spot at the window as he ran down the steps, and I felt a brief rush of relief before I realized he wasn't leaving. He stooped low to grab a melon-sized garden stone and came back up the stairs, fury in his eyes.

I had no time to react as he pulled back his arm and aimed at the window on the other side of the couch. I braced myself for a shattering crash but stared in wonder as the stone bounced harmlessly off the window like the panes were made of rubber, and ricocheted back at Fletch. The rock hit him dead square in the forehead, and he fell like a sack of potatoes to the porch floor, knocked out cold.

The sound of an engine tore my attention away from him, and I nearly cried in joy at the sight of my daddy's pickup zooming up the driveway. My legs wobbled as I stood and made my way to the front door, where I saw that I hadn't been wrong—the door was unlocked. And suddenly I knew Fletch hadn't mixed up his keys, either.

I closed my eyes and pressed my cheek to the cool wood. "Thank you."

The house let out an exasperated breath that felt an awful lot like an embrace. A stiff-armed embrace, but one nonetheless.

"Sarah Grace!" my daddy yelled.

I pulled open the door. "I'm here."

My mama, ashen white at the bottom of the steps, saw me and burst into tears.

My father pulled me into his arms and held me tight. "We got here as soon as we could. He tore out after you the minute you were out the door. We tried to call, but you weren't answering. The police are on their way, too."

Even as he said it, I heard sirens. Daddy let go of me, and I went down the steps.

"I don't think I've ever been so scared in my life," Mama said as she briskly wiped tears from her eyes.

"I'm so sorry for all the fuss, Mama. I'm sorry for everything."

She pressed her lips together and nodded, but hardness crept into her watery eyes. "It's been a long day, Sarah Grace, and I have a headache. Pack a bag. You're staying with us tonight."

At her disappointed gaze, guilt twisted through my stomach. I didn't think I could bear seeing her look at me this way the whole night—and morning—long. "Maybe it's best I stay here."

After a long moment, she said, "Fine. Do as you wish. I'm going home."

Daddy, oblivious to the tension between Mama and me, stood over Fletch, who was still out cold. "Dang, you have good aim, Sarah Grace."

"I didn't throw the rock," I said, watching my mother walk away. "He did . . . But it bounced off the house and hit him in the head."

Daddy's eyes went wide, and then he smiled. "Karma—that's what that is."

I glanced at the house and could hear it chuckling quietly. Karma, indeed.

After all was said and done, Fletch had been carried off to the hospital, Daddy told me to give Mama time to come around, and I'd talked to three police officers about what had happened—none of them Shep Wheeler, thank the heavens above. Not one of them had believed the rock story until they viewed the video from our doorbell camera, which I suddenly didn't despise nearly so much.

Long after everyone had gone, I walked through the quiet house straight to the kitchen where I took eight crystal tumblers from the cabinet and placed them into a paper sack. I folded the top over neatly, creasing the edge of the paper just so.

Guided by the dim light of a thin crescent moon, I carried the sack into the backyard, marching myself around patio furniture toward the outdoor fireplace. For a moment, I watched lightning bugs flit around the gardenias, dazzling in the darkness. Then, I drew in a deep breath and swung the bag, slamming it against the bluestone chimney. I took heart at the sound of shattering crystal. I swung again and again until the bag split and glass rained down on the patio, tinkling like an old, mournful melody.

As the crystal glittered at my feet, I dropped the bag, turned, and went back into the house, locking the door behind me.

Chapter
12

In his chambers, Judge Quimby glanced at the grandfather clock that stood sentry aside the door, the swing of the pendulum suddenly sounding a lot like *tsk*s. It was past quitting time, and he should be getting home. Mrs. Quimby was making a chicken potpie—one of his favorites.

Yet, he dragged his feet.

Persy Bishop was weighing on his mind this evening. Word had whispered its way through the courthouse that she could be the mother of the babe found in the woods. It didn't sit right, this news. By all accounts, Persy and Blue were close. Why keep the pregnancy secret? If Persy didn't feel she could raise a child, why not initiate a private adoption between her and her sister? Kinship adoptions weren't uncommon. He'd signed a fair share of petitions over the years.

If she was indeed the babe's mother and Persy hadn't wanted Blue to know, it was a wishful, foolish notion that the relation would stay secret forever. It seemed every day he read another story about DNA analyses from genealogy sites revealing such family secrets, shining a spotlight on philanderers, sperm donors, abandoned children, undisclosed adoptions, and even murderers.

No, it didn't sit right. His instincts told him the police were barking up the wrong tree where Persy was concerned. He shook an antacid from its bottle, hoping to ease his stomachache before it ruined his supper.

Time would tell if he was right about Persy Bishop.
Eventually, DNA always spoke the truth.

Blue

Early the next morning, Flora was making noises like she was
fixin' to start wailing, and I paced with her in my arms while
singing her a lullaby under my breath.

My shirt was damp from spit-up and needed to go straight
into the wash, Flora was unusually fussy, and so was I. My
worries had kept me tossing and turning last night instead of
sleeping, and when I had drifted off, I'd dreamed of glittery
threads being pulled apart.

I stepped into my studio, which was half-packed, but until
police techs finished scouring the farmhouse, I couldn't take any
of my supplies over there. Shep had said it would be a day or two.

I opened the curtains and noticed Moe sitting on the deck
next door, reading the morning paper upside down. Last night
I'd asked Marlo whether she and Moe had paid the restitution
for the fire at the high school, telling her about the conversation
I'd had with Sarah Grace. She'd denied it, saying that it had already been paid when she inquired about it, and I believed her.
But her response left me more confused than before. Who'd paid
the bill on my behalf?

"Does this look like a giraffe to you? Because it's looking
like a snake with arms to me," Persy said from her spot on the
couch, staring with a critical eye at the orange balloon animal
she'd created. Her gaze darted between her handiwork and the
YouTube instructional video she was watching on her phone.

"Are you sure you still want to go today?" I asked. I'd actually been looking forward to the festival before all this had
happened.

This. Persy and police and DNA tests and principles compro-
mised in the name of love.

My chest ached, a pain that had started when I'd picked up that ribbon the day before. I had the feeling it wasn't going to go away until Shep finished his investigation. A field test had confirmed that it was diluted blood on the sofa, and he agreed it was likely that Persy's and my old bedroom was where Flora had been born. He'd sent the sofa off for more testing, cordoned off the farmhouse, and then asked to talk to Persy.

She twisted the balloon a different direction. "I told you I do. I don't care what people are saying. I know I'm not Flora's mother. The DNA test will prove it. Let them talk. It doesn't bother me."

Persy hadn't batted an eye when Shep had asked her to take a DNA test. He swabbed her cheek right here in the keeping room, and she'd been as calm as could be. He'd swabbed my cheek as well as a precautionary measure. In case Persy's test came back negative, he'd be one step closer to identifying all the DNA samples in the room.

It was Persy's calmness that bothered me most. Persy, who freaked out at any hint of impropriety. She followed speed limits to a frustrating degree. She wouldn't pick up a dollar on the street out of concern that whoever lost it would come back looking for it. She would rather eat nails than return a library book late. Once, she'd broken into tears when I accidentally turned the wrong way down a one-way street, fearing I'd be arrested and thrown in jail.

I said, "Then tell the kids the balloon is a snake with arms. A hybrid. They'll love it."

For Persy to stay perfectly calm when there was a police officer in the house questioning her was suspicious. Highly suspicious. It was as if she had known that moment would come. She'd prepared for it. Otherwise, she'd have been a ball of nervous energy.

"A snake with arms." She nodded. "I like it."

Since Flora's was a high-profile case, Shep said it would take only twenty-four to seventy-two hours for the rapid DNA test

to come back. I could only hope that once it came back negative, he'd drop any inquiries into her involvement. After all, if
not for that phone call, he wouldn't have any reason to look
into Persy's behavior at all.

An *anonymous* phone call.

Who had it been from?

My mind spun, twisting thoughts and suspicions until they
knotted. My theories weren't giving me anything but a headache.

Marlo stepped out onto the deck, carrying Moe's breakfast
plate. Faint golden wisps fluttered around her like nervous but-
terflies as she set the plate in front of him and placed her hands
on his shoulders.

I watched in dismay as Moe swatted her hands away, but
she kept replacing them. This went on and on a few times until Moe seemed to forget what he was doing. The golden haze
surrounding her gradually faded, and after a moment, Marlo
stepped aside and slumped into her chair. Moe smiled and
turned the paper right side up.

I watched Marlo for a second, noticing her exhaustion. The
moon had started to wane, which had weakened her healing
hands—so she was having to use more and more energy to help
Moe. I was grateful for the approach of the new moon, as it
would provide a respite from moon dancing. She needed to re-
charge before she was the one who needed to be healed.

I dropped a kiss on Flora's head and placed her into her cradle and set it rocking. I needed to change, eat something to
settle my stomach, then head over to the festival.

As I ran upstairs, Moe's voice chased me up the steps.

*What she hasn't learned yet is that she's hurting herself by
keeping herself closed off. Opening up is the only way she'll
find her happiness.*

For Flora's sake, I was determined to be myself at the festival today. To keep an open mind. To meet people. To let Mrs.

Tillman introduce me to the Buttonwood Moms. To step out of my comfort zone.

And I hoped to the heavens above that I wouldn't regret it.

❧

"Snakes don't have arms!" a little boy shouted at Persy a few hours later as she tried to hand him a balloon.

She glanced over at me, an eyebrow arched, and I shrugged as I finished painting a unicorn horn onto a small girl's forehead.

At the last minute, I'd balked at taking Flora with me today, suddenly worried about the heat and the crowds and protecting her. I'd called Marlo to bow out of attending and was surprised when she offered to watch Flora for me and insisted I go.

"You're not going to be there?" I asked.

"Nope. The town needs to see Henry in charge, not me. I'll come by later on, for the last session of story time, and will bring Flora to you then. Moe's aide is here to keep an eye on him, a godsend she is, so I can give my full attention to little Flora."

I'd been at the festival for three hours now, and even though I'd been enjoying the day, I missed Flora and couldn't wait to get back to her.

Persy was holding up well under the scrutiny of our neighbors, who hadn't been as nosy as I feared. Mostly because they were too busy talking about Sarah Grace and Fletch's big fight last night.

As soon as I heard about it, I'd called her, but she hadn't answered. I hadn't quite known what to say to her voicemail, so I'd hung up. I couldn't get any scoop from Kebbie, either, as she was absent from the tent today, calling off with what she now thought was a bad cold, not allergies.

"There you go," I said, holding a mirror up to the girl's face as I set down my palette. "A prettier unicorn I never did see."

"Thank you, Miss Blue!" she said, hopping off the stool.

As soon as she galloped off to talk to her mother, Henry sat down on the vacated stool. "Do you see many unicorns?"

"What? You don't? We need to work on your imagination."

"We can start with a little paint." He pointed to his face. "What should I get done?"

"You're not serious."

"I am. Perfectly."

I smiled. "All right, then. Since we're working on your imagination, you tell me what you want."

"Hmm. Let's see. A snake with arms?"

"Hey!" Persy said. "I heard that."

I laughed. "I think I'll leave those to Persy."

She stood up. "While there's a lull, I'm going to grab some cotton candy. Do either of y'all want anything?" When we both declined, she said, "I'll be back in a couple of minutes."

"Fine, fine. A clown?" he suggested.

I winced.

"No? How about a mask? Like Zorro?"

I shook my head.

"A blue bunny?"

I rolled my eyes. "Don't go borrowing my imagination. It's like you're not even trying."

"All right, then. How about a rabbit with blue eyes and dimples asking a certain blue bunny on a date?"

My heart skipped a bit as I glanced down at the palette, and said, "That's a *little* better."

"You're a hard judge, Miss Blue."

Opening up is the only way she'll find her happiness. I placed my hand under his chin and turned his face toward mine. I dipped a paintbrush into the brown on the palette, then swirled it with white and brought it to his face. With a few strokes from his jawline to his forehead, a tall rabbit with long, straight ears took shape. "Where would the blue-eyed rabbit think of taking her? Answer carefully."

His dimples deepened as he smiled. "He's thinking a picnic, somewhere quiet. A park. The woods. A lake. We'll talk books and movies and families because we'll be trying to get to know one another and where we come from, the good and the bad, because they're big parts of who we are now. So, if he asked . . . what do you think she'd say?"

"Henry, I—"

It was on the tip of my tongue to say no. We'd just met. There was Flora to consider. There was so much we didn't know about one another. But then I thought about sitting with him on a blanket on a sunny day, watching the clouds drift by, and I didn't want to say no. I wanted to learn more about him. Not just more. I wanted to know everything.

I quickly finished the painting and held the mirror up to him. "She'd say don't forget the kite."

The rabbit on his cheek held a kite that soared onto his forehead, drifting upward into a sea of clouds that blended into his hairline.

He grinned at his reflection, and the curve of his cheek made the rabbit look like he had a potbelly.

"Blue! Hello!" Mrs. Tillman sailed into the tent with two older women trailing behind her. "Oh my. Did you paint that rabbit, Blue? It's splendid."

I stood up. "Thanks, Mrs. Tillman. Have you met Henry Dalton? He's the new owner of The Rabbit Hole."

Mrs. Tillman held onto his outstretched hand and grinned. "Welcome to Buttonwood, Henry! We surely will miss seeing Marlo and Moe every day, but it's nice to know such a beloved shop is in good hands."

"Thank you, ma'am."

She pivoted and said, "Henry, this is Mrs. Judy Rudolph and

Mrs. Clem Weese, two of the judges for today's dessert competition. Judy is also Buttonwood Baptist's organist, and Clem is the president of the local mother's group."

"Even though I'm a meemaw now," she said as she held out her hand. "Pleasure to meet you, Henry."

Mrs. Tillman sent a conspiratorial wink my way before saying, "Sadly, the third judge for the event today, Mrs. Janet Ogilvie, has come down with a cold and had to forfeit her judging chair. Blue, we were hoping you'd take her place."

I pressed my hands to my chest. "Me?"

She smiled. "You're an upstanding member of the community, we trust you can be fair and impartial, and we know you bake. Marlo's raved of your cookie recipes for years. It won't take but half an hour. Can you spare her, Henry?"

"We can make do," he said, glancing at me. "But the decision is up to Blue."

Truly, the thought of being a judge made me queasy. Sitting in front of my neighbors, with them watching my every move, hanging on my every word.

It seemed more like a nightmare than an opportunity.

But then I saw Sam Mantilla's serious eyes and heard him telling me how important community was for Flora. A half hour of my time and discomfort suddenly seemed a small price to pay for this town to start seeing me as my own person.

"Your name is so familiar to me, Henry," Miss Judy said to him as they all waited for me to make up my mind. "Is it possible we've met before?"

"It's possible," Henry said. "My family used to visit Buttonwood when I was a boy, and I spent a few Sundays sitting on church pews here. Well, squirming if I'm telling the truth. I've never been one to sit still too long."

"Dalton, Dalton . . ." She shook her head.

The air in the tent suddenly stilled, the mood darkening as Oleta Blackstock headed straight toward me, her sturdy black block pumps soundless on grass that seemed to wilt under each of her steps.

If there were a personification of Southern Gothic, it would be Oleta. Dressed in one of her overly starched, vintage short-sleeve shirtwaist dresses with matching pillbox hat, she was altogether nightmarish with her nearly skeletal figure, short gray hair, black eyes, sharp cheekbones, barbed tongue, and utter self-righteousness.

I fought the urge to hide under a table.

"I see the rumors are true," Oleta said as she approached, her dark gaze darting between Henry and me.

"Oh hell," Henry whispered, then coughed.

I threw him a look at the strange reaction.

"Good afternoon, Miss Oleta!" Mrs. Tillman said. "Beautiful day, isn't it?"

She raised a darkly penciled eyebrow. "No. It is not."

Mrs. Tillman's mouth fell open, and she glanced around like she didn't know what to say to that.

Oleta jabbed a finger at me. "Just so you're aware, Blue *Bishop*, I fully believe that baby you found is your sister's illegitimate child and you've concocted finding the baby to try to hide the truth. And I'm not the only one thinking it. I've been hearing talk all morning." Cold, black eyes shimmered with hatred that she polished with every fiery breath she took.

"Oh dear," Mrs. Tillman said, covering her mouth with her hand.

I could take Oleta's viciousness, but she had no right to drag Persy into her attacks. Anger built, flowing hotly from the tips of my toes to my ears.

"Lolly, stop," Henry said sharply.

Lolly?

She turned her finger on him. "I'll get to you in a moment."

"No." He stepped in front of me. "This stops with me right now."

Oleta straightened, pulling her shoulders back. "I'll remind you to mind your manners, Grandson. Respect your elders."

A collective gasp echoed through the tent.

I backed up a step, looking between Henry and Oleta. My breath hitched, and I cursed the moisture in my eyes and the stinging in my nose, hating that I couldn't hide the pain, the *hurt* that overwhelmed me at the force of the truth. "You're a *Blackstock*?"

"Lordy be! You're Aubrey's boy," Miss Clem cried. "I didn't realize you were one of Buttonwood's own! Why didn't you say so?"

"Yes, why?" I asked, my heart feeling like it was near to breaking flat open.

"I can explain, Blue," he said. "Let's take a walk."

I could feel everyone watching me, and suddenly I didn't want to hear what he had to say. I wanted only to be swallowed whole by the earth. My head swam, and I felt faint. I grabbed my knapsack and quickly said, "I have to go home. Tell Persy where I went."

"Blue, wait," Henry said, reaching for me. "Stay. Please stay."

Oleta clamped onto his arm and pasted on a brittle smile. "Let her go."

As I ran through the crowds, tears streaming from my eyes and embarrassed heat flooding my cheeks, I could hear Moe's voice in my head again as he asked Henry if he'd planned on hurting me.

Never. I like her.

Well, Henry might not have planned it, but he'd gone and done it anyway.

Chapter
13

Former town council member Ezra Atherton sidled up to Judge Quimby at the country club bar and pinned him with a glassy-eyed stare. "This is a fool's game you're playing, Quimby. Re-election is in five months. Your constituents, including me and my bank account, don't want you to make the wrong decision when it comes to that baby Blue Bishop found. You'd do best to terminate her guardianship."

Judge Quimby could only assume Ezra meant to intimidate with the pointed look, but he succeeded only in making the judge want to go fishing. No question Ezra's slightly bulging eyes, big loose lips, and slightly green cast to his flaky skin reminded the judge of a largemouth bass.

He ordered a whiskey neat. "I appreciate your concern, Ezra, but my decision will be based on what's best for the child."

"I know we ain't always seen eye to eye, Quimby, but I can't believe you're even considering letting Blue adopt that girl. Don't you remember the fire Blue set in high school? How she got out of that mess I still don't understand. The Bishops don't have a decent bone in their bodies. Bad to the bone. There's other *good* families to consider."

Of course he remembered the fire Blue set. It was the only time she'd been inside his courtroom. But he also knew that Ezra, who was well-known for taking kickbacks and accepting bribes, should be the last one, in the judge's opinion, to cast stones.

In this town, your last name could make sins vanish. Everywhere except in his courtroom.

Sarah Grace

Storm clouds hung low in the sky, and the threat of rain lurked in the humid air early Sunday morning as Hazey set our snail-like pace, sniffing every bench, rock, and tree trunk along the paved paths that snaked through the park.

Doc Hennessey had released her into my care yesterday morning, and Hazey and I had spent the day together at home, playing ball, watching movies, and throwing Fletch's clothes into trash bags that I piled in the garage. I'd kept my phone off, and I hadn't answered any knocks at the door. I had wanted to be alone with my dog and my newfound freedom.

The park was quiet at this time of the morning, a little before seven. A few people milled about, cleaning up after yesterday's festival. By nightfall, the Ferris wheel would be disassembled along with all the tents and booths, and the park would be back to normal.

I wished it were as easy to put my life back together. It wasn't meant to be, however. Soon people would be waking up to get ready for church. They'd start their coffee, put some bacon on, and go out to the front porch for the *Buttonwood Daily*.

Where an article about the fight I'd had with Fletch had received front-page coverage. The headline had read,

Buttonwood Mayor Mum on Domestic Dispute

I hated that headline writer, whoever it was, for making it seem like the incident involved my father. When I'd turned on my phone this morning, I'd had a dozen voicemails from reporters across the state looking for an interview. Any hopes of keeping quiet what had happened between Fletch and me had been obliterated. It was only a matter of time before those reporters started digging into my and Fletch's lives, turning over all we'd tried to keep hidden for so long.

I'd called my father as soon as I'd seen the headline this morning, and I wasn't surprised to find him already awake. There was going to be an emergency meeting this afternoon at campaign headquarters. Damage control.

Fletch had left a message as well, telling me that he'd be at the house later today to pack his stuff. Little did he know I'd already done some of it for him, so hopefully his would be a quick visit.

I let out a huff of breath, thinking about the mile-long to-do list I had that included calling Blue. I was hoping to meet with her today to sign the house contract. It had been forgotten in the aftermath of Shep showing up at the farmhouse the other day, and right now the thought of working on the Bishop farmhouse was the only thing I was looking forward to this week.

Well, that and playing with Hazey.

Fletch's and my house had shocked the heck out of me with its excitement at having a dog running through the hallways. So much so that I instantly felt guilty for never having had a pet before now. Doc Hennessey was thrilled that Hazey had already gained a pound and was responding well to her antibiotic. As she slept next to me in bed last night, her head on my thigh, I couldn't help thinking that she'd been the one to rescue me. If it hadn't been for my resolve to adopt her, the fight with Fletch that had spilled out most of my secrets in front of my family might never have happened, and they'd all still be bottled up inside, suffocating me.

Hazey tugged at her leash and barked at an oncoming jogger. I pulled her in, letting the runner pass without the threat of being licked to death. Her tail fanned the air around my legs as she glanced up at me. I patted her head, and she set off again, sniffing the clover along the pathway.

I had yet to see anyone I knew, but it was only a matter of time before I heard the whispers behind my back. I'd already decided to skip church today, which was probably the wrong choice, but the thought of everyone staring . . . No thanks. By next week, most of the chatter will have died down, and Daddy's team will have come up with talking points to use in which I would say a lot about nothing at all.

Hazey barked at another jogger, and I about fell over when I saw it was Shep who was approaching.

His eyes flared when he saw me, and I silently begged him to jog on past, but he slowed to a stop and pulled earbuds from his ears. "Hey, Sarah Grace."

"Hey, Shep. I didn't think you ran anymore."

"What can I say? You inspired me."

"Right. Because nothing says inspiration like copious amounts of sweat."

"You wore it well. Who's this?" he asked, crouching down to let Hazey lick his face.

He wore black running shorts and an emerald-green T-shirt that made his eyes look like frosted sea glass. Sweat darkened the hair along his forehead and around his ears and created a light sheen on his tattooed arms.

I didn't understand how it could feel like only yesterday that I'd stood in front of a justice of the peace and pledged my forever love to this man. Ten years had gone by, but it was as if those years were nothing but the blink of an eye. We were different people now. I shouldn't still feel anything for him, other than fondness. Yet . . .

"Hazel. I call her Hazey. She followed me out of the woods the other day, and long story short, I adopted her yesterday."

"You finally got a dog. Good on you."

He knew full well I'd never had a dog because of my mother's allergies. He and I had always talked about getting a dog after we settled down in a place of our own. A family-friendly rescue that'd grow up with our little one. I closed my eyes against a sudden wash of tears, hating how easily old, painful memories could sneak up on me.

"She's a beauty," he said, and I could feel his gaze on me even with my eyes shut. I always could.

I blinked away the past and saw that Hazey seemed taken with Shep. She'd flopped onto her back and offered up her belly like she'd found a new best friend.

He gave her a good rub, then said, "I heard at work what happened with your husband. I tried to call you, but it went straight to voicemail. I went by your house, but you weren't home." His gaze burned. "Is that how you hurt your hand?"

I glanced at the gauze wrapped around my palm. "No. I cut myself cleaning up some glasses I broke. It's not deep. The cut, I mean."

"Glasses? Plural?"

I shrugged. "Slipped right out of my hands."

His eyebrows went up. "Are you okay? I mean . . . from what happened Friday night?"

The incident had been labeled as a domestic dispute, but no charges had been filed since no actual threats had been made and Fletch had only hurt himself, though not seriously. He'd been released once he sobered up.

I didn't know where Fletch was staying, but I could guess. I hadn't heard anything from him other than his voicemail, though I knew my father had been keeping tabs on him and had made it clear, in no uncertain terms, that Fletch wasn't to show up for work tomorrow morning.

"I'm okay," I said. "I promise I am. But you should know my family knows about you and me. It all blew up at dinner the other night with Fletch. It's likely the whole state will know soon, since reporters are now asking questions."

His jaw fell, and he let out a low whistle. "I have to say I'm glad it's out. It was a hard secret to keep, because it never felt shameful to me, like it did you. Proudest day of my life was when I married you."

Lord, help me, but I wanted to cry. "I was never ashamed of marrying you, Shep. I was ashamed I hid it from my family instead of telling them flat out that I loved you. We shouldn't have run off to elope. We should've had the wedding here first, with everyone invited, then left town, like you wanted. If we had just done that . . ." I gave myself a shake before I became bogged down by regrets. I held up a hand.

"If we'd just done that, what?"

I blew out a breath. "I'm sorry. I can't have this conversation right now. Everything's too raw."

He folded his arms across his broad chest and said, "I agree this isn't the time or place for that conversation. I'm not entirely sure how we ended up there. I only meant to check on you, to make sure you're okay."

"I am."

"At least you don't have to run from the past anymore."

"Exactly," I said softly. "Now I can run simply because I want to. I hear my sweat is inspirational."

Instead of smiling, like I'd expected, his eyes clouded. "Are you staying with him, Sarah Grace?"

The catch in his voice almost did me in. "No. He's coming by today to pack his stuff—my father will be there, too, so don't go worrying that I'm meeting with him alone. And I'm meeting with an attorney this week."

Shep's chin dropped, and he stared at the ground for a long moment before looking back at me. His green eyes were misty as he oh so slowly smiled. "Then I guess I'll be seeing you around. Maybe out here running in the early mornings?"

My heart beat a little faster. "Maybe so."

He set his earbuds back in his ears, and with a nod, he jogged off.

I let out a deep breath and smiled. I'd taken only two steps before I heard, "Hey, Sarah Grace?"

I hid my smile and turned around. "Yeah?"

Shep jogged in place. "Do you mind if I stop by tonight?"

My pulse picked up, and my hands turned clammy. "Tonight? Why?"

"Work. I'm hoping that, like Blue, you'll also consent to a DNA test since you were in the bedroom at the farmhouse. The more profiles we can establish, the better, in case Persy's test isn't a match to Flora's. I can bring a kit by. Won't take but a minute."

"Isn't it easier just to wait and see if Persy's a match? Her test will be back soon, won't it?"

"I could wait," he said, his eyes sparkling in the shadows of the cloudy morning, "but then I wouldn't have an excuse to see you tonight, would I?"

My heart swelled with hope. "Well, I'd hate to stand in the way of good police work, so sure. Come on by. I'll be home all night."

"I'll let you know when I'm on my way. See you then."

He started to turn away when I said, "Hey, Shep?"

He held my gaze. "Yeah, Sarah Grace?"

I smiled. "I'll probably be hungry by then. Maybe bring a pizza with you and stay longer than a minute or two?" I longed to sit with him, to talk until there was nothing left to say.

It took a moment before he nodded. "Extra pepperoni?"

"Of course. Is there any other kind?"

He laughed, and it sent warmth flowing through me. God, how I'd missed his laugh.

"Some things never change," he said, then threw a hand up in a wave as he ran off.

I watched him go for a few seconds, waiting for my heart to realize we weren't still crazy in love.

But like he'd said: some things never change.

≫⼃

"If looks could kill," Fletch said as he watched my father give him the evil eye as he walked Hazey around the front yard. "I'm guessing I won't be on the Christmas card list."

I sat opposite him on the porch steps—a good three feet separating us. "Probably not. No doubt Mama crossed you off the minute you ruined my grammy's heirloom tablecloth."

Fletch had his elbows on his knees and his hands clasped together. There was a painful-looking black-and-blue goose egg on his forehead and dark circles under his clear eyes. "Did I?"

"You don't remember spilling wine?"

"Honestly, Sarah Grace, I don't remember much of what happened at all. Was it bad?"

I wrung my hands. "You could say that."

"Did it have anything to do with that dog?"

That dog. "Her name is Hazey," I said, trying not to lose my patience. I'd already told him her name when he'd been surprised to see her here. "And some of it, yes."

He flexed his fingers. "I can't believe you adopted a dog without talking to me about it first."

I lifted an eyebrow. "The proverb about throwing stones seems truly appropriate right now, considering all you've kept from me."

The house chuckled.

Anger flashed in his eyes. "I'm not the only who's kept secrets, Sarah Grace."

Obviously he had remembered *some* of what had happened on Friday night. "Don't," I warned. "I'm not getting into this with you again. Not now, not ever."

My father looked over, and I gave him a small smile, letting him know I was okay.

Fletch stretched out a leg. "I have an old college buddy down in Florida who runs a Division II football program. He's been trying for years to get me to sign on as an assistant. I called him yesterday and took him up on the offer. I found a condo down there and will be moving by the end of the week."

I almost let out a whoop of relief. He was moving away. Thank heavens. "Okay."

"I won't be moving alone."

I nodded. "Didn't think you would be."

"Look, Sarah Grace—"

I held up a hand. I didn't want to hear his reasons or excuses for cheating, and I certainly didn't want an insincere apology. "What's done is done."

"All I was going to say is this doesn't have to get nasty. You have my word you'll get your fair share in the divorce. It might get a little sticky where my trust fund is concerned, but we'll work it out."

I decided not to point out that his word held little value and that it had already gotten nasty. "I don't want any of your trust fund, Fletch. In fact, I don't want—" I cut myself off. I'd planned to tell him I didn't want anything. I had my own money. My own business. I wanted a clean cut from him, nothing binding us together at all. But as I sat here on the front porch, fully aware the house was listening to every word, I realized there was something I wanted very much. "The only thing I want is the house. That's it."

Behind me, the house let out a sigh of relief, and I knew I'd made the right decision. Long term, this house wasn't for me. There were too many bad memories here. But I'd stay until life settled down a little; then I'd make sure a nice, loving family moved in. A family with a dog. No, two dogs.

Out with the despair, in with happiness. Funny how I'd been thinking that about the Bishop farmhouse, but it pertained to this house just as much. Maybe more.

"You're serious?" he said. "That's it?"

I could understand why he was shocked. The value of the

house was a drop in the bucket compared to his net worth, and since he'd cheated on me *and* I had video evidence of him being an angry drunk, I definitely would've received my fair share in divorce court. Maybe more than fair.

"I get the house; we go our separate ways."

"Fine. That works for me." He stood up and looked back at the house. "There are only a few pieces of furniture I want to keep that I can't take with me right now. I'll make a list and send for them when I get settled. I couldn't find my granddaddy's crystal tumblers—did you pack them?"

"No," I said, trying my hardest to keep a neutral expression.

"Where the hell would they be, then?"

I shrugged. "I don't know. If I find them, I'll mail them to you."

His tongue rested in his cheek pocket as he studied my face. After an excruciating moment, he said, "My lawyer will be in touch with yours. Without either of us contesting anything, the divorce shouldn't take long. A month or two. But you already know how quick a divorce can be, don't you?"

I stood up and leaned against a porch column. I was done playing his games. "Yep. And I also know what it's like to be madly in love. Awkwardly, it wasn't with you."

His nostrils flared, and he strode off down the walkway. He pulled open his car door and looked back at me. He said nothing, and after a second he got in and slammed the door.

Which was fine by me. There wasn't anything left to say.

As Fletch drove off, I hoped that he'd be able to leave behind his family's harrowing legacy and his own personal demons here in Buttonwood, smashed up alongside those crystal tumblers— if only for the sake of his new baby.

There were some heirlooms that shouldn't be passed on.

Chapter
14

Blue

Sunday had dawned dull and gray and had stayed that way, a perfect complement to my mood. I glanced at the clock. It was almost noon, the time when the bookshop opened on Sundays, and I tried telling myself that I didn't care about Henry or his dimples in the least, but I wasn't fooling myself. I cared. I didn't want to, but I did. Even still, I couldn't imagine facing him today. Or any day ever again.

My gaze drifted to a small basket of oak galls sitting on the corner of my desk in the sunroom. I'd found them on the table on the front porch this morning, along with a worn copy of *Poppy Kay Hoppy Finds a Friend* and a note from Henry. A note I'd read at least twenty times already.

> *I'm sorry, Blue. I didn't tell you straight off because I didn't want to scare you away. I know in your mind Oleta might be worse than Jack the Ripper. The last thing I ever wanted was to hurt you. Please forgive me.*

Mixing crushed oak galls soaked with iron sulfate, a recipe that dated back to medieval times, would yield a lovely deep purple-black ink. I had a store of it already, but I could always use more. It was clear Henry had put some thought—some imagination—into his apology.

And begrudgingly I admitted, if only to myself, that Oleta

wasn't as bad as Jack the Ripper. She hadn't *killed* anyone. That I knew of, at least. Still, she was the most horrid person I'd ever met.

Please forgive me.

I let out a long, weary breath. I didn't know how to forgive him. Especially not right now, when the hurt was still so intense. But if I was being brutally honest, I didn't know how to forgive at all. I'd been trying for years to forgive my family, and I had never managed to find a way.

Flora and I had skipped our walk in the woods this morning, and the wind was still howling about it. But I hadn't had it in me to go looking for lost things since I was feeling a little lost myself, which was counterproductive at best.

I needed to find the lost thing with no name so I could get out of this town. Away from the embarrassment and the shame. I wanted to get away from my family's long, dark shadow and stand in my own light and start over somewhere new. Someplace where Flora could grow up without people like Oleta Blackstock always making her feel like she'd never fit in.

Fighting an overwhelming urge to run away, I glanced down at Flora and soaked in the wonder of her, and my love for her edged out my heartache.

I finished buttoning the snaps of her sleeper and smothered her in kisses. Her legs kicked as I scooped her up. I'd already given her a bath, clipped her fingernails—a task I despised for fear I was going to hurt her—and brushed the wisps of her hair.

"Henry tried to warn you," Persy said from her spot at the dining table. She had a couple of textbooks open, a pen in hand, and a notepad at the ready.

So far she'd taken zero notes, instead focusing her energy on getting me to give Henry another chance.

"True, true," Marlo echoed from the kitchen. "He sure did. He was planning to tell you—he just didn't get the chance."

She was dressed in her Sunday finery, having recently returned from church with Moe, who was snoozing on the couch.

They'd come over with take-out barbecue from my favorite place in town, and I recognized the tactic for what it was: they were trying to cheer me up.

Unfortunately, I wasn't very hungry—not even for cookie comfort. And I wasn't in the mood to be cheered, either, but I appreciated the attempt.

"Frankly, Blue," Persy added, "it's a bit hypocritical of you to be mad at him at all."

I clenched my jaw as I faced her. "Why's that?"

She tapped her pen against the pad of paper. "You don't want to be judged on your family, but you're judging him on his."

Marlo clucked in agreement.

"It's not the same thing," I insisted, even though I suddenly questioned if it was . . . and decided it wasn't.

Persy rolled her eyes. "Oh, okay. If you say so."

"He kept the truth from me. I never did that to him. You kept it from me, too, I might add," I said to Marlo as I wrapped a blanket around Flora.

Marlo had known all along who Henry was and hadn't said a word.

"What would you have done, Blue honey, if you knew from the start that he was Oleta's grandson?"

I took a moment to think about it. "Probably offer my con-dolences."

Persy laughed.

Marlo shook her head and said, "You'd have done no such thing, because you'd never have met him face-to-face. You'd have kept your distance, thinking he was the same as his grand-mother."

"Maybe. Maybe not. I'm friends with Sarah Grace, and she's a Cabot."

"But you've known Sarah Grace your whole life. You can't paint the two with the same brush, honey. And it only proves what I've been telling you all along. People will judge you for *you* if you give them a chance. Are you going to sit there and tell me you don't still like Henry even though he's a Blackstock? Hmm?"

I took a deep breath and prayed for patience. This day was doing its best to try me. I felt nothing but wrung out and put up, and it wasn't even noon yet.

Flora stared at me, her eyes trying to focus on my face. According to the books I'd read, newborns had lousy vision, but I could already see the progress she'd made with focusing in only a week. Her eye strength would continue to grow along with the rest of her, and by about three or four months she should see everything clearly. I was looking forward to the day when she'd look at me and smile. The mere thought of it filled me with happiness.

"I didn't hear your answer, Blue," Marlo said, laughing lightly.

"I'm done talking about it," I singsonged. I scooped up Flora and set her in a bouncy chair in the sunroom. Shep Wheeler had called this morning to let me know the farmhouse had been cleared—I was free to move my studio over there, and I needed to finish packing. He'd also let me know that the anonymous phone call that had come in about Persy had been traced to Buttonwood Baptist, but no one saw anyone make the call and the phone had been wiped clean of fingerprints. It was a dead end.

"Oh, come on. Go see Henry, Blue," Persy urged. "Give him another chance. You two are so cute together."

I was saved from more talk about Henry with a knock on the front door. Sarah Grace had arrived just in the nick of time. I pulled open the door, and my mood lifted a little when she smiled. She had a leather messenger bag over one shoulder and a leash in hand.

"I hope you don't mind that I brought Hazey," she said. "It's official. I'm keeping her. And I can't bring myself to leave her home alone yet."

I held out my hand and Hazey sniffed, then licked it as her tail dusted the porch. "I'm so happy for you both. Come on in."

"Glory be," Marlo said, her arms open wide to Sarah Grace. "Come here, child, and give me some love. It's been too long. I didn't know you were coming over. Are you hungry? There's plenty to eat."

Hazey trotted over to sniff Moe's feet as Sarah Grace stepped into the embrace and said, "Marlo, I forgot how your hugs can make everything feel right in the world, but no, I'm not so hungry right now. Thank you, though."

"I've heard about what's been going on with you—saw that article, too." Marlo pulled back to study Sarah Grace's face. "You okay?"

"I actually am," she said with a hint of a smile.

Marlo motioned for another hug. "All right, good. But you come by anytime you need a hug."

"I will; thanks, Marlo." She looked over Marlo's shoulder and said, "Hey, Persy. It's good to see you again. It's been a while."

Persy's cheeks flushed a dark red. "Yeah, it has been a hot minute, hasn't it? Hazey's a total sweetheart—we all fell in love with her at the clinic."

I wondered why Persy was blushing as Sarah Grace said, "She's definitely lovable."

Persy snapped her textbooks closed. "I'll bring these upstairs and come back to set the table."

Sarah Grace said, "I didn't mean to interrupt your lunch. I can come back later."

"You're not interrupting anything but my packing," I said. "Sunday dinner isn't formal around here. Heck, stay and help me pack my studio. Maybe you'll work up an appetite. Marlo wasn't kidding about how much food there is."

"Did Shep clear the farmhouse?" she asked.

Nodding, I glanced around. "I just need to figure out how to get all this over there."

Moe mumbled something and sat up, rubbing his eyes. He stared at Hazey, who sat at his feet. "Skitter?"

"Her name's Hazey," Sarah Grace said as she kissed Moe's cheek. "The newest member of my family."

But I'd be darned if Hazey didn't start wiggling her butt in excitement and put her head on Moe's knee like she'd done it a hundred times before. Moe kept staring, tears in his eyes, as he petted her head.

Confusion and anxiety flashed across Sarah Grace's face. "Marlo, did you and Moe lose a dog? I didn't even know you had a dog."

Marlo put an arm around her and said, "No, we don't have one. I have the feeling this here dog is an old friend of Moe's. An old, old friend he hasn't seen in a good fifty-five, sixty years. This happens sometimes when he first wakes up."

Realization dawned in Sarah Grace's eyes, warm and soft. "She's a good girl."

"My best friend," Moe said, still petting and loving and living in another place and time. "I thought she'd done run off for good."

"I think I will stay awhile," Sarah Grace said, "and let these two old friends catch up. And, Blue, we can use my truck to move everything over to the farmhouse."

"You wouldn't mind?" I asked.

"Not in the least."

Sarah Grace's phone rang, and as she checked the readout she frowned and silenced the call. "It's a reporter who doesn't like taking 'no comment' for an answer."

Oh no. She'd been so worried about her father's campaign, and I imagined that concern was still weighing on her mind, especially now that the story had gone statewide.

"It'll all blow over soon enough," Marlo said. "You just need to ride out the storm until you can stand in your own light again."

Sarah Grace took a deep breath and nodded. "Ride out the storm. I can do that, but I have the feeling it's going to be a long storm. The worst of it hasn't hit yet."

"I see." Marlo put her arm around her. "In that case, my little rabbit, while you're waiting for those storm clouds to pass on by, you might consider changing your phone number."

Sarah Grace

"I can't work here. There's no way." Blue stood in front of her desk, unpacking colorful pots of paint, jars, brushes, tubes, and tins. "I don't know what I was thinking."

I set the final box from my truck onto the floor. "You were thinking about clear passageways and rooms not being used for two purposes."

Glancing over, she smiled. "Right. Now I remember. But the farmhouse as a solution was a mistake. I can't work here every day."

"Is it the smell or the memories scaring you off?"

"Honestly, right now it's the smell. It's always at its most potent after a hard rain. I can't subject Flora to the scent of old cigarettes and mildew for hours every day. If the court investigator thought my sunroom was unacceptable . . ."

"But if not here, where? Will you rent a space in town?"

With her eyebrows drawn low in concentration, she glanced around. "As I've been unpacking I've realized that relocating my studio is really a logistical problem more than anything. I can draw and paint with only a few items, easily locked away. I mean, it's not ideal, but it's doable in the short term until I can build a backyard studio. It's the *storage* component of my work that needs a new home, and the farmhouse fits for that. I can come and go to pick up anything I'll need on a day-to-day basis—without needing to spend hours at a time here." She began setting aside items. Small pots and tubes, brushes and tins.

"Is that going to fly with the court investigator?"

"I don't see why not. I can work at the dining room table at home and lock the box of my supplies away when I'm not using them. Long term it's not feasible, but it's manageable for a few months."

With a nod, I looked around. "We can tarp this area to keep it as dust-free as possible. And I can help with the backyard studio, too, if you want. Once you have some plans drawn up, it shouldn't take too long to build. A month or so."

"Really? That'd be great. Thanks, Sarah Grace. And thanks again for helping me move all this stuff. I was running out of time fast."

I couldn't help the thread of warmth that ran through me at the happy glow in her eyes. "Well, thanks for selling the house to me. I can't wait to get my sledgehammer on it." We'd signed the contract earlier, and demolition couldn't come soon enough. "You know, I have to admit I'm surprised you picked this bedroom for your studio. The dining room has the best light."

She laughed and said, "The choice was easy since this room is the cleanest. The dining room would take two days to scrub down. Where do you think you'll start with your renovations?"

I glanced up at the water stains on the ceiling. "No doubt, the roof. If I don't do that first, anything I do inside might be ruined with the next rain."

Blue set her hands on her hips. "I guess I need to get the rest of the house cleared out this week. After Twyla died, I didn't have the heart to empty the place." A closet door squeaked as she opened it, and she took a step back from the smell that wafted out. "Apparently whoever cleaned this room knew her limits. This closet hasn't been touched in years."

By the smell, I hazarded a guess that mice—or rats—had nested under the threadbare sheets and ripped backpack on the closet floor.

She stood on tiptoes and reached up to grab a plastic box on the shelf above a slanted closet rod. The box had BLUE written on it in black marker.

"Mementos from my childhood," Blue said as she put the box on the desk. The top crackled and popped as she pried it off.

The box smelled faintly of dust and vinegar, and was barely half-full.

"Twyla put these boxes together for Persy and me after we moved out but wouldn't let us take them to my house. She liked looking through the things she'd saved over the years, which wasn't much, obviously, because we'd had so little. Persy claimed her box after Twyla's funeral, but I . . ." She shook her head. "I suppose it's time to take it now."

"You're welcome to borrow my truck for moving things. And I'll have a dumpster delivered this week for anything you want to throw out."

There was a twinkle in her eye when she said, "I hope it's an extra-large dumpster because that would be almost every piece of furniture. There's nothing salvageable, really." She pulled out a few rocks from the box. "These are some of my earliest painting attempts. I can't believe Twyla kept them."

"They're adorable. Very folk artsy."

She smiled at the cross-eyed pig and the chicken with oversized eyes, then sobered as she reached in and pulled out a wooden button.

SEND THE GIRLS TO THE RABBIT HOLE.

I gasped. "Did you know?"

Her voice was thick as she stared at the button. "No."

The button appeared burnished, as though it had been frequently handled. "How old were you when you first went to the bookshop?"

"Eleven. It was a few months after the bank robbery."

The bank robbery, not the deaths of her brothers. I wanted to hug her until the painful memories faded. "Wow. I wonder what advice Twyla had sought from the tree." I imagined her going to the Buttonwood Tree, so lost in her grief that she didn't know how to take care of her two young daughters.

But the Buttonwood Tree had known.

"I don't know, but it was the best thing Twyla ever did for Persy and me." Blue closed her hand around the button, then put it back into the box. She replaced the lid without looking at the rest of the items and quickly packed a large zippered portfolio with supplies. She slung the strap over her shoulder and picked up the box of mementos. "I should be getting back home to Flora. The rest of this can keep until tomorrow."

I wasn't sure if she meant the contents of the box or the room . . . or both.

As we went down the stairs, my phone buzzed with a text message. "It's Shep. He's coming over tonight." Her eyebrows went up, and I quickly said, "He's coming by to get my DNA sample, since I was in the farmhouse, too. But"—I tried not to blush—"he's bringing a pizza."

She grinned. "Are you following your heart, Sarah Grace?"

"Maybe," I said as I pulled open the front door. "My heart is a bit all over the place at the moment. It doesn't quite know what it wants. The easy answer is Shep. It always has been, and there's really no point in denying it, but he's just part of a bigger picture."

"What kind of bigger picture?"

I closed the door behind her as we stepped onto the porch. I felt a bit silly as I said, "I want to be different. I want to be bold. Brave. Open. Spontaneous. I want to make decisions on what I want, not on what other people want." They were all things I'd stifled for so long. "I want to be *me*. I think that's truly what my button meant."

Blue put the box in the bed of my truck and faced me. "From

what I've seen in the past week, I think you're well on your way. Are you happier?"

I took a second to really think about my answer, and I could feel the bubble still floating around my chest. I smiled. I smiled so wide it made my cheeks hurt and tears pool in my eyes. "There's definitely room for improvement, but yeah. I'm happy."

As I said the words, I sent a silent thank-you to the Buttonwood Tree, because I realized my curse had finally been broken.

Chapter
15

Adelle Rae Dockery stuck a stainless steel scraper into his mouth and said, "Judge Quimby, I heard tell you're in the thick of things with Blue Bishop and that little girl she found." She tsked loudly. "That's something, ain't it? Finding a baby in the woods?"

"*Arghghgh*," he said, trying to talk around her fingers in his mouth.

Why dental hygienists tried to hold a conversation during appointments, he'd never know. Adelle Rae was a chatterbox, used to carrying on one-sided conversations—at least with him. She was fifty if a day, and she'd been working here for as long as he could remember, starting out as Adelle Rae Whitford before marrying Dr. Dockery some thirty years before.

He'd thought for certain that she would've quit when they married, but she made it known that she enjoyed her job working alongside her husband. For a moment he allowed himself to imagine Mrs. Quimby working with him and held back a chuckle. No doubt she'd have left him before the end of the first day. He was a picky, particular boss.

"I don't know Blue real well," Adelle Rae said, "but I was shopping at Publix once about ten years back when— Have I told you this story?"

He shook his head, trying to ignore the feeling of the scraper against his teeth and gums.

"Well, there I was minding my own business as I pushed

my buggy through the store when I happened to look down to see my engagement ring was missing. I about died. It's a Harry Winston, don't you know? Worth more than the house I grew up in. I don't wear it here at work, but it was a weekend, and I'd been all over town that day running errands. I had no idea where I lost it. I had a bit of a meltdown, I confess, and in the middle of it, Blue Bishop comes up to me, calms me down, and tells me she'd just turned in a ring to the front desk that she'd found in the potato bin not ten minutes before. On my mama's grave, I've never been more grateful in my whole life. Ain't that something?"

"*Arghgh.*"

"I know. I still can't believe it. The thing that stays with me all these years later is how easily Blue could've pocketed that ring. Hocked it. She needed the money—everyone in Buttonwood knows that—but she turned it in. I tried to give her a reward, but she wouldn't accept it. So now I buy her whole series of books for every baby shower I'm invited to. Such sweet books. Such a nice woman. She'll be a great mama to that baby she found. Don't you think so, too?"

"*Arggh,*" he said, afraid she'd prod him with the scraper if he remained silent.

She nodded. "I knew you'd agree. I just knew it. Now tell me how often you're flossing."

Blue

It had started raining after Sarah Grace dropped me off at home late this afternoon, and it had been raining since. I watched raindrops track down the windows in the sunroom for a few moments before forcing myself back to work at the dining room table. It was a little past ten at night, and the rest of the house was dark. Persy was upstairs, and I could hear the rumble of her voice as she talked on the phone.

I still didn't know who she was talking to.

A task light illuminated my sketch as I dipped my paintbrush into a small pot of blue gouache and carried it to the rabbit drawn on the watercolor paper before me. I used small, steady strokes to fill in Poppy's blue fur. Her lop ears brushed the ground. Her long, black whiskers were stiffly horizontal, giving the impression that they, too, were paying rapt attention to the ballet teacher's instruction. Determination glowed in her persimmon-orange eyes as she stood with two others, a cat and a chubby raccoon. Her leotard and tutu were purple, and I added more water to soften the outline of the tulle skirt, making it appear billowy. The illustration of page thirty was slowly coming to life, the color adding dimension to my drawing.

Art supplies were scattered across the dining table, which I was using as a makeshift desk. Water, an alcohol solution, brushes, a rag, paper towels, small plastic pots of gouache, a palette of watercolors, my homemade inks.

Someone knocked softly on the back door, and I nearly jumped out of my skin. I hadn't heard any footsteps on the deck, but sure enough Marlo's distraught face was framed in the glass pane.

I jumped up and opened the door. "Is it Moe? Is he okay?"

"He's missing. I don't know how he got past me," she said, exhaustion causing the skin under her eyes to sag. Her shoulders bowed, and her steps were heavy as she came into the sunroom. "I swear that man is like smoke and can slip through a crack in a doorway. Will you help me find him?"

Missing? I realized I'd been caught off guard by the knock because the wind hadn't been howling with urgency, like all the other times Moe had wandered off. "Of course, but there's no need for us to both be out in this weather. Let me just ask Persy to keep an eye on Flora."

Marlo looked relieved by my offer as she said, "No need. I'll stay here with our little flower and wait for you."

With a nod, I went to the front closet and shoved my feet into my tennis shoes. I grabbed a raincoat and a flashlight. I had no idea which direction to turn, so I said, "Any idea where he might have gone?"

She worried her hands. "No, and I don't know how long he's been gone, either. After spending the afternoon with Flora, he was a lot more like his old self. It's as though her new life gives *him* life. He'd been so clearheaded when he turned in to-night that I allowed myself to relax a little. I fell into a deep sleep on the couch only to awaken to find him gone. If I hadn't been awoken by the rain, I might have slept the whole night through."

"You needed the rest." I slipped the flashlight into my pocket and took hold of her hands, stilling them. "We both know that it's not just Flora giving him renewed energy. It's taking a toll on you, Marlo. It's literally draining you. I'm worried that one morning there'll be nothing left. You're killing yourself to keep him alive."

She squeezed my hands and held my gaze. "Blue, my sweet child, some things are worth dying for."

Impulsively, I threw my arms around her. "But aren't some things worth living for? I don't want to lose either of you, but I don't know if I can bear losing you both."

She held me close. "Don't you see, Blue? Loving us means that you'll never lose us. We'll always be part of you, same as your mama, daddy, and brothers are in the things you do, in the things you say, in the way *you* love."

"No, I'm not like them at all," I insisted, trying not to think about how I'd almost walked out of the farmhouse the other day and not looked back after I found that pink ribbon.

She pulled back and looked into my eyes. "'You can't pick out the pieces you like and leave the rest. Being part of the whole thing, that's the blessing.'"

It was a quote from *Tuck Everlasting*, and I didn't have the energy to pick it apart right now. All I could do was keep shaking my head, my emotions raging.

"Now, get on with you." She pushed me to arm's length, and I nearly sobbed at the sight of the golden sparkles in her eyes, tears glittering with love. "Bring Moe home to me."

Sniffling, I tried to choose one of a thousand protests that would convince her to change her mind. What would be the magic words to make her *stay*?

"Go on," she said, walking me to the door. "Go find him. I'll take care of sweet little Flora."

Without another word, I slipped on my hood and plunged into the darkness. Thunder rumbled in the distance as I jogged down the sidewalk heading to the town center. In the past, Moe's nighttime journeys had taken him all over, perhaps retracing familiar routes. I'd most frequently found him at the bookshop, the church, the Buttonwood Tree, the barbershop, and the park. Every so often I'd find him at the library or at Publix. Each time he'd had no idea that he'd even been lost, and I didn't know whether that was a blessing or a curse.

But each time he'd gone missing, I'd had the wind at my back, guiding me to him.

Tonight, the wind was still, and panic bloomed that I wouldn't be able to find him and bring him home. That he'd be lost forever.

I couldn't let that happen.

My lungs burned with exertion as I frantically searched everywhere I could think to look. As I reached the intersection where Poplar dead-ended at a county road, I slowed to take a decent breath.

I glanced all around, my gaze searching. Moe wasn't lurking in any doorways and wasn't sitting on the bench at the corner or under any tree. No match for the storm's darkness, the streetlamps did little to illuminate the landscape. Shadows closed in and tears welled. I was drenched, soaked to the skin despite my raincoat. Lightning flashed and thunder crashed. "Moe?" I shouted.

Twin dots of approaching headlights in the distance appeared in the darkness. The sky lit up once again, and electricity sizzled in the air, lifting the hair on my arms. In the brightness, I caught an unnatural silhouette melded to a traffic pole. The outline of a man.

"Moe!" I yelled, the relief in my voice all but drowned out by the thunder.

I sprinted across the road just as he stepped away from the pole to walk in the overflowing street gutter. With his dark skin and dark clothes, I had trouble seeing him in the rain and shadows, even though I knew where he was.

"Moe!" I shouted again as I sprinted toward him. "Get out of the road!"

The twin specks of those headlights were growing bigger, and a murky outline revealed itself. A tractor trailer headed south.

Panic drove each footstep as I watched the truck's approach. If it drifted too far, it could clip Moe, who seemed oblivious to any danger he was in as he strolled slowly, sloshing his way toward a destination known only to him.

I was five feet away when Moe's meandering path began to veer to the right—into the road. One more step, two, and he'd be in the truck's path. There was no warning horn, no brakes. The driver obviously didn't see him.

I didn't think twice as I lunged for Moe, grabbed his arm, and yanked for all I was worth. We both fell backward with the force, and the truck's engine roared as it rumbled past and kept going, not knowing what could have been.

But I knew.

I started shaking as the what-ifs ran through my head in fast-forward. What if I hadn't been strong enough to pull Moe back? What if I'd been hit, too? In a blink, my life could've been gone. I hadn't had time to think before I reacted, but I knew I'd have made the same choice.

LOVE IS WORTH THE RISK.

Sitting in the gutter with water rushing over my lap, I helped Moe into a sitting position. There was an angry scrape on his cheek, but otherwise he seemed unfazed.

I burst into tears as I hugged him, this man who had taken me and Persy under his wing without batting an eye at the strange situation. This man who'd first read me *The Wind in the Willows*, voicing the characters so perfectly that I could hardly bear to hear anyone else read the story. This man who'd openly and generously shared his life, his livelihood, his love. This man who had nurtured, advised, taught, consoled me. This man who was slowly slipping away, a cruel, heartless disease carrying him away piece by piece.

"Ah, Blue," he said, patting my back. "Come now, stop that fussin'."

Snuffling, I pulled back to look him in the eyes, surprised by the distinct clarity I'd heard in his tone. Despite the rain and darkness, I was close enough to see that his eyes were clear, unclouded—Marlo had been right. He seemed like his old self.

The truth of his journey tonight hit hard and fast, knocking the wind out of me. It hadn't been the disease that led him to the path in front of that truck, and my heart cracked open right there on the side of the road.

The wind hadn't been able to lead me to him . . . because he hadn't been lost.

The rain washed away the tears falling from my eyes, sweeping them into the gutter, and I wished it would take my pain, too, carry it far away. "Why, Moe?"

He found his feet, held out a hand to me. "Had a dog once. Skitter. A true mutt."

I took his hand, felt its warmth, its waning strength, and I clung to it like my life depended on it. No. *His* life.

He put the hood that had fallen back on my head and looped his arm around my shoulders. Thunder rumbled in the distance, and the rain let up a piece.

The worst of the storm had passed.

We began our trek back home as he said, "I loved that dog somethin' fierce. I was fifteen when she started running away from home. You see, she was sick. Real sick. My pa said it was a dog's instinct to hide when they're feeling poorly, and to let her be, but I couldn't stomach the thought of her dying alone. I always found her and brought her back."

Raw emotion clogged my throat. "It was the right thing to do."

"Was it? After a time, it didn't feel like it. It felt I was interfering with what she wanted most in the world."

As the words settled, they sparked a fire, making me simmer. We walked a block in silence before I thought I could talk without lashing out. "I had a daddy once. Also a bit of a mutt, if I'm being truthful. I loved him something fierce. He was sick. Real sick. I was eleven when he ran off to die alone, thinking it was better for us not to watch him die, and there's not a day that passes that I don't wish I could've gone out and found him to bring him back home." I faced him, so he could look me in the eyes. "You can count on me tracking you down every dang time you wander off, Moe. Every. Time."

"It's not the same, Blue."

My voice rose with my temper. I couldn't stop myself from yelling. "Sounds the same to me. You're sick. I get it. It's not fair what you're dealing with. You want to go on your own terms. Fine. Okay. But going off alone? Not okay. Not by a long shot. And don't say you're trying to spare us the pain of watching you die, because it's a big, ugly lie. When you go, you should have all of us gathered around you, telling you how much we love you, sending you off right and proper. We shouldn't have to go out looking for you, or get word from the county sheriff that they found a body that needs identifying, or have to scrape you off the goddamn road! Don't you smile at me. Don't you dare. I'm so mad right now I could spit nails."

I hated getting angry, and I couldn't remember the last time I'd actually yelled, but I couldn't help myself. Moe had to know he was wrong. So very wrong.

"Can't help myself. It's so rare to see you all fired up. I've always thought you should show your feisty side more often. Let the Bishop in you shine. It's good to see you standin' in that light."

I huffed, frustrated beyond reason. "This isn't about me."

"Isn't it?"

"*Moe.*"

"That's a pretty picture you painted, everyone being gathered around me when I go and all, not the road part." He pulled a grim face. "Have to confess I didn't think that one through beyond the obvious."

"Don't make light. It's not the least bit amusing." But his tactic had worked. My anger had fizzled, replaced now with a deep ache.

He kissed my forehead. "Tonight wasn't about me going out on my own terms or sparing anyone from seeing me pass on."

"No? What was it, then? Please explain it to me, because I'm at a loss."

"Why'd you pull me back tonight? Why'd you stop me from stepping in front of that truck? Why, when you could have been killed, too? It was a damn foolish thing for you to do."

The anger came rushing back, flooding me. "What do you mean *why*? Because I love you. It was instinct to keep you from getting hurt."

He nodded slowly. "Exactly. Don't you see? Tonight wasn't about me at all, Blue."

It took me a moment to figure out what he was saying. When

I did, my anger whooshed out of me like a popped balloon. I should've known. It was just days ago that I was willing to sacrifice myself to save someone I loved. "Marlo."

"She won't let me go, not on my terms, not on any terms. How else do I stop her? How? Because I refuse to let her die on my account."

I ached to my marrow. "I don't know how, Moe, but I'll figure it out. There has to be another way, because what you tried tonight isn't the way. It's *never* the way. Promise me, Moe. Promise you won't do this again. Give me time to find a solution."

"All right, Blue. All right. But you need to be finding it fast, because if there's one thing we don't have, it's time."

Chapter 16

Sarah Grace

"Look at all this," Shep said, wandering around my office space early Monday morning.

If he noticed the wall colors were the same hue as his eyes, he didn't say. I kind of hoped he noticed—and knew there had been rarely a day he hadn't crossed my mind in ten years.

Last night he hadn't stayed long at my place, only an hour or so, but it had been nice to catch up with him. To see him smile. To hear his laugh. We'd talked about his mama, whose health was failing quickly, and I admired Shep for coming back to try to make peace with her before she passed. But I hurt for him knowing that Mary Eliza would probably never understand why he was there.

When he left after dinner, he'd given me a hug before walking out the door, and I could practically still feel his arms around me now.

This morning when I'd seen him at Kitty's Diner, it had been so nice not to turn around, to run away, before he noticed me. To approach him and acknowledge that he was part of my life, old and new. After we ordered coffee, he'd offered to walk Hazey and me to work, and I had the feeling I smiled the whole way here.

"How many houses are you currently working on?" he asked.

I unclipped Hazey's leash, and she began sniffing every corner of the room. "I just wrapped up a project late last week, so only one until I close on Blue's house."

He smiled. "How do you manage it all?"

I tried not to get flustered by his appreciative stare but could feel my cheeks heating. He was dressed for work, in dress pants and a button-down shirt, and his badge and gun were at his waist. I'd been dying to know if he'd had any new leads in Flora's case, but I'd promised myself I wouldn't ask. I didn't want any hint of impropriety hanging over our heads as we explored our new relationship. Whatever that proved to be.

At the sink, I filled a dog bowl with cool water. "I'm a bit of a workaholic, not that you'd be able to tell from the past week. I have a great team of subcontractors, and if I find myself in over my head, I'll use a general contractor to manage the project, like the one that's going right now. No one even thinks twice about me picking up a nail gun these days. Early on, it took some convincing."

"I've seen you shoot skeet. They had reason for concern."

"Fair enough." I grinned. "But I've yet to maim anyone with the nail gun. Wait." I held up a finger. "No. That doesn't count as a maiming. It was only a flesh wound. A scrape, really."

He laughed, a deep rumble that washed over me and made me want things I couldn't have. Not yet at least. I was determined to take things slow between us.

His phone buzzed, and as he looked at the screen, his eyebrows dipped low, and concern tightened all the lines of his face.

"Everything okay?" I asked.

He messaged something back to the sender and said, "Persy's and Blue's DNA test results are in. I need to get going."

"Is something wrong?"

He gave me a half smile, and I realized I wasn't going to get any more information. He'd probably already said too much, though I wanted to know more. Like why the results were cause for such consternation. I let it go for now. I could find out easily enough from Blue later on.

I set the bowl on the floor. "Well, thanks for walking Hazey and me to work."

"You're both welcome." He opened his mouth, then closed it again and headed for the door. Finally, he said, "You up for a run tomorrow morning?"

"Sure. If you can keep up."

He shook his head and laughed as he walked out.

I watched him go, wondering if he had the same feeling in the pit of his stomach that I did. It was a gnawing ache, a growing ache, an ache that came from falling headfirst into love.

Back into love.

I pressed my cool hands to my hot cheeks and forced myself away from the door. Kebbie was due in at nine, more than an hour from now, and I hoped she was feeling better than she had been on Friday night.

I was planning to spend most of the day catching up on paperwork before having a late afternoon appointment to meet with a lawyer to talk about my divorce. I tried not to think about all the time I'd wasted trying to make my relationship with Fletch work and vowed never again to put appearances before my feelings.

With that thought, I threw myself into work. This week I had a meeting scheduled for Thursday morning with my contractor and several meetings on Friday with potential tenants for the house that had undergone its final inspection last week, and I had a dozen applications to review.

I didn't look up from my paperwork until Hazey rolled, stretched, and yawned loudly. I smiled and made a mental note to buy a dog bed for the office. When I glanced at the clock, I was surprised to see it was a little past nine. Kebbie should've been here already. I reached into my workbag for my cell phone, and Hazey's tail lazily grazed the floor.

I patted her head and checked to see if I had any messages—and found a text from Kebbie that I hadn't heard come in: RUNNING LATE.

I texted back an "Okay, see you soon" and leaned back in my chair.

To keep my brain occupied, I called up local real estate listings online, looking for new houses on the market—foreclosures and auctions. I didn't have extra cash right now to buy—but looking never hurt anyone.

A half hour later when Hazey clambered to her feet and ran to the door, her tail wagging like crazy, I picked up the sound of footsteps on the deck. I fully expected it to be Kebbie, but instead my father came inside carrying a tray with three take-out cups of iced coffee from Kitty's.

"Down, Hazey," I said as she raced figure eights around his legs.

He gave her a good petting, rubbing the side of her neck, and then handed me a cup. "Is it Keb's day off? I thought she was supposed to be working."

"Thanks for this," I said as I held up the drink. "Kebbie's running late. She'll be in soon—I'll put her drink in the fridge. I know she hasn't been feeling well lately. Is she any better?"

"She spent most of the weekend sleeping, trying to fight her cold, but she must be feeling better if she's coming in. I didn't see her before I left the house this morning. I had to be at the office early."

"Ah yes, the war council." Deliberations about the end of my marriage were continuing. "Is it already over? I thought you'd be on lockdown all day long."

He dragged Kebbie's chair over to my desk and sat down. "We're taking a short recess."

I sipped on the coffee, enjoying the ice-cold caffeine. "How goes it?"

"It goes." He took the lid off his coffee and drank it straight from the cup, without a straw. "More bad news is coming. A reporter from Mobile found out about your first marriage, and a local reporter caught wind that Fletch has a pregnant girlfriend. I expect we'll see headlines about both tomorrow."

I winced and rubbed my temples. "How's Mama taking the news?"

He shook his head. "Not well."

"I'm sorry," I said for the hundredth time, wondering if she was ever going to talk to me again.

"Stop apologizing, Sarah Grace. You didn't do anything wrong."

"I eloped and divorced without telling you."

A small smile pulled at the corners of his lips. "Questionable but not wrong."

"Daddy."

"Sarah Grace," he said, echoing my frustrated tone.

"Stop trying to make me feel better about it."

"I'm not." He pulled his right foot onto his left knee. "You didn't commit any crimes. You didn't hurt anyone."

I wasn't convinced that last bit was true, but I didn't argue.

"My advisors are suggesting I put out a press release that mentions your split from Fletch and references your previous divorce. Blah, blah, divorce from her second husband, respect our privacy, blah, blah. *Transparency* is the catchword of the day."

"How badly is this hurting your campaign?"

He stared into his cup. "It's too soon to tell. We need to be as honest as possible without giving away too many details, blah, blah, blah."

My bubble of happiness started to free-fall. "That's a lot of *blah*s."

He glanced over the rim of his cup. "Sure is."

"For what it's worth, I think your advisors are right. About the transparency, that is, especially since all our secrets are leaking out. Eventually, this storm will blow over," I said, echoing Marlo.

"But where does it stop? When does transparency start to equate to intrusion? Can nothing be kept private anymore?" He dragged his hands through his hair and oddly sounded like he was detached from what he was saying, as if they were words placed in his mouth. Words that strangely sounded like they'd come from my mother's lips. If anyone valued family privacy, it was her, and I could see her pushing him to agree. When it came to advisors, there was only one in his orbit that could bend his will.

"It's exhausting keeping secrets," I said. "If I'd been *transparent* from the get-go, none of this would be happening."

In fact, I'd probably still be married to Shep, with a houseful of little ones, dogs, and happy chaos. My heart panged with regret, and I told myself to let it go. To forgive myself for the decisions I'd made, once upon a time. But all that was easier said than done.

Daddy stared into his cup for so long that I was starting to think that he hadn't heard me. "It's not you, Sarah Grace. It's—" He cut himself off and stood up. "It's nothing. I need to get back to work. They're expecting me."

I stood, too, suddenly concerned by his demeanor. "Are you sure it's nothing?"

When he glanced at me, he looked so sad that I wanted to cry. "Daddy?"

"I'm tired is all. Secrets *are* exhausting." He came over and kissed my cheek, then headed for the door. "I'll check in with you at the end of the day to let you know what's decided."

With that, he left, and I sat down, wondering why I felt like he'd been talking about his own secrets, not mine.

But no. My father was an open book.

Wasn't he?

Blue

Flora was starting the week off unusually fussy and the wind extraordinarily calm.

My world had somehow tipped out of balance.

Usually this time of morning, the wind called for me to scout the woods, but not today. Today, it was eerie in its silence, which made me nervous. There'd never been a day of my life that I hadn't felt the pull to search the woods. Why today, of all days, had the need dissipated?

I paced the sunroom, hoping the movement would help set Flora at ease—and me, too. It was hard to believe that it was only a week ago that I'd found her. She was such a presence in my life that it felt like she'd always been here.

Sam Mantilla had just left and had given the sunroom his stamp of approval. My temporary guardianship of Flora had been extended thirty days, and for that alone it was worth moving my work space over to the farmhouse.

Although the sunroom felt much more spacious, I couldn't deny that I missed having my studio here. With all the natural light, the view of the backyard with its flowers, colorful lights, and knowing Moe and Marlo, who forever inspired me, were right next door.

It was bigger, yes. But empty, like it had lost a piece of its soul.

I blew out a long breath.

"What's with you today? You're so restless," Persy asked as she bustled around the kitchen, setting her breakfast bowl into the dishwasher and refilling her mug with coffee.

"The wind is calm."

She threw a look to the backyard. "It does look peaceful out there."

I didn't mention my suspicion that the stillness meant anything but tranquility.

"I thought maybe you were fighting the urge to go see Henry at the bookshop this morning."

There was that, too. Not that I'd admit it, just to hear Persy say she told me so. As the image of Henry's kind eyes and dimples flashed through my head, I realized I'd become accustomed to our early morning meetups. I was going to miss sharing coffee and talking books with him, but I wasn't ready to face him. Not yet. Not until I worked through my feelings.

"Mmm," I said noncommittally because Persy was staring at me, waiting for a response.

She laughed. "You're being stubborn."

She's been hurt a fair time or two, and she's closed herself off from most people. To protect herself, you see.

As Moe's voice echoed in my thoughts, I tensed. I didn't know how to open myself back up after being hurt. I didn't know how to forgive or how to let the hurt go.

Flora wiggled and let out a squawk, and I shifted her in my arms, trying to settle her before she started all-out wailing.

"Here, let me hold her for a bit before I have to leave for class." Persy held out her arms for Flora, and I carefully transferred her into her care.

If the doctors at the hospital had correctly aged Flora, she was eleven days old today. She hadn't grown much, but her skin had cleared, the nub of her umbilical cord had fallen off, and she was stretching her arms and legs more often. She was eating a little more, sleeping a little less, and she didn't look so much like a little old lady anymore but a healthy, beautiful baby. "She's clean, fed, and burped. I'm not sure what's wrong."

Flora let out a pathetic mewl, pushing her bottom lip out in the most adorable pout I'd ever seen, and Persy said, "Could be she's just in a mood. We've all been there, haven't we, Flora?"

I stretched and rolled my neck to loosen a kink, and my gaze went to the trees in the backyard, to their motionless branches. No leaves rustled. There wasn't a lick of a breeze.

The morning sun was hiding behind wispy clouds that seemed to be moving at a good clip, which made no sense to me since there was no wind blowing down here. My anxiety kicked up a notch.

On the deck next door, Moe sat reading his upside-down paper, and my chest squeezed so tightly I couldn't take a deep breath. When I brought Moe back last night and told Marlo what had happened, she shut down. Wouldn't talk about it at all. Simply gave me a hug and a kiss and took Moe home.

Loving shouldn't hurt so much. It just shouldn't. But there was no denying that it did—because I hurt. I had only a few days to try to make her see reason, since the new moon was tonight, and she couldn't moondance without the moon, which meant she couldn't heal him.

Persy followed my gaze. "Why won't Marlo let Moe move to Magnolia Breeze? It's a nice place."

It was, and Moe would appreciate its focus on palliative care. "She's trying so hard to keep him home that she doesn't even like to talk about care facilities."

"Do you think it's because of money?" Persy asked as she swayed with Flora. "I know those places can be expensive."

Marlo came out with a breakfast tray and set it in front of Moe. She reached over and turned the newspaper around, but his forehead furrowed deeply in annoyance. He turned the paper upside down again.

Dejected, she sat down next to him.

"I don't think it's about money."

It was because she knew she couldn't save him.

She'd been saving people for so long. She mostly saved with unconditional love and acceptance, and sometimes with a little moonlight. She didn't know how to accept that this time . . . there was nothing she could do. No amount of love. No amount of healing.

And if she couldn't help him, no one could. No hospital, no

nursing facility, no nothing. She was bound and determined for him to die at home. To die with her at home.

I wished for her to understand that his death wouldn't be her failure. She shouldn't be so focused on his dying, but rather on the way he'd lived his life. A life full of love and happiness.

Moe glanced her way and startled as if only now noticing she was sitting there. Smiling, he patted her hand, ignored his breakfast, and went back to reading the upside-down paper.

As if she sensed she was being watched, she looked across the yard, through the window, and straight at me.

The clouds shifted. Sunbeams emerged and slanted against the pergola, dressing them both in prison stripes.

I held her unwavering gaze for a long moment before turning away.

Flora let out a wail and Persy picked up a pacifier and offered it to her, and she angrily sucked it into her mouth, her light eyebrows drawn low. "I see you're learning early that Mondays stink, Flora. But at least you don't have calculus. Be glad. You know, Blue, you should save this pacifier when she outgrows it and put it in a box like Twyla made for us."

I liked the idea of a keepsake box for Flora and hoped the police would return the Buttonwood Tree button that said to give her to me.

In the quiet aftermath of finding Moe last night, I'd chosen to go to bed instead taking a trip down memory lane by finishing my exploration of the box I'd taken from the farmhouse, but now . . . Now I had the time.

I picked up the box from its spot next to the hearth, set it onto the dining table, and lifted its creaky top. I showed Persy the rocks and the button and kept digging. There was a small wooden squirrel my daddy had carved from a birch tree that had toppled in the yard during a tropical storm. The power had been out for nearly a week, and he'd literally whittled away the time. There was a prairie rag doll, Agatha, so loved her clothes were faded and tattered. I'd carried that doll everywhere when I was little. I found a folder with papers that I set aside.

There were no pictures, no baby shoes, no tiny footprints, but there was a small knitted pink baby hat, the band rolled up almost to the hat's peak. It looked familiar, and with a start, I realized it looked a lot like the hats Mary Eliza had been knitting last week at Magnolia Breeze. I unfolded the brim looking for a tag and something fell to the floor and rolled under the table.

I reached for it and was surprised to see another Buttonwood Tree button. It was dark gray with age and grime, the writing hidden by layers of dirt.

"What's it say?" Persy asked as she continued to poke through the box.

I showed it to her. "It's too grimy to tell." I took it to the kitchen and quickly gathered a few supplies. I dipped a cloth into a small bowl of white vinegar and rubbed the disc of wood. "It's going to take time. I don't want to fully soak it, because it'll distort the wood, which might make the letters unreadable."

Looking at the clock on the microwave, she said, "Well, hurry, because I need to leave soon."

I rubbed a little harder.

"Hey," Persy said, holding up one of the papers from the folder. "Did you see this? It's a death investigation report from the army."

"No, I've never seen it before." I didn't particularly want to see it now. Everyone knew how Mac had died—I didn't need to see it written out in black and white. As she kept reading, I kept scrubbing the button. "I think one of these words says 'family.'"

"Blue, this report says that Mac died honorably."

My hands stilled. "What?"

She looked over at me. "Yeah. See for yourself."

I walked around the counter and took the paper from her, my gaze skimming over paragraphs.

Mac had stopped a man from assaulting a woman in an alley behind a bar, and the man had turned his knife on my brother. The woman had escaped unharmed, but Mac had died as a result of his injuries.

"Why didn't Twyla tell us?" Persy asked.

"I'm not sure." I tried to soak in this new information. I flipped the paper over and back again, hoping it would reveal more secrets. "Maybe it didn't matter to Daddy and Twyla how he died, only that he was gone. Or it could be because they weren't great readers. Maybe they couldn't make out what all this meant."

I shuffled through the rest of the papers in the file. Mixed in with a few school papers and some of my early drawings, I saw that my parents had received a check from the army, too, when Mac had died, enough to cover funeral costs with a little left over. Also in the folder were daddy's death certificate and a booklet on how to raise chickens.

Persy said, "Maybe it wasn't important to them, but I like knowing he was protecting someone, that he didn't die in vain."

I liked knowing, too. I set the papers back into the file and held out my hands for Flora. "You're going to be late."

Persy looked at the clock and groaned.

As she ran around, stuffing her backpack, I went back to the button in the kitchen. "It definitely says 'family.'"

Persy ran over to me to look for herself. "Yep. And that word after it says 'yours.'"

"But there's a word in between. *If*? *Is*? *As*? And I think this says 'choose love.'"

"I see it," she said.

Flora yawned, seemingly unimpressed with our efforts to decipher the hidden message. There were bits of other letters showing, but they were too camouflaged to make out specific words. This discovery effort was going to take longer than I thought so I switched tactics. I stuck a corner of the cloth into the bowl of vinegar, soaking it. I set the button onto a plate, then set the saturated cloth over the top of the wood. "I'll let it sit for a while. This method should soak through the rest of the grime but shouldn't make the wood swell."

She slung her backpack over her shoulder. "You'll text me what it says?"

"You shouldn't be texting during class."

She rolled her eyes as she grabbed the car keys and muttered, "Cruel."

My phone rang as I laughed. "It's Shep."

Persy froze midstep.

Suddenly worried that I didn't want to know what Shep had to say, I forced myself to answer. The call was short and to the point, and it wasn't even a minute before I hung up. "The tests are back."

"And I'm not Flora's mother. I know. Those tests were a waste of time."

"Actually he said there was something in the results that he needed to discuss with us in person. He'll be here at ten."

Her whiskey eyes flared. "This is ridiculous. I'm not Flora's mother. I can't believe I'm going to miss class for this." She dropped the keys and headed for the stairs.

My heart had lodged in my throat as I said, "Maybe you're not Flora's mother, but that doesn't mean you're not involved with her birth."

With one hand on the stair railing she looked back at me. "What're you trying to say, Blue?"

"I think you know exactly what I'm saying, Persy. I thought you had a secret boyfriend with the way you've been staying out late and talking to someone in the middle of the night. Now I'm thinking it wasn't a boy at all, was it? I'm worried about you. I'm worried *for* you."

She tried to look me in the eyes but failed. "Let it go, Blue."

With that, she ran up the steps.

Let it go. If only it were that simple.

I couldn't let it go. Not until her name was cleared for good. All it was going to take was one warrant for Persy's cell phone records to blow open this whole case.

Flora yawned around her pacifier, and I put her in the bouncy seat so I could clean off the dining table. When I picked up the pink hat, I wondered if it was possible that Mary Eliza had made my baby hat.

And if she had, why did that thought fill me with more uneasiness than Shep's visit?

Chapter 17

Judge Quimby believed paperwork would one day be the death of him. He stacked another file on the corner of his desk as Willow Eakins, his administrative assistant, tapped softly on his door and stepped into his chambers.

There was another blasted file in her hands that she laid on the desk in front of him.

Though he forced himself to thank her, he rather wished she'd run the folder through the shredder.

It was, perhaps, time to schedule a vacation.

He glanced up when he realized she still stood in front of his desk, wringing her hands.

Willow had worked with him for nearly seven years, and he'd never known her to dawdle. "Something on your mind, Willow?"

"The Bishop family."

He wasn't surprised. Motioning for Willow to sit, he said, "What about them?"

She perched on the edge of the seat as if ready to take flight at a moment's notice. "With you being involved with Blue's guardianship of the abandoned baby, I feel like I need to tell you that I once had a relationship with Wade Bishop."

"Did you?" he said, trying to act as if he hadn't known.

"It was a long time ago. Almost thirty years."

"Wade's reputation didn't bother you?" he asked.

It was quite a reputation, too. Before Wade had seen eighteen

years on this earth, he'd been arrested multiple times for under-
age drinking, truancy, petty larceny, vandalism, and disorderly
conduct. The more Wade acted out, the more convinced the
judge had been that he was doing it only because no one expected anything else from him.

Shrugging, she said, "Maybe a little, but not so much that
I wouldn't date him. And he was working on turning his life
around. When we met, I was working at Publix and going to
school at the community college, and he had just started working as an electrician's apprentice. We'd been dating only six
months when he asked me to marry him. He wanted to settle
down and start a family straight off." She glanced at her hands.
"We were both only eighteen at the time, and I wasn't sure I
was ready for all that. I thought it was all too fast, too soon, to
be real. I was scared, so I told him no."

"That is awfully young to be settling down if you have
doubts."

"We ended up breaking up, and I moved around some before coming back to town about ten years later. I called Dodd's
Electrical to install porch lamps on my new house, and I was
shocked when it was Wade who showed up. He was a full-
fledged electrician."

Not many had seen any hope in Wade or given him a chance
to prove himself capable of something other than accruing misdemeanors until Ray Dodd had come along.

"Wade and I quickly picked up where we'd left off, and I
thought for sure we were headed back to the altar . . . but then
the bank robbery happened."

"I'm so sorry."

She nodded as she stared at her hands. "To this day, I don't
know why he did it. He had everything going for him. His reputation had been cleaned up, he was making a good living, we
were planning a future . . . and then it all went up in flames.
At the very least, it's a small comfort to me that when he died,

he knew how much I loved him. I just wish I'd had more time to show him how much. Anyway, I wanted to let you know in case it comes up."

"I appreciate it, Willow."

After she left, he stacked his files and locked them away. There was nothing that couldn't wait until tomorrow. Right now, he felt an urgent need to get home to Mrs. Quimby to let her know just how much he loved her.

Blue

"What time did Shep say he'd be here?" Marlo asked as she pulled the pitcher of sweet tea from the fridge.

"Ten."

I had a bad feeling about this visit. All because of the wind and its silence.

Its deafening silence.

My gaze drifted to Flora, curled in a ball in her Moses basket. She'd finally fallen asleep, and her face was slack with peace. I put cookies on a plate and glanced out front. Moe's health aide was walking with him around the neighborhood, as he'd been insistent that he had to go look for his beloved Skitter.

The scratch on his cheek had disappeared overnight, but his eyes had been cloudy, hinting that he'd been taken to another place and time. When I questioned him about what had happened last night—and about keeping his promise—he hadn't seemed to know what I was talking about. Until today I hadn't realized exactly how much Marlo had been helping him. No wonder she was drained.

Since her healing had been minimal these last few days, it was clear to see now how far down the rabbit hole of dementia he'd traveled, and I hoped to the heavens that he didn't feel lost. That he somehow knew where he was, even if he was the only one who knew it.

Marlo followed my gaze and said, "Moe's been extra tired this morning. Perhaps a nap with Flora later is just what he needs."

A nap with Flora and her energy.

I squeezed so hard on the cookie I held that it broke, sending crumbs flying across the countertop.

Marlo, always intuitive to my feelings, put her arm around me, absorbing my hard anger into her soft curves. Her inner light glinted in her dark eyes. During this forced hiatus from healing Moe, her body was trying to heal itself. "I'd rather go with him, Blue, than live without him. I've been at his side for more than fifty years, so long that I can't hardly tell where he ends and I begin. No use in separating us now."

I wiped my hands. "Why?"

She seemed startled by the question. "I love him. Is it so hard to understand?"

"Love is a shallow answer, Marlo, and you know it. You love me. You love Persy. Yet you're still willing to go."

"Then what's the deep answer, honey? Tell me."

"You're scared to live without him, plain and simple. But someone pretty special once told me that those we love live inside us. He wants you to stay. *He* wants you to keep on living because he knows he'll be with you still. It's his way of staying alive, too. What would *you* want if you were Moe? Have you put yourself in his shoes? Would you want him to die for you?"

She opened her mouth but snapped it shut when someone knocked on the door. It was just as well. I wasn't sure there was anything else I could say that could possibly change her mind, and I was starting to think I was going to have to accept that I'd soon lose them both.

Persy came stomping down the stairs as I opened the door.

Shep took off his sunglasses as I invited him inside. He gripped a folder tightly. "Sorry for the short notice."

"It's fine," I said. "I'm glad to get this over with."

Marlo came over to him, and he gave her a hug. He was yet another of her little rabbits.

She said, "Would you like some sweet tea, Shep? Cookies?"

"No, thanks, Marlo."

I checked on Flora in her basket, then gestured around the living room. "We should probably sit down."

Despite her mood, Persy sat next to me on the couch, shoulder to shoulder. Marlo sat on the other side of me, and I felt bookended by love. It was a lovely feeling, one I'd have savored if not for the anxiety sweeping through me.

I couldn't help thinking that Shep was about to change my life forever.

I knew it by the stillness of the wind.

And by Shep's expression.

I said, "You look like you're here to deliver a death sentence. You should see the look on your face."

Persy nodded. "It's grim."

He tapped the folder against the palm of his hand. "I don't know an easy way to say all this."

"Just spit it out," Marlo said, "before I up and die from the suspense. Is Persy Flora's mother?"

"No," he said. "There's no relation between them at all."

Persy crossed her arms. "I told you so."

"Then why all this fuss, Shep?" I asked.

He took a deep breath and opened the folder to remove several pieces of paper. "Autosomal DNA comes from both your parents. It's the test traditionally done to establish a DNA profile. When your test came back with an interesting result, Blue, the lab also ran a mitochondrial DNA, mtDNA, test—that type of test is often used to verify *maternity*, since mtDNA is passed down through maternal lines for generations."

Verify maternity? "You tested me to see if I was Flora's mother?" I asked, trying to follow along with what he was saying. "Why? I'd certainly know if I gave birth to her. I didn't."

"And the tests prove that." He held my gaze. "But, Blue, the test proved that you *are* related to Flora."

The wind suddenly breathed a gusty sigh of relief that whistled down the fireplace and swept through my soul, stirring the familiar pull to the woods. It beckoned, begging me to hurry. But I couldn't leave. Not yet. I looked down at Flora, at the familiar shape of her eyes. I had believed the similarity to be a coincidence. "How?"

"You and Flora come from the same maternal line." His eyebrows furrowed as he leaned forward, as if the gravity of the situation was pulling him downward. He set his elbows on his knees. "But, Blue, you and Persy do not. There is no possible way that you and Persy have the same mother. And further examination of both your results shows that in all likelihood, Persy is actually your aunt—and one of your brothers is your real father. Twyla and Cobb are your grandparents, likely adopting you as their own when you were born. It happens in a lot of families. Sometimes the kids know; sometimes they don't."

"Gad night a livin'," Marlo said under her breath.

Persy stiffened. "Say what now?"

I stood up, too flustered to sit still, jolted by Shep's words, summoned by the wind. My mother wasn't my mother, and my father wasn't my father? "This is nonsense. The tests are obviously wrong. Contaminated or something."

The wind roared in my head, threatening to drown out every thought other than running into the woods. I planted my feet to the floor so I wouldn't run for the door.

"There was no contamination. I'm sorry, Blue," Shep said, true remorse shining in his eyes. "I know it's a lot to take in."

Persy's face had drained of color, and her mouth hung open like she was trying to speak, but no words were coming out.

Shep said, "The amount of DNA you share with Flora is about the same as you being her first cousin once removed. Do you know if any of your brothers had illegitimate children?"

"Besides me, you mean?" I said, my voice high with disbelief. He winced.

"Ty would've been only seven when I was born," I said. "Wade was eighteen, so it's possible he'd gotten someone pregnant, I suppose. I don't know much about Mac's life. He was in the army and died a few months after I was born."

Marlo nodded and said, "Wade dated someone pretty seriously back then. Asked her to marry him. Willow Eakins. She works for Judge Quimby now."

Persy glanced at me, looking pained. "Twyla always did say you came as quite a surprise."

Twyla had never liked to talk about my birth at all, and now I wondered if that was because she didn't *know* the details. I couldn't believe what I was hearing, but it didn't feel wrong. Why didn't it feel wrong?

"And," Persy added, "wasn't there an issue with your birth certificate at one point?"

There had been. I'd been held back a year because I hadn't had a birth certificate when Twyla tried to register me. An oversight, she had said, since mine had been a home birth with no witnesses, and she hadn't bothered to fill out the necessary government paperwork. We'd had to get a "delayed" certificate of birth, and by the time everything was sorted out I'd already missed too many days of classes and was forced to wait until the next school year to start kindergarten.

Shep made a note on one of the papers. "I'll talk to Willow."

I paced. Two steps forward. Pivot. Two steps back. The wind gusted, urging me to follow it. I froze, midpivot, listening to it calling.

Marlo came to stand next to me as if recognizing that I was prepping to flee. "This is all too fantastical to be real, Shep. If there was no contamination, could the tests have been mixed up? You took Sarah Grace Fulton's DNA too, right? Maybe the two tests were mixed up accidentally? Could be *she's* Wade's love child."

My jaw dropped. Was it possible? Was Sarah Grace a *Bishop*?

Persy shot off the couch. "Sarah Grace took a DNA test? *Why?*" Panic pulsed off her in manic undulations, banishing the wind's plea, forcing me to focus on her. She looked near tears at the news, restless as she gestured madly at nothing in particular.

Shep slowly rose from his chair. "She took it for the same reason as Blue, to help with the case." His eyes had darkened and narrowed. A cop who was seeing cause for concern. "Why does that upset you so much, Persy?"

Placing a shaky hand to her forehead, she mumbled under her breath. Tears gathered in her eyes. Her chest heaved, and her breath came out in tiny huffs as she fought to keep her composure.

Finally, she said, "Blue, your DNA test and Sarah Grace's were definitely mixed up." Her bottom lip pushed out, trembling. She looked between all of us, her gaze lingering on Flora, before she bolted for the door. She flung it open and was gone in a flash.

Stunned, I looked at Shep. His eyes were closed as if he was praying. When he opened them, regret poured out in shiny green waves. "I'll be in touch," he said in barely a whisper before he, too, went running out the door.

Sarah Grace

I was drowning in a sea of invoices when the office door flew open, making me jump nearly out of my skin.

"I stopped by Kitty's for muffins," Kebbie said as she came inside, kicking the door shut with her foot. "A peace offering. Sorry I'm so late."

At the sudden noise Hazey barked and scrambled to her feet. She whined and ignored my commands to get down as she excitedly jumped on Kebbie, nearly knocking her over. Her purse, its contents, and the bag of muffins went flying.

"Down, Hazey, down!" I grabbed her collar and she finally sat, though not until after she grabbed a blueberry muffin that was rolling by, eating it in two big bites.

Kebbie righted herself, fixed her dress, and then let Hazey sniff and lick her hand. "I didn't know she was here or I would've knocked a warning first. Hi, Hazey, I'm happy to meet you—aren't you a pretty girl? I'm sure glad I bought extra mufflers."

"Mufflers?" I asked with a smile.

Kebbie cocked her head. "What?"

"You said mufflers, not muffins."

"Oh. Did I?" She frowned. "Weird. Slip of the tongue, I guess."

Her reaction was weirder than her original comment. A humorous slip of the tongue should've been cause for a laugh, but she didn't seem to recognize that she'd made the mistake in the first place. "I'm so sorry about Hazey jumping on you. We'll work on her manners." I gave Kebbie a once-over, suddenly extremely worried about her. "Are you okay?"

"Fine. No harm, no foul." She took a second to catch her breath. "Hazey barely touched me before you grabbed her."

"No." I shook my head. "You're breathing heavy. And you look . . . Maybe it's time to see a doctor, Kebbie. Whatever you have is more than a cold."

She chuckled and fluffed her hair. "Gee, thanks, Sarah Grace."

Her hair was done—her makeup, too. But it did little to hide that her skin was ghastly white dashed with mottled redness. Her face was puffy, too, especially around her eyes.

I bent low to help pick up the contents of her purse. "How long have you been sick now? A week?"

"I'm fine. And I can pick all this up," she said, sucking in a breath and wincing in pain as she crouched down.

"And I can help." She most certainly wasn't fine. She looked like death warmed up, spit out, run over, buried, and resurrected. "Are you having trouble breathing? And what hurts? I saw you wince in pain."

"This conversation is pretty painful. Drop it, Sarah Grace."

"No." I reached under her desk for her phone that had skidded underneath it. I handed it to her, and when she took it, I noticed her hand shaking. I took hold of it—felt its heat. She was burning up. "Do you have a fever? Why're you shaking?"

She tugged her hand free. "I'm just a little marshmallow."

I stared at her. "Marshmallow?"

She stared back, looking thoroughly confused. "S'mores on your mind, Sarah Grace?"

It was clear she had no idea she was randomly saying the wrong words. "That's it. We're going to collect the rest of your things; then we're going to the doctor." I knee-walked over to my desk, reached under, and came back with a prescription bottle.

"No, we're not," she said, reaching for the bottle. "That's mine."

I snatched it away before she could grab it and stood up. "What is this about, Kebbie?"

I held the bottle toward her, the label facing outward. It was clearly a prescription for Persy Bishop, a seven-day supply of acetaminophen with codeine. Painkillers—I recognized the name from when I had my wisdom teeth removed a few years ago. "Why do you have Persy's pain pills?"

Kebbie stood up and swayed slightly before grabbing onto the edge of her desk. She lifted her chin and said, "She gave them to me."

"Why?" The medication had been prescribed by the same

doctor who I saw for my birth control pills. And this prescription had been filled the same day I'd seen Persy in the doctor's parking lot. The same day an anonymous tip had been called in to the police that Persy was Flora's mother. Had that tip been called in to purposefully shift the suspicion toward Persy and away from someone else?

Someone like Kebbie?

My breath caught as the truth hit me hard, nearly knocking me over. "Oh, Kebbie. Oh no."

"No one needs to know," she gasped, the words coming out as broken as she was.

I ran over and threw my arms around her. "We'll fix this. It's fixable."

Finally letting go of her emotions, she cried into my shoulder as she clung to me, her feverish body shaking violently against mine. Tears flowed from my eyes, soaking into her hair as I held her. We needed a plan. Our own war council. Damage control.

Run. We needed to run. Just until we could figure out what to do.

I ignored my mother's voice in my ear whispering, *Do better. Be better.* It wasn't as though we were running away forever. We'd be *temporary* fugitives. "We talked about going away for a few days. Let's do that now. Right now. We don't even need to pack. We can get what we need down at the beach, including a doctor. We need some time to figure out how to face this, and to find a good lawyer."

"No. We can't tell *anyone.*"

"Oh, Kebbie." I hugged her tighter. This wasn't a secret I could keep, even if I wanted to. She didn't know I'd taken a DNA test. The proof would be back soon enough. Proof that would lead straight back to her. "It's too late for that, Kebbie."

When I told her what I'd done to help Flora's investigation, she cried harder, folding in on herself from the weight of her secrets and the knowledge that the truth was coming for her.

I grabbed her purse, shoved everything I could into it. I clipped Hazey's leash to her collar and picked up my workbag. Hazey danced, excited by this turn of events as I took hold of Kebbie's arm. "Let's go."

"Wait . . ." Her voice trailed off as her body went limp. Her eyes rolled to the back of her head, and she dropped to the floor.

Horrified, I fell to my knees and shook her. "Kebbie!"

She didn't budge, and I couldn't see or feel her breathing. *Oh God, please, please help her.*

Her pulse was fast but weak under my fingertips at her throat, and fear shot through my body as I stumbled for the phone to call an ambulance.

Please.

Chapter
18

Sarah Grace

Bleak.

The word floated through my head, set adrift by long faces and waning spirits. We'd been at the hospital for close to seven hours now and were drained of energy and filled with weariness. We'd been shuffled from the emergency department to a well-appointed visitor lounge outside the medical intensive care unit, where Kebbie had been transferred an hour ago. An hour that felt like days, the time dragging by so slowly that at one point I thought the clock was broken.

There were a few strangers in the room, family members of others who, like Kebbie, were the sickest in the hospital. Among those gathered here in the lounge, watching TV or getting a snack, were my mother and father, who sat side by side in upholstered armchairs, bonded together in silent anguish. Mama stared straight ahead at nothing at all, and Daddy focused intently on the floor as if to find answers in the sparkling flecks of quartz in the terrazzo tiles.

We were waiting to be taken back to Kebbie's room, which would happen after she was situated and assessed by the ICU doctors and nurses. She'd been slipping in and out of consciousness most of the day and had been started on intravenous broad-spectrum antibiotics to fight an infection and the widespread inflammation caused by postpartum sepsis that was wreaking havoc in her body.

Postpartum.

I'd been by Kebbie's side most of the time in the emergency department, and in moments of wakefulness, she'd burbled delirious confessions. She was Flora's mother. She'd given birth to her two Fridays ago in the Bishop farmhouse, with Persy there to help her through it.

It was almost too much to wrap my head around.

Shep had been by a few times, but as far as I knew, he hadn't spoken to Kebbie—most likely because she wasn't fully coherent. I knew the questions would come. Questions that had no answers at the moment. The whys.

What we did know was that sometime after giving birth, Kebbie had developed an infection. Left untreated, it had overcome her system, and she was in what the doctor in the emergency room had called severe sepsis. It wasn't the worst-case scenario—that would've been septic shock. But she was close to that now, with her blood pressure unstable. I'd done a quick search on my phone after the ER doctor had given us the news and immediately stopped looking when I saw the mortality rate. The numbers were terrifying.

Nausea rolled through my stomach as I looked out a window at the flat rooftop one story below and listened to the building wax on about the things it had seen and the tales it could tell, like a lonely old man in a diner bending the ear of the waitress.

I tuned it out. Any other day I would have been happy to sit and listen, but not today. Not unless these walls stopped telling me about the horror stories and started talking about the miracles it had seen.

Because Kebbie needed one.

I tipped my neck side to side, stretching it, and then spent a good five minutes picking dog hair off my shirt so my mama wouldn't have an allergy attack. It was bad enough she had barely looked at me since arriving, as if baby Flora were just another secret I'd been keeping from her.

I could only imagine what her reaction was going to be when she found out where Hazey was. As soon as the ambulance had pulled away from the office, I'd called my parents and quickly realized that I couldn't take Hazey with me to the hospital. And I hadn't wanted to leave her at home, alone, wondering if she'd been abandoned again. So I'd done the only thing I could think of and had taken her to Blue's house. She'd opened the door before I even knocked, gave me a hug, and promised me she'd look after Hazey as long as I needed.

I turned away from the window as the lounge door opened and a woman stepped into the room—the intensive care unit's receptionist. "Family of Kimberlee Hastings?"

Mama bounced out of her seat as if it were a springboard, and Daddy stood slowly, as if his body were weighted down by his worries. I walked over and took hold of his hand as we all looked at the woman expectantly. Fearing the worst. Praying for the best.

"Y'all can see her now. Please follow me." She talked as she walked, explaining the procedures to get visitor passes, quiet times, visiting hours, the rules—no using cell phones, no fragrances, food, or flowers—and how we had to wash our hands upon entering and exiting Kebbie's room. After we'd shown her our IDs, we had our passes and were directed through double security doors on our way to room number four, Mama's heels clicking softly on the floor.

A cloud of illness, antiseptic, and solemnity floated in the hallway, along with mechanical sounds, indiscernible voices, and from somewhere beyond the curve of the corridor, jaunty big-band swing music.

The music lightened my dark mood, reminding me that this unit was filled with life, not death, even though most here were knocking on death's door. These were people who lived and loved, who had families, jobs, hobbies. Behind their ominous illnesses were *people*, not just patients. There was hope here. Hope and optimism. I clung to it.

Outside each treatment room there was a computer station with a window above to look in on the patient, and there was a sink. A nurse stood in front of room four and greeted us warmly. She introduced herself as Dominique, Kebbie's nurse until nine thirty tonight. We quickly washed our hands as Dominique explained the presence of monitors, machines, tubes.

"Has Kebbie responded to the antibiotics?" Mama asked, her voice high and reedy, as she dried her hands.

Dominique said, "The next few hours will tell us a lot."

"What are we looking at?" Daddy reached up to shove a clean hand through his hair, then thought better of it and dropped it. "What should we be prepared for? How sick is she? How long should we expect her to be here? Is she going to . . . die?"

My stomach dropped out as I waited for the response to these questions that had spilled out drunkenly after having been bottled inside him for hours.

Dominique held his gaze, empathy shining in the dark depths of her eyes. "Kebbie," she said, picking up the use of her nickname, "is quite ill. The most important thing right now is for her to know you're here. Hold her hand. Read to her. Play her favorite music. She might not always look awake, but you'd be surprised at how much she hears. We welcome friends and family, though the number in the room is capped at three, simply for space reasons. Visit often. Stay for a while. We want you here because we know she wants you here. Studies have shown the great benefits to patients being surrounded by loved ones."

She beckoned us to follow her through a large sliding glass door that opened into a room glowing with waning sunlight. "Miss Kebbie, your family's here to see you, honey," she said cheerfully.

Heaven bless nurses, I thought as I followed along.

I held back a cry at the sight of Kebbie in the hospital bed, looking small and fragile among the vast array of technology surrounding her. There were four IV bags hanging from a pole, an oxygen mask over her nose and mouth, she looked puffy around her eyes and upper cheeks because her kidneys were failing, and she was deathly pale. She wore a blue hospital gown that hung loose at the neck to allow wires and leads, and a standard cotton blanket was pulled up to her chest. Her eyes were closed.

It had only been an hour since I'd last seen her, and somehow she looked physically worse for that time. Yet there was softness to her face that hinted of peace, and I was grateful to see it. Most of the time in the emergency room, she'd been distraught, and I hoped her serenity meant the medications were working.

I picked up one swollen hand, and Mama scooted around the other side of the bed to pick up the other. Daddy stood next to Mama and said, "Keb, darlin', we're right here."

Mama nodded as if Kebbie could see her. "We're not going anywhere anytime soon. I might just pull up a bed right next to you—don't think I won't."

"This place better look out," Daddy said, forcing a laugh. "Aunt Ginny will be running this unit before long."

"Everything's going to be fine," Mama added. "You'll be home in no time at all."

Kebbie blinked open her eyes and found my face first. There was clarity to her gaze that I hadn't seen for most of the day. I said, "If you didn't want to work today, you should've just said so."

"Sarah Grace," Mama admonished, adding a deep sigh.

I grinned at Kebbie.

Through her mask, I saw the corner of her mouth twitch into a partial smile that quickly dissipated. She turned her head to the other side of the bed. "I'm sorry."

Her voice was soft and a bit hollow as it came through the mask but still audible.

Mama kept on nodding. "We know. It's okay, Kebbie. It'll all be okay."

"Promise me," Kebbie said.

"I promise you'll be okay." Mama crossed her heart. "I promise, darling girl."

"No," she said. Her eyes fluttered closed then opened again a moment later. She inhaled deeply. One of the monitors beeped. "Promise me if anything happens . . . if I die . . ."

"You are not going to die, Kimberlee Cabot Hastings. You are not." Mama jabbed a single finger and spoke with a force that dared Kebbie to defy her.

Tears gathered in Kebbie's eyes. "Let Blue keep Flora. Promise me."

"That's not a decision to be made right now," Mama said swiftly. "You're too ill to think straight. That's *your* baby. Your perfect little girl. She belongs with you. With us."

"Ginny," Daddy said quietly in warning.

Kebbie turned her head back to me. With as much strength as she could muster, she said, "Let Blue keep Flora. *Promise.*"

I searched her eyes, saw the determination lurking in the sad pools of blue. I took a deep breath and followed my heart. "I promise you, Kebbie."

Mama glared at me from across the bed, and I pretended not to notice. This wasn't a battle to be had in front of Kebbie, but I should've known it had been brewing. Mama had wanted that baby before she'd even known Flora belonged to Kebbie— and now that she knew that little girl was *family*, there was going to be no stopping her from fighting for custody.

But it clearly wasn't what Kebbie wanted. It never had been, if the choices she'd made were any indication. I silently vowed to carry out her wishes, even if I didn't fully understand them.

With a nod, Kebbie closed her eyes again. When she didn't

immediately reopen them, I borrowed a pen and paper from Dominique, pulled up a chair next to Kebbie, and chatted to her about the playlist I was going to make.

Daddy left to make some phone calls, and Mama pulled up a chair and went back to holding Kebbie's hand. As I wrote, I could feel Mama throwing daggers my way, but I didn't look up.

She wasn't going to change my mind—if there had ever been a time in my life for me to stand up for what *I* believed in, it was now.

Blue

A tin full of mini chewy chocolate espresso cookies rested between Persy and me as we sat on the front porch swing, trying to sway away all our troubles.

I'd made the batch earlier, after Persy came home from running off to warn Kebbie about the DNA results. A fruitless warning, because she hadn't been able to find her. It wasn't until later that we'd learned Kebbie had been taken by ambulance to the hospital. I ate three cookies before Persy finally spoke up.

"You were right earlier—I didn't have a secret boyfriend," she said. "I had a secret friend. Kebbie and I have been hanging out every now and then for about a year now, ever since she started volunteering at the clinic."

"Why keep the friendship secret?"

"Ginny Landreneau."

"Ah," I said in understanding. "But you could have told me, you know."

"I thought about it, but it felt a little like I'd be breaking a promise if I did."

Flora was tucked into her baby sling on my chest and was busy trying to eat her fingers. I smoothed her hair and kept a hand on her back as Persy gave us another push. Hazey lifted her head at the sound, then quickly put it back on her paws. She was keeping watch over the neighborhood, and her ears perked every time someone drove by.

The wind had died down, but I knew it would be back. It had been calling to me all day, nagging, really, and I'd asked it to please be patient. I was being pulled in so many different directions today that I felt close to crying. I knew I eventually had to deal with the emotions surrounding Flora's future, but they could wait. Right now I needed to focus on Persy.

"How long had you known Kebbie was pregnant?" I asked.

"A while. She swore me to secrecy."

Birds chattered from bushes surrounding the porch, and the ceiling fan whirred, stirring the fine hairs on Flora's head. "Who's Flora's father?"

"Kebbie doesn't know. He was some cute guy she met at an off-campus party. He was from out of town, and one thing led to another. It was just supposed to be a fling. She doesn't even know his last name. When she realized she was pregnant, she was embarrassed and ashamed and panicked."

Poor, sweet Kebbie. The community would've been shocked senseless to learn she was pregnant, but I had no doubt they'd have eventually accepted it. Especially since she was a Cabot, one of Buttonwood's founding families.

Persy bit into a cookie. "It was easy enough for her to hide the pregnancy. Big sweatshirts, oversized sweaters in the winter, dresses that flared out over her stomach, and stupid jokes about needing to diet. I'd given her the name of the adoption agency you've been talking to, and she planned to call them a week before she was due, knowing they'd help her figure out where to give birth and all that. She knew how badly you wanted a baby and even talked about how cool it would be if the agency gave the baby to you."

I breathed in the scent of Flora's baby shampoo, wishing it had happened that way.

"She didn't tell her aunt and uncle, because they would've

pressured her to keep the baby—Ginny especially. But Keb didn't feel like she was capable of taking on that kind of responsibility and wanted something more for Flora."

I spotted Marlo watching us from the living room window, and I nodded to let her know we were faring okay. Curiosity had to be driving her crazy. "How did Kebbie end up giving birth at the farmhouse?"

Persy let out a huff of exasperation. "Because we don't know what contractions feel like. We almost always hung out at the farmhouse. You rarely went there, so it was like our own private hideout."

"You two were the squatters." I'd suspected as much but wanted to hear it from her.

She nodded. "We'd watch movies and eat junk food. We bought the inflatable sofa months ago at Walmart because the real couch reeked. Everything did. We set it up in our old room, and I hid it under Twyla's bed when we weren't using it. We were there on Friday night when Keb's stomach started hurting, but we thought it was the junk food. Indigestion or something."

I wiped cookie crumbs from my fingers. "Understandable."

"I really didn't think anything of it," Persy said. "She wasn't due for another few weeks, so contractions didn't even cross my mind. We fell asleep watching TV, and next thing I know, Keb was shaking me awake saying she had to push."

"Why didn't you call for help?"

"Kebbie begged me not to. She didn't want the lights and sirens and attention. Then everyone would've known the truth, and honestly, it happened so fast that by the time anyone would've gotten there, Flora would've already been born. Because of my work at the vet clinic, I knew just enough to help without panicking too much. Flora cried straight off," she added with a smile. "The room was a hot mess, though. I spent most of Saturday cleaning, and I went shopping up in Alabaster for the baby things we needed, like diapers and clothes and stuff. Kebbie decided to skip calling the adoption agency in favor of using the safe-haven law. And because she knew she had a three-day grace period, she said she wanted to spend a couple of days with Flora before she handed her over. I was going to drive Kebbie over to the hospital on Monday, but when I went to the farmhouse that morning, she and Flora were nowhere to be found. Next thing I knew, I was getting a call from you about finding a baby in the woods."

"Kebbie hadn't told you her plan for me to find Flora? Or showed you the button?"

Persy shook her head. "Apparently, she'd taken Flora to the Buttonwood Tree early Monday morning to ask if she should give Flora to a stranger . . . or to you. She really liked the idea of you raising Flora. She always thought you'd be a great mom, and with you raising Flora, then Kebbie could still see her grow up. That's when she got the button that said to give Flora to you. But she still didn't want you to know Flora was her baby."

She'd gone to such great lengths to prevent anyone from knowing she was Flora's mother, and as I thought about her being rushed to the hospital, I couldn't help but thinking what a high price that silence had cost. "So she waited for me in the woods."

"Yep. She knew your routine. That morning, she watched to make sure you found Flora—she'd never just leave her out there—and then she ran home. I still can't believe Sarah Grace chose that week to look at the farmhouse or that she was back there on the day I told you I'd check out the squatter situation. I'd wanted to finish cleaning up and get rid of the sofa, but I panicked when I saw Sarah Grace's truck in the driveway, thinking she was going to figure everything out. But then I had the bright idea that maybe it wasn't such a bad thing if the police thought I was Flora's mom. Because once I was ruled out, maybe they'd stop looking so hard. That sure backfired, didn't it?"

As her words sank in, my jaw dropped. "*You* called in the anonymous tip?" No wonder she hadn't seemed shocked when Shep questioned her that night.

"I hoped I'd be tested, ruled out, and that would be the end of it."

Even though Persy was convinced Sarah Grace's and my DNA tests had been mixed up, I wasn't. A wisp of wind whistled through the trees, reminding me of its earlier relief when Shep had been here talking about the results.

Relief.

Such an odd reaction.

So odd that I was going to ask Shep to retest us both, just to make sure the results were correct.

I said, "The truth would've come out anyway. Kebbie's illness would have told everything."

Tears gathered in Persy's eyes as she told me how Kebbie had complained of cramping a few days after the birth, but they didn't know what was normal and what wasn't. As the cramps worsened and the fever started, Persy went to a doctor in Alabaster and complained about bad cramps to the point where the doc prescribed mild pain pills to see her through her cycle.

"I begged her to go to the doctor. She insisted she was okay, that she was feeling better and that she just needed rest. I should've made her go." A tear tracked down her face. "I don't know how I'll forgive myself if she"—Persy swallowed hard—"dies."

I put my arm around her, wanting more than anything to reassure her that Kebbie would be okay, but it wasn't a promise I could make. "I imagine Kebbie didn't tell you how badly she was feeling, because if she went to the doctor, her secret would be exposed."

"It would have been worth the truth coming out if it meant saving Kebbie's life."

I agreed, though I wasn't sure Kebbie felt the same way.

"I should've told someone," Persy said as more tears fell. Her redness turned to splotchiness as her emotions ran rampant. "I should've told Shep right away what I knew; then maybe Kebbie wouldn't be in the hospital right now."

We could talk in circles all afternoon about would haves and should haves, but there was no changing what had happened. I hugged her more tightly and prayed that Kebbie would get better. "Sometimes when we're trying to protect people we care about, we don't make the best decisions."

"How much trouble do you think I'm in?"

This was new territory for us Bishops—caring about the consequences of our actions. "I don't know. Helping Kebbie when she was giving birth wasn't a crime. You didn't lie to the police, because they didn't ask you if you knew who Flora's mother was—because they thought it was you. You just didn't tell what you knew, and there's no *legal* obligation to do so if it's a misdemeanor crime. Morally?" I wiggled my hand side to side.

Persy had definitely been in between a rock and a hard place with wanting to protect her friend, and Twyla had told us both what happened when in that position. We should've taken the warning to heart.

After a few minutes, Persy sniffled. "Do you think the Landreneaus will let me visit Kebbie?"

A lawn mower hummed from somewhere in the neighborhood as we swayed. "It can't hurt to ask."

The swing glided slowly to a stop. "Blue, what's going to happen now? To Flora?"

"I don't know," I said, hoping my heartache didn't trickle out with the words. "It's likely the Landreneaus will want her, and since they're her family, by blood at least, they'll probably get custody."

The wind blew gently, trying to dry my tears.

"I'm *so* sorry, Blue," Persy cried. "I've really made a mess of everything."

As I held her close I started to think that the name Bishop wasn't only synonymous with trouble—but with heartbreak as well.

≫≪

It was late. Half past eleven, and I was waiting up for Sarah Grace, who said she'd be here before midnight. The dull drone of a TV drifted down from Persy's room, and Flora was sleeping in her cradle next to me. Taking care of her tonight had prevented me from wallowing in self-pity.

I'd been working at the dining room table and had put the finishing touches on the painting of Poppy that I'd started yesterday. I couldn't help smiling at Poppy as she twirled on the page, her ears flying out like helicopter blades. I'd intended to keep working until Sarah Grace showed up, but when I pulled out the final painting for the book, which had already been sketched, I was too listless to start adding color to the cotton paper. I tucked the sheet back into my portfolio, capped my ink bottles and gouache pots, and cleaned my brushes.

Hazey watched my every move from her spot on the couch, and each time I passed by, she thumped her tail. I stopped to stroke her neck, and she rolled over to offer me her belly and almost fell off the couch. I laughed, and she kissed my hand.

She had been the only one tonight to elicit a smile from Moe. He was still calling her Skitter, and as far as we were all concerned, that was her name when he was around. For some reason, it felt like she understood why we were calling her something different. "You're a good girl, Hazey."

Her tail thumped harder.

As I washed paint from my hands, my gaze fell on the button next to the sink. I checked to see if the vinegar had worked its magic yet, but the button was being stubborn in revealing its message. I rewet the cloth and would check again in the morning.

I was reminded of the other button I'd found lately, however, and walked across the room to the mantel, where I'd put the button that had been in the box I'd taken from the farmhouse.

SEND THE GIRLS TO THE RABBIT HOLE.

I closed my hand around the smooth wood, and in my head, I heard Marlo say, *Sometimes being a good mama is knowing when to ask for help—and accepting it when it's being offered.*

I hadn't been a mother for very long, but even so I recognized what it must have taken for Twyla to accept that she needed help, seek it from the only thing she trusted—the Buttonwood Tree—then let Persy and me go.

She'd loved us enough to let us go.

The depth of pain she had to have been in was staggering, and being poor and uneducated and unwilling to ask the community for assistance, she hadn't had the tools to heal herself. She'd coped the only way she knew how.

They'd all coped the only way they knew how. My brothers and my father, too.

Mac fought, raging against the injustices of the world. Wade and Ty hadn't known any other way to get the money to save our father other than robbing the Blackstock bank. And my daddy had cheated, lied, and stolen to feed his family, because he had no other skills.

It had taken listening to Persy talk this afternoon about Kebbie and the choices she'd made out of shame and fear to understand why my family hadn't ever looked for another solution. None of them had known how to ask for help when they needed it most, always choosing to run away from the community instead of looking to see what help it had to offer.

And I was no different. Only yesterday I'd wanted to run away.

It had to stop, and it *would* stop with me.

There would always be people like Oleta who'd look down on me, and I just had to accept that. For whatever reason, she didn't have the skills to get over what happened in the past. But it was people like Marlo and Moe and Mrs. Tillman and even Henry who filled me with hope that I could—I would—become a thread in this community. No. It was people like them that showed me I already *was* one.

Finally understanding *why* my family had done the things they'd done brought a wave of peace and also something I'd been seeking for a long time now: the ability to forgive. I'd spent so long trying to stay out of their shadows that I'd had trouble seeing that mine had been a loving family. A big, flawed, troublemaking yet loving family. I was who I was *because* of them.

I glanced over my shoulder at the photos on the bookcase across the room, and my heart filled with love as I finally realized that standing in my own light didn't mean running away from theirs. It meant sharing it. Standing *with* them.

My gaze drifted from the bookcase to the basket of oak galls on the hearth as my thoughts on forgiveness circled back to Henry.

I missed him.

It had seemed impossible to forgive him only a couple of days ago, but now that I could see our situation a bit more clearly, I couldn't really blame him for wanting to keep his identity a secret for a while. Because truthfully, if I'd been in his shoes, I'd have done the same thing if given the chance.

I never had that chance, though, because he'd already known my family's reputation when he came to town—and it hadn't mattered to him. At the very least I owed him the same courtesy.

My head came up at the sound of a car door, and I hurried to the window. Sarah Grace's truck was parked at the curb, and she was walking up the porch steps. I pulled open the door, and Hazey leaped off the sofa and skidded across the oak floor in her rush to get to Sarah Grace, causing her to smile. She bent to give the dog a hug, and Hazey cried her joy.

"How has she been?"

"She's been great. We all love her. Come on in while I gather her toys. Would you like a drink?"

"Hand to God, I'd kiss you on the mouth for a glass of wine."

"Sarah Grace," I said, trying to sound shocked as I quickly went into the kitchen and pulled the wine from the fridge. "What would your mama say to hear such a thing?"

"Right now, probably nothing." She walked over to the island, Hazey trailing behind her. "She's not talking to me at the moment."

"What? Why? Is it about Kebbie?" I poured the wine, then handed her the glass.

She took a sip and let out a slow breath. "Partly. It's a long story."

It was obvious she didn't want to talk about the disagreement, so I didn't press. "How's Kebbie tonight?"

"Her kidneys are worse, and so is her breathing. There's talk of feeding tubes, intubation, and dialysis. I hated leaving her, but they're strict about the visiting hours, unless there's a dire emergency. They'll call if that happens."

The kind of helplessness that came from watching someone go from perfectly healthy to near death virtually overnight had to be soul crushing. "My word. I'm so sorry, Sarah Grace."

"Me, too," she said softly as she refilled her glass. "Is Flora sleeping?"

I nodded toward the cradle on the other side of the dining table. "She'll be awake soon for a bottle, but I can get her up early if you want to hold her."

She walked over and crouched down. I could only imagine what was going through her head. Flora was part of Kebbie, and I understood why Sarah Grace would want that connection right now. However, there was a pain in my chest, a weight, almost like someone was sitting on me. A pain I ignored. I knew it wasn't anything a doctor could treat. It came from knowing that Sarah Grace had the power to take Flora away from me permanently.

"No, that's okay. Let her sleep. She looks so peaceful." Standing, she abruptly reached out to catch her balance. "Whoa. Woozy. This wine went straight to my head."

"Sit, sit," I said, leading her to the sofa. "Have you eaten today?"

"Breakfast."

Breakfast seemed an eternity ago. No wonder she was dizzy. "Let me make you something. Eggs? Toast? There's leftover pulled pork."

She winced and shook her head. "No—but thank you. My stomach . . . I'm sure I'll be fine if I just sit for a minute."

"Put your feet up, and take as long as you need. But you really should eat something. There's cookies." They weren't the least bit nutritious, but she'd have food in her belly.

Her eyebrow went up at that suggestion. She set her drink on the coffee table, kicked off her flats, then lay down on the sofa. "I'll take one. Thanks, Blue." Hazey jumped onto the couch next to her, somehow finding enough room next to Sarah Grace's legs. "I like your house. So warm and welcoming, like a kind hostess who can't get enough guests to suit her."

I liked thinking of the house that way and hoped one day the house would be full.

Back in the kitchen, I pulled the cookie tin from the cupboard. I set several cookies onto a plate in case Sarah Grace found her appetite, grabbed a napkin, and said, "Would you like some milk? Water?"

When she didn't answer, I turned around and saw that she had fallen asleep, her head nestled against a sofa pillow, the look on her face now serene instead of apprehensive. Sleep was giving her what she needed most right now—a break from reality. The normal thing to do in this situation would probably be to wake her up so she could go home to sleep in her own bed, but I wasn't about to interrupt this much-needed rest.

I put the cookies back into the tin and then called Hazey to the back door so she could go out one more time before I locked up. Once back inside, she returned to her coveted spot on the sofa. I grabbed a lightweight throw blanket and set it over Sarah Grace and studied her face. I supposed if I looked hard enough, we had similar lips and cheekbones. But she looked so much like her mother that all I could see was Ginny.

I left one light on in case Sarah Grace woke up in the middle of the night, then carefully scooped up Flora. At the bottom of the staircase, I glanced back at Sarah Grace, noting how peaceful she looked, all of her worries suspended by sleep, her mind and body resting. Recharging. As I started up the steps, I held on tightly to Flora and could only hope that after the chaos of today, tomorrow would be kinder to us all. But most especially to Kebbie.

Chapter
19

It was quiet in Boon Hardy's barbershop—a rarity. Judge Quimby eyed his receding hairline, wondering how long until he was fully bald. Another year or two, he supposed. "The usual," he told Boon.

Boon had always been an outgoing sort but didn't like gossip, which the judge appreciated. The radio was on, playing an old tune from an era long past. It reminded him of his early childhood, before his parents had passed and he'd been sent off to a home for boys. For a moment, he let himself recall his mama's ham steaks, her laugh, and the scent of his daddy's pipe tobacco. It brought up such a feeling of warmth and comfort that he hoped the song went on for a good, long while.

"Been hearing talk here around the shop about Blue Bishop," Boon said, spritzing the judge's hair with a mister.

"That so? I thought you didn't abide talk."

"Sometimes I let it slide." He combed through the judge's thin hair, then deftly trimmed the ragged ends. "Especially when it comes to the Bishops. I have an affection for the family."

"I didn't know."

"Cobb was a good buddy of mine. He didn't have many around here, so I counted myself lucky. I find him on my mind sometimes, thinking about how his life could've been different if he wasn't so dang proud."

"Proud? How?" The judge didn't hear too many stories from people who liked Cobb.

"You ain't never seen a man so resistant to asking for help. Wanted to prove he was fine, capable of making it through life his own way. Which was well and good except his way involved cheatin' and scamming."

The judge knew. Oh, how he knew.

Boon glanced around as if afraid of being overheard in the empty shop. "The thing of it was, he couldn't read a lick. And because so he flunked out of school, couldn't find a decent job, got indignant and flippant when he had to fill out paperwork."

Couldn't read? The judge hadn't known, but it explained a lot about Cobb's personality.

"He tried to learn from time to time. He told me all about how he was trying to learn along with Blue when she went into grade school. He'd pay special attention while she practiced her letters, and he encouraged her to do puzzles with him where she was the one who did most of the work. He never could quite grasp how to read and was too embarrassed to ask for help from anyone other than a six-year-old girl."

"Did Blue know?"

"Not the full extent of it. I only know because I was his reading buddy in primary school and figured it out on my own. That's how we became friends—I didn't make fun of him." He brushed the hair from the judge's neck and added, "All I'm saying is that when it comes to your dealings with Blue, the sins of the father shouldn't be passed on to his kids just because they share the same name."

Sarah Grace

Early the next morning, I put on a pot of coffee and glanced at the clock. It was almost seven, and visiting hours didn't start until eight thirty. It was hard to believe that just yesterday Shep had asked me to run with him this morning. A date that had been canceled in light of all that had happened.

I was startled by the sound of knocking so early in the morning but then was filled with hope that it would be Shep at the door. I could use his assurances right now about Kebbie's legal future, and if I was being completely honest, I wanted to see him. To be near him. To feel his quiet strength.

I rushed to open the front door, a flutter near my heart, and quickly saw that it was my mama who stood on the porch, looking beautifully put together in a blue floral shift dress that brought out her eyes, and nude sling-back pumps. The flutter fizzled, and I hoped the letdown didn't show on my face.

Trying not to worry about how I looked—unshowered with yesterday's makeup on and my hair not combed—I held open the door. "Hi, Mama. Would you like some coffee?"

I knew why she was here, and I was going to need more caffeine to deal with it.

"Yes, please," she said, following me to the kitchen, her heels tapping out her determination on the wooden floorboards like a warning signal.

I braced myself for the battle about to take place and pulled two mugs from the cabinet.

Mama sat on a counter barstool. "I came by late last night, but you weren't home."

"I fell asleep at Blue's house last night, so I didn't get home until a half hour or so ago."

I still couldn't believe I'd fallen asleep on her couch, but I had to admit it was the best rest I'd had in a while, and chitchatting with her over coffee and toast this morning had been a nice distraction from the day ahead. And I'd been able to snuggle Flora, too.

Sweet, sweet Flora.

Mama said, "At her house."

"Yes, I went to pick up Hazey and nodded off. Blue's taking care of her again today, so I can spend all day at the hospital without worrying about her."

"Hazey, your new dog."

I poured coffee and went to fetch the sugar dish. "Yes, Mama."

"I see." She wrapped her hands tightly around her mug. "Did you see Flora?"

Nodding, I said, "She's cute as can be."

"Do you happen to have a picture?"

I let my guard down a bit at the plea in her voice. No matter our disagreement on Flora's future, the baby was part of Kebbie. I pulled my phone from my pocket. "No, I don't. I'll text Blue."

"You don't have to—"

"Too late." After a moment, my phone buzzed. I clicked on the picture Blue had sent along with the message THIS IS MY FAVORITE.

It was of Flora sleeping in a wooden cradle, her head turned to the side and fisted hands resting on each side of her face. Her cheeks were rosy, her lips pursed. I handed the phone to my mother, and she stared at the photo as if trying to memorize the image.

"She's perfect. Your hair was the same way when you were a baby. Like blond dandelion fluff. Kebbie's hair was dark when she was born, but it lightened over time. What color are her eyes?"

"Right now they're kind of a bluish gray, but apparently that can change."

"I bet they'll be light blue. Like Kebbie's." She pushed the phone over to me. "We need to be on the same page when we go to the hospital today, Sarah Grace. I don't want any tension inside Kebbie's room. It's not good for her recovery."

Here we go. "I'm assuming our positions haven't changed on the matter, so it's probably best if we just agree to leave the tension outside the room."

"Why are you being so stubborn?"

"Why do you not understand what Kebbie wants?"

"Stop being naïve, Sarah Grace. Kebbie is twenty years old. She doesn't know what she wants."

"Really? Because I sure knew what I wanted when I was younger than she was. And so did you. You need to start being honest with yourself. *You* want Flora in our family. You want the picture-perfect Christmas card. You want people to say you did the right thing by raising Flora. You definitely don't want to explain allowing Flora to be raised by a Bishop. But, Mama, there is no right and wrong in this situation. Let people talk. That's all it is. Talk. We've had enough of it lately to know it won't kill us."

"No, but it can hurt us. Your daddy's numbers are down in the most recent poll, and that's before the news breaks about your secret marriage and Fletch's illegitimate child."

"How far down?" I asked, my stomach suddenly hurting.

Her lips tightened.

My heart sank, and a tidal wave of guilt swamped me. I wanted to run to my father, tell him how sorry I was all over again. What a mess of trouble Fletch and I had caused.

Mama said, "Now is not the time to turn our backs on family, and Flora *is* our family. She is Caroline's granddaughter. She *should* be raised by us. Family takes care of its own."

All I could see in my head were Kebbie's beseeching blue eyes. *Promise me.* "Blue is a good mother—the mother Kebbie chose for Flora."

Mama's cheeks flushed crimson. "No, she's the mother the damned Buttonwood Tree chose. I don't understand your sudden friendship with Blue Bishop, and I don't much like it, but you already know that. You shouldn't associate with the Bishops. Why must you defy my wishes? And so openly? Sleeping at her house? My word."

My jaw clenched. "I like Blue. I don't understand why you don't. You barely know her. Besides, I'm almost thirty years old, Mama, and can choose my own friends."

Her fingers tightened around the mug. After a moment, she said, "This isn't about Blue. It's about the Bishops in general."

"Way to be close minded, Mama. Do better. Be better."

Her eyes narrowed. "We're getting off track. I didn't come here to talk about Blue. I came here to talk about Flora."

"We should support what *Kebbie* wants for Flora. It's not our decision. It's hers."

"It was the wrong decision."

My temper flared white-hot. "Obviously, she knew you'd feel that way. You with your endless quest for perfection. You might want to take a moment and look within as to why Kebbie might have kept her pregnancy a secret from all of us."

Mama sucked in a shocked breath. "How *dare* you, Sarah Grace, insinuating that I had something to do with Kebbie's choices. They were her own."

"Really? I don't think so. Trying to live with your demands for perfection was—and is—impossible. I eloped because I couldn't bring myself to tell you I loved a man you wouldn't approve of, and not only that, but I was pregnant out of wedlock. I knew you'd be disappointed in me for not fitting into your perfect world. For embarrassing you. I imagine Kebbie has felt the same way these past nine months. She went to great lengths to make sure Blue raised Flora. She was so certain of the decision she was willing to *die* for it, to protect it."

"Neither of you have any idea how I would've reacted, because I wasn't given the option of voicing an opinion."

I cracked a joyless smile. "We know exactly how you would've reacted. You proved it after what happened with Fletch and me. The silent treatment is hardly supportive and comforting."

Mama pushed her mug away and lifted off the stool. "I'm done here."

"We're not a perfect family, Mama. Taking Flora from Blue isn't going to change that fact. Just because we *can* take Flora away doesn't mean that we *should*."

Mama's jaw jutted. "I've contacted a lawyer. There will be an emergency hearing in front of Judge Quimby in a couple of days. We'll have guardianship of Flora before the weekend."

"*Mama.*"

She held up a single finger. "Not another word. That baby is ours. She is not going to be raised by a Bishop, not if I can help it."

My voice rose. "Kebbie should have our support, not our divisiveness. I will fight for what she wants until she's well enough to do it for herself."

"So be it. I'm leaving now."

She started to walk away, and I said, "You don't get it, do you, Mama?" She didn't stop to listen, letting her heels punctuate her displeasure. I followed her to the hallway. "When Kebbie gets better and finds out what you've done, you're going to lose both of them. Her and Flora. Are you prepared for that?"

Mama stopped momentarily before opening the door and walking out, not once looking back.

꙳

My head was pounding by the time I walked out the front door an hour after my mama had stormed out, and I nearly fell down the front steps when I saw Shep leaning against my truck. He was dressed for work and looked like he hadn't slept a wink last night. Still damp from a recent shower, his hair was combed back off his drawn face. Dark circles rimmed his eyes.

"What're you doing here?" I asked.

"Trying to make myself leave. I shouldn't have come."

I made my way over to him, forcing myself to walk, not run. "Then why did you?"

He stuck his hands in his pockets. "I needed to see how you were doing."

As much as I wanted to sidle right up close to him, I kept a good two feet between us. "I've been better."

"Any word on Kebbie this morning?"

"Holding steady from last night, which is huge for a critical-care patient." I couldn't help thinking about after she'd come to live with us, sad and lost as she mourned her parents—and the life she'd once known. It had taken a long while before her enthusiasm for life gradually eased aside her grief to let in some happiness. My heart ached for what she must have been going through these past months, keeping such a big secret. A secret that could have killed her. One that still could.

"I'm scared senseless for her. She has a long fight ahead of her to get better, and when she does, she'll still have to deal with the legal ramifications of what's happened and face the judgment of the community." I sighed. "First things first, I suppose, but I can't help thinking of all the challenges ahead."

"If it sets your mind at ease, legally speaking there are cases on record similar to Kebbie's situation, one not too long ago here in Alabama. Cases where no harm was meant for the infant, and since Flora was well cared for and healthy when she was found, that's in Kebbie's favor. A good lawyer is necessary, but I seriously doubt Kebbie will face jail time. Probation, maybe, but not jail."

This information should've reassured me, but in my head, I could only see the tubes and machines keeping Kebbie alive. Was she strong enough to fight? Was she willing? After all, she'd been willing to die. *Perfectly* willing. I told myself to stop thinking about it and said, "My mother's contacted a lawyer, but I think it's a family attorney. She wants custody of Flora."

"By the pained look on your face, I take it you don't agree with her decision."

"I think we should support Kebbie's choice, but Mama thinks Flora should be with family, no matter what the emotional cost is to get her."

His green eyes glistened like fresh dew on new grass. "Family isn't always the best choice. No one knows that better than I do."

Unable to stop myself, I stepped forward and reached out to cup his cheek. I wanted to take all his pain away. His emotional scars ran deep. Soul deep. Mary Eliza had been a cruel, heartless mother.

He took hold of my hand, closed his fingers around it, and before I knew it, I was in his arms. He brought his lips to mine, and for a moment I was living in an old memory, lost in wonderful feelings and never wanting to be found again.

All too soon, he pulled back and took a step away as though he didn't trust himself. By the mournful look in his eyes, I suddenly felt like I was losing him all over again.

"I can't come back, not like this, until this case is closed," he said, his breath ragged.

"How long?"

"Don't know."

I fought tears, refusing to cry over this. He wasn't leaving forever. He'd be back. I'd see him through his work on the case, around town, on the jogging paths.

Yet I was bereft, my yearning for him on full display, open and raw. No words would come, so I nodded my understanding. He was caught between a rock and a hard place. As was I.

"But, Sarah Grace, if you need me, I'll be here, no matter what. Just call."

"Your job . . ."

"No matter what."

With that, he turned and walked away. Away from me. Away from us. I watched until he disappeared out of sight; then I climbed into and started the truck. It was barely eight in the morning, and I already wished the day were over, so I could be back at Blue's house with Hazey and Flora and snuggles and kisses, among friends who felt a lot like family.

Chapter 20

Blue

It was half past eight in the morning, and as Flora, Hazey, and I walked the woods, my thoughts were being pulled in so many different directions that they'd knotted. They were a jumbled mess of Flora and Persy and Moe and Kebbie . . . and Henry.

Determined to set things straight between us, I decided I'd stop by to see Henry at the bookshop on my way home. I was new to forgiveness and wasn't sure where it would take us, but I wanted to find out. He was worth figuring it out.

Flora's cheek was pressed against my chest, and she squeaked every so often as we walked as though she were testing her voice. I stopped to check the progress of the burgeoning flowers on a wild hawthorn bush, and the wind kicked up. Nudging. Nagging. Urging me to keep looking for the lost thing with no name.

I'd awoken with a new restlessness in me that I couldn't quite identify, and the wind had been unruly to the point where I hadn't been able to ignore its summons. So, after Persy left for class this morning, I let the wind lead the way, fully expecting a detour from my usual route, but the wind had me walk the same path I'd taken for years.

As my gaze scanned the woods, zipping past trees, under ferns, over moss and mushrooms, the wind kept pushing me forward.

When I approached the narrow trail that led to the farmhouse, I paused for only a moment before turning toward my old home. Hazey kept an even pace as we walked single file, stepping over roots and rocks. I steered her away from the reach of a poison ivy branch, and before long we were in the farmhouse's backyard.

The restlessness in me grew, making me antsy. The wind howled, agitated, but didn't settle.

There was nothing new to find here.

"Come on, girl," I said to Hazey, calling her away from the old chicken coop. We stepped back onto the path, my footsteps a little more hurried now. Back on the main trail, we stopped at the Buttonwood Tree, where I checked the button hollow out of habit and found nothing. I took a minute to give Hazey some water, peeked into the empty rabbit hole, and then carried on, taking the trail to the north side of town.

The wind died down, disappointed, as I followed the well-worn side path that spilled onto a paved walkway that ran alongside Buttonwood Baptist, which marked the end of my daily hike. I glanced back at the woods. What was I missing, day after day?

Hazey pulled on her lead, and the retractable leash stretched to its limits as she ran forward to greet a man who sat on an iron bench next to the path.

Henry.

At the sight of him, my chest squeezed a little as if I were seeing an old love after a long absence. How had this man worked himself into my heart after so little time?

He let her sniff his hand then scratched her chin before lifting his gaze to meet mine. "Hi, Blue. I didn't know you had a dog."

Hazey's burnt-orange coat gleamed in the sunlight, and her tail wagged with excitement. "I'm dog-sitting. Hazey belongs to my . . . friend, Sarah Grace. She's also Kebbie's cousin."

I ignored the rush of emotion at even saying the word *friend*, yet she was truly my first outside my immediate family, which of course included Moe and Marlo.

He stood up and pushed a hand through his dark hair. "Word's been going around town about what happened. It's hard to believe. Is Kebbie going to be okay?"

I adjusted the sling to protect Flora's face from the sun. "It's too soon to know."

"Can we send flowers? Something?"

I studied his face. His earnest blue eyes. The faint hint of stubble on his cheeks. Those dimples. He truly was a good guy, and I'd been ready to walk away from him simply because Oleta was his grandmother.

"She can't have flowers in the ICU, but I'm sure we can think of something." I glanced around. "You're out early."

Hazey wandered off to sniff a trash can as Henry nodded. "I was waiting for you. I hope you don't mind—I wanted to talk to you, face-to-face."

My heart kept on squeezing. "How'd you know I'd be here?"

He smiled, and his dimples widened. "Seems everyone in this town knows your route and decided to share it with me. Nearly every day, rain or shine, you go back and forth between the church and your house."

Something he said snagged on my inner uneasiness and stuck there like a sticky burr, but I couldn't place what it was exactly that had bothered me. For the moment, I let it be and said, "Everyone? Why?"

"Well, maybe not *everyone*, but it felt like it. People were dropping in all day long at the bookshop yesterday to talk to me about you. The stories I've heard . . ."

A jab of irritation had me frowning. "What kind of stories? You already know all about my family and their exploits. Was there really need to rehash them?"

"The stories weren't about your family. They were about

you. Well, mostly. The Kehoes did subject me to a ten-minute photo presentation of their cat Vera, who you found once and returned to them. They're mighty grateful, by the way. I've heard how you're a great marble player, how you take cookies regularly to Mrs. Widdicomb, and how you used to paint rocks."

Flora squeaked, and I patted her back. "Why on earth would they tell you all that stuff?"

"They were giving me advice on how to get you to forgive me."

It wasn't the answer I'd been expecting, and a rush of warmth took me by surprise, nearly making me tear up. "Henry, I was g—"

"Now, Blue"—he held up a hand—"hear me out. I think I've earned that much—did I mention the ten-minute photo presentation of a cat?"

I was about to tell him that I'd been going to see him, to talk to him, but I found myself caught up in his smile. "Vera can't help it if she's photogenic. She's a beautiful cat."

"Yes, quite. She's also getting older and is starting to have urinary problems. And I think I agreed to supper with the Kehoes next week. Please tell me they don't have a slide projector."

I dropped my head and laughed. Hazey's curiosity of the trash can faded, and she trotted back to me. I patted her head. "There's no slide projector."

He sagged. "Oh, thank God."

"Because they put all their old slides onto DVDs. There are thousands of pictures of Vera. You'll be there awhile. You might want to pack an overnight bag."

He held my gaze, and suddenly I was twelve years old again wondering if falling in love felt like you were going to throw up, cry, and dance for joy all at once.

"I'm sorry, Blue."

I looked down at my dusty tennis shoes, then back up at him.

"I shouldn't have run off. I should've let you explain. I'm sorry, too." I nodded toward the woods. "Do you still want to see the Buttonwood Tree?"

His blue eyes shimmered in the sunshine as he held my gaze. "Yeah, I do. Very much so. I can take the leash if you want."

I passed Hazey's leash over to him, and we headed for the tree line. The dirt path was wide enough for two, so we walked side by side, with Hazey leading the way.

"Families can be so complicated, can't they?" I said as we walked into the woods, the welcoming shade dropping the temperature a degree or two.

"Some more than others. I can't tell you how many times I wanted to walk away from mine and never look back. Blind ambition seems to be a family trait, an ugly one at that. Success equals money, and it doesn't matter who's hurt in order to get to the top. Only money matters."

Flora's eyes drifted closed, then popped open again as if she were afraid she was going to miss out on something important if she fell asleep. "Why didn't you walk away?"

Pain skipped across his face. "I love them. I'm often embarrassed of the things they do, ashamed even, but it doesn't change the love I have for them. They're a part of me, and I'm a part of them. It's as simple—and as complicated—as that."

It truly was.

Hazey stopped to sniff a tree trunk, and I saw that Flora had lost her battle with sleep. I kissed the top of her head. "'You can't pick out the pieces you like and leave the rest. Being part of the whole thing, that's the blessing.'"

"What's that from?"

"*Tuck Everlasting.* Marlo quoted it to me not that long ago when we were talking about how people we love, our families, are still within us even long after they're gone. When she told me, I of course didn't want to hear it, and I certainly didn't want to believe it was true, but it stayed with me. She was right—she usually is. After all these years you'd think I'd have learned that by now."

"Knowing and accepting can be two vastly different things."

I knew. Oh, how I knew. "You say blind ambition is a family trait, so why don't I see it in you?"

"Early on, I realized I wasn't like the rest of my family, but I was caught in their wake, not sure how to break away from a future that had already been planned for me. But then, one summer here in Buttonwood when I was fifteen, I saw some kids teasing a local girl, and the devastated look in her eyes about tore me up. I ran them off but lost track of her until a stiff breeze blew me straight into The Rabbit Hole. There, the girl, who has the prettiest eyes I've ever seen, invited me into her private world for the afternoon. Afterward, I asked around about her and heard her story—heard her family's story, too. I knew that after all she'd been through, that if she was strong enough to walk a different path from her family, then surely I could find that strength within me, too. So I carved my own path in my ambitious family, one I hope my niece and nephew will travel as well. You see, sometimes it takes someone else to help you find another way, to help you find yourself. You were that someone for me, Blue, and I hope to be that someone for them."

His words wrapped around me like a hug, and I glanced over at him. Oh so slowly he smiled, and then I smiled. A thread of joy wound around us, binding us together, and it was as though the world ceased to exist for a moment. A wonderful, incredible moment.

"Did a breeze really blow you into The Rabbit Hole?" I asked, wondering if it was possible it was the same kind of wind that guided me on these hikes every day.

He nodded. "Strangest thing I've ever experienced."

I watched Hazey zigzag on the trail, trying to sniff everything in sight. "It doesn't sound strange to me at all. It sounds normal. This is the South after all, where there's always a touch of magic in the air."

We walked on, standing closer to each other now, our arms brushing. It was a silence filled with hope, with promise, with forgiveness and understanding.

As we approached the clearing surrounding the Buttonwood Tree, Henry looked skyward at the tree's vast canopy and said, "I've been fascinated by the legend of the tree since I first came to Buttonwood as a little boy. Mostly because Oleta warned me against believing such nonsense."

"Why am I not surprised that she doesn't believe in the Buttonwood Tree?"

He smiled. "What's that Dahl quote? 'Those who don't believe in magic will never find it.' But her warning only encouraged my fascination, so I suppose I should be grateful. The more I heard about the tree, the more I wanted to hear. I sought stories any place I could find them around town. From time to time, I play with the idea of writing a book about Southern folktales that features the Buttonwood Tree. I don't think it gets more folklorish than how a woman's grief turned her body into a tree, her determination into a crow, and her resolve to help others into the wind. But I've never gotten past chapter one."

Chill bumps swept up my arms. "Her *resolve*? Is that true? I've never heard that before."

The wind. Could it be this whole time the wind that summoned me into these woods every day had been Delphine's resolve to *help* me? Why? What was so lost that she'd spend years trying to help me find it?

"I can't quite remember who mentioned it to me. It was a long time ago. Did you know she also had a daughter? That's a little-known fact as well."

Stunned, I said, "She did? The legend talks only of her son and husband."

"She had a daughter, Celene. By all accounts I heard she

was in her late teens when tragedy struck her family." Henry stepped over bulging roots to place his hand against the tree's bark as if feeling for a pulse. "Celene missed her mother so desperately that she dug a hole beneath the tree to sleep near her."

My eyes widened. "The rabbit hole. What became of her?"

"No one I ever talked to knew."

My mind was spinning with this new information. "Do you still think about writing a folklore book?"

"Sometimes, but the other Southern folktales I've studied don't hold my attention like the Buttonwood Tree, and there's not enough material on it for a whole book."

"Maybe you could switch your focus. You could always document the advice on the buttons given to people and follow up on whether it was taken or not. There are a lot of human-interest stories held within those buttons."

He glanced up at the tree. "That's actually a good idea. But aren't you worried about Buttonwood being overrun with people seeking advice from the tree if the book is published?"

I put my hand next to his on the bark. "I'm not so worried about that. It's like you said earlier with the Dahl quote—only those who believe in magic will find the tree, and I think Delphine would approve of people seeking her help."

He tipped his head side to side, then smiled. "Then maybe I'll give writing the book another try. See where it takes me."

I was about to offer him my help when my phone rang, and I wiggled it out of my pocket hoping it was good news about Kebbie. I frowned at the readout, however, when I saw the name that popped up. "It's Shep Wheeler, the investigator for Flora's case."

The wind swirled as I answered, and Shep said, "Blue, could you meet me at the hospital at noon? There's a conference room outside the ICU, to the left of the lounge. Just come on in."

There was a command hidden in his invitation, and I didn't dare disobey. "Only me? Not Persy?"

"Just you."

"I should be able to make it if I can find someone to watch Flora—because I can't take her with me to the hospital."

"I can watch her," Henry offered. "We get on well, the two of us."

My eyebrows dipped low. Henry was great with her, but I wasn't sure I could ask that of him. Hopefully Marlo and Moe would be back by the time I needed to leave for the hospital. "What's this meeting about, Shep?"

"Finding the truth. I need your help."

Hazey nudged my leg as if sensing my distress. "I've found lots of things, Shep, but the truth has never been one of them." As soon as I said the words, my skin prickled with awareness. The restlessness I'd been dealing with eased up a little.

The truth?

The wind circled around me like it was cheering me on. Was the truth what I'd been searching for in these woods all along?

My gaze went straight to the Buttonwood Tree, always at the center of my treks through the woods, taking me from my house—both current and former—to the church.

I didn't understand how they all related to each other, but I suddenly knew that they did.

"There's a first for everything, Blue," Shep said. "I'll see you soon."

Finding the truth about what, though? Flora's case was all but closed. We knew who her mother was, and why she'd been left in the woods.

"Was Shep calling about Kebbie?" Henry asked, concern causing his forehead to furrow.

I put my phone back into my pocket. "No, he wasn't. I honestly don't know what he wants, but I'll find out soon enough. I need to get home."

What truth? The question ate at me, pushing me along the path. Flora squirmed as if sensing my adrenaline, and the tender skin between her eyebrows bunched up as she frowned in her sleep. Using the pad of my thumb, I gently rubbed away her concern, and her lips puckered in a satisfied pout as she kept sleeping.

He nodded to Flora. "I was serious about watching her. I don't mind at all. I want to help."

"I appreciate that, Henry. If Marlo's not home soon, I may have to take you up on your offer. Maybe you can come with me to the hospital and wait outside, away from all the germs. I can even hook you up with the baby sling so you can be hands-free."

He gave me a wry smile. "I can just hold her."

"You still don't trust the sling, do you? It's secure."

He looked unconvinced, and I laughed.

As we approached my house, my gaze skipped ahead to Marlo's driveway and her car parked there—she was home. I was surprised my reaction wasn't one of relief—but recognized I'd wanted to spend more time with Henry today. When I turned back toward him, my gaze caught on something shiny on my front porch. Tied to a column, balloons danced in the breeze.

IT'S A GIRL balloons.

Not only that, but the porch was covered in gifts, each dotted with a small pink bow. Hazey ran ahead to investigate, and I climbed the steps slowly, trying to take it all in. There was a basket of eggs from the Widdicombs. A stuffed animal from the Kehoes—a cat. Watercolor paper from Mrs. Tillman. A bag of marbles from the Granbees. Baby booties from Mrs. Dodd.

"No, Hazey, no. Sit," I said, my voice thick as I pulled her away from a box of produce gifted by the Dockerys. Among a dozen gift bags filled with clothes and toys, there was a stroller from Buttonwood Moms Club, a wooden sign that said I LOVE YOU TO THE MOON AND BACK from Marlo and Moe, and a colorful kite from Henry.

There were tears in my eyes when I turned to Henry. "What's all this?"

"It's a baby shower of sorts. Everyone wanted you to know that they support you and Flora. There's even talk of a fundraiser if you need help paying for a lawyer."

"Did you plan this?"

"Not me. It was Marlo." He came up a step and smiled as he cupped my face, his hand warm against my skin. "But I want you to know, Blue, that I'll do everything I can to help. I don't know what the future will bring—all I know is that I want you in mine. And I can only hope you want me in yours."

I swallowed hard. "Oleta . . ." She shouldn't have an influence on my life, but her hatred was enough to scare me away.

"I'll talk to her, Blue. She's hard and bitter, but I'm hoping underneath it all there's still a heart. Give me a chance. Please. Give *us* a chance."

I glanced away, then looked back at him. On separate steps, we stood eye to eye, nose to nose, lips to lips, with one sleepy baby between us.

LOVE IS WORTH THE RISK.

It was. It definitely was.

I whispered, "You do know how to change diapers, right?"

He laughed as he leaned in to kiss me. "I'll learn."

My heart swelled as love whirled around us, glittering like moondust.

Chapter
21

"Not too long after the bank incident and Cobb's unexplained disappearance, I woke up to an uproar in the backyard, my chickens yelling bloody murder. I thought a fox had gotten into the coop, so imagine my shock when I threw open the back door and found Twyla Bishop out there, two of my best broody hens in her arms. Lordy, I still don't know how she'd wrangled them both."

"What did you do?" the judge asked from his chair on the third-base side of the field. His five-year-old grandson was currently on the bench, awaiting his turn at bat. The judge had been trying not to fall asleep during the never-ending T-ball game when Carey Widdicomb sat her chair next to his.

"I threatened to call the law, of course. Before this happened, I'd had eggs going missing and suspected someone was stealing them. Twyla, apparently, decided that day she'd had enough of taking the eggs and went straight to their source."

"Did you call the police?"

"No, sir. I couldn't bring myself to because she looked me dead in the eye and told me she was only trying to feed her girls. A few of us around town had dropped off food and offered help any way we could, but Twyla always sent us away, saying she could take care of her own. That moment, when she told me she was trying to feed her girls, was the closest she'd ever come to asking for help, and I had the feeling it near about killed her to do so. I sent her off with eggs that morning, and the next day, my husband and I showed up at the Bishop farmhouse with a coop, feed, four hens, and a book on how to raise them. We didn't ask if Twyla wanted them—we just did it. The day after that I found a stack of molasses cookies wrapped up in a napkin on my back porch, tied with a piece of twine. Same thing happened the next weekend, and the weekend after that. Finally, I went by the farmhouse to tell Twyla she didn't have to keep thanking me—that she didn't owe me anything. Turned out it hadn't been her bringing the cookies. It had been Blue. Little eleven-year-old Blue. It was like to break my heart."

It was like to break his, too.

"I kept checking in on Twyla and the chickens, bringing by more feed in case she couldn't afford it, and eventually we became friends. I truly think I was her only one. She was an interesting, complicated, flawed woman, and I miss her." She shook her head. "Anyway, to this day Blue still brings cookies by the house once in a while. Twyla would be right proud of that girl and how she turned out. I know I am. Oh look, here's my grandbaby at bat."

The judge thought about what Boon Hardy had said about Cobb not liking to ask for help, too. Apparently it was a Bishop family trait. One he prayed hadn't been passed down to Blue.

Sarah Grace

The ICU had enforced quiet-time hours between noon and one, and again between five and six in the late afternoon. The lights were dimmed in the hallways, doors were closed, conversations were hushed, and family members were asked to wait in the visitor lounge. While the nurses spoke about how this benefited patients, I thought there was value to visitors as well. A time to step away to eat, or call friends, nap, or in my case, escape my mother's disappointed, sad gaze.

I could handle the disappointment. It was the sadness that was eating away at me like acidic guilt.

The thing of it was I understood why she wanted custody of Flora. I truly did. And if Kebbie had come to us and asked us to take in her daughter, I'd have been the first in line with my arms open wide. But Kebbie hadn't. My desire to support *Kebbie's* choice outweighed everything else. Her voice needed to be heard, even if we didn't like what she had to say.

Daddy had been subdued today, closed off and quiet. I had the feeling he didn't agree with Mama's plans to take custody of Flora, either, but was going along with whatever Mama wanted—flotsam caught in a rushing river. Of course, he was also dealing with his campaign and those dismal polling numbers. When I'd tried to bring up the topic and apologize again, Daddy had shut down the conversation with a single shake of his head.

As Mama, Daddy, and I walked through the double doors leading into the reception area, I was surprised to see Shep standing next to the doorway of a private consultation room. He held a black expanding folder in his hands and wore a solemn expression.

He straightened, came forward, and shook hands with my father. Giving me only a fleeting glance, he said, "I need to speak with all of you. The conference room is available for our use."

"Now?" Mama asked. "Shep, it's been a long morning. Can't it wait? Kebbie isn't going anywhere."

He held her gaze. "This isn't about Kebbie, ma'am."

Daddy raked a hand through his hair. "Then what's it about?"

"I'll explain soon enough." He gestured to the conference room, and Mama and Daddy exchanged worried glances before walking through the doorway.

I touched his arm—I couldn't have stopped myself from touching him if I tried. "Should I be worried?"

At the sound of fast-approaching footsteps, I turned and saw

Blue headed our way in a tizzy. Her hair was pulled up in a topknot, but loose pieces curled around her flushed face. She wore no makeup, and her eyes were bloodshot as though she'd been crying recently.

"I came as fast as I could," she said in a jumble of words. "I even took the stairs because the elevator was taking so dang long. Did I miss anything? Sorry I'm late. I hate being late."

"No worries. You're not late," Shep said. "We haven't started yet. Let's go in and get this all sorted out."

He put his hand on my back, guiding me, but it seemed to me he let his fingers linger there longer than necessary. As soon as Blue and I walked into the small room, Mama's eyes darkened like storm clouds. Blue sat across from Daddy, and I sat next to her, facing Mama's disappointed sadness straight on.

Shep closed the door behind him and stood at the head of the table. He opened the file folder and shuffled through papers.

"Hello, Blue," Daddy said in the growing silence, ever polite. "I didn't expect to see you here today."

"That makes two of us, Mayor Jud," she said. Her gaze shifted to Mama. "Hello, Miss Ginny."

"Hello," Mama said with no warmth whatsoever. Her thunderous look swung to Shep. "Is this meeting about Flora? Did Sarah Grace sweet-talk you into mediating? I'm not changing my mind about seeking custody. I've already contacted the court for an emergency hearing." Her chin lifted with strong-minded defiance.

Blue's soft gasp broke my heart, but when I glanced at her, I was proud to see fortitude shining in her amber eyes. She sat straight and her voice was loud and strong when she said, "I'm real sorry to hear that, Miss Ginny, but you should know I'm not letting Flora go without a fight."

"I wouldn't expect anything less." Mama sounded resigned more than anything else. "Since you're a Bishop."

"Ginny," Daddy said, his voice tight, stretched so thin it was like to snap in two.

Blue smiled. *Smiled.* I thought for a moment she'd done lost her mind, but her tone was clear, even, and steady when she said, "That's right. I am a Bishop. Mine was an imperfect family, but a good family full of love for each other, and that's nothing to be ashamed of."

Shep interrupted their stare down by saying, "Something unexpected came up in the investigation of Flora's case, and I need to explore the matter further to see if it merits a separate criminal investigation." He spread several pieces of paper on the table and stared at me as though looking straight into my soul. "Sarah Grace, as you know your DNA was taken to aid in Flora's case, as was Blue's."

"What?" Mama rocketed out of her chair. "What on God's green earth possessed you to give your DNA to the police, Sarah Grace?"

For a moment, I wanted to answer pizza with extra pepperoni simply to break the suffocating tension, but the fear on her face stopped me. "Why wouldn't I?"

Daddy tugged Mama back into her seat, and I swore I heard him whisper, "Pandora's box," leading me to recall the conversation we'd had at the Bishop farmhouse the day I decided to buy it.

Truth be told, Sarah Grace, you need this house more than it needs you. There's a lot to be learned here once you start peeling back the layers. Valuable lessons. But it could also be a Pandora's box you ultimately wish you'd kept closed. Are you sure you're ready to take that risk?

Suddenly I had the uneasy feeling he hadn't been talking about the house at all.

Shep went on, still talking directly to me. "When I was discussing the DNA findings with Blue yesterday, there was speculation that her test had been mixed up with yours, because some of the results didn't make sense."

Blue reached for my hand, and when I looked over at her, confusion sparkled in her eyes.

Mama stood up again. "Are we obligated to stay here?"

"No, ma'am," Shep said. "But one way or another, this matter isn't going away. Answers are needed, and there's more to this story to be told."

"Let's go, Jud." Mama pulled at his elbow.

Daddy clasped his hands on top of the table and shook his head. "No. We knew this day might come. I never wanted to keep it quiet. We should've been more transp—"

Mama held up a finger. "So help me if you say the word *transparent*."

My heart hammered. "Mama, please sit down and tell me what's going on."

She sat, but she didn't say anything. Fat tears rolled down her cheeks.

Taking a deep breath, Daddy said, "Sarah Grace, the truth of the matter, what that test shows, is that I'm not your biological father. Your daddy is Mac Bishop. When he and your mama were younger, they had been dating secretly, since her parents didn't approve of him. They were planning to be married, but he passed away before that could happen. I always promised him I'd take care of your mama if something happened to him while he was in the military . . . so I asked her to marry me. I adopted you at your birth, and I tried to raise you up the way Mac would've. I definitely know I love you as much as he did, but man alive, I wish to God above that you could've met him. He was a hell of a good man."

Mama's face hardened. "If he was so good, he wouldn't have gotten himself killed by picking a fight, would he? He'd promised me he wouldn't fight, promised me he wanted better for himself, but he just couldn't help himself, could he? *Bishops*," she muttered before her shoulders started shaking from silent sobs.

The words echoed around the small room, becoming fainter and fainter as the pulse in my ears became louder and louder. My body grew heavy, thick, like I'd gone completely numb from head to toe. I didn't know what to think. What to feel.

I heard Blue's breath hitch as she fought not to cry. "He didn't pick the fight. He was defending a woman who was being assaulted. When Mac died, the army did a death investigation. I just found the official report yesterday in a folder of old papers. He died with honor."

At this news, Mama closed her eyes tightly and folded into herself as if trying to block any more pain. Mascara streaked her face as she fell apart.

How many times had she warned me to keep away from the Bishops? To do better. Be better. Now it all made sense. She'd been trying to protect me . . . from myself.

Bishops can't stay out of trouble. It's in their blood.

I stared at her as if I didn't even know who she was. She'd been so angry with me, giving me the silent treatment, over the revelation of my secrets, yet she'd been keeping her own much bigger ones. It was hypocritical at best and damned hurtful now that I knew the truth.

"I had a feeling there was more to that story," Daddy said. "Mac only fought in self-defense or in defense of someone else. He hated people who picked on others just because they were bigger, stronger. He embodied the saying about how strong people stand up for themselves, but stronger people stand up for others. Why didn't Twyla or Cobb say what really happened?"

Blue lifted one shoulder in a shrug. "We'll likely never know."

The room was starting to spin, turning round and round with my thoughts. Feeling queasy, I took deep breaths and fought the urge to run.

Daddy's gaze swung to Shep. "There's nothing criminal about what happened between Ginny and Mac. I legally adopted Sarah Grace. I don't know why you gathered us together like this, when you could've waited. We're a family in crisis, and you've only added to our emotional load."

Shep's eyebrows went up. "I understand you're upset, Jud, but it's best to remember who truly bears responsibility for keeping Sarah Grace in the dark. We might not be here now if the truth had always been spoken. The fact remains this meeting couldn't wait. As I said, there's more to this story, and it involves Blue."

"Me?" She sniffled loudly. "How?"

His tone softened. "Your DNA test."

"Do I need to redo it since my test was mixed up with Sarah Grace's?"

"No, Blue. There was no mix-up at the lab."

"How can you say that after all this?" She gestured around the table.

He said, "I know it wasn't mixed up because I dropped off Sarah Grace's test at the lab late on Sunday, and it wasn't yet completed yesterday morning. And this is where the criminal element I talked about comes into play. Because those results I shared in your living room *were* yours."

Blue

"Impossible," I said, shaking my head. "There's been some kind of mistake."

"All the tests are here before me. Yours, Sarah Grace's—which was completed this morning—Persy's, Kebbie's, Flora's."

I kept shaking my head, but as if it had sneaked into the hospital and slid under the door, I could feel the wind's relief just the same as I had yesterday, when it rushed down the chimney and wrapped around me.

Relief at the truth finally being revealed.

The truth of who I was.

"Your test is nearly identical to Sarah Grace's. Twyla and Cobb are your grandparents. Persy is your aunt. Flora is your first cousin once removed."

Everyone's eyes were on me as if seeing me for the first time—even Ginny's. And for once, she wasn't looking at me with disdain.

"How can that be?" I asked.

Compassion was written all over Shep's face, in the softness of his eyes, the tilt of his jaw. "Blue, your test is so similar to Sarah Grace's because she's your sister. Your parents are Mac and Ginny."

There was dead silence in the room. It yawned and stretched and stole all the air.

I put my hands to my face as I tried to breathe, even as the wind wrapped its arms around me, trying to console.

"No. Im-impossible," Ginny stammered. "What kind of cruel joke are you playing, Shep?"

"The DNA tests don't lie," he said to her. "Sarah Grace and Blue share the same parents. They're full sisters. There are no records of an adoption or guardianship on file for Blue, and she didn't even have a birth certificate until she was five. I need to know how she came to live with the Bishops. Did you ask them to raise her? Did Mac?"

Ginny's face had drained of all color. I had her chin, I realized. *My God, I had her chin.* A sob caught in my throat, and I couldn't take a deep breath.

I felt a hand on my back, rubbing it, much like I soothed Flora. Sarah Grace.

My *sister.*

"I think it's time to leave." Jud slid his chair away from the table. "This conversation has gone on long enough."

Undeterred, Shep asked, "Miss Ginny, do you deny having

a baby in December of 1990?" He glanced at the paperwork. "December eleventh?"

She opened her mouth, and it hung open as her gaze suddenly swung to me. I wasn't sure what it was I saw in her widening eyes. Horror? Disbelief? A mixture of the two? "I—Oh. Oh my God. She told me you'd *died*. She told me you *died* and that she buried you. Why? Why would she do that? I chose love. A perfect family was mine! I shouldn't have been cursed!"

She *chose love*. The phrase nagged and the wind whirled around me, circling round, like I was suddenly caught up in a funnel cloud. Everything spun, all the words and emotions and feelings I'd had since finding Flora—she'd been the key to unlocking the truth. To righting a wrong. Without her, I would've never known the truth. *My* truth.

"'A perfect family is yours. Choose love,'" I said. "That's what the button says, doesn't it?"

Ginny's face crumpled. "You have the button? She told me she'd buried it with you."

"I have it." My hands were shaking, and I pressed them together. "I found it yesterday, too, in the same box as Mac's papers, a memory box that Twyla had put together for me a long time ago. The button was hidden in the brim of my baby hat."

She bent in half as if the truth had broken her. Jud put his arm around her, pulling her close. He kept looking between me and Ginny like he couldn't believe his eyes.

"Who?" Shep asked. "Who are you talking about? Who told you Blue had died? Twyla?"

"No." It hurt to speak the name, because I knew it was going to cause him pain. "It was Mary Eliza."

Ginny's head came up, her face ravaged with emotion, and she nodded before she turned to Shep. "Your mother stole my baby."

In my head, I could hear Mary Eliza's rantings.

The wind, the wind! The wind knows! Blue is trouble.

Trouble, trouble. The wind, the wind! Took the baby. Trouble! Took the baby! The wind knows! Atone, atone!

That night in her room at Magnolia Breeze, she hadn't been accusing me of stealing Flora—she'd been confessing to taking *me.* The wind had been trying to get her to tell the truth before she took it to the grave.

And with this final piece of the puzzle, suddenly I knew deep in my soul that I'd finally found what I'd been looking for my whole life long.

The thing with no name was *me.*

I'd simply never realized it, because I hadn't known I'd been lost.

Chapter
22

Blue

As I walked up my front walkway after time spent at the hospital, the wind blew about, but there were no messages in it. No summons. No nudging to action.

All lost things in my world had been found.

I opened the front door to the heady aroma of garlic, onions, and spicy sausage and saw Marlo in the kitchen, stirring a pot on the stove.

Henry was lying on the couch, reading *The Wind in the Willows* to Flora. He glanced up when I came in and gave me a sweet smile before going back to the book to finish his sentence. He was doing the voice of Badger exactly like Moe, and a lump formed in my throat as my gaze swung to Marlo.

Moe would live on in Henry. And, in turn, Flora. He'd live on in every child that he'd read to in The Rabbit Hole over the years. Did she see it? His influence at work? His legacy?

She watched me like she knew exactly what I was thinking, but didn't comment on it. Instead, compassion lit up the golden flecks in her eyes as she tipped her head to the side and said, "I know you're probably not hungry, but you should eat something. You've had a day of it. I've made some red beans and rice, one of your favorites. It's almost ready. Another fifteen minutes or so."

A day of it was putting it mildly, but it was nothing like what Kebbie was going through. My stomach immediately declined the offer, but I didn't want to disappoint Marlo, so I said, "Thanks. I can try to eat a little something."

Outside, I saw Persy and Moe playing fetch with Hazey. Earlier, I'd called Persy to let her know what was happening, and she'd met me at the hospital for moral support. While I spoke with a new investigator called in to take over for Shep, Persy sat with Kebbie for a while, sharing the whole shocking tale, even though there was no sign she'd heard a word of it. And when it seemed like I was going to be at the hospital for quite a while longer, Persy had decided to head on home to break the news to everyone else.

I dropped my bag, quickly washed my hands, and walked over to Henry. He had set the book on the coffee table and was already standing up to hand Flora over to me. I took her, carefully holding her head as I brought her to my chest and breathed in the scent of her, resting my cheek on her head. "How's she been?"

"A little fussy, but reading to her has calmed her down some. How're you?" he asked, his troubled gaze sweeping over me as if I'd been physically injured by today's revelations.

The longer I spent turning over in my mind what had happened, the more I began to think maybe the truth would be the start of healing. For a lot of us. "I'm not sure. It's all a little too new to sort out my feelings yet. I feel like I'm operating on autopilot for the most part."

Marlo came to stand next to me. She put her arm around my shoulders, and I leaned into her. She'd been my foundation for so long that I instinctively counted on her for comfort—and she always seemed to know when I needed it most.

Henry stuck his hands in his pockets. "Looks like you're in the best hands now. I should probably get going to the bookshop, unless you need me to stay. Just say the word."

He hadn't had to stay at all—Marlo had been here the whole time. It meant a lot that he'd kept the bookshop closed half the day to be here for me. "Why don't you come back after closing time? I'm sure there'll be plenty of leftovers, and I wouldn't mind if you read a little bit of *The Wind in the Willows* to me, too."

He smiled and said, "Sounds like a good plan to me." He kissed Marlo's cheek, then mine, then the top of Flora's head.

When the door closed behind him, Marlo looked at me with her eyebrow raised.

As a blush settled in my cheeks, I said, "If I didn't know better, I'd say you planned this all along. Henry and me."

Grinning, her eyes widened, flaring dramatically, and she pressed her hands to her chest. "Me? Why would you think such a thing?"

I shook my head and sat on the sofa with Flora, watching her as she pushed her tongue against her lips. I hated the thought that I might have to hand her over to the Landreneaus, but my gut twisted painfully at the thought of someone *stealing* her away.

"A police officer came by to pick up the button you had by the sink," Marlo said, easing herself down on the cushion next to mine. She put her arm around my shoulders.

"It's evidence now, but I highly doubt it'll ever be used at a trial. Mary Eliza is in no condition to talk, never mind undergo questioning."

And I believed she said all she'd intended to the other night. *Atone.*

I added, "I hope Ginny eventually gets the button back. It's rightfully hers. I know I'd want it back."

I held Flora closely as I told Marlo the whole story. How, a few months after Mac had headed off to boot camp, Ginny discovered she was pregnant. She and Mac already had plans to get married the next summer and leave Buttonwood, but she started resenting that he was gone and that she had to deal with the pregnancy alone. She went to the Buttonwood Tree for advice. *A perfect family is yours. Choose love.* So Ginny did. She chose love. She also chose to keep the pregnancy a secret for as long as possible, since, well, Mac was a Bishop.

"Makes sense since Bishops were the enemy of the Cabots," Marlo said. "It's amazing to me that Ginny was brave enough to *choose love* with Mac. She had to have known the stir marrying him would cause in her family since Cobb pretty much stole the farmhouse."

By choosing love, she had risked the wrath of her family. She had risked all, truly, and I could only admire her for the decision. To stand for what she believed in, no matter the cost. To shine in her own light.

"Ginny was due with me in early February, so she and Mac moved up wedding plans to January, when he next had leave, so they'd be married before I arrived. She hoped her family would forgive her and learn to love Mac as she did."

"February? But your birthday is in December."

Flora grabbed my finger and held on tightly. "The week I was born, Ginny hadn't been feeling well for a few days but hadn't thought anything of it. She was in church when her water broke. She'd rushed to the restroom—and that's where Mary Eliza found her sobbing. The whole story came out. Ginny begged Mary Eliza not to say anything—and showed her the Buttonwood Tree button. Mary Eliza took Ginny to the parsonage to rest, change, and try to talk her into going to the hospital. But to both their surprise, I was already well on my way."

"You do like to be early," Marlo pointed out. "I guess Flora gets that from you."

"Maybe so."

I continued on, telling Marlo how I'd been born right there in the parsonage. I'd been tiny, but Mary Eliza assured Ginny that I would be okay. She'd wrapped me in a pink blanket, put a hat on me that she took from a yarn basket next to the bed, and placed me in Ginny's arms. Mary Eliza had urged Ginny to sleep while she cleaned everything up—and that when she woke up, they would come up with a plan to tell the Cabots what happened. Ginny trusted her, so she slept. She wasn't sure how long. An hour, two at the most.

"When Ginny woke up, her arms were empty. Mary Eliza told her that I had passed away, and that I must've been too little after all. She said she'd buried me in the church graveyard and that she was just heading out to get Ginny's parents—and for her not to worry about telling them what happened. Because even though they'd be disappointed with her sinful behavior, she was sure they'd forgive her and help her to lead a more faithful life from there on out."

Marlo shook her head and *tsk*ed. "Playing on Ginny's emotions and fears like that—she knew Ginny would stop her from notifying her parents."

"Exactly. And she did stop her. Mary Eliza took Ginny home, and as far as her parents knew, she'd come down with a stomach flu. Ginny did her best to hide her grief and carry on."

"Had Mary Eliza run you to the farmhouse while Ginny slept?"

Flora yawned and stretched her hands over her head. "I don't know. There are some parts to the story we'll never know. I don't know if Mary Eliza talked to Twyla and told her I was a Bishop, or if she simply left me on the porch with my hat and button for someone to find. All I know is what Twyla has told me my whole life. I was tiny and blue when I arrived in her world."

"It's a blessed miracle you survived."

"I think so, too. Ginny said Mac was as devastated as she was by the news of what had happened. When he came home on leave at the end of January, they both agreed to go back to their original summer wedding plans, to give themselves some time to grieve. But little did they know that before he went back to Fort Jackson, Sarah Grace had been conceived. And then the unthinkable happened when Mac died a couple of months later."

"Lordy, Lordy. I can hardly believe what all I've heard to-day."

"That makes two of us." Flora let out a displeased bleat, and I put her against my shoulder and rubbed her back. "It's all so tragic."

"Endlessly tragic. How's Persy taking the news?"

I glanced out the window and saw her chasing Hazey around the yard, trying to get a stick out of her mouth. "I don't think the news was as shocking to her as it's been to others, because she already experienced the initial surprise when Shep was here yesterday, telling us about the DNA tests. Now it's more about accepting."

"For both of you."

I thought about the devastation I'd seen on Sarah Grace's face. Ginny's. Jud's. Even Shep's. After all, it was his mama who was at the heart of this tragedy. "Not just us."

"What's all this mean for you and our little flower?"

"I'm not sure. Ginny mentioned fighting for custody, so I need to get a lawyer as soon as possible, because I'm not handing her over willingly."

"You have a lot of people wanting to help you, Blue. You don't need to be fighting alone."

I closed my eyes against the memories of my family not reaching out to the community when they needed help the most. When I opened my eyes, I glanced around at all the presents that had been piled onto my porch earlier but were now scattered about the room. "I'll take—and be grateful for—all the help I can get, Marlo. And I never did thank you for all this," I said, swallowing hard as I motioned toward the gifts.

She waved a hand of dismissal. "I didn't do anything. This is all you, Blue honey. People want you to know they support you.

We think Kebbie picked the best mama for Flora that there is. Did you see her at all? Kebbie? While you were at the hospital? Persy didn't say much when she got home, and I didn't want to push."

My throat was thick as I said, "I visited with her for a little while. She looks so . . . broken. There are so many wires and tubes that she's all but lost in that hospital bed."

"Poor, sweet girl." She made a soft clucking noise of sympathy. "I remember the first time she came into the bookshop after her mama and daddy died in that plane crash. I gave her a hug, and she didn't let go for a good hour. She came by every single day for a month, and I'd sit with her on the couch, my arm around her much like it is with you right now, and I'd read to her. We went through the whole Harry Potter series in no time flat. There's no better escape from real life than into a book."

"And there's no better comfort than being in your arms." Kebbie's immense grief had always floated around her like a cloud, except when she was with Marlo. "It's like Sarah Grace said. Your hugs make everything seem right in the world. They're a gift you share freely, and I know I'm grateful for them, and I imagine Kebbie is, too. You've helped so many of us. All your little rabbits," I said, smiling.

"All my little rabbits," she murmured, then tightened her arm around me.

Our heads came up at a knock on the door, and I passed Flora to Marlo and stood up to look out the window. "It's Shep."

I pulled open the door. He'd changed out of his work clothes and into jeans and a tee, but his green eyes still held the same haunted looked from earlier. "Shep? Something wrong? Is it Kebbie?" I held my breath as I waited for the answer.

"No, no. She's holding steady." He dragged a hand down his face, and added, "I don't suppose you've seen Sarah Grace?"

"Not since I left the hospital. Why?"

"I've been looking for her. Jud said she went out for air to gather her thoughts, and an hour later she still hasn't come back. I've looked at her house, her office, the park, the trail. No sign of her. I want to make sure she's all right. I thought she might be here."

Have you ever felt a connection to a place that you don't quite understand? It's just this feeling, deep inside, that you're meant to be there?

I debated whether to tell Shep to look at the farmhouse, wondering whether she simply needed some time alone, before deciding to take the risk. "She's not, but I have a feeling I know where she could be. You might want to take Hazey with you. A little Hazey therapy can only help."

Minutes later, he drove off, and I hoped I hadn't made the wrong choice in sending him to the farmhouse. But I had the feeling that Shep was who Sarah Grace needed most right now.

Sarah Grace

Welcome home.

The house had said that to me the first time I'd come here, and it had said it to me again today.

It had known the truth all along, but as I knew, houses were the best secret keepers. They kept all skeletons in the closet until those secrets were exposed by others.

The sun beat at my back as I leaned as much weight as possible into the screwdriver and turned my wrist. When the screwdriver spun but the screw didn't, I stepped back. The screw was stripped.

Great. Fantastic.

A wasp buzzed past my ear, and I watched as it disappeared underneath the kitchen windowsill.

"Don't get comfortable," I told it. "You'll be evicted soon enough."

I stepped back to study the screen door that hung askew at the back of the farmhouse. I'd thought the screw just needed tightening, but the issue went deeper. I wiggled the hinge plate, feeling how much it gave way. One good tug, and I'd have it in my hand.

Wiping my forehead, I walked around to the front of the house for more supplies from my truck, taking note of all the changes I wanted to make. I'd originally wanted to take the house back to its original footprint, but the more time I spent here, the more I wanted to either fix what already existed—or add to it. Keep the first-floor addition but turn it into a half bath. Add more windows. In my head, I could see the yard take shape. There'd be a new patio, a flower and vegetable garden—and the return of a functioning chicken coop. There was nothing quite like fresh eggs.

I wasn't sure how this old farmhouse had recognized me as a Bishop, but now that the truth was out, the house was quite talkative, assigning blame for every dent or blemish. I listened carefully, trying to soak in a history I should've already known. A history I'd been denied.

Arms laden with supplies, I returned to the back door. I used a piece of railing that had broken off the front porch to level the door, and then I pried the hinge from the door frame, but kept it attached to the door, where it still held tight.

I was drilling into the hole, widening it, when I heard barking. I dropped my hand and listened.

"Sarah Grace?"

"Back here," I called, jumping off the rickety steps. I walked around the side of the house and saw Shep coming toward me with Hazey. As soon as she spotted me, she whimpered with excitement and bolted forward, stretching the leash to its limits. I braced myself for impact as she jumped and licked my face, and though I should've corrected the behavior, there was plenty of time to practice her manners later. I held on to her for a good, long while and finally turned toward Shep.

"Don't shoot," he said with a smile, hands in the air.

I hadn't even realized I still held the drill gun. "Don't worry. I have lousy aim, remember?"

"I went by Blue's looking for you, and she suspected this is where I'd find you. She thought you might be in need of a little Hazey therapy, too."

Blue. My *sister*.

As we walked back to the rear steps, Hazey walked around the yard, sniffing every weed. The house was curious about the newcomer, its only pets having been the mice in the walls and the raccoons in the attic.

I held back a wince at the raccoon news.

"Should you be here?" I asked, climbing the steps to finish the door project. "With me?" I jammed the drill bit into the second hinge hole and squeezed the trigger.

He waited until I'd finished before saying, "I'm off the case. Conflict of interest is an understatement."

I put down the drill and picked up a hammer. I stuck a dowel into the hole and pounded it in. I probably should've coated the dowel in glue first, but I hadn't had any in the truck, so this had to do.

"How're you doing?" he asked. "You had quite a sucker punch today."

That was also an understatement. I pounded a second dowel into the bottom hole, the hammer strikes so forceful I felt the reverberations in my shoulders.

He laughed as he sat on the lower step. "I guess that answers my question. You need any help?"

"Nope."

Hazey barked at something in the tall grass, and I was certain I didn't want to know what it was. Shep reeled her in a little bit as I maneuvered the hinge plate over the holes in the door frame. I used a new screw to marry the two, then repeated the process for the second hinge hole.

The shiny screws looked out of place against the old wood and the rusty hinge plate, but given time they'd weather and no one would ever know they were new and hadn't been here all along.

If Shep was wondering why I was wasting my time trying to fix a screen door that would undoubtedly be dumpster bound in a few weeks, he didn't say. The whole door frame was rotted and needed to be replaced, but I couldn't take seeing this door hanging for one more minute.

I stepped down and let the screen door close, and while there was still a gap between the door and the frame, it was no longer hanging loose. "This was supposed to be a simple project. Just tighten a couple of screws, but it didn't quite turn out that way."

"Sometimes what looks simple on the surface turns out to be quite complicated underneath."

I knew he wasn't talking about the hinge. "Like?"

He shrugged. "Lots of things. Like falling in love. Like investigating the case of an abandoned baby. Like forgiveness."

I moved the hammer aside and sat next to him. My shirt stuck to my back, and my hair was matted to my head. I was going to have to run home to shower before going back to the hospital. "My mother's been texting and calling. My father, too. I know I should answer, but I just can't right now. How're you? You had quite a sucker punch today, too," I said, nudging him with my shoulder.

Hazey ran over, her butt swaying with happiness. I patted her neck; then she was off again to investigate a patch of clover.

Shep stared at his hands. "Actually, it didn't feel like a sucker punch. More like a gentle shove. As I stood in that room hearing the details, all I could think about was how I wasn't shocked by what was being said. Not even a little bit. My mother is more than capable of such a despicable, heartless act."

I reached over, took hold of his hands. Our fingers intertwined. I'd broken a nail at some point today, and his thumb kept running over the break, as if trying to heal it by touch alone.

The sun was merciless in its assault, and I made a mental note to add a sunporch to my plans. "Do you think she thought she was doing the right thing? What she felt was best for Blue? For my mother?"

"Undoubtedly. She lived by a twisted moral code. It was sinful for a young woman from a good family to take up with the town ne'er-do-well and get pregnant out of wedlock, but it was perfectly fine to kidnap a baby and tell the mother the child had died."

I blamed the heat on why I found what he'd said amusing. "*Ne'er-do-well*?"

He glanced over at me, and I smiled.

Dropping his head down, he let out a huff of laughter. Then he put his arm around me and pulled me in close to him.

"You once told me you felt like you could be yourself around Blue and couldn't understand why. Do you think deep down you sensed a connection to her? Kind of like how you've always felt a connection to this house?"

Shep was one of the few who knew exactly how special my relationship to houses was. That my house whisperer nickname wasn't all in fun. When I first told him how I could hear what houses had to say, he said only that he'd known from the moment he met me that I was extraordinary.

I used to tease him about that once in a while when he'd question my judgment about something mundane, like putting ketchup on a hot dog. "Hush now. I'm *extraordinary*."

"Maybe so." I took a big breath. "Part of me understands my mama's thinking by keeping my father a secret. She wanted to protect herself. And me. But the other part of me is just so angry about it. I feel a part of me was stolen as well, but by my own mother, not yours."

"I get that, but do you think knowing Mac is your father would've changed who you are now?"

I looked deep inside, to who I truly was. The woman who loved to run, to get her hands dirty, who admired the delicate intricacies of her grandmother's tatted lace. I thought of the influence my daddy had on me, especially my love of real estate and nature.

"Probably not, but I missed out on knowing the Bishops. Twyla Bishop is my grandmother! I won't ever have her teaching me how to make cookies. I'll never do word puzzles with Cobb. I'll never play marbles with Ty or fish with Wade. And Mac . . . even though I feel like I kind of know him, thanks to my daddy, I've never even seen a picture of him. I know the Bishops had their issues—I'm not trying to revise history. But I should've been a part of that history, the good *and* the bad. I know I should just accept what's happened, because there's no changing it, but it seems impossible, and I'm mad about it. I can't pretend otherwise. I refuse to pretend otherwise."

He kissed my temple. "Give yourself time, Sarah Grace. No one's expecting you to put on a happy face and pretend your life wasn't changed forever today. And you're right—there's no changing all those things, but you still have Blue. She's your connection to all those people, just like you're her connection to the Cabots. You have each other to lean on and to learn from."

"I always did want a sibling," I said after a long moment. Back in high school when Blue took the blame for the fire, I had no idea that it had been my older sister looking out for me. Part of me wanted to believe, deep down, that she'd somehow known, and I liked the idea so much that I allowed myself to believe it true.

I swatted away a mosquito and said, "I should get going. I need to get back to the hospital, not that I'm particularly looking forward to facing my mama." *Forgiveness*, Shep had said earlier. There was a lot of it needed right now, but I found my-self struggling with the concept at the moment.

"Do you want me to keep Hazey for you? Or should I take her back to Blue's?"

With all my might, I wished she could come to the hospital with me. "Could you take her home with you? Blue's already done so much, and I imagine she might want a quiet night."

"I'm happy to. It'll be good to have the company."

I didn't particularly want to be alone tonight, either. "Do you want me to bring a pizza by when I pick her up?"

His gaze softened. "Yeah. I'd like that. Extra pepperoni, of course."

I allowed myself to lean into him for a good long moment before I stood up. "I'll text when I leave the hospital."

He called for Hazey, I gathered up all my tools, and soon we were walking side by side toward the front of the house, where Shep's truck was parked behind mine on the gravel drive. After I'd put all my supplies away, I looked back at the house.

"What is it?" Shep said, following my gaze. "You see some-thing?"

I nodded. "I'm going to talk to Blue about tearing up our contract."

"You're serious? You don't want to buy the house anymore?"

"Oh, I want it more than ever. You asked me what I see . . . I see white paint with black trim. I see ferns hanging from the front porch and planter boxes spilling over with color. I see a stone walkway to the backyard. A swing set. A tree house. A chicken coop. Another dog for Hazey to play with. A baby. Or two. Or three. I see love and happiness. I see *home*." I glanced over at him, following my heart to what I wanted most. "The contract with Blue is with Sweet Home. I want it to be in my name. Our names, you and me. I want this house for us. Because if home is where the heart is, it wouldn't be home without you."

As I waited for his response, all my hopes and dreams hung between us, sparkling like silvery stars in the night sky.

When he pulled me against his chest, heart to heart, I knew all would eventually be okay in my world. And as he kissed me, I heard the house cheering in the background.

Chapter
23

"Excellent choices, Judge Quimby," Josephine Pease said in low tones as she stepped up next to him in the nonfiction section of the Buttonwood Library.

He had Rick Bragg's latest tucked into the crook of his elbow and was reading the dust jacket of an Alexander Hamilton biography.

Miss Jo had been running the library for years and spent so much time there that even on her days off she carried with her the smell of old books, like the scent had burrowed into her skin. Her name badge hung from a lanyard and swung side to side when she held out another book. "Might I suggest this one as well?"

He lifted an eyebrow as he took the book from her outstretched hand. "I'm a bit above the reading level, don't you think?"

"Children's books aren't only for children. There are lessons to be learned for all."

"And what does"—he adjusted his reading glasses—"*Poppy Kay Hoppy Finds a Friend* need to teach me?"

Written and Illustrated by Blue Bishop. He stared a moment at the book's cover and felt a surge of pride at her accomplishment.

"Did you happen to see Blue reading to the children at the Buttonwood Festival?"

"No, I didn't," he said, uncaring whether his exasperation

came out in his tone. Why did everyone in this town feel the need to voice their opinions of Blue Bishop?

Miss Jo narrowed her eyes as if he were a naughty child who'd just ripped a page from a book. Properly chastised, he sighed and said, "What did I miss?"

"I have to admit I wasn't sure Blue was the best choice to represent The Rabbit Hole, being that she's a Bishop, but especially considering the gossip going around at the time. It took me only a good minute to come to my senses. In no time flat Blue was surrounded by littles, their small faces completely enraptured as she read book after book. The kids had started out a good distance from her chair on the lawn but slowly crept right on up to her feet."

The judge eyed the eight-hundred-page Hamilton biography and suspected he could finish the tome by the time Miss Jo finished what she needed to tell him.

"The last book Blue read that afternoon before the scene with Oleta Blackstock was this one," she said, tapping the book he held. "The story is about Poppy Kay, a shy, lonely rabbit who simply wants to find a friend to play with. She's hesitant to talk to others, not only because of her shyness, but because she's different. She doesn't look like other rabbits."

"How so?" he asked, curious despite himself.

"She's blue, for one," Miss Jo said, nodding to the cover. "Her whole family is, which sets them apart from others—and not in a good way—but unlike her family, she has overly long lop ears. She feels like she doesn't fit in. Not with her family, not anywhere."

Clever, clever Blue, the judge thought. "How does she end up finding a friend?"

"You'll have to read the story to find out," Miss Jo said with a smile. "And take some time studying the illustrations. The emotion Blue captures in her drawings is inimitable. Truly special."

He stifled a sigh and added the book to the pile in his arms.

She gripped her name badge, swinging it to and fro. "I learned a hard, painful lesson this past weekend about judging others."

"Sometimes the hard lessons are the most valuable."

"Yes, indeed. I'm a bit ashamed that it took me so long to see in Blue what the children saw straightaway. No offense to your profession, but don't you agree that little ones are the best judges of character?"

He glanced at the blue rabbit on the book cover, the sadness in her eyes cutting to his soul. "No doubt."

Sarah Grace

The next morning I woke early to make sure I could go running. I had a lot of pent-up energy and emotion to jog off, and I needed to do it before visiting hours at the hospital.

The sky was streaked with pink as the sun rose, and Hazey loped alongside me as if she'd been doing it her whole life long. Other than Shep, I couldn't think of a better running partner.

Shep.

It amazed me how easy it was to be with him—I'd forgotten the comfort that came with true, pure love. It was as though our hearts had recognized each other as old long-lost friends and picked up where we left off. We'd decided to let the past rest in peace to focus on our future together. It had been hard to leave him last night, to go home to my big, empty house, when I'd wanted more than anything to stay. But I'd had the feeling that if I stayed, I'd never leave again.

Which, I was starting to think, wouldn't be such a bad thing. Let people talk. I loved him—I'd always loved him—and I didn't care who knew it.

I was halfway through the park when I spotted my mama in the distance, walking toward me with steady determination.

She had swapped her designer pumps for slip-on skimmers, which were part loafer, part tennis shoe, and had on knee-length blue cotton shorts and a short-sleeve blouse.

I felt a surge of anger at seeing her and debated whether to turn around, since I didn't have the energy to fight with her, not now. Not when I'd just found a peaceful foothold in this mixed-up world of mine. But when she called out my name, I simply didn't have the heart to turn my back on her.

I slowed to a stop, and Hazey circled back to me in confusion. I patted her back and told her to sit as Mama approached.

As she neared, Mama lifted her sunglasses atop her head, and I saw she'd been crying. Her eyes were puffy and bloodshot, and she wore little makeup to cover her emotions. "I went by your house late last night, but you weren't home, so I thought I might find you out here this morning. Can we talk, Sarah Grace?"

I shouldn't have been surprised to see her. She'd tried many times to talk to me at the hospital last night, but I'd cut her off at every turn, wanting—needing—time to work through my emotions.

I still wasn't sure I was ready to talk about everything that had happened, but I couldn't keep putting off the inevitable. "I was at Shep's until late, and I'm not sure we can talk without fighting. I don't want to argue with you."

Hazey licked her hand, and Mama's eyes flew open wide in surprise before she tentatively petted Hazey's head. "I know you're angry . . ."

I looked away from her, across the grassy field still dented from the carnival rides that had been set up last weekend. In time, the ruts would fill in and no one would ever know the damage that had been done.

Time had a way of healing almost everything, and I thought it best to give Mama and me time to let things settle a bit before tearing down our walls to expose all our damage.

"When Mac died, I was so angry with him for fighting, for getting himself killed. I blamed him for ruining our perfect family, because it was the only way I could get through my grief. I tried everything I could to break my curse, going overboard with trying to find perfection. I'm mad at myself. I failed Mac. I failed you. I failed Kebbie. Goodness, how I failed Kebbie," she said, her voice strained. "I'm sorry. I'm so sorry, Sarah Grace."

A perfect family is yours. Mama had tried so hard to make her life with Daddy and me as perfect as it could be. But her attempts had been doomed to failure, because that button hadn't been meant for the three of us. It had been meant for Mama, Mac, and Blue.

This morning I'd woken up wondering if she'd even been cursed by the Buttonwood Tree, as she'd always believed, because technically, she'd followed the tree's advice. In light of everything that had been revealed, it seemed to me she'd cursed *herself* by not forgiving Mac for breaking her heart. Every decision she made from that point on had led us to where we—Mama, Kebbie, and I—were today.

"Do you think you'll ever be able to forgive me?" she asked.

She stood before me with a look of remorse on her face, pain in her blue eyes, and the air was chokingly thick with significance. Our broken pieces hung in the balance between us. We could put them back together or let them be taken away with the leaves blowing across the pathway.

I let out a sigh. "Of course I will, Mama. I just need time to sort through my feelings."

"Time," she said with a nod. "Okay. How much time are you thinking?"

"*Mama.*"

She held up her hands. "I'm sorry, but it's eating me up thinking about how much you hate me right now."

"I'm upset, but I don't hate you. I'm actually kind of glad to know how alike we are. It's a bond that wasn't there before."

Hazey nudged Mama's hand for more petting, and she obliged despite her allergies. "We can't get much more similar."

We'd fallen for men we believed our parents wouldn't have approved of, gotten pregnant, and made rash decisions in the face of personal tragedy.

We were women who'd kept secrets in the name of protecting people we loved when in truth we were protecting only *ourselves*. From embarrassment, shame, humiliation, awkwardness.

Foolish women, because trying to save ourselves only put us in a prison of our own making, one constructed of lies and pain and heartache.

"Instead of pretending we've led perfect lives all this time, we should've owned up to our mistakes. Learned from them. Grown from them. We could've shown that we're not defined by those mistakes and would've taught others that they're not defined by theirs, either. People like Kebbie. What happened with Flora could've turned out so differently if we'd just been more open about our own pasts."

Mama lifted her chin. "I know. I see it so clearly now. But we can start right over, can't we? It's like that saying: Some lessons are taught, others learned. Now we know what we need to do."

Hazey eyed a squirrel, and I kept tight hold of her leash so she couldn't give chase. "You sure you're willing to deal with the gossip?"

"It's just talk, right? Someone once told me that it won't kill me."

"But it could hurt."

A tear leaked from the corner of her eye. "I doubt it hurts more than what I feel right now. If I survive this week, I can survive anything."

Suddenly I hurt for my mother. I couldn't imagine hearing that a child you had mourned was very much alive—and had been living less than a mile away the whole time. Never mind how she'd treated Blue all these years, or finding out that she'd judged Mac unfairly. Or how her perfectionist attitude might have influenced Kebbie.

I pulled her into a hug. "You don't have to deal with it alone, Mama. You have me and Daddy and Hazey. She's real good at therapy. We'll help you through it best we can. Everything is fixable with a little forgiveness and time."

She nodded into my shoulder. "I love you, Sarah Grace."

"I love you, too, Mama."

She held on to me for a long minute before pulling away and wiping her eyes. She straightened her shirt and said, "There's somewhere I need to go, but first I want to hear a little more about Shep. You still love him, don't you?"

"I've never stopped loving him. Not for a single second. You're not going to lecture me, are you?"

She gave a half smile. "No lecture. Only some advice. That kind of love is rare. Special. Once in a lifetime. You two have been given a second chance. You owe it to yourself to see if you can make it work with him. Because true love is worth all the hard times. It's *everything*."

"I've come to learn that myself." I squinted at a jogger in the distance. "Is that Daddy?"

She turned around. "What's he gone and done?"

He was dressed in knee-length athletic shorts, a moisture-wicking tee, and what looked like brand-new sneakers.

"Daddy?" I said as he approached. Hazey zipped over to him to say her hellos. "What're you doing?"

"I'm jogging. I think. Am I doing it right?"

He glanced tenderly at Mama, and she rolled her eyes and gave him a kiss. Their marriage might not have begun with love, but it had grown over the years. And it might not be a perfect union, but it was a happy one.

I smiled. "I'm not sure there's a wrong way. When did you start running?"

"This morning. I thought maybe we could do it together once in a while."

My heart melted right there on the pathway, puddling around my feet. "That sounds nice."

Mama said, "I need to get going. I'll see you two at the hospital in a little while." She glanced at Daddy. "Please don't hurt yourself."

"I'll do my best."

As Mama walked away, he patted Hazey, then fell in step with me as I started jogging. I'd slowed my pace down considerably, but he was still struggling to keep up. His breaths came out in painful-sounding *whooshes*. Half a lap around the park, I took mercy on him and said, "Are those new running shoes?"

"Bought"—*puff, puff*—"them last night."

"I thought that might be the case. We should probably stop after this lap, then, or you might get blisters." He had on thick socks, so I thought he'd be just fine. Blisterwise, leastways. His heart was another matter. The last thing I wanted was for him to have a heart attack from his attempt to prove that he'd always be here for me.

His bristly eyebrows rose, and relief flowed across his eyes. "I didn't . . . even . . . think of that."

"How about we get some coffee instead?"

He nodded and sweat rolled down his plump cheeks.

When we finished the loop, he bent double and sucked in air.

"It gets easier," I said, patting his back.

"Liar."

I laughed. "It's true. And it means a lot that you'd come out here to run with me."

He straightened and wiped his brow. "Well, you mean a lot to me."

I kissed his damp cheek. "I know." We started walking toward the diner. "Will you do me a favor?"

"Anything, Sarah Grace. Name it."

"Will you tell Blue all your stories about Mac? She hardly knows about him at all, which doesn't seem fair."

He faced me. "Absolutely. I'd be honored to."

"Thank you."

We walked in companionable silence the rest of the way to the diner. Once there, I tied Hazey to a post near the door and assured her I'd be right back.

Daddy held the door open for me, and the patrons inside all fell silent as we walked in. My chest tightened as Daddy called out hellos to people we'd known all our lives. Hushed whispers flew through the room as we walked to the counter.

Kitty Malone took our orders and wouldn't make eye contact. I didn't know which made her uncomfortable, the rumors of my divorce or Kebbie's news, but it didn't much matter. Let them talk. The gossip would die down soon enough.

Daddy, apparently, didn't feel the same way, because he suddenly climbed onto a chair and said, "Who has questions? Air them now. Come on. Out with them."

"Is Kebbie really that baby's mother?" someone asked in the back.

I leaned against the counter, using it for support. Lord a'mercy. Mama would keel over if she saw him like this. Despite her insistence that she could handle any gossip, I was certain she hadn't considered my father would be standing on a chair in the diner, dressed the way he was, airing our family business.

"Yes, ma'am. She was embarrassed of her predicament and thought she was doing what was best for her and the baby. Fear clouds a person's judgment sometimes, because she should've known we'd all still love and support her, no matter what. Am I right?"

It took a moment, but the room echoed with "Yessirs."

Peer pressure wasn't always a bad thing, I reflected, watching him in awe as he guided our friends and neighbors to the destination he wanted them to see.

He added, "It's not like all of us haven't made our own questionable choices from time to time. Another question?"

Someone else said, "Sarah Grace, did Fletch really knock up a waitress from the Dishwater?"

"Well," I said, "I don't rightly know if she worked at the bar, but Fletch is now living with a woman and their unborn child in Florida."

A gasp went around the room, and Daddy looked at me with a twinkle in his eye.

"And while we're talking questionable judgment," I went on, emboldened, "you all might have heard by now that I eloped with Shep Wheeler when we were eighteen years old, and we divorced not long after. But I never stopped loving him. So if you see us together around town, just know that we're doing the best we can to make sure this second chance sticks."

Jaws dropped around the room, including my father's.

I almost laughed. Swear to God, I almost did.

"In more serious news," Daddy began in a low voice. Everyone leaned forward. "You'll be hearing a lot of talk about this soon enough, but I want you to hear it from me first. It's time to confess that I am not Sarah Grace's biological father. Ginny and Mac Bishop were once in love. Sarah Grace is their child. As is, it turns out, Blue Bishop."

After the ensuing uproar calmed, Daddy explained what had happened in such a way that he and Mama were going to have casseroles and floral arrangements on their porch in no time flat.

Daddy stepped off the chair and said, "Fortunately for us all, humans are forgiving creatures. We love, we learn, we grow. We're going to need your assistance to help our family heal. Sarah Grace and Blue, especially, have been given quite a shock, and I'm sure they'd appreciate your kind support as they adjust to it all."

As we walked toward the exit, drinks in hand (on the house),

Mrs. Weese stood up and hugged me. It started a chain reaction of hugs and handshakes. It took five more minutes before we were able to leave.

Outside, Daddy said, "Transparency. I like it."

I untied Hazey and we headed off down the street. "Mama's going to skin you alive."

"Worth it, to get it all out at once and stop the rumors."

"Well, if nothing else, it was probably good practice for the campaign trail."

He glanced down, then back at me. "I'm dropping out of the running, Sarah Grace."

I froze. "What? No. Daddy, *please*."

He gave me a sad smile. "One day, maybe, I'll run again, because I've spent a lot of time mulling it over, and I realized *everyone* has something to hide. No family is perfect. No one is perfect. We all have flaws. We all have strengths. The things we do in the name of love might not be our proudest moments, but they're actions that come from the heart. Trying to achieve perfection in any form is harmful in the long run. If I can take what's happened to us to show that even the most loving of families have problems, then hopefully it will help other families going through their own issues. Help them to be more transparent. Help them to heal. But right now, I need to be here to help my own family heal. I'm so sorry, Sarah Grace, for keeping the truth from you. I love you more than you can possibly know."

"I love you, too." I hugged him tight and never wanted to let him go. "You'll always be my daddy."

Chapter
24

Blue

"She looks like one of Marlo's moonflowers," Moe said as he sat on the sofa, holding Flora in his arms, gazing at her like she was the most beautiful flower he'd ever seen, and she was looking at him much the same way. "What's her name?"

"Her name is Flora," I said, then kissed his soft cheek.

It was the third time he'd asked in twenty minutes. It was a little past eight in the morning, and I'd been trying to sort through all the gifts I'd found on the porch yesterday—that were now scattered throughout the dining room—so I could write thank-you notes. But sitting with Moe seemed more important, so I was curled up next to him on the couch.

Marlo had asked if I could keep an eye on him this morning while she ran an early errand, and I couldn't help wondering where she'd gone. She hadn't said, and when I asked, she'd only smiled and told me she'd be back soon.

It was the second morning in a row she and Moe hadn't shared breakfast on the deck, but Moe didn't seem upset by the break in his routine. There was no glow about him at all, only that distant look in his eyes that made my heart ache. Flora's newborn magic didn't seem to be helping, either. How long until he was lost to that distance, never to return? A week? Two?

I rested my head on his shoulder. "I love you, Moe."

He touched his hand to his cheek where I'd kissed him and smiled at me. "You're a nice girl. What's your name?"

My chin quivered as I said, "My name is Blue Bishop."

He scratched his chin. "Bishop. I know that name. Good people."

Nodding, I sat next to him for a while, trying to make peace with my emotions, until Flora started to complain, making him agitated. I scooped her up, bouncing her in my arms. "Are you hungry, Moe? Breakfast is almost ready."

He nodded and patted his stomach. "Like a bear."

"It's almost ready. Another minute or two," Persy said from the kitchen, where she was making breakfast. Scrambled eggs and sausage.

She was planning to go see Kebbie later on this morning, and after coffee with Henry at the bookshop, I was looking forward to a quiet day here with Flora. I hadn't seen or spoken to Sarah Grace since yesterday at the hospital, but we'd texted, and it was like nothing had changed between us.

And for that, I was grateful. We'd become friends over the past couple of weeks, and I had the feeling that friendship would only grow stronger now that we knew the truth of who we were and how we were related.

Persy would likely see Ginny today at the hospital, and I could only hope she'd be civil. Ginny had been on my mind a lot this morning, and I couldn't quite bring myself to think of her as the enemy, even as a custody battle loomed. We wanted the same thing—for Flora to grow up happy, safe, loved. I just wished it could all have been different. That I'd get to know Ginny outside of a courtroom.

She was my mother.

I could barely wrap my head around the notion. She'd been so terrible to me growing up that it was hard to feel any kind of warm and fuzzy feeling about the revelation, yet part of me now understood why she'd acted so badly. She thought Mac had failed her and that all Bishops were well and truly bad at their core.

I'd spent a lot of time thinking about Twyla, too. Thinking and wondering.

I couldn't imagine a day when I would think of her as anything other than my mother, so I decided I wouldn't even try. She was and always would be my mama. My Twyla.

The wind had been still this morning, and I tried to imagine a life without finding things. Without my foraging. Without the family I'd been raised with. Without the lessons that had come from the hardships I'd endured. Without the wind's guidance. Without Marlo and Moe as surrogate grandparents.

It was all . . . unfathomable.

Everything that had happened to me had shaped me the same way the wind carved rock, slow and steady: The way I didn't take a single day for granted. The way I baked. The way I used art to influence, not arguments. The way I longed for a big family. The way I loved.

All this time I'd wanted to be normal because I cared so much about what others thought of me, of my family, when it truly didn't matter. Because it only mattered what I thought. I was proud of who I was, and I loved my family. I wasn't going to let anyone make me question my place in this community ever again. Because I belonged here as much as anyone else.

And with that, I knew I'd be staying in Buttonwood. I'd come to realize that moving didn't make for a fresh start. It was a mind-set. One that had taken me a while to figure out, but now that I had, I couldn't wait to see where it would lead me.

I kissed Flora's head and danced with her around the living room, earning a smile from Moe. Flora was getting sleepy, her body growing heavy as I glided past the dining table. I stopped to critique the last of the Poppy paintings. I'd finished it this morning, and I was happy with the way it had turned out. I smiled at Poppy Kay in the dance studio, her arms out, her legs stretched in a position that looked a lot like a mix between tai chi and ballet. I'd scan all the paintings and send them to my editor later today, since my scanner was at the farmhouse.

I flipped open my sketchbook and glanced at the crow that stared back at me. I'd had an idea for a new book based on an advice-giving crow, whose guidance was sometimes misunderstood by those receiving the messages. I had two rough sketches done—one of a black crow and the other of a golden crow. I was leaning toward the golden one as my main character. Ideas swirled, and while I longed to sit down and continue sketching, I didn't have time. There was too much to do this morning.

"Blue," Persy said softly and motioned with her chin toward the couch.

Looking over, I saw Moe starting to nod off. I walked over and pulled a blanket onto his lap. I took a long look at him, trying to memorize everything I possibly could. Because I couldn't help but feel I didn't have much time left with him.

I held Flora close as I walked to the sunroom, searching for solace as I gazed out at the backyard flowers, letting the colors soothe. I waited to feel the pull to the woods, but it didn't come—there was no reason to, now that I knew the truth. But I found I missed it and promised myself I'd go for a hike soon. Maybe with Henry again. Or Marlo. Or Sarah Grace. When I did, I'd be sure to stop by the Buttonwood Tree to give thanks.

"Should we eat outside this morning to keep Moe as close to his routine as possible?" Persy asked as she scraped eggs onto a serving plate.

"Good idea."

At the sound of my voice, Moe blinked awake and looked around like he didn't know where he was.

"Are you hungry, Moe?" I asked loudly, knowing he'd probably forgotten I'd already asked. Flora didn't so much as flinch at my voice. She was sound asleep.

"Yes, ma'am," he said, trying to stand up. "Surely am."

Persy rushed over to help him up, then walked with him onto

the deck. A few quick trips between the kitchen and deck, and we had the patio table set. I was about to lay Flora down in her cradle when there was a soft knock at the door. When I peeked out the window, I was taken aback to see that it was Ginny who'd knocked. She stood on the porch holding a small gift bag. Taking a deep breath, I opened the door.

Her gaze flitted between me and Flora before she said, "Hello, Blue. I hope I haven't come at a bad time. I was hoping to talk with you."

"We were just getting breakfast ready." Flora's heart beat against my chest, little flutters, tiny reminders that grief and pain didn't have to make you hollow, burned from the inside out. There was room enough for forgiveness. For healing. "Come on in."

Ginny took a step backward. "Are you sure? I can come back another time."

I was impressed she'd shown up in the first place. Twyla would've taken to her bed for days after getting the devastating news Ginny had heard yesterday. It was simply Twyla's way. To retreat, to nurse her wounds alone. I silently told myself to avoid comparing them. They both had their strengths . . . and weaknesses. "I'm sure. Stay. I'm not hungry, anyway. Can I get you something to drink?"

"No, no thank you."

She glanced around as if trying to soak in everything in one look. She said nothing about the smattering of gifts around the room but tipped her head to the side when she saw my artwork on the table and walked over for a closer look.

"These are lovely."

"Thank you."

"Is this Delphine?" she asked, tapping the picture of the crow.

"Not exactly. It's loosely based on her, though. A new story idea."

"I saw the crow once, up close. It was beautiful. This black crow captures it perfectly, except for the eyes."

"Really?" The crow never came close to people, preferring to watch from high above.

"It was—" She swallowed hard. "It was after you were born. I'd gone to the Buttonwood Tree. As I sat crying on the cold ground, she landed next to me, and when I looked over at her, I saw she was crying, too. She had gold eyes and was crying golden tears. I've never told anyone that before now."

Golden tears. My skin prickled, and I rubbed away chill bumps while trying not to disturb Flora.

Ginny's yearning gaze dropped to the baby, and I couldn't ignore the silent request. "Would you like to hold her?"

"Could I?"

"She drools a little when she sleeps. Let me grab a cloth for your blouse."

"It'll be fine," she said, setting the gift she'd brought onto the table. "A little drool never hurt anything."

It sounded so much like something Twyla would have said that I smiled. Could they have been friends if given the chance? I wasn't sure. And I'd never know.

I passed Flora into Ginny's arms, and there were tears in her eyes when she looked up at me. "She looks so much like you and Sarah Grace when you were born. That hair is definitely all Cabot."

"My hair was that light?" I'd only ever known it to be a dark blond.

She nodded. "Your color now is just like Mac's, though. You look so much like him that sometimes it's been hard for me to look at you at all. Seeing you brought back such painful memories."

I thought about all the times she'd evaded me my whole life. I thought it was solely because I was a Bishop, but it went deeper.

It was because I looked like the man she'd loved and lost. "And now?"

"It still hurts, but for entirely different reasons." She sniffled as she held Flora tightly. "That bag is for you. You mentioned you found your hat and my button in a box of childhood mementoes. I'd like to add a few things to it, if you don't mind."

Curious, I opened the bag and pulled out a stuffed white rabbit that had thin strands of silver threads woven through it and a flat hand-carved maple bird, hollowed in the center to hold three wooden loops.

"Mac made that teether for you not long after I learned I was pregnant, right around the same time I bought that rabbit for your eventual nursery."

My throat clogged with emotion. "You kept them all this time?"

"Of course. You were gone, but you most certainly were never forgotten. I want you to know, Blue, that if I had any idea you were mine, I would've come for you. Nothing would've stopped me. I know you didn't have an easy upbringing, and I can hardly bear thinking of you having to struggle when I was so . . . oblivious."

I held up a hand to stop her. "My only regrets from my childhood come from losing people I loved too soon. They weren't perfect. But I was loved."

"I wish I'd known the Bishops better, but Mac and I needed to keep our relationship secret. He spoke fondly of them, but he wanted better for himself. For his own family. He didn't have the best grades in school—he was a different kind of learner. He could carve wood, fix an engine, and take apart a toaster, rewire it, and put it back together. When that judge offered him a way out, he jumped at the chance. He thought the military was the best way for him to learn skills he could then use for a career." She shook her head. "If he'd just stayed here in Buttonwood . . ."

"I know from experience there's no use playing the *what if* game. If he stayed, he could've been in the car with Wade and Ty when they crashed."

Maybe one day I'd tell her why my brothers had robbed that bank, but I wasn't ready to open myself up like that quite yet. I gestured to the couch. "Please, sit down. Flora gets heavy after a little while."

She sat and gazed at Flora's slack face. "Is she a good baby?"

"The best." I suddenly wanted her back in my arms, but I forced myself not to ask.

"Sarah Grace and I had a long talk this morning," she said.

"How's she doing?"

"She's angry."

I nodded. "I think we all have cause to be angry."

"Yes, that's true. I made mistakes, I admit. No one is perfect, though heaven knows, I tried to be. I thought I was cursed to a lifetime of unhappiness, so I tried extra hard to prove the tree had no power. To prove I could still have a *perfect* family."

I wanted to say there was no such thing, but the Buttonwood Tree said Mac, Ginny, and I would have been one. I tried to picture the three of us together, and I simply couldn't.

"In that quest for perfection, I hurt so many people. I did my best to hide the Bishop in Sarah Grace out of fear, but really all I did was make her feel like she was *less than*, a disappointment, which couldn't be further from the truth." Her brows knitted. "In turn, she made choices and decisions she regrets . . ." She shook her head. "And it's likely Kebbie would've made different choices recently if she hadn't been afraid of what I'd think or do . . . and I don't think I'll ever forgive myself for making her believe she couldn't trust me. I hope one day she'll be able to forgive me. Which leads me to Flora."

I stiffened.

"I had no say in Mary Eliza taking you away from me. You were just . . . gone. Kebbie did—does—have a say in what she wants for Flora, and I've been trying to take the decision away from her because I thought I knew better. Just like Mary Eliza believed she knew what was best for me." Her chin quivered as she smoothed Flora's hair. "I would love to raise this little girl, but she's not mine to raise. She's yours. I'll support Kebbie's choice. I'll support you. But I do hope you'll allow me to be part of Flora's life. And your life, too."

I wiped away a tear that snaked down my face. I didn't know what life would look like as part of the Cabot family, but I was willing to figure it out. To stand in my light as part of that family as well. "I'm not sure what to say other than of course you can be part of our lives."

Her chin was still quivering as she smiled at me.

I had her smile, too. I wondered how many other traits of hers I'd discover and suddenly realized I was looking forward to finding out.

A phone rang from inside her purse, and she carefully juggled Flora in order to answer it. She frowned at the screen and said, "It's the hospital. Hello?"

My stomach knotted as she spoke, terse one-word answers to questions I couldn't hear. When she hung up, she stood and kissed Flora's head as she handed her back to me. "We need to go. Grab Persy, too. Kebbie would want her there."

Panicked, I said, "What's going on?"

Her face lit up like she was glowing from the inside out. "Kebbie's taken a turn for the better. She's awake and asking for us."

Chapter
25

"Judge Quimby, what a nice surprise bumping into you," Oleta Blackstock said as he came down the courthouse steps on his way to his car.

It could've been his imagination, but it seemed she'd been waiting for him. He'd seen her earlier pacing this stretch of the sidewalk, her blue dress and pillbox hat unmistakable. "Good afternoon, Miss Oleta." He lifted an eyebrow at her sturdy black pumps.

"I was hoping for a moment of your time to talk about Blue Bishop."

"I do believe you've said your piece already."

She waved a hand. "My thoughts get jumbled sometimes. I'm old. It happens to the best of us. I'd like to offer a revised opinion on the matter of Blue Bishop and Flora."

Despite what she said, there wasn't a sharper mind in all of Buttonwood than Oleta Blackstock, which made him curious as to what she had to say. He took in her gravity-defying hat and coal-black eyes that burned with ferocity. "Go ahead."

Her hands curled into fists, and it seemed as each word was being unwillingly pulled from her lips as she said, "I've perhaps misjudged Blue Bishop. If my previous opinion has swayed you in any manner, then I retract the statement. Let it hold no bearing at the upcoming hearing."

"Why the change of heart?"

Her cold eyes flickered warmly for only a moment before she said, "Sometimes family is more important than pride."

He suddenly knew her grandson, Henry, had his hands in this conversation. Good for him, the judge thought. "I'm of the belief that family is more important than most anything."

She lifted a thin eyebrow. "I've never much cared for such saccharine sentiments."

And it showed, not that he dared mention it. "Viewing life with a little sweetness can make a world of difference."

She seemed to think on that for a moment before she nodded. "Yes, well, thank you kindly for any future toothaches," she stated, then stomped away.

He watched her go, thinking he probably should have started their conversation by mentioning the canceled hearing but was glad he hadn't. He just wished that Blue had seen Oleta take up for her, even if it hadn't been her idea, because it had been a sight to behold—and one he never thought he'd see in his lifetime.

As he headed for his car, he hoped one day baby Flora would know how her arrival was changing this town and its people.

For the better.

Blue

Persy said, "*Blue*. Have pity on me and sit down. You're making me dizzy."

We were waiting our turn to see Kebbie. Sarah Grace, Ginny, and Jud were in with her now. From a high window in the visitor lounge, I watched Henry walk the grounds with Moe and Flora, and I smiled with fondness at how easily he'd agreed to come with us this morning. I planned to make him his favorite cookies—butterscotch—as a thank-you.

On the window ledge, four crows had gathered and were cawing loudly.

None had golden eyes.

"It's weird, isn't it?" she said.

I sat down. "The crows?"

She looked at me oddly. "No. Not the crows."

"Sorry." I laughed. "I have crows on my mind lately, and I swear those four are staring at me. What is it you find weird?"

"You at the moment," she joked.

The humor in her eyes brought me happiness.

"I've been thinking a lot about everything's that been revealed," she said. "If it weren't for Flora, we might never have known the truth about you. And by the way, I fully expect you to call me Auntie Persy from now on."

This was the first time she'd spoken to me about the DNA revelations and how they changed our familial relationship. On paper, at least. "Not happening."

"What? That's outrageous. I think Auntie Persy has a nice ring to it."

"We'll have Flora call you that. You'll always be my little sister, Persy. Knowing where I come from doesn't change anything between us."

"You're a Cabot. I still can't believe it."

"I have Cabot blood, but I've always been and always will be a Bishop." The truth wasn't going to change that. Not even a little bit. "You know, I always wanted a big family of my own. I just never realized I was going to find another half of a family tree."

She smiled. "That's what you get for always finding things."

I hoped I'd still be able to—I enjoyed helping others in such a unique way.

"But seriously, I've been thinking a lot about our family and about labels. Aunts, sisters, cousins. They're just biological definitions." Her voice shifted into monotone. "Aunt: a sister of a person's father or mother."

She really had been thinking a lot about family if she was

quoting dictionaries. I wasn't sure where she was going with all this, and I wasn't certain she knew, either. I was going to let her talk it out, because it was obviously very important to her.

"It's love that truly defines family. At least to me. Like how sometimes friends turn into family. And then you happen to find out they *are* family. But Blue, if I'm being completely honest, I never really felt like you were my sister."

My jaw dropped. "How can you say that?"

"You're misunderstanding. I always knew you were going to be a great mama someday. I knew because you've been a great mom to me. I never needed a piece of paper to tell me how I was related to you before, and I certainly don't need one now."

With tears in my eyes, I hugged her. She set her head on my shoulder, just like she used to do when she was a baby and I'd rock her to sleep at night. I didn't regret any moment of caring for her. I only felt sorry that Twyla had missed out on so much when she was lost to her grief.

The door to the lounge opened, and Sarah Grace walked in. "Oh! I can come back."

"No!" Persy and I said at the same time and then stood up.

Sarah Grace smiled. "Y'all can go back now."

"Go ahead, Persy," I said. "I'll be right there."

She rushed through the door, and Sarah Grace said, "Is she okay?"

"Yeah, I think she is. You?"

"All things considered, yes. I heard you and Mama talked this morning. Kebbie was so happy to hear Mama wasn't going to fight for custody of Flora. And so shocked about the DNA tests that I thought for a minute there that it was a good thing she was in the hospital in case she needed resuscitation."

"She's doing that well?" I asked.

Sarah Grace nodded. "It's a near miracle if you ask me. Her labs are almost normal. She'll likely be transferred out of the ICU later today or tomorrow. She's still facing challenges ahead—dealing with the police and all that—but medically, the doctors say she'll be just fine in time. How're *you*, Blue?"

I let the news about Kebbie sink in a little before I said, "It's a lot to take in, but I think it's all going to be okay."

The receptionist buzzed us through the locked double doors that opened in the unit.

"A *lot* to take in," she repeated with a smile. "But I'm happy about you and me. I truly am."

"I am, too, Sarah Grace."

Sisters.

As we walked into Kebbie's room, Persy was sitting on the edge of Kebbie's bed, talking a mile a minute. I was taken aback when I looked at Kebbie and nearly stumbled.

Not because she was sitting up in bed, holding her own with the conversation.

But because she was surrounded by a beautiful warm glow, and I swore there was a glimmer of golden light in her eyes.

Moonlight.

꙳

It was the kind of day in Buttonwood, Alabama, where the breeze soothed, bringing welcome relief from the heat of the day and a promise of a warm, springtime shower. Leaves on the massive oaks and sky-high hickories looked to be waving hello at Marlo, Flora, and me like we were long-lost kin as we passed by, making our way along the trail that led to the Buttonwood Tree.

Marlo was moving along at a good clip, which was surprising considering the healing she'd done this morning. It had to have taken quite the effort to bring Kebbie back from the brink of death. The abundant moonlight in that hospital room told me that Marlo had to have had a store of light to use this morning—not solely the piddling amount she'd pulled from last night's waxing moon. A few days' worth at least, which meant she hadn't been using her moonlight lately.

"How long?" Marlo asked.

Lost in my thoughts, I was startled by the sound of her voice. We'd been walking in silence. Not an awkward silence, but a comfortable one. One that came from knowing each other so well that there was no need for words. "How long until what?"

"Until you tell me why you asked me to walk with you this afternoon. Don't you dare deny there's a reason. I can see purpose in your eyes, shining bright as the sun in the sky."

I made a mental note to wear sunglasses more often and said, "I was just thinking that it's been eighteen years since I walked into The Rabbit Hole with Persy perched on my bony hip. You took us in, you fed us, clothed us, cared for us, taught us, supported us, loved us, healed us, saved us. You became part of our family. Treasured, beloved family."

A squirrel darted across the path in front of us, a nut in its mouth. Flora snuffled in her sleep within her wrap, and I could feel her drool seeping into my T-shirt.

A little drool never hurt anything.

Both my mothers were right about that.

"You practicing your eulogy, child?" Marlo asked, a twinkle in her eyes.

"Not hardly. Especially since I think I have some time before one is needed, don't I?"

"Perhaps." There were tears in her eyes when she said, "Moe will be moving into Magnolia Breeze this coming weekend."

I stopped walking, took her hands, and held them tightly. I knew it had been the most difficult, painful decision she'd ever made. "When did you decide to use your healing to save Kebbie?"

She gave me a sad smile. "All my little rabbits."

It took me a moment, but I remembered the conversation we'd had about Kebbie.

Your hugs make everything seem right in the world. They're a gift you share freely, and I know I'm grateful for them, and I imagine Kebbie is, too. You've helped so many of us. All your little rabbits.

Marlo tugged on my arm, and we continued walking the well-worn path, the gentle breeze pushing us along. "I couldn't bear to think of Kebbie suffering when I could help, and I know Moe would give his life for her if he could. I'd been saving up my moonlight to give Moe one big burst of healing, but Kebbie's illness was the push I needed to finally let him go the way he wants to go. Without me. He knew all along that others need me, but I was too stubborn to listen."

"It wasn't stubbornness. It was love." It was instinctual to protect the ones we love. To help them. And in some cases, to heal them.

"Perhaps a bit of both."

"He'd be so proud of you if he knew you helped Kebbie."

"I hope so."

"I know so."

"I don't know how I'm going to be able to say goodbye."

I closed my eyes against the pain that came merely from the thought. "I don't know how, either, but I do know you'll have a big family around you to support you. All your and Moe's little rabbits."

"All *our* little rabbits. He'd like that."

As we stepped into the clearing around the Buttonwood Tree, Flora wiggled, trying to stretch. I took her out of the wrap, and her arms shot upward. She blinked, and in the light filtering through the canopy I could see blue starting to edge out the gray in her eyes. I set her against my shoulder and rubbed her back. "Hey, Marlo?"

"Yes?"

"How'd you get in to see Kebbie before visiting hours?"

Her eyes twinkled. "I know people, some who're willing to bend a few rules."

"And how come no one else in the hospital room seemed to notice Kebbie's glow?"

"Only certain people can see it. A trusted few. In time, I'll teach someone else the healing ways of the moon. Kebbie, perhaps, now that she knows its full power."

I touched the tree trunk and listened to the wind rustle the leaves above my head. "You know, I had an interesting conversation with Henry yesterday, while we walked these woods."

"Oh? It wasn't all goo-goo eyes and sweet nothings?"

"*No,*" I said, feeling heat rise to my cheeks.

Marlo laughed. "It's no surprise to me that he fell for you. You're a lovable sort."

I smiled. "And you're slightly biased."

"Hogwash."

"Anyway," I said, pressing on, trying to calm Flora as she whimpered. "He mentioned how he's thought about writing a book about the Buttonwood Tree."

"Is that so?"

"He shared an interesting tidbit I'd never known about Delphine's family."

"Do enlighten me."

I glanced at her as she emphasized *enlighten*, and saw her teasing grin. She knew where I was going with this. "Did you know that Delphine had a daughter? Celene? When her mother turned into the Buttonwood Tree, apparently she burrowed under the tree to be close to her." I glanced at the rabbit hole beneath the tree, and though it should've been dark as night, there was a faint glow within. "I looked up the name Celene online. It means moon."

"Hmm. Now that you say so, I might've known that." She held out her arms for Flora, and I passed her over. Marlo shifted foot to foot. Dancing, I realized. She was doing the moondance without the hand gestures. Flora quieted.

"I don't suppose you know what happened to Celene? Did she have children? Grandchildren? Great-grandchildren?"

"Don't suppose I do know. Do you?"

I watched her sway, my heart full of love. "I have a feeling I do."

She smiled, and the light in her eyes shimmered. "You might be right, but let's keep that feeling between you and me and this here little flower, okay? Now, let's dance." She held out her hand for me, and I stepped up next to her, trying to match her graceful movements.

The wind swirled in step with us while we danced just south of the Buttonwood Tree, and when I heard a faint caw, I looked up to see a black crow perched on a high branch, looking down at us with pride shining in her golden eyes.

Chapter 26

Judge Quimby spent Thanksgiving morning in his home office. The room was scented with roast turkey, pecan pie, and traces of his pipe's vanilla tobacco. On the TV, large inflatables floated down Sixth Avenue in New York City, but the sound was muted as he unlocked a desk drawer and pulled out a file labeled simply with the letter *B*.

B for Bishop.

Into it he added the picture of himself and Flora Cabot Bishop that Blue had sent him in a thank-you note. Flora's kinship adoption had been finalized late last week. It had taken a fair amount of time, due to the nature of the unknown father. Four months had to pass, and notices had to be published in newspapers throughout Alabama before his rights could be terminated. No one had ever come forward, and as the judge thought about that young man never knowing he was a father, he felt a twinge of sympathy.

He sifted through the papers in the file, glancing over various arrest reports, Cobb's autopsy report, and a recent newspaper clipping about Blue's kidnapping. The old adage that truth was often stranger than fiction came to mind, and he wholeheartedly agreed. Kidnapped. It still shook him to his core. Mary Eliza Wheeler had passed on only a week after the truth had come to light. She'd never been formally questioned in the matter and had taken her side of the story to the grave with her.

He set a mug shot of Mac Bishop on his desk, studying his eyes. He saw what he'd seen decades ago when Mac had appeared in his courtroom: The plea for help. The plea for someone to just cut their family a break. The desperation of not knowing how to change his circumstances.

The judge had recognized it, because he'd once been that boy. If not for a loving, adoptive family that had taken him in, he wouldn't be where he was today.

Mac Bishop hadn't been in the same position, in need of a family. But he had been in need. So the judge had decided to help, to give him a second chance instead of sending the boy to jail.

The judge rubbed his eyes as he skimmed Mac's obituary, and for what felt like the millionth time, he questioned whether he'd done right by Mac. Had there been another way? A way that wouldn't have led to the boy's death?

Guilt ate at him now, exactly as it had done when he'd heard the news of Mac's death.

It was that day that he'd vowed to do what he could to help the other Bishop boys change their circumstances, so they wouldn't suffer the same fate as their older brother. Wade, especially, had struggled, until the judge had pressed Ray Dodd into giving Wade a chance as an apprentice. And when Ty started stealing, he'd convinced Mrs. Quimby to plant seeds with Mrs. Granbee about giving Ty the option of working on their farm the next time he fell in trouble at the general store.

That's all those boys needed—a chance.

Or so he'd believed. Until the bank robbery happened, and he'd wondered what had gone wrong. How had he failed so badly?

The truth had come by way of Cobb's death certificate. He'd ordered a copy as soon as it had become public record. Hindsight was a bitter pill to swallow. The judge had been so focused on helping the boys that he hadn't noticed Cobb falling into ill health. To be fair, Cobb had kept it well hidden. Even now, very few in the community knew the cause of Cobb's death.

But he knew. When he found out, he went digging for answers and found the medical bills. Bills that should've been covered by state aid but had been denied due to a form not having been filled out properly.

Because, as the judge now knew, Cobb Bishop had been barely literate.

The judge bristled at the unfairness of the world. Of how one injustice could lead to one desperate decision after another, causing a ripple effect. He'd been bound and determined that the ripple ended for the Bishops with Cobb's death.

He set his pipe on the ashtray and placed the pictures back into the file and glanced at a note he'd written to himself about getting a job for Twyla at Dulcette's Orchard. He'd kept an eye on Blue and Persy as they grew, pleased that they were doing well in school and keeping out of trouble.

Until Blue's senior year of high school.

He had a feeling there was more to the story of the fire at the high school, since Blue refused to confess but didn't deny the charges. It was a story he'd never likely hear, but it didn't much matter. She'd been a good student and a model citizen, and there was no reason at all to suspect the fire had been anything but accidental. Yet the high school principal, a pea-brained, mealymouthed toad, had a grudge against the Bishops. So focused on reparation for the ruined prom, for which he'd received much contempt and hostility from angry parents and the school board, he wouldn't drop the matter and had been intent on seeing Blue arrested and sent to jail. Ridiculous. After some legal arm-twisting, a civil agreement had been reached. Two thousand dollars to cover the damage at the school for dropped charges.

From the file, he lifted a certified check receipt, a copy of the original that had been submitted to the court. Two thousand

dollars paid anonymously to Buttonwood High School on behalf of Blue Bishop.

As he thought back to the confident, successful, happy
woman who'd stood in his courtroom last week holding a beautiful blond baby girl, he decided that two thousand dollars was
the best money he'd ever spent.

Persy getting mixed up in the abandoned-baby case had
taken him by surprise, too. He'd been set to twist some arms
and throw his weight around, damn the ethics of it all, to make
sure she'd be assigned the best public defender in the county,
but it hadn't come to that. His worries had been set at ease
by a quick hallway chat with the DA, who'd declined to file
charges against Persy for sharing her painkillers, given the circumstances of the case.

He suspected all Blue's and Persy's wild oats had now been
sown. But just in case, he'd continue to keep tabs on them. With
that, he closed the file and locked it away. He put out his pipe,
shut off the TV, and headed for the kitchen, hoping Mrs. Quimby would let him sneak an early taste of the pecan pie.

Blue

"If you don't stop picking at the turkey, I will ban you to the
chicken coop," Sarah Grace said, shaking a finger at Shep.
"Don't think I won't just because we're newlyweds."

She looked so much like her mother in that moment that it
made me smile.

Our mother.

Six months after I learned the truth, it was still sinking in.

He pulled her close and kissed her. "I dare you."

She growled, then laughed. "Go on. Git. Don't you have
football to watch? Henry!" she yelled. "Come get Shep, will
you? Dinner's in *five* minutes. You'll survive till then."

Henry walked into the kitchen, his head bent at an angle, since Flora had a handful of his hair. She was in a grabby stage. At six months old, she was simply the most beautiful child I'd ever seen, and no one better dare tell me otherwise. Blond wisps floated around her chubby face and big blue eyes gazed at everything around her, trying to take it all in. She was curious. So very curious.

"Ooh, look at that turkey," Henry said. He reached out to steal a bit and Sarah Grace smacked his hand with a spatula.

I laughed, then Flora laughed because I was laughing, and I had tears in my eyes and a stitch in my side in no time flat.

The sounds of the football game carried in from the living room as I washed my hands. I glanced out the window over the kitchen sink and into the grassy backyard. Gone were the weeds, replaced with sod and a paver patio. In the corner of the yard stood a small chicken coop and fenced pen for Sarah Grace and Shep's four chickens, which had been the inspiration for the book I was working on in my brand-new backyard studio. *Poppy Kay Hoppy Finds a Chicken Coop.* I was still fussing with my golden crow book—taking extra time to get it right before sharing it with my agent.

Kebbie and Marlo stood at the chickens' fence, arms linked as they cooed to the birds. I studied Marlo, watching her carefully, just as I'd been doing these last few months since Moe had died. He'd gone peacefully, surrounded by us all—including Hazey standing in for his beloved Skitter—and every time I thought of him, I ached from missing him.

Marlo had taken to walking with me nearly every day, and she still worked part-time at the bookshop. Nights were harder for her, but she still danced with the moon, and every day she seemed to have more of her old glow about her. The glow that came from loving Moe, not just mourning him.

Kebbie was dealing with some aftereffects of being ill,

something called post-intensive care syndrome, but she was working through them with professionals. She'd been arrested after being discharged from the hospital and charged with a Class A misdemeanor. She pleaded guilty and was given probation in lieu of jail time. She'd signed guardianship of Flora over to me pending the search for Flora's biological father, and after that time was up and he hadn't come forward, she'd terminated her rights as well. Flora's adoption had been finalized last week in a packed hearing at the courthouse. There'd been applause and tears by the time all was said and done, and Judge Quimby had been gracious enough to stick around and pose for endless pictures.

Flora would always know her birth story—it was important to all of us to have the truth be known to her from the get-go. As she grew, we'd answer any questions she had as openly and honestly as possible. Kebbie would always be part of her life, and I was happy about that. Flora was one lucky little girl to have an abundance of family who loved and adored her. I couldn't ask anything more for her, truly.

Kebbie had withdrawn from college, though she often talked about going back one day, and was working full-time with Sarah Grace. Doc Hennessey's twenty-two-year-old son had asked Kebbie out a few times now, but so far she kept turning him down. She was interested, though—I could tell by her blush every time she talked about him.

Sarah Grace and Shep had done an amazing job on the farmhouse, a complete transformation in only five months' time. Yet it still felt like the house I'd grown up in. Fixtures and flooring could be changed, walls moved, and windows added, but there was no taking the love out of the house. However, I was glad the sadness had faded.

As I scraped mashed potatoes from a pot into a serving bowl, Persy sailed into the kitchen to pick up the next platter of food to deliver to the sideboard, a basket of cranberry oatmeal cookies that Sarah Grace and I had made together that morning. Hazey was right on Persy's heels, followed by a small mutt with curly hair, a bent tail, and a gentle spirit. Almost five months ago, the wind led me to him at the Tuscaloosa flea market, and Sarah Grace had ended up adopting him. She'd named him Obie.

He was the first thing I'd found since the wind stopped summoning me every day, and I'd nearly cried with joy that I hadn't lost the ability altogether. Since then, I'd found a few other things as well.

Namely, love.

As if sensing I was looking at him, Henry glanced over at me and smiled.

"They keep hoping I'll drop something," Persy said. "And I'm thinking about it. How do you ever say no to those eyes, Sarah Grace?"

Persy had turned nineteen two weeks ago. She was dealing with her own aftereffects of what happened with Kebbie—namely, guilt. Guilt that she hadn't spoken up. Guilt that she hadn't been punished the same as Kebbie. She was working through it in her own way—volunteering on campus and coming home as often as possible to hang out with Kebbie. They had plans to travel to Europe next summer and talked endlessly about which destinations they were most excited to explore. One would think *they* were sisters with how close they were.

Sarah Grace laughed. "I don't. They're spoiled rotten."

"What can I do to help?" Ginny asked, walking into the kitchen.

Sarah Grace glanced around. "We just need to move everything to the sideboard at this point and open another bottle of wine."

Ginny set her hand on Sarah Grace's arm. "Go easy with Oleta's glass. She's already had two cocktails and has challenged your father to see which of them can do more push-ups."

I couldn't help but laugh. "My money's on Oleta."

Ginny smiled and whispered, "I think that's why Jud won't accept the challenge—he thinks he'll lose."

"Hey," Sarah Grace said. "He's now running two miles without stopping. He might surprise you yet."

"Are you talking about me?" Jud yelled.

"Why would you think that, honey?" Ginny said as she grabbed the basket of rolls and headed out of the kitchen.

I carried a fluted casserole dish of dressing to the sideboard, stopping to admire the table's centerpiece, a beautiful arrangement of oleander that Oleta had brought.

Henry sidled up next to me. "Thank you again for inviting Oleta."

I glanced into the living room. Oleta was sitting ramrod straight on the couch, wineglass in hand, as she stared bitterly at the football game. "I couldn't stand the thought of her being all alone today."

"I'm hoping she'll be on her best behavior, despite the flowers."

"Oh, come on." I laughed. "Nothing says 'Happy Thanksgiving' like poisonous flowers. It's almost supper time—could you go let her know?"

Giving me a hug, he said, "She's coming around. She's just taking her sweet time about it."

He was right—she was. She hadn't glared at me in months, but she still called me by my full name. Even so, she had accepted my invitation to join us today. It was a start. A small start, but one nonetheless.

Oleta wasn't one of my favorite people, not by a long shot, but Henry was, and I'd do just about anything to help Oleta find the path he'd created and walk it with him.

As soon as Henry headed for the living room, Shep stepped up next to me with a bowl of creamed collard greens. There was an air of peace about him that had come after his mama's death back in May. She'd never even been formally questioned in the matter, not that it would've changed anything.

I banished a brief surge of anger and pain—there was no point in holding on to it. As Sarah Grace had told me often, the damage had been exposed. Now was the time to rebuild.

"I've been meaning to get this to you." He put his hand in his pocket and came out with a button. "Now that the case is closed, I thought you might like to have this back."

GIVE THE BABY TO BLUE BISHOP.

I ran my fingers over the letters and closed my hand around the button. I wasn't sure whether I'd put it into Flora's baby book or frame it, but I knew I'd always treasure it.

I gave him a hug. "Thanks, Shep."

As everyone settled into their seats, I tucked the button into my pocket and went back to the kitchen to make sure everything had been brought out, and I heard Sarah Grace say to the empty room, "I know, I know. I'm happy, too."

"Sarah Grace? Who're you talking to?"

She laughed and said, "An old friend of yours. I'll tell you all about it sometime."

I picked up the green bean casserole and said, "I'll nag you until you do, you know. Don't think I'll forget."

"Oh, I know. You're such a pesky older sister."

We shared a smile then joined the others. Taking a moment, I looked at those gathered around the table, laughing and joking, in the house where I'd grown up with so much sadness. If someone had told me a year ago where I'd be now and with whom, I'd have laughed myself silly. Oleta? Ginny? Jud? At the same table as me?

Marlo caught my eye and smiled, as though she knew exactly what I was thinking.

As I stood in a puddle of light by my chair, I noticed how the sunbeams reflected off the glasses and flatware, casting beautiful glittery silver threads throughout the room, a complicated web that wrapped around everyone gathered, binding us together as family.

ACKNOWLEDGMENTS

Thank you so much to my agent, Jessica Faust, for her steady, enthusiastic guidance; to editor Kristin Sevick, whose wise suggestions changed this book for the better (much better!); and to everyone at Forge Books, who make my books the best they can be. Such a great, supportive team, and I'm so grateful to be part of it.

To good friend and author Jess Montgomery, who didn't even blink when I discussed with her the book I was working on about a magical buttonwood tree that dispenses wisdom, who then suggested that wisdom should come out via actual buttons. Perfect. Thank you, Jess!

For my readers, thank you so much for picking up this book, reading it, and following me on this crazy, wonderful, magical writing journey. I hope that when you finished the last page you felt the same heartwarming sense of peace that my characters eventually found within this story.

And last but not least, thank you to my family, who bring a steady source of love and magic into my life. Much love.

1

Sadie

"Whereabouts are you from, Sadie?" Mrs. Iona Teakes asked as she deftly chopped pecans on a wooden cutting board in her sun-steeped kitchen, the summery afternoon light spilling through a bay window overlooking the Coosa River.

Across the yawning stretch of water, the main street of a small town fluttered with activity as people went about their day. Before coming to Mrs. Teakes' charming home, I'd stopped for lunch at the local burger place, not only for something to appease my grumbling stomach but also to get a feel for the town. Its people. Its mood. Its potential. Its heartbeat.

I'd been looking for a place to call my home for so long now that I was beginning to think I'd never find it.

But Wetumpka, Alabama, had promise.

A revitalization initiative was in full swing, and the heart of the community was evident in the rebuilding that had taken place in the years since a tornado swept through, uprooting trees, buildings, lives. Heart was my number one requirement when it came to a hometown.

"I was born and raised about an hour and a half north of here. In Shelby County."

Curiosity burned in Mrs. Teakes' watery eyes as her gaze shifted to my hair, then away again, but she was much too polite to ask any prying questions, for which I was grateful. I'd rather not talk about myself at all, but especially not about my hair and the circumstances of how it had come to be this particular color.

My mama has often said my glittering silver tresses reminded her of starlight, as though all the stars in Alabama had fallen directly onto my head, leaving me with a sparkly crown, a stunning glow. Time and again, I'd pointed out that Alabama's famous fallen stars had been meteorites, and if they'd crashed onto my head, I'd be dead, but Mama always argued the fact that I *had* died the night my hair turned color, and who was to say it hadn't been the *stars* that had caused my brief death.

It hadn't been the stars. It had been a watery accident. But Mama wasn't one for accepting small truths, favoring bold exaggerations instead.

Stars bested water, plain and simple.

I'd drowned that summer night nearly eight years ago in Lake Laurel, at just eighteen years old. But I'd been saved. Brought back to life. Brought back to a *new* life. To a new normal. All these years later, I hadn't quite figured out who this new Sadie Way Scott was exactly. Or why I had been saved. No matter how far I ran away from my hometown of Sugarberry Cove, Alabama, that particular *why* haunted me, following my every move, because there had been a reason. I felt it, deep down, like a pulsing bubble of pressure that kept me searching, seeking.

"Is there anything I can do to help, Mrs. Teakes?" I needed a diversion from my thoughts or else I was bound to fall into a deep mud hole of self-pity. I'd already set up my cameras, three in all, to frame specific shots of the homey kitchen that breathed vintage charm, which was easy to do since it hadn't been updated in at least sixty years, possibly more. The room was painted a cheerful blue, and the scent of vanilla floated in the air, as if being exhaled by the colorful floral wallpaper that served as a backsplash. The bulbous white fridge, covered in family photos, postcards, and old newspaper clippings, hummed loudly, its long chrome handle gleaming. The wide stove with side-by-side ovens had two storage drawers at the bottom, and I could only imagine the stories it could tell of the meals it had cooked.

But those stories would have to wait. The focus of today's video was on a dish served cold. Several small glass bowls were lined up along the ceramic tile countertop, each filled with different ingredients. Shredded coconut. Mandarin oranges. Sour cream. Maraschino cherries. Pineapple chunks. Mini marshmallows. Once the food prep was complete, I'd be the one asking all the questions for the sake of the video, which would be posted the following week on my YouTube channel, A Southern Hankerin'.

The videos were about more than Southern cooking. At their heart were human interest pieces featuring people across the South willing to share a family recipe and the story behind it. Last week, I'd had an in-depth preliminary phone interview with Mrs. Teakes, and today, I'd film her while she told me how, in the late 1960s, she'd captured the heart of her late husband with her recipe for ambrosia salad.

During the interview I'd be sure to mention how the South proudly labeled some desserts as salad. To those who lived here, this came as no surprise. After all, this was the land where mac and cheese was considered a vegetable. But my audience wasn't limited to the South. I had viewership that spanned the globe, a fact that amazed me—though it shouldn't. People tuned in for the heartwarming, relatable stories, which were needed in the world more now than ever.

Mrs. Teakes set down her knife and flexed age-spotted hands. Intelligent brown eyes, framed in an abundance of delicate wrinkles, assessed me, while their softness begged for more information. "Not much left to do, only these pecans to finish chopping. Whereabouts in Shelby County?"

I fussed with a camera setting that needed no adjustment. "Sugarberry Cove."

The river water below Mrs. Teakes' kitchen churned with happiness, white-crested rapids pushing and pulling and racing. Farther down the river, the water calmed, gradually rolling into stillness near a bridge with five arches that created circular reflections on the water's suddenly smooth, glassy surface.

Still waters that reminded me what used to be my home.

"On Lake Laurel? How wonderful! I've been several times for the water lantern festival. A lovely little town. So enchanting. Do you still live there?"

Much like the rapids, my stomach churned as I glanced at the clock on the countertop microwave, wishing time away. My gaze shifted to a tarnished brass teakettle that rested on a stove eye, then to two teacups that dangled on hooks under a golden oak cabinet, one cup with *Mr.* stenciled on it, the other *Mrs.* The former looked pristine in condition, the latter well-used, well-loved, with its tea-darkened interior and chipped handle. Hung askew on the wall by the fridge was a framed, stained cross-stitched cloth with the words HOME IS WHERE YOUR HEART IS.

Old wounds ached at the simple words, and I turned to look out the window instead of the phrase that haunted. Mocked.

"No, ma'am, but I still have family up that way. My older sister, her husband, and their little boy live up there. And my mother owns a bed-and-breakfast cottage on the lake and my great-uncle, who's more like a granddaddy to me, lives and works at the cottage, too. " I bit my lip to keep from saying any more, from spilling my heart onto the cutting board next to the pecans. Why was I revealing so much?

But I knew why.

The water.

I missed Sugarberry Cove.

I missed my *old* home.

The home, the family, that I'd had before my accident had changed everything and everyone. Most especially me.

Mrs. Teakes picked up the knife once more. "Where *do* you live, Sadie?"

I turned my back to the window and on old memories. "Here and there and everywhere. I travel a lot, and I'm still looking for the right place to settle down. This seems like a nice area. Wetumpka, I mean."

"Indeed it is. I grew up here, and I wholeheartedly recommend it." She chopped another pecan, the sharp knife slicing nutty brown flesh into small pale pieces. "The water lantern festival is coming up soon, if memory serves. The weekend after next? Will you go back for that? Such a special event."

"No, ma'am." Truly, it was the last place on earth I wanted to be.

Setting the knife down again, she faced me. Slim, graceful fingers fiddled with the top button of her pale blue cardigan as she said, "No? The lady of lake, Lady Laurel, might be especially generous this year, granting multiple wishes. You don't have any wishes to set afloat?"

The lanterns at the festival carried wishes across the lake, which came true only if Lady Laurel pulled the floating vessel from the surface of the dark water to fill her underwater home with light born from the purest wishes of a person's heart.

Deep lines fanned across her cheeks as Mrs. Teakes smiled, and the warmth in her eyes pulled at my heartstrings, making me want to tell her the whole story, start to finish, about how sometimes during the water lantern festival it was important to be very careful what you wished for.

"The festival will make do without my wishes." Faking a smile, I picked up the knife to finish chopping the pecans, etiquette be damned. The sooner I could stop talking about myself, the better.

Mrs. Teakes' gaze slowly drifted to my hair again. "I've heard told several stories of Lady Laurel's kindness, not always having to do with the lanterns. There's been rescues, haven't there?

Boaters? Swimmers? Didn't she save a young woman once from drowning?"

The glimmer in her eyes made me suspect she already knew why my hair was this color. There had been a flurry of media interest after my accident, but it had died down fairly quickly, thankfully. I'd hated the attention. Everyone stared. Whispered. The doctors had been mystified by my hair, but ultimately chalked up the change in color to a traumatic shock reaction. These days the looks my hair garnered were a sight easier to deal with because most people assumed I purposely dyed it this color. To be edgy or artsy or as a *brand*, to set myself apart from a zillion other online creators. But back home in Sugarberry Cove everybody knew its true source: lake magic.

I'd been saved by Lady Laurel, the Lady in the Lake.

There were many days I cursed the wish I made the night I'd fallen into the water, the wish that had ultimately caused my accident and its aftermath. I'd love nothing more than to go back in time to make a different choice. But there was no going back to what used to be. It was gone, left behind in the lake after I'd been pulled out, floating away on a water lantern carrying a wish that had changed life as I knew it.

In the span of a few short weeks, I'd died, been brought back to life, dropped out of college, shattered people's belief in me, suffered crushing heartbreak, and begun drifting around the state in search of odd jobs to keep afloat until I eventually started making videos to tell other people's stories. Now I lived out of a suitcase as I traveled the South for A Southern Hankerin'.

Why had I been saved?

Using the blade of the knife to sweep pecans from the chopping board into a glass bowl, I winced as the knife bit into the side of my thumb. A spot of red blossomed instantly.

I quickly folded my fingers over the wound, pressing tightly.

Mrs. Teakes gasped and set her hand on my arm. "Oh dear. I'll fetch a bandage."

"No need. It's only a nick, and I'm a quick healer." An understatement, to be sure. "It didn't even hurt."

"Nonsense. I'll be just a moment."

As Mrs. Teakes hurried out of the room, an incoming text message vibrated the phone in the back pocket of my jeans. I pulled the phone free and saw the message was from my sister, Leala Clare.

Sadie Way, you need to come home. Mother's okay but had a minor heart attack. She's at Shelby Baptist.

My stomach lurched into my throat, and my hands shook as I stared at the screen. At first I was disbelieving that my sister would *text* me this news, but then I remembered I'd asked her to always text before calling in case I was filming. And even in the face of something so important she hadn't ignored my request. Leala was nothing if not a rule follower.

"Sadie, are you all right? You've gone ghostly white."

Mrs. Teakes stood before me, concern flaring in her eyes, bandage in hand.

"I'm okay, but I'm sorry, I need to go. There's been an emergency." I quickly gathered my cameras and notes. As I headed out the door, I said, "I'll call to reschedule our interview."

"Anytime, dear. Anytime."

A few minutes later, I turned down the jazz playing on the car radio and backed carefully out of the narrow asphalt driveway. Mrs. Teakes stood on the front porch, waving, the bandage fluttering in hand like a tiny white flag. My gaze dropped to my thumb on the steering wheel, to the spot where the knife had pierced. The wound had already disappeared, the skin as smooth as it had been before being sliced.

As I headed north toward the home I'd barely seen in years, I couldn't help but wish that my emotional wounds could be so easily healed as well.

2

Leala

"Stay true to yourself," I said to the bathroom mirror, trying not to notice the panic-induced storm clouds gathering in my gray eyes. I carefully placed a small bottle of shampoo into a specific sleeve of a toiletry bag and turned the container so the label faced outward. I did the same for bottles of conditioner, moisturizer, eye drops, sunscreen, and hair spray.

"You'll be fine, Leala Clare," Connor said from the bedroom, his deep voice loaded with impatience. "You'll be there only a few days."

He barely tolerated my affirmations, which I'd adopted not long after I started practicing yoga, six months after Tucker's rough birth. Often, the simple phrases were the only things that got me through the days when I started questioning decisions I'd once been so sure about.

"Do I need to mention," he added, "how much you sound like your mother when you do it?"

I poked my head out the bathroom doorway so he could see the dirty look I was shooting him. "Are you trying to pick a fight?"

Without looking my way, he shrugged. "I'm just saying."

Early morning summer sunlight filtered through the curtains, casting the master bedroom in a soothing orange haze, and I took a deep breath and tried desperately to find some inner peace. Or any peace at all. I was on edge. A nervous wreck.

I nibbled a thumbnail, then forced myself to drop my hand. It had been years since I'd bitten my nails.

Connor sat in the king-size bed in a tight-fitting white T-shirt and blue boxer briefs, his back against the tufted headboard, his laptop balanced on a pillow on his lap. Thick brown hair stood in disarray, as it did in every morning until he showered. He was a fitful sleeper, and the tossing and turning gave him extreme bedhead.

"Well, stop saying, please." I was nothing like my mother. She was an F5 tornado while I was a light breeze.

He turned his head slightly to give me a brief smile, then glanced back at his computer screen. Stifling the urge to cross the room to smooth his unruly hair into place, which he'd hate, I tightened the sash of my robe and picked up two romance novels from my nightstand. I carried them to the upholstered bench at the foot of the bed where an open weekender was waiting to be packed, and said, "I need all the pep talks I can get to survive the next few days without losing my composure. Or my mind."

Or myself.

I'd worked too hard on all three to lose sight of them now.

I placed a pair of pajamas into the bag. "You know how my mother brings out the worst in me."

Mother's heart attack had been treated with what the cardiologist had called "clot-busting" drugs to clear the sixty-percent blockage in her artery, and I'd been grateful no major surgery was needed. After recuperating for two days in the hospital, she was to be discharged early this afternoon, and Sadie and I had agreed to spend the weekend with her—mostly to give our great-uncle Camp a well-deserved break and to make sure Mother rested as the doctor had prescribed, because Susannah Scott rarely did what she was told.

Saying nothing, Connor continued to peck at the computer's keyboard. Deep worry lines creased the skin between his blue eyes as he concentrated on the screen. At thirty years old, he was a senior associate at a big law firm in Birmingham, trying to make partner this year, and his work consumed his every waking moment. Or at least it seemed that way.

I picked off a loose, long blond hair from the arm of my robe. My hair tended to shed when I was stressed, and after these last few days of dealing with my mother and seeing Sadie I was surprised I wasn't yet bald.

The last time I'd seen my little sister had been at Easter brunch four months ago, here at my house. The stretches between her visits were growing more and more distant. If not for Mother's cardiac situation, Sadie might not have come around again until Thanksgiving.

Even though we were four years apart in age, we'd once been so close. Thick as thieves, tied at the hip. We'd done everything together growing up, mostly because Mother had designated me Sadie's keeper while Mother was busy with the cottage—or with her then boyfriend, our neighbor Buzzy Hale—which was always while I'd been in high school. I'd hated the forced responsibility, but loved Sadie enough to accept it without much argument, because for one, I wasn't much of an arguer. And two, if not me, then who'd watch over Sadie, keep her safe? Certainly not Mother. She had a proven track record of being negligent.

As Sadie and I had grown older and Mother and Buzzy's public displays of affection intensified, we'd take off to escape the embarrassment of it all. We'd go swimming or biking or spend long hours at the library, giggling as we read romance novels hidden behind *Teen* magazines. We'd drifted apart some when I went to college, but we still managed to make time for each other. Weekend spa dates. Movies. Long lunches.

Then, the accident happened and nothing had ever been the same. At the thought of that lantern-lit night, guilt twined through my stomach, making it ache. I pressed a hand to my belly and said, "As much as I hate to be away for three nights, this weekend will be a good time to have another heart-to-heart with Sadie moving back to Sugarberry Cove for good. I can't remember the last time we spent more than a few hours together."

Connor didn't look up from his computer. "You'll be wasting your breath. Sadie doesn't want to move back. She's made that quite clear."

It was true that every time I brought up the subject, Sadie shut down the conversation quickly, trying to hide the sadness in her eyes. "Maybe this time will be different, since she'll be *here,* in Sugarberry Cove." Right now, she was staying at a hotel close to the hospital. I'd asked her to stay with me, but she'd declined saying she wanted to be near Mother. "I know the lake is a painful reminder of what she went through, but staying away isn't helping her any."

Of course, Sadie never blamed the lake outright for her desertion, instead claiming she simply loved to travel and that her career was on the road—but I wasn't buying it. She was escaping—just like we used to do when Mother and Buzzy got too touchy-feely with each other. Sadie's job was nothing but a front. She had dubbed herself a *content creator,* and I couldn't help but roll my eyes even thinking about the title. I truly didn't even know how she was making ends meet.

If she wanted to see what hard work truly looked like, she should spend some time with Connor. He'd had a hardscrabble upbringing, earned a hardship scholarship to college, and was top of his class in law school down in New Orleans, where we'd lived for three years before moving back here, to my hometown.

But I knew better than anyone that Sadie would hate spending time with Connor more than being back in Sugarberry Cove, a place she once loved with her whole heart, near family and old friends, all whom had become virtual strangers.

I plucked another long hair off my sleeve. "Since Sadie will be staying at the cottage, she won't be able hide from her fears. Three days isn't a lot of time, but maybe being so close to the water, she'll finally be able to start healing. That's all she needs. A *start*. Don't you think? Every day is a chance at a new beginning."

"*Mm*," Connor grumbled.

He'd obviously tuned me out. Sometimes I wanted to get rid of our internet altogether. There was something to be said for unplugging once in a while. Suddenly irritated by his distraction, I picked up a pile of three blouses from my side of the bed and tossed them into the open weekender, having instant regrets as soon as they landed in a loose heap. I quickly refolded the shirts into a neat stack. "Maybe I should take Tucker with me this weekend after all."

At this, Connor finally glanced up. "A two-year-old at the hospital? And underfoot at the cottage while your mother convalesces? You think that's a good idea?"

His tone stated that this was a ridiculous idea, and maybe it was. But I liked it better than Tucker staying here with a distracted Connor.

"A cottage under renovation, at that," Connor added.

Truthfully, the renovations were the least of my worries, as they were confined to two guest rooms on the first floor that had been water-damaged by a burst pipe. The restoration work was almost done, due to be completed just in time for the water lantern festival.

I said, "It's not ideal, but you're busy with work."

"We've been through this. I took today off, didn't I?"

We had been through it. I'd insisted Tucker come with me. Connor insisted Tucker stay home, away from hospitals and illnesses and recuperations. It wasn't as if I wanted Tucker exposed to the hospital and its germs, either. And I certainly didn't want Tucker exposed to my mother's quirks for any great length of time. Except for our monthly dinners, I managed to keep our visits quick. In and out in less than half an hour.

But at the cottage, at least Tucker would be with me, where

I could keep a close eye on him. I'd offered Connor a compromise—dinner at the cottage tomorrow night—but he had dismissed it straight off, saying he wanted the weekend alone with Tucker. Which on the surface was all well and good, but underneath there was one big flaw with his plan: Connor's inability to unplug from work.

"We both know that a vacation day isn't really time off," I said. "You'll be on call. You'll check your email. You'll be easily distracted. Like you are now." In truth, I could do naked cartwheels in front of him, and he probably wouldn't look up from his computer long enough to notice. Or care.

I wasn't sure which was worse.

Drawing in a deep breath, I glanced around at the big master bedroom with its vaulted ceiling, so cavernous that it sometimes made me feel small and lost. I had a successful husband, a beautiful little boy, and a fancy house that was so big we'd hired a service to help clean it. I should be happy. Content. Especially since I'd worked so very hard on being happy and content.

Yet . . . I felt restless in the one place where I should feel most comfortable: home.

And truly, I should be thankful for Connor's job. His hard work had allowed me to quit my job as a healthcare accountant to stay home full-time, something I'd always wanted to do once we had a child. Or thought I wanted. I shook my head, not wanting to go *there* right now.

But instead of thankful, I was resentful. Because somewhere along the line I'd lost Connor. The man I'd fallen in love with. The man who'd shared my hopes and dreams. And sure, those dreams had shifted over the years, blurred, and changed course due to unexpected bumps in the road, but the grand plan, the happy, close-knit family part, had never altered.

But somehow, over the eight years we'd been married, he'd lost sight of what we'd always wanted, too engrossed in billable hours to see that he was slowly erasing himself from our lives. I missed him, and I didn't know how to bring him back to us, to make him understand all he was losing by working all the time. Somehow Connor Keesling, the man I loved with my whole heart, had become the thing I despised most in the world.

A workaholic.

Uneasy, I shifted my weight and added two pair of shorts and yoga pants and a yoga mat to the bag. "It takes only a moment for a two-year-old to wander away or find trouble. Not even a moment. A split second. If you're glued to your phone or laptop all weekend..."

I couldn't even finish the sentence as all the what-ifs flew through my head, flashes of the worst-case scenarios that often gave me insomnia and nightmares.

I knew how fast a world could be turned inside out.

ABOUT THE AUTHOR

HEATHER WEBBER is the *USA Today* bestselling author of more than thirty novels and has been twice nominated for an Agatha Award. She loves to spend time with her family, read, drink too much coffee and tea, bird-watch, crochet, watch cooking competition and home improvement shows, and bake. Heather lives in southwestern Ohio and is hard at work on her next book.

heatherwebber.com
Instagram: booksbyheather
Facebook: HeatherWebberBooks
Twitter: @BooksbyHeather